Delores Fossen, a *USA TODAY* bestselling author, has written over one hundred novels, with millions of copies of her books in print worldwide. She's received a Booksellers' Best Award and an RT Reviewers' Choice Best Book Award. She was also a finalist for a prestigious RITA® Award. You can contact the author through her website at www.deloresfossen.com

Carol Ericson is a bestselling, award-winning author of more than forty books. She has an eerie fascination for true-crime stories, a love of film noir and a weakness for reality TV, all of which fuel her imagination to create her own tales of murder, mayhem and mystery. To find out more about Carol and her current projects, please visit her website at www.carolericson.com, "where romance flirts with danger."

Discover more at millsandboon.co.uk

HER CHILD TO PROTECT

DELORES FOSSEN

THE DECOY

CAROL ERICSON

MILLS & BOON

First Published in Great Britain 2021
by Mills & Boon, an imprint of HarperCollins*Publishers* Ltd
1 London Bridge Street, London, SE1 9GF

www.harpercollins.co.uk

HarperCollins*Publishers*
1st Floor, Watermarque Building,
Ringsend Road, Dublin 4, Ireland

Her Child to Protect © 2021 Delores Fossen
The Decoy © 2021 Carol Ericson

ISBN: 978-0-263-28332-7

0421

HER CHILD TO PROTECT

DELORES FOSSEN

Chapter One

Sheriff Barrett Logan aimed his flashlight in the ditch and looked for a dead man.

There were no signs of him, but then Barrett hadn't believed there would be. That was the problem with getting an anonymous tip. It could be a hoax. However, since he was the sheriff of Mercy Ridge, Texas, checking out hoaxes was part of his job description.

Especially this one, which had come in the text he'd gotten from an unknown number.

There's blood near the county marker. She finally did it. She murdered him.

Barrett didn't know who this *she* was, but that wasn't the only word that had stood out for him. *Blood*, *finally* and *murdered* had also grabbed his attention. If this was indeed some kind of prank, then the person who'd sent the text had clearly wanted to embellish the details in such a way to make him jump right in and investigate.

Keeping watch around him, Barrett moved away from his truck that he'd left parked on the road. He'd put on his emergency flashers and kept on his high beams in case someone was out this time of night. Not likely, though. This was a rural road with a mile or more separating the sprawling ranches that dotted the area. Plus, it was nearly one in the morning, and most folks had long gone to bed. Mercy Ridge wasn't exactly a hotbed of partying and such.

Barrett fanned the flashlight over the sign that the texter had mentioned. The sign wasn't just to let drivers know they were entering another county but also to mark the lines of jurisdiction. Barrett and his deputies policed this side, but if the supposed body was beyond the sign, then that would fall under the jurisdiction of the Culver Crossing PD.

The cool spring rain spat at him, soaking the back of his shirt and his jeans. Thankfully, though, his Stetson was keeping the water out of his eyes, making it easier for him to see a long stretch of the ditch. Definitely no body and no blood in there, but he did see something else.

Footprints, maybe.

Someone or something had trampled down the weeds on the other side of the ditch. Weeds that practically arrowed toward a thick cluster of trees and underbrush.

Avoiding the trampled down parts, Barrett jumped across the ditch, his boots sinking into the wet ground, and he adjusted his flashlight again. However, before he could follow the trail, he heard the sound of an approaching vehicle. One that braked to a screeching stop right behind his truck. It was a Culver Crossing cruiser, and Barrett started muttering some profanity before the deputy stepped out.

Della Howell.

She was definitely someone he hadn't wanted to see tonight. Or any other night for that matter. The last time they'd spoken nearly two months ago, she had made it crystal clear that she hadn't wanted to see him, either. Yet, here she was.

Barrett hadn't expected her to have changed much in these two months, and she hadn't. Well, except for that troubled look she was giving him. Then again, Della often looked troubled, and there was often plenty of wariness in her crystal blue eyes.

The rain had already gotten to her, he noticed. There were strands of her shoulder-length dark brown hair clinging to the sides of her face and neck. Her shirt was doing some clinging, too. Definitely something he hadn't wanted to notice.

Della pulled in her breath and released it slowly, the kind of thing someone would do when steeling themselves up. It didn't seem to help, though, because at the end of it, there wasn't much change in her expression.

"Did you get a text telling you that a body was out here?" she asked.

Her voice and expression were as cool as the night rain, and it reminded Barrett that it hadn't always been that way. Of course, the noncool times had happened when she'd been in his bed. Since that was another reminder he didn't want or need, he pushed the thought aside.

"Yeah," he verified, and purposely turned back to his search.

He tried to look unruffled by all of this, but his thoughts were going a mile a minute. Why had someone texted both of them? Was this some kind of sick ploy to get them back together? If so, heads were going to roll. Of course, he couldn't actually come up with anyone who'd want that. Certainly not his brothers, because they knew he was still stinging from having Della put an end to their *relationship*.

As Barrett had done, Della fanned her flashlight over the ditch and surrounding area, and she stopped on the trampled down weeds. She hopped over the ditch, moving right behind Barrett. Too close to him, but then she was likely trying not to disturb the area that had alerted both of them.

"If an animal did that, it would have to be a big one," Della muttered.

Yep, but there were some bears in this area, or it could have been deer. However, it didn't seem like that, and an uneasy feeling settled in Barrett's gut. Since he'd been a lawman for over a decade, he'd learned not to dismiss that feeling, and that's why he rested his right hand over his sidearm.

With Della right on his heels, Barrett continued walking, moving slowly along beside the trail that something or someone had left. He still couldn't pick out actual tracks or footprints, but then the rain could have washed them away.

And then something caught his eye.

Barrett kept the flashlight on the object for a few seconds, making sure he was seeing what he thought he was. It was a woman's purse.

Della obviously saw it, too, because she stepped around him, going closer. She stooped down to examine it, and even though she didn't ask any questions, Barrett could practically feel them going through her mind.

Who did this belong to, and how'd it get here?

The cream-colored leather handbag was lying on its side and was wet with rain, but it wasn't damaged. Nor did it look as if it'd been there for a while. In fact, it looked as if someone had dropped it there very recently.

"It's open," Della said, angling her head so that she could see the contents. "There's a wallet."

Good. Because once they knew the owner, they could figure out how it got here. And why.

Della looked up at him, his flashlight spotlighting her expression. It was a mix of dread and Texas-size concern. "I recognize it." She swallowed hard. "It belongs to your mother."

That took Barrett's uneasy feeling to a full gut punch. Hell. This wasn't going to be good. He hadn't seen or spoken to his mother in years, and to the best of his knowledge, she didn't stray this close to Mercy Ridge.

"No," Della said, as if reading his mind. "Alice wouldn't have come here."

And Della would know that about her. Unlike Barrett and his brothers, Della was close to Alice. Or rather she had been when Della and he had still been together. He figured that hadn't changed because, unlike him, there wasn't bad blood between Della and his mother.

Bad blood.

It was an expression that people threw around a lot when it came to estrangement, family feuds and such, but it was deeply personal for Barrett. Even after all this time—over two decades—he could still see his father lying on the floor of his office. Could still feel the vicious punch of grief and the instant realization that nothing would ever be the same again.

And his mother had been the one who'd caused that.

"Alice wouldn't have had a reason to come here," Della added.

Barrett welcomed the sound of her voice. It drew him back to the only place his thoughts should be right now and that was figuring out what had gone on here. Bad blood, old memories and an attraction for Della shouldn't be playing into this.

"No, but someone could have stolen the purse and ditched it here," he argued.

It was the most logical theory he could come up with, but it still didn't make sense. If someone wanted to toss away a stolen purse, there were a heck of a lot of easier ways to do it. Just throwing it into the ditch would be faster than coming into these woods.

Barrett glanced around them again, looking for any signs of the person who might have left the purse. Nothing. No sounds, either. Just the steady rain and the pulsing of his own heartbeat in his ears.

Della slipped a thin plastic glove from the back pocket of her jeans, and once she had it on, she looked at the wallet. When she had it open, Barrett had no trouble seeing his mother's driver's license.

Muttering some profanity, Della put the wallet back in the purse and took out her phone. Of course, his mother's number was there in her contacts. Had been for as long as Barrett could remember. It had been one of the many sticking points between Della and him when they'd been together.

Even though Della didn't put the call on speaker, Barrett had no trouble hearing it go straight to voice mail, and he got a jolt of memories when he heard the recording of his mother's voice. Bad memories. As he'd done with his body's reaction to Della, he pushed that aside.

"I'll text Jace and ask him to go out to Alice's house ASAP to check on her," Della said as she did just that.

Jace was Della's boss, Jace Castillo, the sheriff of Culver Crossing. Since that was also where Alice lived and Jace and Alice were friends, it was a logical request. But the *ASAP* also let Barrett know that Della was plenty worried. So was Barrett. Just because he didn't care much for the woman who'd given birth to him, it didn't mean he wouldn't do his job. If something had happened to her, he wanted to find out.

"Jace will head over to Alice's place now," Della relayed when she got a response from him.

Good, but Barrett didn't intend to just wait around. He turned his flashlight to the ground around the purse. The weeds and grass had been trampled here, too, and that continued, the trail leading deeper into the darkness and toward that thick clump of oaks.

He started walking again but then stopped when he heard a sound. Maybe a moan, and it was coming from that area by the trees. Della must have heard it, too, because she hurried after him when he picked up the pace of his steps. And despite the rain and darkness, Barrett spotted her.

The woman lying in a heap on the ground.

It was his mother, all right.

That got both Della and him moving faster. It also got Barrett glancing around to see if anyone else was there. He wasn't sure what they were dealing with, and he didn't want to be ambushed.

As far as he knew, he didn't have anyone gunning for him, but as a lawman, that was always a possibility. Some people just stayed riled to the core even when they'd gotten what they deserved, and someone could have used this to lure him out here.

His mother was lying on her side, her legs drawn up into a fetal position, and her arms and hands were pressed over her chest like a shield. She made another moan, the sound of pain, and that's when Barrett saw the gash on her forehead. It was still bleeding, but the rain was washing it away.

Other than that wound, he didn't see any more injuries. However, she was soaked to the bone, her yellow dress clinging to her.

"Alice," Della called out on a rise of breath, hurrying to her. She didn't try to pick Alice up but did lift an eyelid, causing his mother to moan in pain again.

"I'll get an ambulance," Barrett said, making the call.

He estimated that it would take the EMTs about fifteen minutes to get there, and during that time he hoped he'd have answers as to what had happened to her. Hoped, too, that he could tamp down the worst-case scenarios going through his head.

God, his mother looked so weak. And hurt. While Barrett wanted to be immune to the feelings that caused inside him, he wasn't.

"Why are you out here?" Barrett asked her. His lawman's tone came through loud and clear, and it caused his mother to open her eyes again. She looked in his direction, her gaze spearing his.

"Barrett," Alice muttered. Her voice was watery and weak, just like the rest of her.

"Why are you here?" he repeated, his snap earning him narrowed eyes from Della.

His mother shook her head, groaning at the movement, and she glanced around as if seeing her surroundings for the first time. "I don't know."

Hell. That wasn't the answer he wanted, and he moved in closer to get a whiff of her breath. No scent of alcohol, but her eyes looked a little glazed. He'd never heard rumors of his mother being a drug user, but maybe that's what was going on. Of course, that still didn't explain squat.

"You think she was in a car accident?" Della asked him.

Maybe. But there'd been no other vehicles on the

road, and Barrett was pretty sure he would have seen a car that'd crashed into a tree or a pasture fence.

"Oh, God." Della practically gasped that out, and it definitely got Barrett's attention. However, it took him a moment to realize why Della had said it.

The blood.

She had eased back his mother's arms, no doubt to see if there were any other injuries, and there apparently were. The front of her dress had blood on it, and probably because of the way she'd been holding her hands, the rain hadn't washed it away.

Della kept her movements gentle, but she continued to move Alice's arms and leaned in to examine her. When Della looked back up at him, there was a whole new wave of concern in her eyes.

"Her dress isn't cut," Della said, her voice shaky now. "I don't think it's her blood."

Barrett cursed before he could stop himself, and the words from the text came back to him. *There's blood near the county marker.* Yeah, there was. What the person who'd sent that text hadn't mentioned was that it was on his mother.

But why?

How?

Getting those answers was a high priority. So was the ambulance. Once it arrived, then he could collect Alice's clothes and have them processed at the lab. For now, though, maybe the woman herself could give them some info.

"Think hard. Did someone bring you out here?" Barrett asked.

Alice just gave him a blank look. Not Della, though. Barrett thought there was a different kind of alarm on her face.

"Did, uh, Robert have anything to do with this?" Della whispered to his mother.

Barrett didn't ask who this Robert was. He knew it was likely Robert Casto, a rich rancher from Culver Crossing. Along with having a reputation for being a heavy-handed jerk, Robert was also his mother's lover. Or rather he had been last Barrett had heard, but then he didn't keep his ear to the ground for gossip about Alice.

"Robert," Alice repeated, but she didn't add any more to that. Her eyelids fluttered back down.

"Keep questioning her," Barrett told Della, and he took off his hat to hand it to her. "And hold this over the blood." The rain was already washing away enough of it, and he wanted to preserve the scene—even if he didn't know exactly what this *scene* was.

"Where are you going?" Della asked when he started to step away.

"I want to have a look around," he mumbled, and then added, "Keep watch."

That brusque order had likely offended Della. After all, she was a cop just as he was, but at the moment she was a distracted one. A woman she considered a friend was wounded, in a place she shouldn't be, and she had blood on her.

Yeah, they needed to keep watch.

In the distance Barrett heard the sirens. They'd made good time, but he still had a couple of minutes before the EMTs would arrive on scene and reach his mother. Della would no doubt take care of that, too, and could guide them to their position by using her flashlight.

Barrett used his own flashlight to look at the ground beyond the trees. There were more trampled weeds, and the sight of them put a harder twist to the knot in his gut. What the hell had gone on here? He'd assumed his mother had come here from the road, but maybe she'd come through the woods. But that didn't make sense, either. The nearest house was a good mile away, and there was no trail or back road that led from Culver Crossing to here.

Behind him, he could hear Della continue to ask his mother questions. Could hear the sirens getting closer, too. But Barrett kept moving, kept fanning the light over the rain-soaked ground.

And then he saw it.

Another person. A man this time, and like Alice, he was lying on the ground in a crumpled heap. He was beneath a thick oak and was on his side, his face turned down so that Barrett couldn't tell who it was.

Barrett didn't run to him. His lawman's training kicked in, and he approached from the side so as not to disturb the trail that led directly to him. There could be prints or trace on that trail, things that he might need later when this turned to a full scale investigation. There was no *if* about that. There would be an investigation.

The man was wearing dark pants, cowboy boots and a white shirt. Or rather some of it was still white. The thick oak had done a decent job of sheltering him like an umbrella, and because of that, Barrett could see what was all over the man's clothes.

Blood. And lots of it.

Barrett could also see the gleaming silver handle of the knife that someone had plunged into the man's chest.

Chapter Two

Della wanted to go after Barrett, but she had to take care of a few things first. Alice was her top priority. The woman was too pale, and every inch of her was shaking now. She was injured and in shock. And the scene had to be preserved, too.

Even if any potential evidence didn't lead in a good direction.

Mercy, why had Alice been attacked? And who or what was at the end of the trail that Barrett was following?

"Don't move," Della told Alice, and despite the woman's moaning protests, Della hurried away from her to the ambulance that had just stopped behind Barrett's and her vehicles. The driver angled the ambulance so that the headlights were illuminating the ditch and grassy area where Della waited for them.

Two EMTs quickly got out, and Della didn't bother asking their names. However, she did identify herself, tapped the badge clipped to the waist of her jeans, and she motioned for them to follow her.

"Walk here so you don't disturb the scene," she said, pointing to the makeshift path that Barrett and she had created.

Della ran back toward Alice and was glad that the

EMTs did the same. "The victim is Alice Logan, age fifty-seven. She has a head injury," she explained, and judging from the sounds they made, they recognized the name.

Of course, they did. The EMTs were from Mercy Ridge, and everyone there knew Barrett and his brothers. Everyone knew the scandal that Alice had created, too. It didn't matter that the scandal had happened a long time ago because gossip about that and the aftermath would go on forever.

And Della should know.

She had personal knowledge of family tragedies.

When they reached Alice, the EMTs rushed to her and immediately started to examine the woman. While they did that, she went after Barrett, trudging through the underbrush that scraped her boots and jeans. He wasn't hard to find since he had stopped only about twenty feet away, and he had his flashlight aimed at something.

No, at *someone*.

With her attention frozen to the man on the ground, Della automatically slowed her steps until she reached Barrett's side.

"I've already called this in," he told her. Unlike her, he was firing glances all around, and that's when she noticed he'd drawn his gun.

Della did the same, her service weapon sliding against the leather when she pulled it from her shoulder holster. Just the fact that she needed to take such measures sent her heart rate soaring even higher than it already was. Whoever had done this to Alice and this new victim could still be out there. Ready to attack her and Barrett, too.

"He's dead?" Della asked, already knowing the answer. He certainly wasn't moving, and even though she could only see the side of the man's face, it wasn't the skin color of the living. Plus, the knife appeared to be right in his heart.

"He's dead," Barrett verified. Then, he paused. "That's Robert Casto."

Sweet heaven. That jolted through her like a lightning bolt, and Della frantically shook her head, hoping that it wasn't true. But all it took was a closer look for her to verify it. And the verification caused her to realize that things had just taken a very bad turn for Alice.

"I arrested Casto just yesterday for assaulting your mother," Della blurted out, and she turned to Barrett to see if he'd known that. Judging from the profanity he growled out, he hadn't. "He made bail right away," she added.

That had surprised no one, including Della. Casto had plenty of money. Plenty of attitude, too, making Della wonder why Alice had ever gotten involved with him in the first place. A shrink would probably say that Alice wanted to punish herself, and if so, Casto was a surefire way to do that.

"Did Casto put that cut on her head?" Barrett asked.

"Maybe. But if so, she didn't have it yesterday when I arrested him. According to her statement, they'd gotten into an argument. Then, he'd grabbed her by the hair, slapped her and tried to stop her from getting in her car to leave. Alice managed to get away from him, and she came straight to the police station. She was pretty shaken up, but the only visible injury she had then was a red mark on her left cheek."

The moment Della mentally repeated what she'd just said, the words in the text came back to her.

She finally did it. She murdered him.

Had the person who'd sent that message been talking about Alice? Mercy, she hoped not.

"Alice didn't do this," Della insisted. But she figured Barrett wouldn't believe her. And he didn't.

"Try to stay objective," Barrett said, and it was a warning. One that stung because she knew he was right. Being impartial was part of being a good cop, but it was impossible to override what she knew in her gut.

"Alice didn't return blows when Casto hit her," Della quickly added. She was careful not to say *your mom*. That would be like poking a stick at a coiled rattlesnake. "She was scared but not hotheaded and stupid." Della stopped, reconsidered. "Unless this is a case of self-defense."

Della could see that playing out. Maybe Casto had kidnapped her, brought her here, and Alice had gotten away. They could have fought, and in order to save her life, Alice might have stabbed him.

"You said they'd argued yesterday," Barrett reminded her. "About what?"

This certainly wasn't going to make Barrett believe Alice was innocent, but Della couldn't withhold evidence. She had to believe that when all the pieces of this were put together, the facts would clear Alice.

Even if at the moment, it didn't look as if that would happen.

"Alice wanted to end the relationship," Della said. "Casto apparently didn't care much for that and got physical with her. He had a history of that. Not with women, not that I know about anyway, but he's punched several of his ranch hands."

Barrett didn't question her about that, but she figured he'd want more details later. Right now, he was likely doing the same thing she was, trying to piece this together. If Casto had a history of violence, then it could have come back to bite him.

Or rather kill him.

Della stooped down to get a better look at the body so she could see if there was anything to back up her theory. There was so much blood. Casto's shirt was covered with it, and it was dripping off the fabric and seeping into the ground. The flashlight made it look as if it were on display. And it slung Della right back to another place, another time.

Another violent death.

Her best friend and fellow deputy this time. Francine Silva. Francine's killer had also used a knife. It had left a pool of blood. Lifeless eyes. A senseless death, and her killer hadn't been caught, hadn't been punished.

Somehow, that was the hardest part to take.

Francine had been murdered by an unknown assailant. An intruder who'd broken into her house and killed her when she'd surprised him. Or rather that was the theory. Ironic that even though Francine had been a deputy and had lived her life surrounded by cops, her murder was still unsolved.

Sometimes, the deepest cuts came from not knowing who'd done it. And from not having been able to stop it.

Della shook her head, pinched her eyes shut a moment and tried to will away the images. It'd been over a year since she'd had a panic attack, and she didn't want to have one now. She was a cop, she reminded herself. Armed and trained. And she needed to do her job. If she didn't, then heaven knew what would happen to Alice. Despite Barrett's warning about her staying objective, she doubted he'd do the same when it came to his mother.

"Are you okay?" Barrett asked.

Della groaned softly because she heard something in his voice that she didn't want to be there. Sympathy. She saw it in his dark eyes, too, when she stood and met his gaze head-on.

A shared sympathy had first brought them together. That and the attraction. Cold, dark pasts colliding with a bright scorching heat. It had been the right mix for them to share a bed on a regular basis. Not enough, though, for them to get beyond, well, themselves and the baggage caused by their pasts.

Now that he didn't have on his cowboy hat, the rain covered his thick black hair and his face. A warrior face, she'd always thought. Tough and angled. Hot. Yes, Barrett had gotten a darn good deal out of his gene pool when it came to his looks.

Barrett's gaze stayed locked with hers, maybe trying to decide if she'd told him the truth about being okay. She wasn't, of course. It wasn't just the blood and the fear for Alice, but Della had to deal with something else.

She felt a tug of the old attraction.

Thankfully, it quickly cooled, though only because of the footsteps she heard coming their way. They both pivoted in the direction of the sound, and she soon spotted a familiar face, making his way toward them.

Barrett's brother Daniel, who was also a Mercy Ridge deputy.

Since Daniel was keeping on the same path Barrett and she had taken to get to Casto's body, he'd no doubt seen his mother.

Daniel gave Della a nod that was neither friendly nor hostile, and he went to stand by his brother. The family resemblance was strong, not just in their faces but also their tall rangy bodies, and Daniel's stance showed their united front.

Alice wouldn't be getting any warm fuzzy hugs from either of them. Heck, neither would Della. Barrett might not have spilled the details of their breakup to his brothers, but they wouldn't need to know the facts to be on his side. They'd always be on Barrett's side.

"Any idea what happened here?" Daniel asked Barrett.

"Not yet. But the dead guy is Robert Casto."

Daniel swore under his breath, shook his head. "She killed him?" He hitched his thumb over his shoulder in the direction of their mother.

"No," Della said.

At the same moment Barrett answered, "That's to be determined." Barrett tossed her a scowl and took out his phone. "Someone texted both Della and me this about thirty minutes ago." He showed Daniel the message that she had already memorized.

There's blood near the county marker. She finally did it. She murdered him.

"She," Daniel repeated, and Della had no doubts that the deputy believed that it referred to his mother.

"Yeah," Barrett verified as if he'd read his brother's mind. "You were just with Alice?" he asked, and Daniel nodded. "Did she say anything useful?"

Daniel shook his head. "She's unconscious at the moment. The ambulance is about to take her to the hospital. I figured as soon as the doctor checks her out, you'd question her."

"I will," Barrett confirmed.

"I want to be there for that," Della insisted, causing both Daniel and Barrett to look at her.

The two didn't exactly give her glares, but it was

close enough. Della might get the real-deal glares, though, when she insisted that Alice not be questioned until she had her lawyer present.

"The medical examiner is on the way," Daniel explained several moments later. "I can wait here for him and start processing the scene." He glanced around and tipped his head toward Alice. "I believe she's on Mercy Ridge land, but it'll be close. Not so sure about the dead guy, though. I think the boundaries for Culver Crossing start right about where he is."

Sweet heaven. What a mess if that was true.

Daniel's attention settled on Della again. "Will your *boss* give us a hassle about who'll have jurisdiction on this?" he asked.

He said *boss* in the same tone as discussing a bad cold. There was no love lost between Jace and him, and again it went back to Alice. The Logan brothers wouldn't want Jace on their turf, but Della seriously doubted that Jace would just stay away—even if it turned out that this wasn't in Culver Crossing's jurisdiction. Of course, Barrett likely thought if Jace and she got control of the investigation, they would look the other way at anything wrong Alice might have done.

"Sheriff Castillo will give us a hassle," Barrett concluded before Della could figure out how to answer that. "But call a reserve deputy to help you figure out who'll be primary on this case. Or if we'll have to share the investigation."

Della winced at the idea of sharing. Jace and Barrett could hardly be in the same airspace without snarling at each other, and it wouldn't help that Jace would also be trying to protect Alice. Both Jace and Barrett were good cops, and they would do their jobs, but adding Alice to the mix would fire tempers on both sides.

And Della would be caught in the middle.

Della tried to push that aside, and she followed Barrett when he made his way back to the ambulance. The EMTs already had Alice loaded in the back.

"Restrain her until we know what we're dealing with," Barrett called out to them.

"Restraints?" Della protested. "Is that necessary?"

"It is if Alice is a killer. Or even a suspected one—which she is. Right now, she's the prime suspect in her estranged lover's murder, because I'm pretty sure Robert Casto didn't commit suicide."

Of course, Della had known that, but it felt like another gut punch to hear it. *Alice was a murder suspect.*

Barrett motioned for the EMTs to head out. He started toward his truck, no doubt to follow the ambulance, but he stopped and looked at her.

"I should probably not waste my breath, but there's no reason for you to come to the hospital right away," he said. "It'll likely take the doctor a while to examine her, and that'll give you enough time to go home and change into dry clothes."

Della wasn't sure if he was genuinely concerned about her or if it was his attempt to keep her out of this. Either way, it wouldn't work.

"I'll be fine," she assured him, hoping she sounded a lot stronger than she suddenly felt.

"Suit yourself," he grumbled a split second before he got in his truck and drove away.

Della got in her cruiser, but she didn't follow him. Not right away. She started the engine and took a moment to gather her breath. Then, another moment to try to tamp down everything inside her that she was feeling.

Oh, mercy. Why was this happening now? The timing couldn't have been worse. Barrett and she were already at odds. Odds that she had decided she was going to have to mend. She couldn't see a way around that.

For now, though, mending would have to wait. But soon, very soon, Barrett was going to need to know the truth.

That she was pregnant with his child.

Chapter Three

"Hell," Barrett grumbled under his breath, and he thought that one word described this mess.

He had a dead body, an injured suspect who happened to be his mother, a looming jurisdiction dispute. And Della. No way to forget her since she'd been right on his heels when he arrived at the hospital. She'd stayed on his heels, too, as Barrett had gone to the ER, where Alice had already been carried into an examining room.

Hell was definitely the right word.

Della's breakup with him was still too fresh for him to completely put away his feelings, but he had to try so he could focus on what could turn into a nasty tangled investigation. Still, it was impossible not to remember that she'd ended things so she could get on with her life.

Yeah, her exact words.

Get on with my life.

Translation: Della wanted the whole shebang. Marriage and kids. Barrett could have possibly given her the first, *possibly*, but not the second. Considering he'd had to practically raise his younger brothers, he was about as far from being daddy material as one could get.

Barrett went to the examination room and tapped. With Della looking on, a nurse opened the door. He knew her, of course. Gina Corona. She was scowling, probably because she didn't appreciate the interruption, but when she saw that it was Barrett, her expression softened.

"I need her to stay restrained," Barrett told Gina. "And I have to Mirandize her."

No softening of her expression that time. Gina sucked in a hard breath. "I see." She gave an uneasy glance over her shoulder. So did Barrett, and he saw the doctor, Lyle Tipton, already starting his exam. "She's not conscious right now."

Barrett nodded. "As soon as she's awake, come out and get me. I don't want her saying anything until I've read her her rights."

Gina gave a shaky nod and shut the door. And speaking of *shaky*, that applied to Della, as well. She didn't challenge him, though, on the restraints or the instructions he'd just given Gina. Della just stepped away from the door and him.

Since he was going to need as many allies as he could get on this investigation, he took out his phone to call his other brother, Deputy Leo Logan. Along with the county CSI team, Daniel would take care of supervising the processing of the crime scene. The ME would deal with Casto's body, but there was other legwork to be done, and he could rely on Leo for that.

"I heard about the murder," Leo said the moment he answered. "Just got off the phone with Daniel. What do you need me to do?"

"Plenty." Barrett dragged in a long breath that he figured he was going to need, and he moved even farther away from Della.

Since the ER waiting room wasn't that big, she'd likely still be able to hear him, but by turning away from her, he wouldn't have to see that stark look on her face. A look that conveyed she was no doubt worried about his mother.

The one good thing about this was there was no one else in the waiting room, so prying eyes and ears wouldn't get any juicy gossip fodder. But since someone could come walking in at any second, Barrett decided to spell this out fast to Leo.

"There was no vehicle anywhere near the crime scene," Barrett explained. "I need you to call out every reserve deputy we've got to go through the area and find out how Alice and Robert Casto got out there. Concentrate on the back roads and ranch trails. I also need you to try to trace a text I got. I'm sending it to you now. Yeah, I know it's a long shot," he added after he'd forwarded the message to his brother.

"I'm on it." Leo paused a heartbeat. "Anything else?"

"Daniel will request it, but you push, too, to get the results as fast as you can. I want to know if there are prints on the knife that killed Casto."

"Got it." Leo paused. "You really think Alice murdered him?"

Barrett glanced at Della to see if she'd heard that, but if so, she didn't have a reaction to it. She was sitting in one of the chairs, the heel of her right palm pressed to her forehead. Her eyes were closed, and her breath was coming out in short gusts. She looked sick or something, and he decided it was probably the *or something*. Seeing all that blood had probably triggered some flashbacks for her. It certainly had triggered some for him.

"I don't know if Alice killed him," Barrett answered honestly. He knew Alice was capable of doing some cruel things. Things that cut to the core. But murder.... He just didn't know.

"What about notifying Casto's next of kin?" Leo continued. "You want me on that?"

"I'll have Daniel do that after the ME confirms the ID." Of course, they all knew the dead guy was Robert Casto since both Della and he had done a visual identification, but Barrett wanted to go by the book on this one.

"Do you even know who his next of kin is?" Leo pressed.

"Don't have a clue. I just wasn't interested in Alice's latest bedmate." And yep, there was bitterness in his voice. Barrett had long given up trying to remedy that.

"Are you okay?" Leo asked a moment later.

Barrett figured he'd be getting that question from his grandfather, Ben, and anyone else who knew that this would eat away at him. "I'll focus on the job," he assured his brother. The badge had always grounded him, and Barrett was heavily counting on that happening now.

He ended his call with Leo and glanced around, looking and listening for anyone who could give him answers as to Alice's condition. Nobody was there except for Della. If he didn't get an update soon, he'd go back into the examining room to see what was going on.

"There was so much blood," Della muttered, and judging from the way her eyes flew open, she hadn't intended to say that aloud.

If they'd still been lovers, or even friends, Barrett would have pulled her into his arms and tried to comfort her. But since she'd been the one to put an end to their relationship, there wasn't much chance he could provide any comfort now. However, it punched at him some to see her like this.

"Yeah," Barrett said, sinking down in the chair next to her.

Both of them had certainly seen their share of spilled blood. Della on the night a man had murdered her best friend, Francine. Barrett, on the clear spring day when Alice had walked out on her husband and her sons so that she could run to another man's bed. Barrett hadn't known all of that, though, before he'd gone into his father's office at their family ranch and found him lying dead on the floor. A self-inflicted gunshot wound to the head.

There was no way for Barrett to turn off the image of his father. No way to erase the emotions.

No.

Since that day when he'd been only twelve years old, it was always with him. And while it was the reason he'd become a cop, it was also why he saw and felt the past every time he thought of Alice. His so-called mother might not have pulled the trigger for his father, but she had certainly put the tragic events of that day into motion.

"You're the only person I know who's as messed up as I am," Della said. The burst of air that left her mouth was a little like a hollow laugh.

Barrett made a sound of agreement and hoped that would be enough to stop her from saying more. It didn't.

"At least I was an adult when I found Francine," Della went on. "You were just a kid when your dad died."

He had been indeed, and Barrett knew that had added an extra layer of grief. Grief that sometimes felt so thick he was surprised others couldn't see it coming off him in waves. Still, he'd survived and had been damn lucky that his father's dad, Ben, had stepped up to take in Barrett and his brothers. If not, they might have been forced to go with Alice, to live with the woman they blamed for their father's death.

Of course, Barrett didn't blame only Alice. No, she shared that "honor" with the man she'd run to when she'd left her husband and her kids.

Jace's widowed father, Brett Castillo.

Alice had not only run to her lover, Brett, she'd also moved in with the man and Jace. Had mothered Jace when she hadn't bothered with her own kids. Even after Brett had died in a car accident just a few years later, Alice had stayed in Culver Crossing.

"I go over Francine's file at least once a week," Della went on. "I look at every clue, every photo. I think of all the things that I could have done to make sure her murder didn't happen."

Hindsight could be downright mean, and it wouldn't do any good to tell Della that there was nothing she could have done to stop Francine from dying. That's because Barrett, too, knew all the details of the case since he'd pored over it with Della. In fact, that's how they first landed in bed.

Almost two years ago, shortly after Francine's death, Della had come to him as a friend and fellow cop. First, to have him go over the investigation with a fresh eye. Then, she'd poured out her pain and misery to him, cried on his shoulder, and they'd ended up becoming lovers. Barrett had never been under any illusions that it was more than friendship and comfort between them, but sometimes he wondered if they hadn't both been so *broken* if things would have been different.

The sound of footsteps yanked Barrett out of that miserable mental trip down memory lane, and he immediately got to his feet. But it wasn't a doctor or anyone else on the hospital staff. It was Sheriff Jace Castillo.

Tall and imposing, Jace glanced around the room as if he owned it—at least that was Barrett's take—and he went straight to Della when he spotted her.

Jace didn't ask her if she was okay, but he put his hand on Della's shoulder and gave it a gentle squeeze. However, there was no trace of gentleness when the lawman shifted his gaze to Barrett.

"You've already questioned your mother?" Jace asked, and again it was Barrett's take that he emphasized those last two words.

"Not yet, but I will as soon as the doctor clears her." Barrett made sure he emphasized the "I." He didn't want to go into that examination room and have three cops trying to question Alice. Or worse—one doing the questioning and two treating her with kid gloves.

Jace volleyed some glances between Della and him as if he was trying to decide how to handle this. Barrett decided to clarify things for him.

"Alice was found in Mercy Ridge," Barrett explained. "The dead guy likely was, too, but just in case he wasn't, the prime suspect was taken into custody when she was in my jurisdiction. Even if this turns out to be a joint investigation, I want the suspect's statement on record."

"So do I," Jace assured him. "I'm not looking to cut corners. In fact, I have some of my deputies out scouring the area, and I've instructed them to stay on the Culver Crossing side."

There was a smart-ass edge to Jace's tone. One that Barrett didn't have time to respond to because the door to the examination room finally opened, and Gina gave Barrett the come-forward motion with her hand. Della immediately got to her feet, no doubt to follow him.

Barrett ground out some mumbled profanity. "You can watch and listen, but she talks to me first."

Jace obviously took that as an invitation because he went with Della. However, they stopped in the doorway. Maybe because of the warning glare that Barrett shot them.

Dr. Tipton stepped to the side, adding some notes to a medical chart, and Barrett went closer to the examining table. Lying on her side, Alice was awake, but her eyes looked filmy and unfocused. She had fresh stitches on her forehead. No restraints, though. Something that didn't please Barrett. But at least Alice didn't seem ready to try to bolt right out of there.

"Barrett," Alice murmured, her voice much the same as when he'd found her on the ground. "Thank you for being here."

He nearly tapped his badge to remind her that his being here wasn't by choice, but instead he turned to Gina. "I want her clothes bagged," Barrett instructed the nurse. Then, he looked down at Alice's hands. No signs of injury, and there didn't appear to be anything under her fingernails, but he'd have them checked to make sure.

Dr. Tipton looked up from his notes, his gaze sliding to Della and Jace before he shifted his attention to Barrett. "It's okay if they're here?"

"For now," Barrett grumbled.

The doctor nodded. "Mrs. Logan has a concussion and some contusions on her right side and buttocks."

Barrett had to get past the sucker punch of hearing Alice being called Mrs. Logan. As far as he was concerned, she'd given up the right to use that surname twenty-three years ago. Still, it was legally hers.

"She also has a lump on the back of her head," the

doctor went on. "It didn't need stitches, but it appears someone hit her. Or maybe she got it in a fall."

In other words, it clarified nothing.

"She said she hadn't been sexually assaulted," Dr. Tipton added a moment later.

"I wasn't," Alice verified, and her voice was a hoarse whisper. She cleared her throat and repeated it, this time loud enough for all of them to hear.

Behind him, he heard Della's breath of relief. The idea of sexual assault had occurred to Barrett. Hell, lots of things had occurred to him, but first and foremost was that Alice had rammed that knife into Casto's chest.

"The EMTs restrained me," Alice went on. "They must have thought I did something wrong."

So, Alice didn't know about Casto. Or rather she was pretending not to know.

"I didn't do anything wrong," the woman insisted, looking past Barrett and at Della and Jace.

Alice's allies.

Barrett held up his hand to stop Alice from saying anything else so he could Mirandize her. As he said each word of it, she looked even more unsteady, and Barrett could practically feel Jace's glare drilling holes in his back.

"Do you understand your rights?" Barrett asked Alice when he was finished.

Alice nodded. "But I don't need a lawyer. I just want to tell you what happened so we can clear all of this up."

Barrett doubted that it would be that simple. "How'd you get out in the woods tonight?"

Alice opened her mouth, closed it. For someone who wanted to spout her story, she sure took her time getting started. "I don't know," she finally said. "I don't remember."

Barrett managed not to groan, but even a woman in a partially dazed state had to see the frustration and skepticism on his face. "Exactly what do you remember, then?" he pressed.

Again, she took her time, moistening her lips first. "I was in my garage, getting out of my car, and I heard a rustling sound behind me. Before I could turn around and see who it was, I got hit on the head." She touched her fingers to the spot and moaned softly. "He hit me again right as I fell. This time on my forehead."

"He?" Barrett immediately questioned.

"I believe it was a man, but I didn't get a good look at him because the light was out in my garage."

Barrett would check that out to see if someone had tampered with it and if there were any signs of struggle.

"What happened then?" Barrett continued.

Alice shook her head and winced a little. "I don't remember anything else until I woke up outside. It was dark and raining and someone was dragging me through the grass."

"Who was dragging you?" Barrett asked, knowing he was going to get another head shake from her. And he did. "Was it Robert Casto?"

Alice hesitated as if considering that. "No." Her gaze darted away from him, and Barrett didn't know if that's because she was lying or just embarrassed that she'd been involved with someone like that.

Someone who was now dead.

"The man was bigger than Robert," Alice went on. "A lot bigger, and he was wearing black pants and shirt. And boots," she added as if just remembering that. "Not cowboy boots but the steel toed ones that lace up."

"But you didn't see his face?" Barrett pressed.

Alice stayed quiet a moment. "Just glimpses. I didn't recognize him. I don't know who he was."

Maybe. Barrett still wasn't buying this. He shifted his position, leaning in so he could see Alice's expression when he asked her the next question. "Did you kill Robert Casto?"

There hadn't been much color in Alice's face, but what little there was drained completely. "Robert…" She shook her head. "He's dead?"

Well, if she was faking surprise, she was doing a darn good job. In fact, her reaction went past mere surprise to shock.

"He's dead," Barrett verified, his voice flat. "Someone killed him. Was it you who did that?"

"No. God, no." The words rushed out of her mouth, and Alice pushed herself up to a sitting position. Not easily. She was clearly still wobbly. "Robert's dead," she muttered, lifting her trembling hand to the doorway.

Barrett wasn't sure who Alice was reaching for, but it was Della who came forward, and she took hold of Alice's hand. "It'll be okay," Della whispered, and it sounded like a promise.

One that Barrett knew Della couldn't keep.

If Alice had lied and had been responsible for Casto's death, she would pay. And Barrett would have to be the one to make sure that happened.

Jace stepped closer, too, sending Alice a sympathetic look, but he moved back to the doorway when his phone rang. Barrett ignored him and kept his attention on Della and Alice. It was possible that Alice might say something to her friend that she wouldn't say to the son she'd abandoned.

"Robert's really dead?" Alice asked. Her eyes filled with tears.

"I'm sorry. It's true." Della paused. "Alice, he was murdered. Someone stabbed him."

Alice sucked in a hard breath, her hand flying to her mouth, and those tears didn't stay in her eyes. They spilled down her colorless cheeks.

"I can't hug you," Della murmured when Alice reached out to her. "The lab will need to process your clothes."

Barrett saw it then. Even though he'd Mirandized Alice, it was obviously just now sinking in that she was a murder suspect or at least she'd come in very close contact with the killer. He wasn't legally required to spell that out for her just yet unless he actually arrested her, but he would have told her exactly that if Jace hadn't spoken first.

"I need a word with you," Jace told Barrett.

Barrett felt the annoyance from the interruption slide through him, but he went to the doorway while keeping an eye on Della and Alice. If Alice said anything else, he wanted to hear it.

"That was Glenn Spence, one of my deputies, on the phone," Jace explained. "He was searching the old ranch trails near the crime scene and he found an SUV parked there."

That got Barrett's full attention. "Does it belong to Casto or Alice?"

"Neither. It's a rental, and it appears to be on the Mercy Ridge side of the woods." A muscle flickered in Jace's jaw. "There was a guy inside. No ID on him, but he was dressed all in black and was wearing black steel toed boots."

"I want to talk to him," Barrett insisted.

Jace shook his head. "You can't. He's dead."

Chapter Four

Dead.

That was not what Della had wanted to hear. Right now, they needed answers to keep Alice out of hot water, and this boot-wearing man might have been able to provide them with that. But at least they had his body and his vehicle. Once they knew who he was, they could go from there, and maybe fill in some of those much needed answers.

"I'll head out to the dead man's SUV," Barrett said before Della could volunteer to do just that. It was a reminder that the location of the vehicle was in his jurisdiction. "If Alice says anything else, I want to know about it," he added to Jace, and it sounded like a warning.

"I want to go with you," Della insisted.

Barrett had already started walking, but that stopped him, and when he turned toward her, she saw the debate in his eyes. A long debate that lasted several snail-crawling moments before he finally nodded. Maybe he thought her going with him was the lesser of two evils and that at least this way, she wouldn't be at the hospital with his mother.

Jace gave her a look, too. One that she didn't have any trouble interpreting. If she learned anything, he wanted her to tell him. And she would. Jace and she might not be able to stay 100 percent objective when it came to Alice, but both of them wanted the woman's name cleared ASAP.

When Barrett and she stepped out of the hospital, Della noticed the rain had finally stopped. That could be a break because it meant there was a higher chance of having the crime scene preserved. Daniel was dealing with that, and he was a good cop. If there was anything to find, he would find it.

"Coming with me isn't necessary," Barrett grumbled as they headed toward his truck. Like Della, he glanced around, looking for any signs of trouble.

"That depends. This way you don't have to deal with Jace."

Though it did occur to her that Barrett might have as much trouble or more dealing with her. Still, it would give them a chance to talk, and while she wasn't looking forward to that, she did want to feel him out. To see how Barrett might handle the baby bombshell she would soon have to tell him. Her guess was that he wouldn't handle it well, but she didn't have a choice about telling him. He had to know.

God help her.

Some movement to their left had Barrett and then Della pivoting in that direction, and she saw a man getting into a car. A man she instantly recognized. She slid her hand over her weapon just as Barrett did the same.

"Wilbur Curran," Barrett said under his breath, and he added some profanity. "What the hell is he doing here?"

Della was wondering the same thing, and the question didn't have her relaxing her hand on her gun. Curran was a wealthy cattleman, and there were rumors that he hadn't used legal means to come by all his wealth. She'd already had too many raw memories tonight, and seeing Curran only added to them. It was no doubt the same for Barrett, since at one time Barrett had been trying to tie Curran to Francine's murder.

"Curran's guilty of something," Barrett muttered. "I just don't know specifically what."

Della considered that while she got into Barrett's truck. "Are you still investigating him?"

"Yeah." Barrett didn't hesitate with his answer, and that loosened some of the pressure Della was feeling in her chest. Despite her having ended their relationship, Barrett hadn't stopped seeking justice for her friend.

Of course, Della hadn't stopped, either. She was convinced that something Francine had been investigating had gotten her killed. But what exactly? Della still didn't know, but Francine had been looking into a money laundering scheme that was linked to Curran. No proof of that link, though. No proof of anything, really, and that's why Curran wasn't behind bars.

Barrett pulled out of the parking slot, but he slowed to a crawl when they passed Curran. The man looked at them, his gaze spearing them, and what she saw was plenty of arrogance and cockiness. In other words, his usual reaction.

"Two days ago I requested a search warrant for Curran's financials," Barrett said, getting Della's complete attention. "His connection to money laundering just keeps gnawing away at me. So does the possibility of him having had something to do with Francine's death. I didn't get the warrant," he quickly added, "but I'm going to keep trying."

"Does Curran know that?" she asked.

"You bet. And that's why he's glaring at me right

now." He paused. "And you're thinking he might have had something to do with what happened tonight. I'm not ruling it out, but for now I'm sticking with the obvious. Casto and Alice were at odds, and now Casto's dead. No need for me to try to connect Curran to this."

No, but Della would look into it.

"Thank you," she said.

Barrett's gaze connected with hers for a few seconds before he turned back to the road. Or rather the road and the rearview mirror. He was glancing behind them, no doubt checking to see if Curran was following him. He didn't seem to be.

"What are you thanking me for?" Barrett asked.

"For not giving up on Francine."

His huff let her know that she'd just insulted him. She hadn't intended to do that, but it just felt as if with each passing day people forgot a good cop had been murdered. Della had no intention of forgetting it, and she was glad for all the help she could get in finding Francine's killer. And Barrett's attempts to help her hopefully meant that he wasn't holding their breakup against her.

Or at least his feelings about that had mellowed.

Della very much needed him to mellow so she could tell him what he had to hear. That in about seven months, he'd be a father.

Since she'd seen the plus sign on the pregnancy test, she'd been trying to figure out how to tell him, and she hadn't come up with a single scenario where she could see him being happy about this. Not once had Barrett ever mentioned his desire for children.

In fact, just the opposite.

His bitter childhood had left him not trusting relationships, not wanting a deep connection to anything that could tear him apart again. He loved his brothers, she was certain of that, but Della suspected he held back his feelings even with them. She didn't suspect, *she knew* that he'd done the same with her.

Barrett had had no problem keeping their relationship at just sex, and he'd reminded her countless times that he wasn't capable of more than that. That's why her baby news was going to shake him to the core.

"I noticed earlier that you were too pale," Barrett said out of the blue.

That certainly pulled her out of her thoughts, and Della hoped that no one else had picked up on that. She didn't want anyone guessing about the pregnancy until she'd told Barrett.

"Are you sick, or has all of this just gotten to you?" Barrett pressed as he drove out of the town and back onto the country road.

There it was. The opening she needed. But the timing was beyond bad. After all, they were heading to a crime scene, their second of the night, and this one had a dead body that could hopefully give them answers as to why Casto had been murdered and Alice attacked. Still, maybe timing was always going to be "beyond bad" when it came to Barrett and her.

Della pulled in a long breath that she was certain she would need, but before she could even get out a word, she spotted the vehicle just ahead. Not driving or parked on the side of the road but rather right in the middle of it.

Barrett obviously saw it, too, because he hit the brakes, his tires squealing and going into a slide on the rain-slick road. He managed to come to a stop just a few yards away from the black SUV.

Because of the dark tint on the windshield, Della

didn't see anyone inside the vehicle, but the passenger's side window was lowered a couple of inches.

"Maybe the driver stalled," Della muttered, but she instantly got a bad feeling in the pit of her stomach.

Apparently, Barrett got a buzz, too, because he drew his weapon. Della reached to do the same, but it was already too late. She saw the hand snake out from the window, and she spotted the gun.

Just as the bullet slammed into their windshield.

THE PELLETS OF safety glass flew at him, and Barrett automatically caught onto Della and pulled her lower onto the seat. His first thought was that he wished they were in a cruiser, where the glass and sides of the vehicle would be bullet resistant. But they weren't. They were in his truck, and the shots wouldn't have any trouble getting through to them.

"Did you see who fired the shot?" Della asked, her voice hoarse and shaky. Despite the shakiness, she had already drawn her weapon and was levering herself up. No doubt to return fire.

But the shots stopped her.

Four more rounds came crashing into what was left of the front windshield, and Della and Barrett could do little more than stay down or risk being hit. They were both cops. Both knew they could face possible danger. However, it caused his adrenaline to soar to know that Della could be killed. Of course, she wouldn't care much for him thinking about keeping her safe, but it was hard for Barrett to fight his instincts to protect her.

Who the hell was doing this? And why? Barrett had to figure that it was connected to Casto and Alice, but that didn't give the reason why someone was now trying to kill Della and him.

Especially Della.

It certainly had him rethinking if his mother was behind this. Alice loved Della, and she wouldn't put her in danger. Of course, maybe Alice had lost control of any thug she might have hired to take care of her now dead lover. It could be that this had all gotten out of hand.

Despite the barrage of shots and his heartbeat drumming in his ears, Barrett managed to hear something else between the blasts. A sort of creaking sound, and even though he couldn't be sure, he thought someone had opened the door of the SUV. If so, that meant the shooter could be coming closer to them.

Trying to go in for kill shots.

"I have to get us out of here," Barrett said, and while keeping hold of his gun, he threw the truck into Reverse and hit the accelerator. The wet road didn't give him the safest surface to speed away, but he didn't have a lot of options here.

The shots continued to come at them, and when Barrett had some distance between them and the SUV, he spotted the gunman. A big bulky shouldered man he didn't recognize. The guy got off a few more shots while he jumped back into the SUV. The moment he was inside, the driver turned his vehicle toward them and came after Barrett's truck.

Barrett cursed because he was clearly at a disadvantage. The broken glass on the windshield cut his visibility. Plus, he was driving backward. The SUV had no such limitations and quickly ate up the distance between them.

"I'll try to stop them," Della insisted.

She didn't wait for Barrett to respond. Della came off the seat, her Glock already aimed, and she fired. Her shots blasted into the SUV windshield, shattering the safety glass as effectively as the gunman had done to Barrett's truck. It didn't slow down the driver, though. He continued to speed toward them, and he bashed the SUV into the truck's front bumper.

The jolt knocked Della and him around like rag dolls, causing her to fly back against the seat. It nearly caused Barrett to drive into the ditch, too, but he recovered as fast as he could, and he sent two shots into the SUV. It swerved. Not enough, though. And the driver made a quick correction to keep coming at them.

Worse, the shooter's hand snaked out again from the passenger's side window.

The gunman returned fire, and while at least one of the bullets missed, one slammed into the truck's side mirror right next to Barrett. Another landed somewhere near Della. Barrett couldn't risk checking to make sure she was okay. He had to focus on keeping them on the road so he could get them the hell out of there.

"We can't have them drive into Mercy Ridge," Della muttered.

Barrett was right there on the same page with her. No way did he want to lead these thugs into town where innocent bystanders could be shot. Unfortunately, Barrett couldn't just turn around and have the gunman chase them somewhere else. That meant he had to try to get the truck onto a side road or trail so that Della and he could make a stand.

"Try to call for backup," Barrett told her.

Della fumbled to get her phone from the equipment bag she had with her, and she sent off a text to someone. The second she finished, she levered herself up again. And she fired. She didn't miss, either. The two bullets blasted into the SUV's windshield, and the driver swerved again and slammed on the brakes.

The SUV went into a skid, but Barrett ignored it and kept trying to put some distance between them and his truck. Della didn't let up, either. She sent three more shots into the other vehicle.

Barrett finally saw what he'd been looking for. An old ranch trail that was wide enough for him to use. He had to brake as well so he could back into it as fast as he could. He threw the truck into Park, freeing up his hands so he could do his own shooting into the SUV.

The gunman ducked back inside the vehicle and, mimicking what Barrett had done moments earlier, the driver put pedal to the metal and started speeding backward. Away from Della and him. Barrett felt a split second of relief that they were no longer under fire. But it didn't last. He couldn't let these thugs get away because they could just lie in wait and attack them again.

"Hold on," Barrett warned Della, and he took off after the SUV. "How far out is backup?" he added when he heard her phone ding.

Della glanced down at the screen. "A minute, maybe less. However long it takes Jace to get here from the hospital."

Jace. Of course, she'd texted him. Then again, it was possible she didn't have the numbers for his brother or the other Mercy Ridge deputies.

Ahead of them, the SUV's brakes squealed, and Barrett saw the driver start turning the vehicle around. No doubt so they could try to speed away. But they clearly weren't giving up on killing them because the shooter's hand came out again, and the guy sent three back-to-back shots at them.

Despite the driver's maneuvering, the shots were dead-on.

One of them smacked right into Barrett's steering

wheel, just inches from his hand, and he didn't want to know how close it'd come to his head. He didn't have time to worry about that, though, because he heard the sharp sound that Della made.

The sound of pain.

Barrett risked looking at her, and he saw something he definitely didn't want to see. Blood on her arm.

"Oh, God," she said, the words fighting with her gusting breath. "I need you to take me to the hospital now. I've been shot."

Chapter Five

Della forced herself to slow her breathing. Panicking wouldn't help and would only make things worse. Still, it was hard to hold it together when she felt the pain stabbing through her and saw the blood.

The baby.

The fear of losing her child roared through her like an unstoppable train barreling at her. The injury wasn't that serious. Definitely not life-threatening. But any loss of blood could also mean a miscarriage.

Della nearly blurted out for Barrett to hurry, that it wasn't just her arm injury at stake, but there was no need. Barrett was already hurrying, driving as fast as he safely could, and he was doing that while on the phone with Daniel to get his brother and a team out looking for that SUV. And for the men who'd just tried to kill them.

For as long as she could remember, she'd wanted to be a cop. And wearing the badge meant facing danger just like this. But everything was different now that her baby was added to the mix. She couldn't lose his child. It didn't matter that the pregnancy hadn't been planned or that Barrett didn't want to be a father. She had to be okay so that her baby would be, too.

She managed to text Jace, to tell him that Barrett and she were heading back to the hospital and that he should do the same. Especially since Daniel would have the pursuit of the gunmen under control. Besides, she wanted Jace at the hospital in case those thugs came after Alice.

"How bad are you hurting?" Barrett asked when he ended the call with Daniel.

Della shook her head, hesitating so that she could try to get control of her voice. "It's okay."

It wasn't, of course. There was pain, but if she tried to describe it to Barrett, she might spill all about the baby. This wasn't the way she wanted him to find out. Later, after she'd been examined. Maybe after the shooters had been caught, she'd tell him then.

Thankfully, they weren't that far from the hospital, only a few minutes, and when Barrett pulled into the parking lot, he drove straight to the doors of the ER. Someone had alerted them, probably Daniel, because the moment Barrett came to a stop, a nurse and an EMT came rushing out toward them. Even though Della could have walked on her own, they put her on a gurney and rushed her into the hospital.

Barrett was right behind them.

There was no sign of Jace, but it was possible he hadn't made it back yet. That wouldn't last long. Della would have texted Jace about the shooting, and he would come to the ER to check on her.

It only took seconds for Dr. Tipton to hurry into the examining room with her, and Della didn't think it was her imagination that he seemed relieved when he saw her injury. Yes, there was blood running down the sleeve of her shirt, but it was all on her arm.

"Cut off her shirt," Tipton told the nurse. According to her name tag, she was Gayla Hayward.

Getting her out of her shirt would be just the beginning, Della knew. She'd likely need stitches, and for that to happen, Dr. Tipton would want to administer some kind of painkiller. That meant she'd need to tell him about the pregnancy.

"Could you please wait outside?" Della asked Barrett.

He blinked, maybe surprised that she didn't want him to see her partly undressed, and that's what Della wanted him to believe. For now, anyway.

"This shouldn't take long," Della added, "and I want an update on anything that Daniel and the others might have found. Plus, Jace will need to know."

Barrett hesitated, studying her face. Maybe trying to suss out why she was lying to him. But he finally got moving when the nurse cut away Della's blouse, leaving her bare to the waist except for her bra.

A black lace one.

It was barely there and more suited for date night than a police op, but it'd been the first thing Della had grabbed when she'd gotten dressed.

"If I'd known I was going to get shot, I would have worn something…more sensible," she muttered.

She hadn't intended for Barrett to hear that, but obviously he did, and despite their situation, the corner of his mouth lifted for just the briefest of smiles. Without saying anything to her, he walked out, shutting the door of the examining room behind him.

"It's a deep gash," Dr. Tipton immediately told her. He likely would have continued with an explanation of treatment, but Della caught onto his arm, turning him so they'd have eye contact.

"I'm pregnant," she whispered. The words sounded so foreign, and she realized why. It was the first time she'd said them aloud. "I haven't had an exam, but I've done pregnancy tests. They were positive."

Dr. Tipton stared at her, maybe piecing together why she'd sent Barrett out of the room. After all, it wasn't a secret that Barrett and she had been lovers. Of course, the doctor could think that she'd gotten pregnant after the breakup.

"How far along do you think you are?" Tipton asked.

"Two months," she answered without hesitation. It wasn't hard for her to remember that since she'd almost certainly gotten pregnant right before she'd ended things with Barrett.

Dr. Tipton nodded. "All right. I'd like to do another test here to confirm it, and I won't use any medication that could harm the baby."

The relief came but only as a trickle. There was a bigger concern here. "What about the blood loss?"

"Obviously, it's not ideal for an expectant mother to be shot, but it should be fine."

More than a trickle of relief that time. It came as a flood, and Della lay back on the table. "I don't want anyone else to know about the baby," she murmured.

"No one will hear it from us." Dr. Tipton began to gently press her stomach while the nurse took over cleaning her arm. "But if you're already two months, you won't be able to keep it a secret for long. And you shouldn't be doing duty that puts you in the line of fire."

Yes to both, and Della was trying to figure out how she would deal with that when she heard voices. Jace and Barrett. She didn't know what they were saying, but judging from the volume and tone, they were arguing.

On a heavy sigh, Della got up from the table, grabbed her cut-up shirt and held it in front of her while she opened the door. "I'm okay," she told Jace.

Jace didn't take her word for it. What else was new? He went to her, combing his gaze over her face, then her arm. Behind him, Barrett was doing the same thing, and Della hoped she looked stronger than she felt. Right now, she was shaken and feeling the nerves in every inch of her body.

A muscle flickered in Jace's jaw. "I'm going after the SOB who did this."

"Good." Della wanted that. Not just for her baby's safety but for anyone else who got in those thugs' line of fire. "It shouldn't take me long to get stitched up, and then I can help." Not with going out on patrol. No way would Jace allow that with her hurt. "I can make calls, check on the APB out on the gunmen."

"You can start with getting some rest when you're done here," Jace countered. "I don't want you to go home."

They were in agreement on that. "I could probably find a place to crash here. That way, I could keep an eye on Alice. How is she?" Della added.

Jace took a deep breath before he answered. "She's got a concussion so they're going to keep her overnight. There'll be a deputy or guard on her door." He paused, that jaw muscle working again. "Barrett and I will work that out."

In other words, there'd be a jurisdiction argument. Perhaps a very brief one, though, since Barrett had to be shorthanded what with so many of his deputies working the crime scene and going after those gunmen.

"Did Barrett tell you that we saw Wilbur Curran hanging in the hospital parking lot?" Della asked Jace.

"Not yet," Barrett provided. He might have said more, but the doctor interrupted them.

"Della needs that wound tended to," Dr. Tipton reminded them. "You'll have to talk later."

She nodded, gave Barrett and Jace what she hoped were reassuring looks and closed the door. Obviously, the two lawmen had some things to work out, and despite their checkered past, they would do what was best for this investigation.

Della returned to the table and tried to block out having her arm cleaned, then stitched. It hurt, but she had no intention of asking for pain meds. She'd read a few articles about pregnancy and knew that most meds in this early stage were a no-no. Of course, so was being in the crosshairs of a gunman. To make sure that didn't happen again, she'd have to work with Barrett. Because someone obviously wanted them dead.

But why?

The latest attack had to go back to Casto's murder and the assault on Alice, and it likely wasn't just a matter of killing anyone in law enforcement who might be investigating what happened in the woods. If so, the deputies and the CSIs at the crime scene would have come under fire. That meant Barrett and she were target specific. Someone wanted to eliminate them.

Which would eliminate her baby, too.

The thought of that felt like a meaty fist squeezing around her heart. It was also a reminder that she not only had to work with Barrett, she also had to tell him about the baby. Jace would help her stay safe, but once Barrett knew she was pregnant, it would be a huge distraction for him. For her as well, since she'd also have to deal with the backlash of whatever Barrett felt over having fatherhood thrust on him like this. After all, he'd made it clear that he'd never wanted children because of the ordeal he'd been through as a kid.

That felt like another squeeze around her heart.

She wanted this child, but she had to accept that Barrett might never feel the same way.

When the nurse was finished with the stitches, she drew a blood sample, which she explained would be used for a pregnancy test. Della was certain it would be another positive. However, it was probably best for her to wait for the results before she told Barrett. That might be chicken on her part, but she was too wrung out to deal with that upheaval tonight.

"You can take Tylenol," the doctor added as he helped Della off the examining table. The nurse handed her a green scrub top to wear. "If the pain gets too bad, come back in."

She hoped that wouldn't be necessary, but with or without the pain, Della wasn't expecting to have a restful night. Not with the nightmarish memories of the attack still firing through her mind.

Della thanked the doctor and nurse, put on the scrub top and went back into the waiting room, where she found Barrett pacing and talking on the phone. He was also sporting a very steely expression. He didn't aim it at her exactly, but she had no trouble seeing the questions in his eyes.

"I'm fine," she told him the moment he ended the call. Della glanced around but didn't see anyone else in the immediate area. "Where's Jace?"

"He got called back to his office. He said to remind you that he wants you to stay here, but if you insist on leaving, let him know, and he'll come and get you."

Jace's offer wasn't exactly a surprise, but Barrett continued before Della could say anything.

Barrett huffed, rubbed his hand over his face. "I want you to come back to my place. It's a lot closer than you going back to Culver Crossing, and I'd rather you not be out on the roads any longer than necessary."

The way he'd braced himself, it was as if he was preparing for an argument. But Della had no intention of doing that.

She nodded. "Thanks."

His braced stance continued, and this time there were more than questions in his eyes. There was suspicion.

"I'm tired," Della said, hoping that it would explain why she would readily agree to go to her ex-lover's house. And that was the truth. However, if the pregnancy test results came through by morning, she wanted to be able to tell Barrett where they'd have some privacy.

Barrett nodded as well, and he took out his phone again to fire off a text. "I'm having one of the deputies bring us a cruiser. My truck is too shot up to drive."

With everything else going on, Della had actually forgotten about that, but he was right. There hadn't been much left of the windshield. Plus, the cruiser would be bullet resistant.

"We got an ID on the dead man," Barrett said, putting his phone back in his pocket.

That got her attention, because this was almost certainly the person who kidnapped Alice. And the one who killed Casto.

"The guy had a record," Barrett went on, "so that's why they were able to ID him so fast. His name is Harris LeBeau."

Judging from the way Barrett was looking at her, he expected her to recognize the name. She didn't. "Who is he?"

"Along with being a former bouncer at a club, he also worked for Wilbur Curran," Barrett finally added.

Della pulled back her shoulders. She definitely didn't like that association, since Curran was likely as dirty as they came. Too bad Barrett didn't have proof of that.

"What did LeBeau do for Curran?" she asked.

"Personal security." Barrett punctuated that with a *yeah-right* sound.

She agreed with his skepticism. Personal security sounded more like hired muscle to her.

"Unfortunately, LeBeau officially quit working for Curran about two years ago." Barrett stopped, made a frustrated sigh. "In other words when I bring Curran in for questioning in the morning, he'll claim that he's had no recent association with the man."

Oh, yes. That's exactly what Curran would say. But it didn't make it true. "Maybe Curran will slip up during the interview. You could even ask him what he was doing here at the hospital tonight." Though she was betting Curran would have an explanation for that, too.

Barrett's phone rang, and his forehead bunched up when he saw what was on the screen. "Unknown caller," he said, putting the call on speaker.

Della's heart started to rev because she thought this might be the shooter contacting them. Obviously, Barrett had considered that as well, and he hit the record function on his phone before he answered it.

"Sheriff Logan?" the caller said. It was a woman, and Della instantly recognized the voice.

"Lorraine Witt," Della provided in a whisper to Barrett.

He shook his head, probably because he didn't know her. "Yes, I'm Sheriff Logan," Barrett answered. "Who is this?"

"I'm Lorraine Witt." Her sob came through loud and clear. "I just heard Robert Casto's been killed. Please tell me that's wrong. Please tell me he's alive." That was followed by another sob.

"How do you know Casto?" Barrett asked.

It took Lorraine several seconds to answer, and it sounded as if she was crying. "He's my lover...*was* my lover," she amended. "Is he really dead?"

"Yes, he's dead. He was murdered earlier this evening." Barrett paused a moment, no doubt to give Lorraine some time to absorb what he'd just told her. The woman wasn't absorbing it well, and the crying only got louder. "Who told you about his death?"

Lorraine didn't give an immediate answer, and when she did, her voice was clogged. "A friend, Jessa Marks. She called me. But I didn't believe her. I *can't* believe her. I loved Robert."

Barrett lifted an eyebrow, turning that silent question to Della. Had Casto been involved with both Alice and Lorraine at the same time? Della had to nod. Barrett huffed, muted the call.

"Casto and Lorraine have been on-and-off lovers for years," Della explained. "It's possible Casto was two-timing your mother."

"Great," Barrett grumbled. "Nothing like adding a love triangle to the mix of a murder investigation." He unmuted his phone. "Miss Witt, do you know anything about Casto's death?"

Her response was another loud sob. "No. No," she repeated. "I have to go," Lorraine quickly added, and she hung up.

Barrett stared at his phone as if considering hitting redial, but he finally just ended the record function. "How well do you know her?" Barrett asked Della.

"Well enough. Culver Crossing isn't any bigger than Mercy Ridge, so you know how it is."

He made a sound to indicate that he did. In small towns like theirs, law enforcement got to know pretty much everybody.

"She's never been arrested, never caused any trouble," Della added. "But I can't personally vouch for her." Even if she had been able to do that, Barrett would almost certainly want to talk to Lorraine and anyone else who'd had recent contact with Casto. Jace would do that, as well.

Barrett's phone dinged, and he read what was on the screen. "The cruiser's here and parked just outside the doors. Are you done here?"

Della nodded and would have fallen in step with Barrett, but someone called out to her. It was the nurse, Gayla Hayward. Gayla had already opened her mouth to say something, but she stopped when she spotted Barrett.

"Uh, I need to tell you something," Gayla said to Della. "In private."

Della's stomach dropped, and she prayed this wasn't going to be bad news about the baby. She went to the nurse, who then led her a few feet away from Barrett.

"Dr. Tipton wanted me to tell you that he'll call you in the morning with the pregnancy test results," the nurse whispered. She handed Della a small brown paper bag. "He also wanted you to have a bottle of prenatal vitamins that you should start right away if the test is positive. And you'll need to schedule an appointment with an OB, of course."

"Of course," Della repeated in agreement. It was something she should have already done, but the shock of the news had thrown her for a loop.

After Della turned away from the nurse, she saw that Barrett had his gaze nailed to her, and he slid suspicious eyes down to the bag she was holding. He didn't ask what was in it, thank goodness, because Della figured her lying skills wouldn't be up to par tonight. She also gave another mental thanks when Barrett motioned for her to follow him to the cruiser.

"Move fast," he reminded her, though Della had already intended to do just that.

Barrett opened the passenger's side door for her before he took the keys from his deputy, Scottie Bronson.

"You're sure you don't want me to follow you out to your place?" Scottie asked.

Barrett shook his head. It was no doubt tempting to take Scottie up on his offer, but there were so many other things the deputy could be doing. Such as finding out who was responsible for the attacks so they could put an end to the danger. Della was certain that's what Barrett and she would be doing.

Well, that and trying to pretend that the old attraction between them was old enough to be finished.

Della hurried into the cruiser, and the moment that Barrett was behind the wheel, he took off. Like Della, he also fired glances all around them, looking for any signs of the gunmen, but no one was around.

Both a blessing and a curse.

Part of her would have liked to confront whoever was after them since they had backup and could probably catch and arrest the guys. However, the serious downside to that would be putting the baby at risk.

Barrett didn't say a word as he navigated out of the hospital parking lot and onto the street. His ranch wasn't far, just a few miles outside of town, but it would probably seem like an eternity before they got there. Della slid her hand over her weapon and intended to keep it there until they were safely inside Barrett's house.

"All right," Barrett said, causing her to glance at him. "Are you going to tell me what's going on?"

Della's heart skipped a beat or two. "What do you mean?" she asked, hoping she sounded puzzled rather than scared of his question.

"You know what I mean." His gaze slashed to the bag that was now in her lap. "I want to know what's wrong, and I want to know *now.*"

Chapter Six

Barrett didn't want to take his eyes off the road or their surroundings for too long, but he made sure he caught Della's expression after he'd just made his demand.

I want to know what's wrong, and I want to know now.

Along with looking as if he'd just pointed a gun at her, she quickly glanced away. Obviously dodging his gaze. "I'm worried about going to your place," she finally said after some very long moments.

Barrett opened his mouth to argue that wasn't it, but he stopped. Because maybe that's all there was to it. After all, Della had broken up with him, and it could be she didn't want to do anything that would hint at them getting back together.

Was that it?

If so, then Barrett hoped this unsettled twinge inside him would soon go away. Still, he had a bad feeling that Della had just lied to him.

Barrett didn't press her, in part because he truly did need to focus on the drive and also because his phone rang. Daniel's name popped up on the screen, which meant this was a call he needed to take. Since he wanted to keep his hands free, he put the call on speaker.

"I just got off the phone with Wilbur Curran," Daniel said. "He'll be in your office at eight in the morning so you can interview him."

Good. If it hadn't been so late, Barrett would have pressed for that interview to happen now, but he'd need a clearer head before he dealt with the likes of Curran.

"FYI, Curran's pissed off," Daniel added. "I'm guessing that won't surprise you."

It didn't, and he made a sound to indicate that. "Did Curran happen to say why he was at the hospital tonight?" Barrett pressed.

"I asked, and he said he'd answer the question when his lawyer was present."

That figured. Curran loved to hide behind his attorneys. And that meant it would be a battle to get anything from him. Still, Curran could be a hothead so he might slip up.

Barrett ended the call and pulled into the driveway in front of his house. He got as close to the porch as possible, angling the cruiser to prevent Della from being out in the open any longer than necessary. He expected her to balk about that, to remind him that she was a cop and didn't need such kid glove treatment. But she didn't utter one word of protest.

"I've never slept in the guest room," she muttered.

Considering that she looked embarrassed over that comment, Barrett guessed she hadn't meant to say it aloud.

That unsettled twinge inside him went up a notch.

He stepped ahead of Della, unlocking the door and disarming the security system. Once he had her inside the house, he immediately reset it and went through the living room and into the kitchen so he could make sure the door there was locked. It was. He'd also check all the windows, but for now he wanted to get Della settled. If *settling* was possible, that is. She stood in the foyer, her nervous gaze darting around, looking at anything but him.

"I don't have any pajamas," he said. Something she no doubt knew since he slept commando. "But there'll be some T-shirts in my dresser. That'll work for tonight, and then tomorrow... Well, we can work out a better arrangement."

She nodded, paused as if she might finally tell him what was bugging her. But she didn't. On a long breath, she started for the hall. "I'll grab a T-shirt and a shower. Good night, Barrett."

He took his own long breath and started checking the windows. His house wasn't that big, only two bedrooms, a home office, two bathrooms and an open living, dining and kitchen area. Definitely no frills, but he didn't have time for such things what with tending to his horses and being the sheriff.

He'd barely finished with his security check when he heard Della in the shower of the guest room. He also heard a vehicle approaching the house, and that put him on full alert. Drawing his gun, he went to the front window, bracing himself for the worst. But it was Leo.

Barrett waited until his brother was on the porch before he paused the security system and opened the door. Leo stepped in, his attention going straight to Barrett's weapon.

"Just wanted to check on you," Leo said, his words trailing off when he heard the shower. "And Della. How is she?"

The hell if Barrett knew, but because he didn't want to discuss unsettled twinges with his brother, he just answered, "I think she's as all right as anyone can be who just got shot."

Leo nodded, paused and then cursed softly. "This is a mess. You think Alice had something to do with Casto's murder?"

"She's connected. But I don't know how. *Yet*," Barrett added.

He understood all the things his brother wasn't saying. Leo was the baby of the family, and while he hadn't actually seen their father's dead body on the floor after he'd taken his life, that didn't mean he hadn't been just as traumatized as Barrett had been. Or Daniel. They'd all been cut to the core after their father's death, and that had all started with Alice. Now the woman was back in their lives, and this time they wouldn't be able to ignore her or pretend she didn't exist.

"If Alice isn't released from the hospital in the morning, I'll go there and have another chat with her," Barrett continued. "I need to ask her if she knows anything about the dead guy, LeBeau."

That was for starters anyway. Barrett wanted a lot more details about the argument she'd had with Casto.

"I've put out feelers to a few criminal informants I know," Leo explained. "We might get lucky and find some proof that Curran hired LeBeau."

Yeah, that would indeed take some luck since Curran would have covered his tracks. If he was responsible for this, that is. The problem would be that Barrett wasn't even sure there was a connection between Casto and Curran, so why would Curran have hired someone to kill him? Unless this was all about setting up Alice. If that was it, then it wasn't a good way to get back at Barrett.

Maybe to get back at Della, though.

And that led Barrett to a question that he'd been mulling over. Had Della been the actual target? If so, why? He'd need to go over her recent cases to make sure this wasn't someone who was out for revenge.

Both Barrett and Leo turned at the sound of footsteps, and they saw Della coming toward them. She stopped as if frozen when she spotted Leo. Obviously, she hadn't expected his brother to be there. And Barrett hadn't expected to have the reaction he did to Della.

A *bad* one.

As he'd suggested, she was wearing one of his T-shirts, a nondescript gray one that was big on her. Still, it managed to skim her body in all the right places. Worse, it hit midthigh, showing plenty of her long legs. That caused his body to react, and it didn't seem to care that Della and he were no longer lovers.

"Sorry to interrupt," she said. "I heard you talking to someone and wanted to make sure everything was okay."

Barrett nodded and would have likely said something had she not fluttered her hand toward the guest room and muttered a goodnight. Della turned and hurried off. The moment she was in the guest room, she shut the door.

Barrett took a moment, trying to rein in the heat that had roped and tied him up. Hell. He didn't want this; he didn't want Della, but apparently certain parts of him had other ideas.

"Are you okay with Della being here like this?" Leo asked, sliding him a glance.

Finally, that was an easy question to answer.

No.

Barrett wasn't okay with it. Far from it. And he knew all the way to his gut that this was not going to end well.

DELLA SILENTLY CURSED the pain in her arm the next morning. And her headache. Since she was off both caffeine and meds, she couldn't do anything about either of them. She could only get dressed and hope that no one tried to kill her today.

Thankfully, there was a toothbrush and some toothpaste in the guest bath. A comb, too. That meant she could at least take care of minimal grooming, but she had no choice about putting her jeans and the scrub top back on. Which she did before making her way to the kitchen.

Barrett was there, of course, and he was also cursing. Not silently, though, as she was doing. He was muttering profanities while he read something on his laptop that he had on the breakfast nook table.

"Good," he said. "Glad you're up. I was about to knock on your door to tell you we'll need to leave soon for the interviews with Curran and Alice."

Those would be stressful. Maybe interesting, too, if Alice remembered anything else that would help them. The interviews also meant that she wouldn't be having that baby chat with Barrett this morning. Maybe after that, though, and she made a promise to herself that she wouldn't chicken out.

"The knife that killed Casto is still being analyzed, and the CSIs are going over the trace and fibers they took from the dead man's SUV," Barrett grumbled, sparing her a glance. "No sign of the two thugs who attacked us." Then, he cursed again when he glanced into his coffee cup. Probably because the caffeine wasn't working.

Of course, caffeine had big shoes to fill if it was to overcome some serious lack of sleep. And Della knew for a fact that Barrett had had as restless a night as she had, because she'd heard him moving around in his room. She'd moved, too, and hurt... Even with the pain she hadn't been able to forget that Barrett was just across the hall. Much too close for her body to forget.

She could say the same now.

It was déjà vu being in his kitchen like this, something that had happened many times when they'd been lovers. They'd had plenty of postsex mornings while they'd discussed the investigations into Francine's murder, Curran's money laundering and any others they were dealing with. They'd been good mornings, and Della missed being with him. Heck, she missed the sex. But she wasn't a fool, and she seriously doubted they could get back to that easy pace.

"There's coffee," Barrett added, tipping his head to the pot.

Since she didn't want him asking why she was skipping her usual cup, she laid her purse/equipment bag on the counter, went to the fridge and got some juice instead. No morning sickness, thank goodness, but she didn't want to risk eating right now.

"Leo didn't stay the night?" she asked.

Barrett shook his head and finally looked at her. He nearly did a double take, and at first she thought that was because she looked a wreck. The pain had to be etched on her face. But there was something else in his smoky gray eyes. Heat. For her. It nearly caused Della to smile in a misery-loves-company sort of way, since there was no doubt some heat in her own eyes.

She considered just blurting out she was pregnant. That would not only cool the fire, but it would get this monkey off her back. But Barrett spoke before she could say anything.

"Jace texted me about an hour ago," Barrett explained. "He had one of his deputies bring you some clothes and toiletries to the sheriff's office."

Della hadn't expected Jace to do that but was glad he had. It did make her wonder, though, why Jace hadn't messaged her. Maybe he hadn't wanted to risk waking her. As if.

Barrett checked his watch. "If you want to grab something to eat—"

"I'm fine. We can go ahead and leave. If I get hungry, I can have the diner deliver something."

She had already put on her holster and gun, and the prenatal vitamins were in her bag. No way did she want to leave those lying around for Barrett to find if things worked out that she didn't come back here.

When they reached the door, Barrett motioned for her to stay back while he glanced around the yard. She immediately spotted Buddy Adler, Barrett's part-time ranch hand, who was by the pasture fence. Buddy gave them a thumbs-up, probably a signal to Barrett that he hadn't seen anyone on the grounds. Good. She hadn't known Buddy would be around, but Della welcomed all the help they could get. Plus, Buddy was a reserve deputy so he could add an extra layer of security.

Barrett and she hurried into the cruiser, and she tried not to wince when the seat belt rubbed her arm. Tried and failed. And Barrett noticed.

"Didn't the nurse give you some pain meds?" he asked.

Since she didn't want to outright lie, she settled for saying, "I don't like taking them."

"I get that, but it'll be hard for you to focus on the interviews if you're hurting."

So true. Still, she didn't have another option. But it occurred to her that Barrett did—about the interviews anyway.

"Did Jace ask you to let me talk to Alice and Curran?" she pressed.

That tightened Barrett's jaw a little. "He brought it up."

Ah, she got it then. Jace had likely said he'd allow her to sit in or that he'd be the one to accompany Barrett. No way would her boss want to be left out of this, since the jurisdiction lines were blurred on this investigation.

Barrett didn't add anything else, and Della didn't push. She needed to aim all her mental energy at making it through this morning and dealing with the flashbacks she was having from the attack. Dealing with the worries, too, about the baby. She wished now that she'd asked the doctor more questions about how the stress could affect the pregnancy.

That last worry stayed in the forefront of Della's mind all the way to the sheriff's office. Leo must have been expecting them because he stepped out, keeping watch, until they were all in the building. Then, he handed her a small overnight bag that he picked up from a desk.

"From your boss," Leo said.

Della took the bag to the small bathroom just up the hall, and she was pleased when she saw that Jace had been thorough. She was also a little weirded out that he, or one of the other deputies, had had to go through her underwear. Still, she had fresh clothes to put on so she couldn't gripe about it. She also hurriedly put on some makeup since she was way too pale. Maybe some cosmetics would prevent people from asking her if she was okay.

The moment she stepped out of the bathroom, Della heard the booming voice, and she followed it to Barrett's office. Wilbur Curran was there. And she automatically scowled. So did Curran, and he aimed that particularly acid expression at both Barrett and her.

Curran wasn't alone, of course. There were two suits with him. Lawyers, no doubt, though she didn't recognize either of them. No suit for Curran. He was wearing pricy jeans and a brown leather vest over a crisp white shirt.

"Well, this is an unholy alliance," Curran commented, keeping his scowl on Della. "I didn't know you'd started crawling back into the sheriff's bed."

Della met him eye to eye. "You've obviously got a lot of spare time on your hands if you're keeping up with my personal life."

His jaw tightened, and he opened his mouth, likely to snap back at her, but one of the suits stepped between them. "I'm Gene Templeton, and this is Blaine Conway. We're representing Mr. Curran and ask that you direct any and all comments and questions to us."

Yep, Curran had thrown up that legal wall again. One that Barrett ignored when he looked directly at Curran. "Come with us now."

Barrett didn't wait to see if his order would be met. He just started up the hall toward the interview room. Della followed, and after a whispered conversation with his lawyers, the trio joined them.

When they were all inside and seated, Barrett turned on the recorder, read Curran his rights and then named everyone in the room so it would be part of the official record.

"This is getting real old, real fast," Curran said the moment Barrett finished. "When are you going to get tired of trying to pin stuff on me?"

"I don't get tired of doing my job," Barrett fired back. "I need your whereabouts last night."

The lawyers, who were seated on both sides of Curran, leaned in as if to whisper something, but Curran answered. "At home and then at the hospital. Because you saw me there, that makes you and Deputy Delish here my alibis."

Since Curran had called her that to get a rise out of her, Della didn't accommodate him. She calmly set her bag on the floor next to her, gave him a flat stare and let Barrett continue to take the lead on the interview.

"Home?" Barrett challenged. "Can anyone verify that?"

Curran smiled. It was slick and oily. "Of course, a couple of my ranch hands saw me. I can give you their names."

"Do that." Barrett slid a tablet of paper his way, though both Della and he knew that anyone who worked for Curran would also lie for him. "Why were you at the hospital last night?"

"Just being nosy." Curran grinned. "I heard that your mama was brought in, and I wanted to see if I could hear any gossip."

That was possibly the truth. *Possibly.* It was also possible Curran had wanted to pump someone for info to see if the murder could be connected to him.

Barrett added a few more questions about the hospital visit, nailing down times. Or rather the times that Curran admitted to.

"Tell me about Harris LeBeau," Barrett threw out there.

Now the lawyers moved in again, and the whispering ensued. Curran, however, nailed his attention to Barrett, and the man appeared to be fighting a smile. A reaction that he might hope would rile Barrett and her.

That's why Della returned the half smile while making sure her eyes were all cop. That shut Curran down.

"LeBeau used to work for me," Curran snapped, while his lawyers were still whispering. "As I'm sure you already know. You also know that I ended that employment two years ago."

"When's the last time you saw him?" Barrett fired back.

Curran lifted his shoulder. "A couple of months ago. I saw him at a club in San Antonio. Or maybe it was Austin. We didn't speak," he added with his poker face back in place.

"You're sure about that?" Barrett, again. "Think hard because I'm looking for witnesses now who can tell me otherwise. If I find one person, *just one*, who saw you exchange a single word, then I'll be able to arrest you for giving a false statement and obstruction of justice."

That got the lawyers started, and they doled out their own threats of harassment. Curran's poker face vanished, and the anger flared through his dust-gray eyes. "LeBeau and I didn't talk," he insisted over his lawyers' objections.

Barrett gave Curran a very skeptical look. "Did you know that LeBeau's dead?"

"Yeah. I heard about that," Curran confirmed. "People in this town just love to talk."

Della couldn't dismiss the gossip factor. It could be how Curran had heard the news, but she was betting Curran still had contacts who'd fed him such information.

"As usual, Sheriff, you're barking up the wrong tree," Curran added a moment later. "If you want to find out who's trying to kill the deputy and you, then you need to take a closer look at your own gene pool."

Barrett leaned back in his chair, stared at Curran. "What do you mean?" Barrett asked.

"Well, I'm not responsible for LeBeau's and Casto's deaths, but I'm pretty sure I know who is." Curran smiled. "You need to be talking to your mother."

Chapter Seven

His mother.

Of course.

Barrett had wondered how long it would take Curran to fan some flames by bringing Alice into this. That said, maybe there was some truth to what he'd just said. And it was because of that possible truth that Barrett figured the interview with Alice would go past the point of just being uncomfortable. Then again, things were never comfortable when it came to his mother.

"Do you have proof that Alice had anything to do with the two murders and the attack?" Della snapped, her narrowed eyes latched to Curran's.

Curran shrugged as if this were a friendly chat. "It just seems obvious to me. After all, Alice had a spat with Casto not long before he was killed. Don't you law enforcement types always look at the spouse or lover?" He threw that out with plenty of smugness but then paused. "But Alice doesn't seem to have the stomach for stabbing and shooting, does she?" His gaze shifted back to Barrett. "Her specialty is doing stuff to others to make them end their lives."

Barrett wished that arrow hadn't found its mark, but it did. Always would. Because it didn't matter how many years had passed, Barrett would never forget his father's suicide. Would also never forget that Alice had brought him to that fatal brink. However, Barrett was old enough, *now*, to accept that the suicide hadn't actually been Alice's fault.

"Come to think of it," Curran went on, "Alice would have needed help for something like this."

Della huffed. "You're saying Alice hired LeBeau?"

Curran made a humming sound as if giving that some thought. "No, hiring someone like LeBeau isn't her style, either. But she could have teamed up with Casto's other woman." He chuckled. "Now, Lorraine Witt's got a hot enough head to help Alice do something like this."

Barrett thought of Lorraine's frantic phone call the night before. Not hotheaded then but very worried. She hadn't sounded like a woman scorned as much as someone devasted by losing the man she loved. Still...

"How do you know Lorraine?" Barrett asked Curran.

Curran blinked as if surprised by the question. "I've met her a few times, and I've heard plenty of things about her. Your mama might have that whole 'still waters run deep' thing going on, but Lorraine wears her heart on her sleeve. She might have gotten fed up with Casto's bed hopping and convinced Alice that he had to die."

Or maybe Lorraine had done this on her own. Barrett didn't know a lot about the woman, but that would soon change. He texted Daniel to do a background check on Lorraine and to have her come in ASAP for questioning. Daniel texted back that he would arrange it and ended the message with:

Alice's injuries apparently weren't serious so she was released from the hospital. She's here.

That was as good a reason as any for Barrett to wrap up this interview with Curran. He didn't think he was going to get anything more from the man, and if something came up in his financials check, he could always bring Curran back in. Of course, Curran would claim that was harassment, but Barrett didn't care. The images of the blood on Della's arm was much too vivid to care about anything other than keeping her safe and getting to the bottom of what was going on.

"You can go," Barrett said, standing.

He considered adding that he would get a warrant for Curran's financials, just to see how the man would react, but it would likely only cause some outrage and blustering about more harassment. Barrett would get the warrant, would dig deep into it and hope that he found a money trail.

Barrett and Della stayed put while Curran and his lawyers left. He figured Della would need a quick breather before facing Alice, but one look at her, and Barrett knew it might take a heck of a lot longer than a moment. Della was way too pale.

"Is your arm hurting?" he quickly asked.

She shook her head, and he could see her trying to steel herself up. Cursing under his breath, Barrett went to her. To do what, he didn't know, but apparently it was going to be his day for stupid things, because he touched her, putting his fingers under her chin to lift it and force eye contact. He didn't like what he saw there.

"Why don't you let me get your pain meds, the ones the nurse gave you last night?" he pressed.

Della gave another shake of her head, which caused his fingers to slide against her skin. And just like that, Barrett had memories of a different kind. Bad ones. When he'd touched Della. When he'd kissed her.

Something his brainless body wanted to do right now.

Worse, he saw more than pain in her eyes. Barrett watched as that slow curl of heat washed over her face. Damn her.

Damn him.

He moved his hand higher, his thumb brushing over her bottom lip. Definitely not a smart thing to do, but he didn't stop, and Della didn't back away. In fact, she sort of moved into it, making it much more than a touch.

This was foreplay, and he was starting to have a lot of bad ideas that he shouldn't have. Thankfully, he was saved by the sound of footsteps. Someone was walking toward the interview room, and a moment later, Daniel appeared in the doorway.

His brother had obviously been about to say something, likely something that had nothing to do with why Barrett and Della looked as if they were guilty of a multitude of things, but Daniel just stood there a long moment. Staring at them. Maybe even waiting for them to explain why there was a scalding hot vibe in the air.

"What?" Barrett practically snapped to get his brother to stop gawking.

Daniel flexed his eyebrows, and Barrett hoped that wasn't amusement he was seeing on his brother's face. If it was, it didn't last. Daniel's expression went heart attack serious.

"You want me to bring in Alice, or do you need a… moment?" Daniel asked.

"Bring her in," Della and Barrett said in unison. Their tones and swift responses didn't make them appear less guilty.

Daniel nodded, then lingered a moment as if expecting some kind of explanation. One that Barrett was certain he wouldn't get. He finally turned and walked away.

Barrett knew he wouldn't have much time to steel himself up and cool down his body. Neither would Della, but she was dealing with a couple of other obstacles that Barrett didn't have.

The pain and Della's friendship with Alice.

A friendship that had developed because Alice and Della lived in the same small town. Probably also because Della felt sorry for Alice since she was estranged from her family. There was also the Jace factor. Alice had had some part in raising Jace so that meant Della had had opportunities to socialize with and also get close to Alice.

It wasn't easy to interrogate a friend, or a mother, but Barrett figured Della and he would do their best. After all, the danger could extend to Alice, too, and Della would want to do whatever it took to make sure the woman wasn't attacked again.

Part of him wanted to pawn this interview off onto someone else, but there wasn't anyone in his department who didn't have a personal opinion about Alice. And those opinions were negative. But Barrett knew he could be objective with the facts, and if he got into boggy ground and lost his objectivity, he'd be willing to ask the Rangers to send someone in to do a more thorough interview.

Barrett put a fresh notepad on top of the interview notes he had from Curran, and he'd just sat down when Daniel brought in Alice. She looked better than she had the night before but not much. There was a bandage on her head, and a nasty bruise ran from her right temple to her cheek.

"Barrett," Alice greeted, and she managed a smile.

An uneasy one that turned more genuine when she looked at Della.

Alice went to Della, moving in as if she might give her a kiss on the cheek, but she stopped, her gaze sliding down to Della's badge that was hooked on her belt. His mother didn't seem to resent that Della was here in an official capacity. However, that badge had to be a reminder that this wasn't the place for hugs.

Something Barrett also needed to remember.

"Jace told me what happened, that someone fired shots at Barrett and you and that you were hit. Are you okay?" Alice asked Della.

Judging from Della's soft sigh, she was tired of hearing that question, but she gave Alice a reassuring nod. "And you?"

Alice touched her fingers to the bandage on her head. "We've both been better." She shifted her attention back to Barrett and then eased down into the chair across from him. That didn't stop her from volleying glances at Della and him. "Are…you two back together?"

Great day. Was he wearing a sign or something? Or maybe Alice just picked up on that same vibe Daniel had.

"No," Barrett answered, and he shifted things back to business. "You didn't bring a lawyer?"

"No." She paused, then softly repeated her answer. "I want to help. And I didn't do anything wrong," Alice insisted.

He could have spelled out that plenty of innocent people had lawyers accompany them to interviews. Plenty of guilty ones, too. Instead, Barrett just Mirandized her again to refresh her of her rights—one of which was for her to have an attorney present. The refresh wasn't legally necessary, but since she'd perhaps been in shock and suffering from her injury during the other reading, Barrett wanted to make sure the ground rules were clear.

"Go ahead, ask your questions," Alice said when he'd finished. "I want to find the person who tried to hurt Della and you."

Barrett noted that Alice had omitted herself from the "finding justice" vow. Casto, too. And that gave Barrett his starting point.

"Did you kill Robert Casto?" he came out and asked.

Alice's eyes widened, and she volleyed more glances at Della and him.

"I thought that man, Harris LeBeau, killed him." Alice's voice was shaky now. "That's what I heard some of the nurses talking about in the hospital."

"I need your answer for the record." He tipped his head to the recorder that he'd turned on. "Did you kill Robert Casto?"

"No, I didn't kill him," Alice said on a rise of breath, and she went from looking frazzled and timid to rattled. Of course, she'd been attacked, too, so maybe that was playing into this.

"You're positive?" Barrett pressed.

Alice paused. Way too long. So long that it caused him to groan. Alice groaned, too, and tears sprang into her eyes. "Some things are still hazy, and I just don't remember if I stabbed him." And with that, her breath broke in a sob. "But I couldn't have killed him. I'm sure I would have remembered that."

You'd think, but then there was the head injury. Barrett would need to talk to her doctor and find out if the injury could have caused memory loss or if that was just a convenient out. He was leaning toward the first one. Not because she was his mother—that didn't play in her favor here—but because it was what made sense. If she'd murdered Casto, he couldn't see her staying around and putting herself smack in the middle of a crime scene.

"Tell me about LeBeau," Barrett said, going for a different approach. "Did you know him?"

Alice grabbed a tissue from the box on the table and wiped her eyes. "Yes."

Barrett didn't know who was more surprised by her answer, Della or him. "How did you know him?" Della asked.

This time Alice didn't hesitate. "I met him at the cattleman's ball, the one that Robert hosted at his ranch about six months ago."

Now, that was an interesting connection. "Casto and LeBeau knew each other?" Barrett pressed.

"Oh, yes." But then she paused. "Robert had done some business with him." Another pause. "Come to think of it, they weren't exactly friendly that night, though, but I figure that's because of Lorraine."

Both Della and Barrett practically snapped to attention. "Lorraine Witt?" Della questioned.

Alice nodded, but then she must have noticed that they'd latched on to something. "Yes. Lorraine and Mr. LeBeau were once engaged."

EVEN WITH HER foggy head, Della could see how the pieces were fitting together. Curran was connected to LeBeau who was in turn connected to Lorraine—which made all of them connected to Alice.

And that in turn made Lorraine, Curran and, yes, Alice suspects in Casto's murder.

Della wanted to put Alice at the bottom of the suspect list, but there was a problem with that.

Some things are still hazy, and I just don't remember if I stabbed him.

Those were Alice's own words, and they could be used to incriminate her. Well, if any corroborating evidence came to light, it would. So far, there wasn't any, but it didn't look good that Alice had been found just yards away from her ex-lover's body. The Mercy Ridge DA could use that to charge her with murder. And that's why Della had to push the woman to do anything she could to clear her name.

Barrett wouldn't understand why she felt a connection with his estranged mother. But she did. The woman had always seemed so sad and lost as if she'd accepted there was nothing she could do to make up for her past. To add plenty more salt to the wound, Della knew Alice still loved her sons. Sons who'd likely never forgive her for what'd happened to their father. Yes, Alice had made a horrible mistake, but Della knew the woman paid for it with her bone-deep grief.

"Tell us more about Lorraine," Della said, figuring that Barrett wouldn't object if she launched into the interview.

Alice nodded, but it seemed to take her a moment to compose herself. "I'm sure you know that Lorraine is Robert's ex." She clamped her teeth over her bottom lip for a second. "And she wants...wanted him back. I could tell. I believe that's why she brought Mr. LeBeau with her to the cattleman's ball, so that she could maybe try to make Robert jealous."

"And was he jealous?" Barrett said when Alice didn't continue.

Alice cleared her throat, blinked back tears. "I'm pretty sure that Robert continued to see Lorraine, maybe even continuing his affair with her. He denied it, but she's one of the reasons we argued. That and he became so controlling."

That meshed with everything Della knew about Casto. Controlling and a cheat. That meant plenty of people could have wanted him dead.

"How much do you remember about last night?" Barrett asked her.

"Only what I've already told Jace and you," Alice insisted. "I remember a man grabbing me in my garage. Then, I woke up outside in the woods."

"No other fragments of memories of something that might have happened in between your being kidnapped and us finding you?" Barrett pushed.

Alice shook her head. "But the doctor said everything might come back. He said this happens sometimes with head injuries."

Della nodded. "Did the doctor mention you seeing a therapist? Maybe someone who could use hypnosis?"

"No." Some of the tension faded from Alice's face. "But I think that's a good idea. I want to remember. No matter what, I have to know."

So did Della and Barrett. Because if Alice hadn't killed Casto and LeBeau, then they could focus on Lorraine and Curran.

"Why don't you go ahead and make an appointment with a therapist," Barrett advised her, and then he glanced at his phone when it dinged. "And I'll want to interview you again."

"Of course," Alice said in a whisper. "You're not arresting me?"

The muscles in Barrett's jaw tightened. "Not at this moment. Once I've finished all the interviews and gotten reports back from the crime scene teams, I'll know whether or not I have probable cause to ask a judge for an arrest warrant."

Nodding, swallowing hard, Alice got to her feet when both Della and he did. Alice moved as if to leave, but then she turned back to Della. "You should get some rest. You look very tired."

Looking tired was the least of her worries. Della was dealing with the pain and the looming reminder that she had to tell Barrett about the baby. Maybe she could do that as soon as the first round of interviews were done.

Not here, though.

She'd need to find some place private for there would no doubt be fallout. Della had been stunned to learn about the pregnancy, but she'd had a day now to work through her feelings. Too bad she couldn't give Barrett that much time. He'd need it, but they'd have to jump back into the investigation.

She followed Alice to the door so she could say goodbye to the woman and try to give her a reassuring look. Della was certain that she failed. So did Alice, who offered her a watery smile in response.

"You're not driving yourself home, are you?" Della asked.

"No. Jace sent one of the deputies, and he's waiting out front for me."

Good. That was a reminder that she needed to thank Jace, something Della was certain that Alice had already done.

After Alice walked away, Della turned back to Barrett. He had gotten up from his seat, but he had his attention nailed to whatever he was reading on his phone.

"The lab reports from the CSIs," Barrett muttered without looking at her.

There was something in his body language that sent

Della rushing to his side, and she soon saw that he'd scrolled through the bulk of the report. However, one thing did catch her eye.

Alice Logan's fingerprints.

Della could have sworn that her heart skipped a couple of beats, and she was still trying to tamp down the panic when Barrett turned to her.

"Alice's prints were in LeBeau's SUV," he said.

The relief came. That could mesh with Alice's statement about being kidnapped. Well, it would if LeBeau had been the one to kidnap her. But the concern quickly tamped down the relief. "Were her prints anywhere else?" And she prayed that Barrett didn't say they were on the murder weapon.

"Maybe." Barrett groaned after his answer. "There are fingerprint smears on the handle of the knife. Maybe Alice's, maybe someone else's. The lab has to do further testing."

So, Alice wasn't in the clear just yet, but since Della believed the woman was innocent, she also had to believe that the evidence would exonerate her. Well, it would unless the real killer had planted Alice's prints there. Considering everything else that'd happened, Della figured that's exactly what Casto's murderer had done.

Barrett and she looked up when they heard a woman's voice coming from the squad room. Not Alice's. But rather Lorraine Witt's.

"I want to see the sheriff now," Lorraine demanded. Judging from her tone, she seemed to think someone was going to prevent that, but Della and Barrett both wanted to see her—and question her.

Barrett stepped out, heading toward the squad room, and Della stayed put a moment to gather her breath. Surprisingly, the pain was somewhat better now, which was a good thing because she needed to focus on Lorraine.

"Why isn't Alice behind bars?" she heard Lorraine ask, and a moment later, both Barrett and the woman came into view. Lorraine was dressed to the nines, as she usually was, in a stylish blue dress that was nearly the same color as her eyes. She had her dark blond hair pulled back from her face. "It's obvious that Alice murdered Robert."

"That's far from obvious," Barrett muttered under his breath. Lorraine rolled over him, repeating her question about why he hadn't arrested Alice, and he read Lorraine her rights.

That stopped her, and Lorraine's eyes widened. "You're arresting me?" she snarled.

"Mirandizing you," Barrett corrected. "It's procedure, and it's for your own protection. I hope you caught the part about you having a lawyer present if you want."

"I don't need a lawyer. I'm innocent."

Della figured that Lorraine didn't know that Alice had said pretty much the same thing. But no lawyer was a good thing because it meant that Barrett and she could question the woman.

"First of all, I'll need your whereabouts for between 6:00 p.m. last night and one this morning," Barrett said.

Lorraine made a sound of outrage, but then she sank down into the chair across from Della and Barrett. "I was home, waiting for Robert. He was supposed to come over, and when he didn't, I got very worried." She blinked back tears. "Obviously, I had a right to be worried. Robert's dead." Now some of those tears fell.

"Was anyone with you?" Barrett pressed. "I'll need someone to verify your alibi."

Lorraine's face didn't show as much outrage as

Curran's had done, but it was close. "My housekeeper, Debra Wallace, was there."

Barrett passed her a notepad. "Give me her contact info so I can call her."

That dried up the rest of Lorraine's tears, and when she wrote down the housekeeper's name and phone number, the pressure from her grip caused the pen to dig into the paper.

"There," Lorraine snapped when she was done. She passed the tablet back to him. "Now that we have that out of the way, I want you to tell me what you're doing to bring Robert's killer to justice."

"I'm questioning any and all persons of interest," Barrett calmly replied, keeping his cop's stare on Lorraine. "Did you murder Casto?"

"No!" Lorraine practically shouted that, but the burst of energy seemed to drain her, and she dropped her head in her hands. "No," she repeated in a much calmer voice. "I was in love with him."

"You loved him even though he was seeing another woman?" Barrett asked.

"Robert didn't love Alice," she quickly answered. "The fact that he continued to see me proves that."

Not really. It only proved that Casto was a womanizer.

"What he felt for Alice was just an infatuation, that's all," Lorraine added. "And he'd already ended things with her. That's why Alice killed him. If she couldn't have him, then she decided no one else would."

"That could be a motive for murder," Della pointed out. "But there's that old adage about a woman scorned. That could apply to both Alice and you which means you have motive, too."

Oh, Lorraine didn't care for that. If looks could have killed, Lorraine would have blasted Della to smithereens.

"I wasn't scorned," Lorraine said through now clenched teeth. "Robert always came back to me, and he would have done that again if Alice hadn't murdered him."

"Tell me about Harris LeBeau," Barrett interrupted, causing Lorraine to shift her scowl from Della to him.

Lorraine pulled back her shoulders. "He's dead. Alice killed him, too."

"Tell me about him," Barrett insisted. "I understand you were engaged to him."

"Yes, years ago. That was long before Robert and I became involved."

Barrett glanced down at the notes he'd taken earlier. "Yet you attended a party with LeBeau about six months ago."

Lorraine obviously hadn't been expecting that, and she blinked in surprise. "That's right. It wasn't actually a date, though. I simply wanted an escort for the party, and he wanted to go."

"And you wanted an escort so you could make Casto jealous?" Barrett said, his tone and expression skeptical.

Lorraine's eyes narrowed. "No. There was no need for me to do that because Robert knew how much I loved him." She paused. "Alice told you about the party." Lorraine muttered some profanity under her breath and got to her feet. "Alice is obviously trying to set me up, and you're too biased to see that's what she's doing. This interview is over. If you have anything else to say to me, you can contact my attorney."

With that, Lorraine stood and stormed out the door. Della waited to see if Barrett was going to stop her. He didn't.

"I don't have any evidence I can use to hold her," he said, and it seemed to Della that he was talking more to himself than to her. "That might change when I dig into her financials. Of course, if she got LeBeau to kidnap Alice and kill Casto, LeBeau might have done it as a favor and not because she paid him."

"True." Della gave that some thought. "But Lorraine might have hired someone to kill LeBeau. Maybe so he couldn't implicate her. If so, there might be a money trail for that."

Barrett nodded. "If you want to help look for that, I can find you a desk and a computer to use."

She was about to suggest they go back to his place and work there, so they could talk. But when she lifted her bag from the floor, the strap caught on the back of the chair, causing the contents to spill out onto the table. One item landed right on top of the others. And the label on the bottle was clearly visible.

Prenatal vitamins.

She reached to scoop it up, but it was already too late. Barrett had seen it, and his gaze sliced from the bottle to her.

"Della, are you pregnant?" Barrett demanded.

Chapter Eight

Barrett tried to rein in the storm of emotions rolling through him. And Della's stunned silence sure didn't help with that. If she wasn't pregnant, then a quick denial should have come out of her mouth, maybe followed by an equally quick explanation of why she had prenatal vitamins in her purse.

But that didn't happen.

Della's eyes widened, and her breath seemed to stall in her throat for a couple of long seconds. Then, he saw the answer in her eyes right before she said the single-word answer.

"Yes." Her voice had barely any sound, but Barrett heard it loud and clear.

His gaze automatically dropped to her stomach. No signs there that she was pregnant, but then he wasn't sure how far along a woman needed to be before she started to show. And then he said something that would change his life forever. The way it'd already changed Della's.

"It's my baby." Barrett's voice didn't fare much better than Della's, but he was damn lucky to have gotten out that handful of words.

Della nodded, but he hadn't needed her confirmation. He knew. Even though Della hadn't been in love with him, he had no doubts that he'd been her only lover for, well, years. Their friends with benefits arrangement had made it easy for them not to risk their hearts with someone else who would have demanded more than just sex.

"I know we always used a condom, but those apparently aren't foolproof. And now I'm two months pregnant," she added.

That sent a new slam of thoughts and emotions, and they raged through him like a fierce battle. Della was pregnant. *With his baby.* That meant he'd be the very thing he'd always sworn he wouldn't be.

A father.

Barrett figured he was going to have to come to terms with that. Soon. And he would, once he could actually think straight. But for now, there was a different concern, and it had to do with that bandage on her arm.

"The gunshot wound…" he managed to say.

She shook her head. "The doctor doesn't think it hurt the baby, but he's scheduled me for an ultrasound. He wants me to make an appointment with an OB, too."

He heard everything she said, her words echoing in his head, but Barrett latched on to the first part. *The doctor doesn't think it hurt the baby.* That was good. However, it wasn't nearly enough reassurance.

Barrett cursed. "I should have never had you in my truck, driving out to a crime scene."

Della shook her head again. "We were both doing our jobs."

That only caused him to curse even more. "You should have told me you were pregnant." But then Barrett paused. "Unless you didn't know then. When did you find out?"

Now it was Della's turn to hesitate. "I did some home

tests yesterday. Before Casto was murdered." She swallowed hard. "The tests were all positive, and while I was at the hospital, the doctor did another test to confirm it."

So, Della had known before she'd responded to that anonymous text that had caused them to go into the woods.

"I'm sorry," she said. "Not sorry about the baby," Della quickly added, "but I'm sorry because I know this isn't what you want."

There it was. All spelled out for him. Except Della had it slightly wrong. After raising his brothers, Barrett had figured that he'd best keep fatherhood off the table. He hadn't failed exactly—both Leo and Daniel had turned out all right—but Barrett wasn't taking any of the credit for that.

His brothers had turned out all right *despite* him.

He'd made plenty of mistakes, as his own father had done, and that'd convinced him that it wasn't a good idea to create another generation of Logans.

"Give me a minute," he told her, putting his hands on his hips and dragging in several deep breaths. It didn't help. No surprise there. This was going to take more than some extra oxygen and a minute to process.

Della gave him that minute. Her eyes stayed locked on him, and she was doing some heavy breathing of her own. Plus, she winced during one of those breaths, and that was a reminder she was having to deal with this along with the aftermath of nearly being killed.

"Okay," Barrett finally said. Of course, it wasn't okay, far from it, but he thought he could finally form enough words to discuss this with her.

"Before you say anything else, I want you to know that I can do this pregnancy alone," Della interrupted.

"If you want to be a part of this, fine, but if you don't, I'll understand."

For some reason her almost congenial offer riled him to the bone. They weren't discussing dinner plans here but rather something that would change everything forever.

"I'm already a part of this," he managed to say, though it was hard to speak through clenched teeth.

Barrett likely would have added a lecture about her not shutting him out even if he wasn't sure how he was going to deal with this, but the sound of footsteps stopped him. A moment later Daniel appeared in the doorway.

His brother had already opened his mouth to say something, but he stopped, no doubt picking up on a different vibe in the room. Not the old heat between Della and him. But rather their new situation that felt as if it could bring him to his knees. Barrett pushed all of that aside, though, for now, because it was obvious Daniel had something important to tell him.

"There's a problem," Daniel started, still eyeing them with plenty of concern. "Someone torched Alice's house."

Della gasped. "Is she okay?"

Daniel nodded, shifted his attention back to Barrett. "The fire department's already on scene, but according to the call I just got, there's plenty of damage. Too much for her to stay there. Oh, and because I know you'll ask, Alice didn't do this. She was on her way home with a deputy."

Yeah, Barrett would have definitely asked about that, especially since there could have been something inside the house that Alice wouldn't want to come to light. The CSIs had already gone through the place, but they might have missed something. Plus, this could also make her look more like the victim that she appeared to be.

"I'm guessing no one saw who did this?" Barrett asked.

"Nope." Daniel gave a weary sigh. "Alice has ranch hands, but they were back in the pasture and didn't see anyone. There's more," he added, that weariness going up a notch. "The deputy who was driving Alice home says someone tried to run them off the road. Two men in an SUV. The deputy called for backup, but the men got away."

"Hell." That was likely the pair who'd tried to kill Della and him. "Please tell me the deputy got the license plate numbers?"

"He did, but they're bogus," Daniel answered.

Of course, they were. Hired killers weren't likely to advertise their identities by driving a vehicle that could be traced back to them.

"Alice is apparently pretty shaken up," Daniel went on. "So shaken up that the deputy is bringing her back here to the hospital." He checked his watch. "They should be arriving right about now. And she said she needs to talk to Della and you."

"Hell," Barrett repeated.

He scrubbed his hand over his face. The last thing he wanted right now was a conversation with his mother, but this could have something to do with the investigation. Maybe she had to tell them something that she didn't want to share with Jace's deputy.

Barrett knew he wasn't going to be able to push aside all thoughts of the pregnancy, but maybe this trip to the hospital could be a "kill two birds with one stone" kind of visit. He could talk to Alice. And confirm that Della's gunshot wound truly hadn't affected the baby.

Of course, he wasn't sure what he would do with the info other than add another worry to his list, but he had to know.

"I can go with Della and you," Daniel offered.

But Barrett shook his head. "I want you to get on those financials. Both Lorraine's and Curran's. Run Casto's, too."

"You think Casto might have hired those thugs?" Daniel asked.

"Maybe." It was possible this was a situation of a hired hit gone wrong. If Casto had paid LeBeau and the two gunmen to go after Alice, then maybe the men had turned on him. Despite the old saying, Barrett hadn't found much honor among thieves. Or would-be killers.

Barrett started toward the front of the building where he'd left his cruiser, and Della was right behind him. He automatically slowed his steps, hoping it would stop her from wincing again from pain. But the wince happened anyway when she put on her seat belt in the cruiser.

"You can't take pain meds because of the baby," Barrett said more to himself than her.

"No. Well, not the pain meds that would actually do much good. It's okay," Della tacked on to that.

He wasn't sure about the okay part. Wasn't sure of much right now. However, Barrett shook his head to try to clear it and kept watch around them as he drove them to the hospital. It wasn't far, just up Main Street, and there weren't any strangers milling around. No vehicles that he didn't recognize, either. He was grateful for being in a small town where things like that stood out. Of course, one of their main suspects—Curran—wouldn't stand out, either, and Barrett suspected the man could be as dangerous and mean as a rattlesnake.

Barrett spotted the Culver Crossing cruiser just out-

side the ER doors, and he pulled to a stop behind it. No
sign of the deputy, but he was likely with Alice. Barrett
hoped so anyway. If someone truly wanted her dead,
then a busy hospital might be the way to try it. He held
on to that reminder for Della, as well. She wasn't necessarily safe here, and while that alone caused him concern, his worries about her had skyrocketed now that
he knew about the baby.

Della and he made their way through the ER waiting area and toward the receptionist's desk, but before
they reached it, Barrett saw Dr. Tipton coming out of
an examining room.

"Alice is in there with Deputy Glenn Spence," the
doctor told Barrett. "I had to give her something to
calm her down."

Great. That meant Barrett might not be able to question her after all if the *calming down* zoned her out. But
he could certainly talk to Dr. Tipton. Since there were
several people in the waiting area, Barrett motioned for
the doctor to follow him to the hall. Not exactly private
space, but it would have to do. Barrett had questions
about Della and the baby. Except he wasn't even sure
how to get started. Della helped with that.

"Barrett knows I'm pregnant," she whispered to Dr.
Tipton. "He's the baby's father."

Even with the good lead-in, Barrett still fumbled
around with what to say. "I just want to make sure Della
and the baby are okay," he finally managed.

Dr. Tipton didn't answer until Della gave him a nod.
"They're doing as well as can be expected. I'm waiting
for her lab work to come back, and as I told her, she'll
need an ultrasound. If you like, I'll try to get you scheduled for that later today."

"Yes, thank you," Della said.

"You can be there for that if Della doesn't mind," the doctor offered Barrett, and then his attention drifted back to the examining room. "I'm guessing you're here to see Alice?"

"She wanted to talk to us," Barrett explained.

"So she said," Dr. Tipton verified. "She insisted, really. Let me go in and make sure she's settled down enough to have visitors," he added when he walked away from them.

Barrett hoped to hell Alice was up to it or this would be a wasted visit. For that part anyway. But not wasted on the info he'd gotten from Dr. Tipton. Della and the baby were okay. Probably.

"You don't have to come with me to the ultrasound appointment," she whispered, her voice tight and coated with an avalanche of uncertainty.

"You can't go alone," Barrett reminded her. "That's not safe."

Of course, that wasn't the same as him saying he wanted to be there for the actual appointment, but he would be. Later, Barrett would figure out how he felt about that, but he didn't need any figuring-out time to know that he had no intention of letting Della out of his sight.

"I feel as if I should say I'm sorry," she continued.

"Don't," he fired back. Not exactly a kind, gentle tone for a wounded pregnant woman, and that's why he gave himself an attitude adjustment. "We both had sex when you got pregnant. Both," he emphasized. "So, if you apologize to me, I'll just have to say it right back to you."

He'd hoped that would relieve some of the tightness on her face. It didn't. On a ragged sigh, Della leaned against the wall as if her legs were too wobbly to stand.

"I'm all right," she insisted, probably when she real-ized he was about to reach for her.

Barrett pulled back his hands. "Funny, you don't look all right."

She shook her head. "It's just piling up on me right now. I'd barely had time to come to terms with this pregnancy, and then we were thrown together on this murder investigation. One where your mother is a sus-pect. Then, we were attacked, and I was shot." Della paused, her breath shuddering. "And tomorrow is the second anniversary of Francine's murder."

Barrett knew he would have remembered that sooner or later. Knew, too, that her friend's murder had to be adding to the flashbacks Della was no doubt experi-encing. There was no good time to grieve a death of a loved one, but Della was right—this was all piling on her. And the timing certainly sucked.

He couldn't think of anything to say to give her any comfort, but he reached out again. This time, he did pull her into his arms. She went stiff, likely questioning if this was a good idea. It wasn't. But she finally let go of her breath and sagged against him. He doubted she would actually cry, but he could almost feel the tears threatening.

Mindful of her gunshot wound, Barrett eased her closer, and he got an instant reminder of when they'd been lovers. The heat came despite everything else. However, it was mixed with something much stronger. This overwhelming need to protect her and the baby she carried. Since she was a cop, Della wouldn't care much for his feeling that way, but he couldn't stop himself.

Mercy, what was he going to do?

Barrett didn't have time to dwell on that, though, because Dr. Tipton came back into the hall. This time

Della and he didn't jolt away from each other. Barrett simply stepped back, hoping that her legs were steadier than they seemed.

"Alice still wants to see you," the doctor said, shaking his head, "but I'm warning you not to upset her. She's right on the edge right now, and along with her panic, she's still dealing with the pain from her head injury."

Barrett and Della gave Dr. Tipton nods of reassurance that they wouldn't upset her, but Barrett had no idea if they could manage that. They likely weren't going to have a pleasant conversation with the woman.

When they stepped inside the examining room, Barrett saw Alice on the table, much as she had been the night before, after the attack. Deputy Glenn Spence was there, too, seated in the corner and looking at something on his phone, but the lanky lawman stood and walked over when he saw them.

"I've got a problem," Spence immediately said. "Lorraine Witt was attacked a few minutes ago. Someone ran her off the road."

Barrett felt the punch of surprise, followed by enough skepticism to cause that punch to fade fast. "You're sure she didn't fake it?" Barrett asked.

Spence lifted his shoulder. "Jace said it looks real enough. There are tire marks before the point of impact, and she ended up in a ditch," the deputy added. "She said two men in a black SUV did it."

Barrett muttered some profanity under his breath. He figured it'd gotten around about the men who'd attacked Della and him, and Lorraine could be using that to make herself look innocent.

"If the attack was real and these were the same thugs

who shot Della, they would have tried to shoot Lorraine," Barrett pointed out.

The deputy nodded. "According to her, they did. She said she saw them point guns at her, but she had a gun, too. She aimed hers right back at them and they sped away."

"I don't suppose there were any witnesses?" Della asked.

"Nope. It happened on a remote stretch of the road between here and Culver Crossing."

Most of that road qualified as a "remote stretch" so that didn't surprise Barrett. "Was Lorraine hurt?"

"She says her shoulder's hurting, and there are some cuts on her face from where the airbags deployed. An ambulance is bringing her here because it's closer than the Culver City hospital. Plus, if it's something serious, they're better able to cope with it here."

That was true. Mercy Ridge was a much bigger hospital. Still, Barrett didn't like the idea of two of his suspects being so close to Della.

"If Jace is dealing with Lorraine's attack and you're here with Alice," Della said, "then we're short-staffed in the office."

"We are indeed," Spence verified. "But Jace insisted you not come into work. He's put you on a mandatory leave of absence since you're hurt."

That was standard procedure, but Barrett knew it was hard to pull two deputies out of rotation. Plus, both Jace and he were facing a firestorm—especially if this latest attack was the real deal.

"Jace wanted to know if you could put Alice in the protective custody of one of your deputies," Spence went on. "Or maybe work it out so that Della and Alice are together, protected by just one lawman. It won't be for long," he added. "A day at most."

Well, hell. Spence maybe didn't know the depth of the rift between Alice and him. Or maybe he did, and it didn't matter. Cops landed between rocks and hard places all the time, and Barrett knew that's where he was right now.

"I'll work something out," he assured the deputy, and when Spence stepped to the side, Barrett went closer to the examining table.

Alice looked even more ashen than she had the night before. No fresh tears, though. Instead, there was a shell-shocked expression that seemed to be bone-deep. He wanted to be immune to that look, to her weary eyes that she lifted to meet his. But he was human, and this was a woman on the brink of a very bad place.

"I remember," Alice said, her voice as drained as the rest of her.

She already had his attention, but that caused Della to move to the other side of the examining table. "Remember what?" Della asked.

Alice's eyelids fluttered down, and she shook her head. Now the tears came. "Everything."

Chapter Nine

Della hadn't thought anything could take her mind off Barrett learning about the pregnancy, but she'd obviously been wrong. Every muscle in her body tensed and she held her breath because she was afraid that Alice was about to make a confession.

Of murder.

"I'm listening," Barrett said, and it seemed to Della that he was also holding his breath.

"I remember that man who kidnapped me," Alice explained. She shook her head. "I was unconscious, but I came to when he was dragging me into the woods. I saw his face."

Barrett took out his phone, pulled up LeBeau's picture from the investigation file and showed it to Alice. "Was it this man?"

"Yes," she answered without hesitation. "He wasn't alone. I didn't see who was with him, but he was calling out to someone. He said something like *Hold your horses, I'll be right there after I take care of the woman.*"

"Take care of the woman," Della muttered, and she wanted to cringe. Because that sounded as if he'd had intentions of killing her. Of course, maybe he'd just meant to set her up, but even if that had been the

plan, Alice could have still been killed by the blow to the head.

"Did you hear this other person speak?" Barrett asked.

"Yes." Again, Alice didn't hesitate. "It was another man. Not Robert, though," she quickly added. "And I couldn't make out what he said. But I heard a sound." Alice shuddered and clamped her teeth over her bottom lip for a few seconds. "It was the sound a person makes when they're in great pain. I think that's when this person killed Robert, and I believe Robert was the one in pain."

Barrett stayed silent a moment, no doubt processing all of that. "You didn't kill Casto?" he pressed.

"No." Alice looked him straight in the eyes when she said that. "I didn't kill anyone."

Della certainly believed her, and she thought Barrett did, too. Plus, what Alice was saying meshed with the evidence. Maybe it would mesh even more if the fingerprints on the murder weapon didn't belong to Alice and the CSIs found proof that someone other than LeBeau, Casto and Alice was in the woods last night. The last one wouldn't be much of a stretch since the two shooters had clearly been in the area because they'd attacked Barrett and her near there.

"There's no need for Alice to stay here," Dr. Tipton said, breaking the silence in the room.

Barrett nodded, adding a soft groan, and he looked at the deputy. "Why don't you help us get Alice to my cruiser?" In other words, keep watch when they were outside in case those gunmen were out there. "I'll take Della and her to my place, and you can get back to Culver Crossing."

Spence blew out what sounded like a breath of relief.

No doubt because he was feeling pressed to get back to work. Della was feeling that same pressure. Jace was a good boss, and she hated that he was shorthanded. Still, Della was feeling an even greater need to make sure her baby stayed safe. It'd be harder to manage that if she returned to the job.

Spence helped Alice off the table, and after she signed some papers for the doctor, they went out through the waiting room and to the exit. Barrett and Spence looked out, checking the parking lot, and they must not have seen anything alarming because they then hurried Alice into the back seat of the cruiser. Della sat shotgun, and the moment Barrett, Alice and she had latched their seat belts, Barrett sped off.

Della hadn't realized she was holding her breath until her chest started to ache, and it twisted at her that just being outside brought on the overwhelming fear. There'd been plenty of times as a cop that she was afraid, but this was many steps past that now, because if something happened to her, it also happened to the baby.

Keeping watch around them, Barrett drove through town and toward his ranch. Della kept watch, too, not just on their surroundings but also on Alice and Barrett. She caught him glancing at her stomach and figured he was giving plenty of thought to the baby. There was no way for him to put something like that out of his mind, but it wasn't good for them to lose focus like this.

"Thank you," Alice said from the back seat. "I know you don't want me to be in your home."

"No," Barrett said, and almost immediately he tacked on some muttered profanity to that blunt admission. "It won't be for long," he added, his tone just a tad softer.

Della wanted to say that she knew how hard this would be for Barrett to have Alice under his roof. Especially since she'd be right there with them. He had so much on his plate right now. Heck, so did she. But despite that full plate, they were going to have to talk about the baby. Maybe by the time they got around to doing that, he would have figured out some things. Maybe she would, too.

Thankfully, there was no other traffic on the road, which helped Della's nerves. Also thankfully, an SUV would stand out here, where most folks drove pickups. Of course, the cruiser would stand out as well, but she hoped that would be in a good way. The gunman had attacked them while they'd been in Barrett's truck—which hadn't been bullet resistant. Attacking them in a cruiser wouldn't be a smart move. Though depending on how much these guys wanted Barrett and her dead, they could still go for it.

Della breathed a little easier when Barrett pulled to a stop in front of his ranch. She doubted that Alice was feeling an easiness, though. The woman looked at the pastures, the barns and the house. A house that'd once belonged to her in-laws, Barrett's paternal grandparents. After Barrett's father had committed suicide, his grandfather had moved into the main house so he could help out with Barrett and his brothers.

"A long time," Alice whispered.

Yes. Over two decades. Still, those memories had to feel fresh to her. At least they wouldn't be staying in the main house that'd once been Alice's home. Leo now lived there with his two-year-old daughter, and Della figured Barrett wouldn't be taking Alice anywhere near there.

Ignoring Alice's comment, Barrett went into cop mode and hurried them all inside, where he immediately locked the door and checked the security system.

It was still armed, but he went to all the windows and doors to check for any signs of a break-in.

"I'm sorry about having to come here," Alice whispered to Della. "I mean, I'm sorry to interrupt anything Barrett and you have to do." Her eyes widened, and she blushed. "I didn't mean it like *that*. I know you said Barrett and you weren't back together, but I meant the investigation. You two probably have plenty to say to each other."

Yes, they did. And only a portion of that applied to the investigation.

Barrett came back out of the hall, and he snared Alice's gaze. "You can use my room. The master bedroom," he clarified. "Della's in the guest room, and I can sleep on the pullout sofa in my office."

Alice was shaking her head before he even finished. "I'm not taking your room. The pullout is fine." And as if to prove that, she headed in that direction, issuing another apology.

Barrett muttered some more profanity, and he lifted his eyes to the ceiling as if asking for some divine help. If it came, Della would certainly welcome it.

"Don't you apologize again," Barrett warned Della when she opened her mouth. But he winced and waved that off. "I haven't worked it all out in my head yet, but then I figure neither have you."

He was right about that. "The only thing I'm certain of right now is that I want this baby, and I need to keep him or her safe."

"Him or her," he repeated, and judging from his expression, those pronouns made it very real to him. A boy or a girl. Their son or their daughter. "Yeah, I want the baby safe, too, and that's why we have to declare a truce. For now, let's take our past relationship off the table and concentrate on finding a killer."

That sounded, well, good. "Is it doable? I mean, us declaring a truce?" Della asked.

The corner of his mouth lifted in that half smile. The one that had always sent her heart and body zinging. It was still plenty effective because that's what happened to her now.

And Barrett noticed.

He shook his head, mumbled something that Della didn't catch and then surprised Della by walking over to her. She'd have thought he'd keep his distance from her. As far as he could get. Instead, he slipped his arm around her and eased her to him. Not too close, though. This was obviously a hug of comfort, and Della very much needed it. She wasn't alone in this ordeal, although sometimes it felt like it. But not when Barrett was holding her.

"Be honest with me," he said. "How much are you hurting right now?"

"At the moment, not much at all." Della winced when she heard her tone. It was breath and silk. The tone of an aroused woman.

He looked down at her, the corner of his mouth kicking up again, and his gaze met hers. Maybe there was arousal in his eyes as well, but there also seemed to be some resignation.

So much for them putting their past on the back burner.

Their past was suddenly right in front of them, and Della felt the heat slide through her. Unfortunately, Barrett felt it, too. She knew that because of the way his grip tightened on her, and he kept his gaze fastened to her face. Specifically, to her mouth.

"I'm going to regret this," he muttered a split second before he kissed her.

And there it was. No slide of heat this time but a full slam of fire. It was as if no time had passed between them. As if they weren't neck-deep in a serious investigation that could get them killed. All of that vanished, and all that Della could think about—and feel—was his mouth on hers.

Barrett obviously hadn't lost any of his kissing skills in the past two months. He claimed her, using his tightened grip to pull her even closer. Until they were pressed together with his chest against her breasts. That upped the heat even more, and the urgency came, her body instantly wanting more.

That was the trouble with them being past lovers. Lovers who'd had great sex too many times to count. A lone kiss could feel like hours of foreplay and could make the need for each other seem urgent and primal.

Della was certainly feeling both right now.

It was somewhat of a miracle that Barrett's kiss could make her forget the pain, their messy situation and everything else other than the taste of him. The feel of him against her mouth. She wanted to sink right in, to feed the heat, to lead him straight to his bed.

But that shouldn't happen.

Della mentally repeated that to herself, but it took a triple reminder for her to finally pull her mouth from his. Even then the need continued to soar, fueled now by the fact that she was looking at his amazing face. Yes, Barrett had always hit the higher rung on the attraction ladder.

"I told you I was going to regret it," he said.

But she didn't see much regret in him. Like her, his breathing was uneven, and she could feel his heartbeat thudding against her chest. Della was certain her own heart was doing some thudding. Along with breaking a little.

"Life has a twisted sense of humor," she told him, and she stepped back. "I ended things with you so I could get on with my life. So I could have the home and kids I'd always wanted. Ironic that I'll have the child, but everything else is a mess."

He made a sound of agreement, but Barrett didn't get to voice it because his phone rang, and when Daniel's name popped up on the screen, he answered it right away. He also put the call on speaker.

"Is Alice really at your place?" his brother asked the moment he was on the line.

"Yeah." Barrett's jaw was tight with that response. "By the way, you're on speaker, and Della's here."

"I figured as much. How'd it happen that you took Alice there?"

Barrett took a deep breath. "It seemed the reasonable thing to do since both Della and she are in danger."

Daniel made his own sound, and Della thought she heard his underlying sentiment. For Daniel and the rest of the Logans, there was nothing reasonable when it came to their mother.

"I was about to call a marshal friend and see if they can arrange a safe house," Barrett explained. "For Alice," he added. "Maybe for Della, too, if I can convince her to go."

"Good luck with that," Daniel grumbled.

Under normal circumstances, no way would Della have even considered being tucked away at a safe house. She was a cop and didn't need such protection. But there was the baby. Which meant she had to at least consider it.

"I've been plowing through the financial records on Lorraine and Curran," Daniel went on a moment later. "Nothing so far is standing out for Lorraine, but I'm having Scottie do a lot more digging there. But Curran's a different story. I found something that really stands out."

Della automatically moved closer to the phone. "What?" Barrett and she asked in unison.

"I figured that'd get your attention. It certainly got mine. Listen to this—over the past six months, Curran has made multiple payments to a private investigator. Rory Silva."

Hearing the name felt like a punch to Della, and she shook her head. "Rory Silva?" she repeated. "As in Francine's brother?"

"Yep," Daniel verified. "I'm guessing you didn't know he'd done some work for Curran?"

"No." Della shoved her hair from her face. "I knew he was a PI, of course." She also knew that Francine and Rory hadn't always gotten along. In fact, they'd argued over their grandparents' inheritance for years.

An argument that'd ended when Francine had been murdered.

Della wanted to force any thoughts of that aside. Rory hadn't killed Francine. He'd had a solid alibi and had been broken up over his sister's death. At least he had seemed broken up. Now she had to wonder why Rory had gone to work for a man who had known criminal ties.

"There's more," Daniel went on. "While I was trying to figure out the financials, I got a call from San Antonio PD. They've been going through LeBeau's place, and they found his phone. Not the burner cell he had on him but rather one he used often. I guess he didn't want to carry it with him while committing multiple felonies."

"Please tell me LeBeau called the person who hired him to kidnap Alice," Barrett said.

"Well, he didn't call Curran," Daniel added. "But he did call Rory. Many, many times. Judging from the frequency and length of the calls, I have to say that Rory and our dead guy were friends."

Chapter Ten

"Rory," Barrett repeated. Then, he cursed. Because this was a connection to the investigation that he definitely didn't like.

Barrett knew Rory, of course. Heck, he'd even talked with the man on several occasions so he could maybe find a new angle for Francine's murder investigation. But Barrett hadn't seen or spoken to him in over a year.

That would change.

"Call Rory and have him come in for an interview," Barrett instructed Daniel. "Don't make it a request. Make it an order, and I want him in ASAP."

"I want to see him, too," Della insisted.

Barrett had known she'd need to be in on something like that, but it gave him a dilemma of sorts. He couldn't leave Alice here alone at his place and didn't especially want to tie up one of his deputies with bodyguard duty. Still, he'd have to do just that, because he didn't want to take Alice outside until moving her to a safe house. It was bad enough that Della would be on the road where those gunmen could try to come after her again.

"I'll get Rory in here right away," Daniel assured him, and he ended the call.

Barrett stood there a moment, working out what this connection between Curran and Rory could possibly mean. Judging from the way Della's forehead was bunched up, she was doing the same thing.

"How well do you know Rory?" Barrett asked her.

"Apparently not well enough." She stayed silent a moment longer. "Francine never mentioned that he had any shady associations. I would have remembered that. But Francine and Rory didn't get along, so it's possible he would have kept something like this from her."

"It's also possible that Rory didn't have those shady connections when his sister was still alive," Barrett reminded her. "Or Rory hid them."

It would have been stupid for Rory to announce to his cop sister that he might be skirting along the edges of the law. Or outright breaking it.

Della made a sound of agreement. "You'll question Curran about this, too," she said.

"Oh, yeah." Barrett turned and went to the table where he'd left his laptop. Good thing, because now he wouldn't have to go into his office—where Alice was—to get it. "I want to check for any lab reports and then do a check on Rory. Then, I can call a reserve deputy to come out here and stay with Alice while you and I go back in."

"If you want to go ahead and make that call, I can start the check on Rory," she offered.

Barrett nodded. Right now, he'd take all the help he could get, and Della was a good cop. She'd be able to do that as fast as he could.

While she booted up his laptop, Barrett considered his options, and he settled on calling in Buddy Adler, who lived just up the road. It would mean dipping into the sheriff's department budget to bring Buddy on board and Barrett might get some flak over that, but this way he wouldn't be pulling his regular deputies away from the mountain of work they were facing because of this double murder investigation.

Before Barrett could call Buddy, however, his phone dinged with a text message from Daniel.

Rory's on his way in. He'll be here in under an hour.

Good. Barrett responded:

Arrange to have Curran back in, too. I want to see him after I've talked to Rory.

Thankfully, Buddy answered Barrett's call right away, and he agreed to come over immediately. Which was good. Until he looked at Della's face. Without the flush of arousal, she just looked tired.

"I can have you watch the interviews from here," Barrett offered. "I can rig it so you can do that on my laptop. You'd even be able to ask Rory questions."

Della shook her head. "I'm going with you."

He'd figured that would be her response, but he had to try. Barrett nearly pressed her to stay and get some rest. He might have won an argument about it if he pointed out that this kind of fatigue wasn't good for the baby. But even if she stayed put, rest likely wouldn't happen. Like him, she was probably revved with the prospect that they might get answers.

"I'll check on Alice," she offered. "And I'll let her know that Buddy will be watching her. She knows him, right?"

"Yes, she does." Something that Barrett hadn't actually remembered. But Buddy had been working for Barrett's family for the past thirty years. The hand would have definitely been around during Alice's departure.

And his father's suicide. That might not make it easy for Alice to see Buddy, but at the moment Barrett couldn't worry about her discomfort.

While Della was with Alice, Barrett went to his laptop to check the lab reports. What he read there had him frowning. The smeared prints on the knife were still inconclusive, and at this point it might stay that way. The lab techs couldn't identify something that wasn't there.

He moved on to the financials next and saw that Daniel had made good progress. Curran had paid Rory a total of nearly eight grand. Not a fortune exactly, but it indicated that Rory had worked plenty of hours for Curran. But doing what exactly? That was something Barrett intended to find out.

The next report showed that San Antonio PD had made progress, too, with LeBeau's cell phone records. Rory and LeBeau had talked at least twenty times over the past three months. Some of the conversations had lasted nearly a half hour. Coupled with the fact that there were no business payments from LeBeau to Rory, Barrett believed Daniel had it right.

LeBeau and Rory were friends.

And while there was no crime in that, it did mean Rory had a connection to a killer. That in turn meant Rory was connected to the current investigation.

Hell.

Barrett hoped this didn't circle back around to Francine's murder. Della had enough to handle without adding a dose of the past.

He heard the sound of an approaching vehicle and automatically drew his weapon. But as expected, it was Buddy. Barrett disarmed the security system to let the man in.

"Thanks for coming so fast," Barrett said just as

Della came back into the room. Buddy tipped his Stetson in greeting before he took it off and hung it on the peg next to the door.

"Alice knows you'll be here," Della explained to Buddy. "She said she'd be sleeping while we're gone, that she's exhausted."

The exhaustion part was likely true, but it could be that Alice just wanted to avoid someone who'd been so close to her late husband. Della wasn't the only one who had enough emotional stuff to deal with.

Della and Barrett gathered their things, and Barrett gave Buddy instructions on how to arm the security system after they were gone. Buddy also wouldn't hesitate to call for backup if needed. In a pinch, he could also alert the other hands who'd be working both Daniel's and Leo's ranches.

There was plenty of open pasture around his house, something that Barrett was thankful for because he was able to check out their surroundings and make sure a gunman wasn't lying in wait. There wasn't. But both Della and he stayed on alert during the drive to his office.

As he'd done on their previous trip, Barrett parked the cruiser right in front, and Della and he hurried inside. He'd thought he would continue to go over the financials and reports, but he instantly spotted Rory, who was pacing in front of Barrett's office door.

"He just got here," Daniel told them in a low voice. "And I'm not sure if he's nervous or if that's the way he usually is."

"Nervous," Della supplied.

She didn't get a chance to add more because Rory spotted them and made a beeline for them. He looked young, younger than Francine had been at the time of her death, and he was wearing jeans and a button-up blue shirt. His black hair fell nearly to his shoulders.

Rory reached out as if he might hug her, but he seemed to change his mind when his attention landed on her bandaged arm. "You're hurt," he said. "I'd heard you were, but I hoped I heard wrong."

"It's not bad," Della assured him. "You remember Sheriff Logan," she added, tipping her head toward Barrett.

"Of course." Rory shook Barrett's hand. The guy's palm was sweaty, proving that Della had been right about the nervous part. Of course, Rory had been summoned to a police station on the heels of a murder.

The murder of someone he knew.

Rory was a fool if he hadn't thought he'd be questioned. Then again, maybe he hadn't believed the cops would make a connection between LeBeau, Curran and him.

"Thank you for coming so fast, Rory," Della said, and she looked up at Barrett. "Should we go ahead and take this into interview?"

Barrett nodded, but he let Della lead the way. A good call, he thought, because Rory fell in step alongside her, and the look he gave Della appeared to be a friendly one.

"I'd intended to call you," Rory told her as they walked. "I mean because of the anniversary of Francine's death. I didn't figure you had anything new to tell me, but I thought it was a good time to touch base."

"I'm still investigating it," Della answered, but there was something in her tone. Something with an edge of a threat.

Barrett knew that Rory had never been a top suspect for his sister's murder, but Francine and he had bickered over family money, so that meant Barrett had never removed the man as a possibility. He'd thought that Della had done just that—eliminated Rory. But maybe not.

They went into the interview room, and Barrett closed the door and set up the recorder. Rory stayed silent until Della started reading him his rights.

"Wait a minute." Rory got out of the chair where he'd just sat. "You're arresting me? For what?" His tone and expression certainly weren't so friendly now, and he volleyed hard looks at both of them.

"It's procedure," Della assured him. "That way if something comes up during the interview, all bases are covered." She finished Mirandizing him. "Would you like to have an attorney here with you?" she asked.

Rory stayed quiet a moment, giving that some thought. "No. Not at this exact moment." His jaw was tight now, and he paused again. "This is about Harris LeBeau's murder?"

So, he had heard about it. Barrett would have been shocked if he hadn't. He nodded, sat. So did Rory and Della.

"Can you tell me where you were between six last night and one this morning?" Barrett started.

"Home," Rory readily answered, but then he cursed. "Alone. In other words, I don't have an alibi. I didn't know I'd need one. But I didn't kill LeBeau. He was my friend."

Good. That was one thing he needed verified. "Close friend?" Barrett pressed.

Rory shrugged. "Not really. He had a lot of contacts that helped with some of my PI jobs, and every now and then we'd meet for a drink."

"LeBeau had a criminal record," Della pointed out. "Were you aware of that?"

"Sure. He talked about getting caught with stolen goods. But I also ran him and knew that he'd been arrested for assault." Rory sighed. "He didn't exactly take responsibility for what he'd done. He claimed he'd gotten mixed up with the wrong crowd, but it'd been four years since his last arrest."

Barrett mulled that over a moment. "So, you used LeBeau as a criminal informant?" he asked.

Another shrug. "Sometimes. But I swear I thought he was clean." His gaze met Barrett's. "But you're going to tell me he was into something bad, and that it got him killed."

Oh, yeah. Whatever LeBeau had been hired to do, it'd likely gotten him killed, but Barrett kept that to himself. "When's the last time you saw LeBeau?"

"About a week ago. And no, he didn't mention that he was about to go off the deep end and do something stupid." Rory leaned forward, resting his forearms on the metal table. "I heard he was there last night when another guy was killed. Robert Casto. Is that true?"

"LeBeau was there," Barrett verified. "Any idea why?"

"None," Rory quickly answered, and he huffed, shook his head. "I'm sorry, but I just don't know anything about it." He went stiff and turned to Della. "Do you think any of what happened has something to do with Francine's murder?"

"We're looking into that," she said. Which was a way of telling Rory pretty much nothing, because they were looking into plenty of things right now.

"Tell me about Wilbur Curran," Barrett threw out there, and because he was carefully watching Rory's expression, he saw the flash of surprise in the man's eyes.

"Uh, I've done some PI work for him," Rory answered, but this time it wasn't fast, and hesitation replaced the surprise.

"Why'd Curran hire you?" Barrett pressed when Rory didn't volunteer anything else.

Rory groaned, shook his head. "I can't discuss Curran with you."

Barrett stared at him. "This is a murder investigation, and you're not a lawyer. You don't have client-attorney privilege." Though Rory could argue that he did have an obligation to keep his clients' business under wraps, and that's why Barrett offered Rory a compromise. "Just give me the broad strokes. I'm not looking for specifics." Not at the moment anyway. But Barrett would if he sensed anything was off here.

Rory glanced at Della, maybe hoping that she would give him an out. The only thing she gave him was a stern cop's expression. Rory finally sighed and shifted his attention back to Barrett.

"Curran wanted me to look into any charges that you might file against him in the money laundering investigation," Rory explained. "He believes you'll continue the investigation against him."

"I will," Barrett assured him. And he gave that some thought. It wasn't a surprise that Curran would hire someone to poke into any possible evidence or links that could be used against him, but he had to wonder how far Curran expected the PI to go. "Did Curran ask you to bend the law in any way?"

Rory's eyes widened. "No." And he repeated his denial while he shook his head. "Curran didn't ask, and I wouldn't have done it even if that's what he'd wanted. I need to keep my PI's license. It's how I make my living."

Maybe Rory was telling the truth, but Barrett would

dig deeper to see if anything was there. For now, though, he went with a different angle.

"Because of your connection to LeBeau," Barrett went on, "I can get access to some of your records. I can and will also talk to any of LeBeau's associates about him…and you. Tell me, Rory, am I going to find out anything that'll make me think you're hiding something or that you aren't being completely honest with me?"

The muscles in Rory's jaw went to war with each other, and he looked away, causing Barrett to groan. There was something.

"Spill it," Barrett demanded.

Rory squeezed his eyes shut a moment. "I have debts," he finally said. "Lots of them, and I'm in danger of losing my house. Losing everything," he added in a hoarse mumble.

"What happened to Francine's life insurance money?" Della immediately asked him. "That was a five-hundred-thousand-dollar policy."

Rory appeared to try to steel himself up when he turned to her. "It's gone. All gone. I used it to pay off gambling debts, but it wasn't enough. I still owe the wrong people a lot of money."

In other words, loan sharks where the interest would just keep piling up. And since not paying them off could result in bodily harm or worse, that made Rory a desperate man. One who might indeed skirt the law for a client who'd help him get the sharks off his back.

"You're sure you didn't do anything for Curran or LeBeau that'd give you the cash you need?" Barrett pressed.

"I'm sure." This time Rory looked him in the eyes when he answered.

Barrett took a moment to consider everything he'd

just heard, and he would have asked a few more questions if there hadn't been a knock at the door. It was Daniel, and he motioned for Barrett to step into the hall with him. He did, and Della joined them a moment later.

Daniel handed him a piece of paper. "This just came in from the lab, and I figured you'd want to read it."

Barrett did exactly that. So did Della. She moved next to him, her uninjured arm sliding against his. Several words practically jumped right out at Barrett.

Alice Logan. Fingerprints. Planted.

"The lab guy said the pressure points aren't right on the handle of the knife used to murder Casto," Daniel summarized for them. "The prints belong to Alice all right, but it's their conclusion that someone held her hand on the knife and planted them there."

The long breath that Della blew out was definitely one of relief. Barrett supposed he should be relieved, too, to have one less murder suspect, but this led him to a critical question.

Who had set up Alice and why?

Probably not LeBeau. No, this likely led back to the person who'd hired LeBeau and those other thugs who'd shot at Della and him. He doubted Rory had been the one to do that, but it was possible the loan sharks— or Curran—had pressured him into putting together something like this.

Barrett handed the report to Daniel, and he was about to go back in to interview when Della's phone buzzed. Since they were still arm to arm, Barrett had no trouble seeing Dr. Tipton's name on the screen.

"I need to take this," Della said, stepping away from them.

Barrett didn't follow her, mainly because that would have made Daniel suspicious. Or rather more suspicious than he already was. His brothers were definitely picking up on the vibe between Della and him, but Barrett seriously doubted that they'd figured out Della was carrying his child.

"You want me to finish up with Rory?" Daniel asked, eyeing Della, who was now having a whispered conversation with the doctor. "I was listening to the interview while I was working so I can pick up where you left off."

Barrett hated to dump this on Daniel, but there was no way he could concentrate until he knew what was going on with Della. He didn't care much for the way he saw her shoulders tense.

"Thanks. I'd appreciate you doing that," Barrett told Daniel, and his brother gave them both one last glance before he went into the room with Rory.

Thankfully, Barrett didn't have to wait long. It was only a couple of seconds longer before Della ended the call. However, when she turned toward him, he got confirmation that something was wrong.

"What happened?" Barrett asked.

"Dr. Tipton wants me at the hospital right now," Della said, her voice shaky. "There are some problems with my lab tests."

Chapter Eleven

Della tried to tamp down her racing heartbeat and breathing. She also tried not to go into panic mode. But it was hard to do because this wasn't just about her.

This could be about the baby.

"Did Dr. Tipton say specifically what was wrong?" Barrett whispered to her as they made their way to the front of the building. It sounded as if he was trying not to panic as well, but his voice was louder and stronger when he told the dispatcher that he had to head out for a meeting.

"No," Della answered once they were out of earshot of the dispatchers and deputies in the bullpen. "He didn't want to get into it all over the phone. Plus, he wants to go ahead and do the ultrasound."

Della considered all the possibilities. Then, pushed those possibilities aside. Just going out into the open could be dangerous, and she didn't want to add to their troubles by being reckless. She kept watch around them as Barrett and she hurried out and into the cruiser.

Problems with lab tests, Della mentally repeated. Well, she knew it wasn't the actual pregnancy test because the doctor hadn't gotten back those results the night before. This had to be something else.

Even though the hospital wasn't far, it seemed to take

an eternity for them to get there. Barrett parked by the ER, and they hurried in, making a beeline up the hall to Dr. Tipton's office. Just as the doctor had said, he was waiting for them and ushered them right in.

"What's wrong?" Della immediately demanded, not wanting to wait for polite greetings.

"It's not that bad," he assured her, and seemed alarmed. Probably because she looked ready to come unglued. "But you're anemic, and your blood sugar's a little higher than I'd like."

"Is that serious?" Barrett said at the same moment that Della asked, "What does that mean?"

"Well, the anemia is a fairly easy fix with supplements I can prescribe. The blood sugar, though, will require some monitoring. We don't want it to get out of control because it can cause complications with the pregnancy and the baby."

Oh, mercy. That definitely wasn't good.

"Your OB will give you this information sheet." Dr. Tipton handed her some papers he took from his desk and motioned for them to follow him out of the office and back down the hall. "But I wanted you to go ahead and have it. For now, your OB will likely want to monitor you more closely."

It was a reminder that she needed to make the OB appointment ASAP. Yes, she had a boatload of stuff going on, but the baby had to be her top priority.

"I managed to squeeze you in for an ultrasound appointment," Dr. Tipton continued, leading them into another room. "After the blood loss and shock you just went through, I wanted to go ahead and get it done. I can have the results sent to your OB. Is your OB here in Mercy Ridge?"

"No, Culver Crossing. Dr. Abernathy. I haven't actually had an appointment with him yet, but he was someone my doctor recommended."

Della had been reading through the info he'd given her, but the moment they stepped inside, she saw the tech was already there, waiting for them.

"I'll need you to take off your holster, lift your top and lower your jeans," the tech said. According to her name tag, she was Amanda Pierce. Amanda then looked at Barrett. "Will you be staying for this?"

"Yes," Barrett answered after glancing at Della.

Della didn't exactly give him the green light, but she was a little surprised that he wanted to be part of this. She doubted he'd resolved all of his doubts about fatherhood. However, maybe his worries for the baby were as sky-high as hers.

It was obvious the tech was in a hurry because she didn't waste any time helping Della onto the exam table. Helping her, too, lift her top and push down the waist of her jeans. Of course, that meant she was showing a lot of skin, including her flimsy black lace bra. Even though Barrett had seen every inch of her naked, it was unnerving now.

The tech smeared some goop on her belly and began to move the ultrasound probe over Della. Immediately, some images appeared on the screen. Exactly what images, Della didn't know. To her it looked like a snowstorm surrounding a small blob. Then she realized that was the baby.

The baby, she mentally repeated, the emotions going through her like a freight train. Della certainly hadn't expected to feel this much, this fast at merely seeing her child, but she did.

She glanced at Barrett to see how he was reacting.

He, too, was riveted to the screen, and she didn't think it was her imagination that he looked a little unsteady.

"It appears you're a little further along than you thought," Dr. Tipton said. "I'm estimating closer to three months rather than two."

So, she hadn't gotten pregnant right before she'd ended things with Barrett after all. She wasn't sure why she found that, well, comforting, but she did. She doubted, though, that Barrett was feeling much comfort about it. After all, she was still pregnant, and he was still going to be a father.

"We can't tell the sex of the baby just yet," the doctor went on. "Probably by next month, though."

Next month. Not long at all. Then she'd know if she was going to have a son or a daughter. It didn't matter to her. But what did matter was that everything was okay.

"Do you see anything wrong?" Della managed to ask.

Dr. Tipton looked over his shoulder at her and gave her a reassuring smile. "All looks well. Of course, like I said, your OB will want to see this."

The relief came, and it was just as swift and strong as her emotions at seeing the baby. Her child hadn't been hurt because of the shooting and blood loss. Everything was okay. For now. Della had to make sure it stayed that way.

The tech finished, and after she'd cleaned off the goop, she helped Della off the table so she could fix her clothes. While Della did that, Barrett asked Dr. Tipton about the high blood sugar issue, and she listened to their conversation while volleying glances at the images of the baby that were still on the screen.

"My advice is for you to make sure Della gets lots of

rest," Dr. Tipton explained to Barrett. "And stop by the pharmacy and pick up those supplements."

The pharmacy wasn't part of the hospital but rather up the street, and Della could immediately see Barrett's hesitation about her going there. "Any chance someone else can pick them up for her?" Barrett asked.

The doctor obviously heard the concern in Barrett's voice and saw it on Della's face. "Sure. I'll call them to make sure they know what's going on. Remember to make that OB appointment," he added as Barrett and she made their way out.

"I'm taking you back to the ranch so you can lie down," Barrett informed her. "You can call the OB on the way."

Normally, she would have bristled at him taking charge like this. At anyone taking charge, she mentally amended. But the truth was, she was exhausted. And it would do both her and the baby some good if she could rest. Of course, for that to happen, she'd have to turn off her mind, something that Della doubted was going to happen. Yes, the baby was at the forefront but so was the investigation. They had to solve this case for them to find any kind of normalcy.

"I'll be able to tell Alice about the prints on the knife," Della said after they were in the cruiser.

Barrett glanced at her as if surprised by the topic she'd chosen. After all, they had plenty else to discuss, including what had just gone on in the hospital. "I'll do that. I meant it when I said you were going to get some sleep. I don't want you reading reports or doing anything else with this investigation."

His offer to tell Alice was huge since Della knew he wanted to avoid any contact with his mother. "I'll have to tell Jace soon," she went on several moments later as

Barrett drove through town. "Tell him I'm pregnant, I mean. He'll put me on desk duty."

That was something that definitely wouldn't have sat well with her if she'd been merely hurt. But being out in the field was too big of a risk.

"Later, after you've rested, you and I can talk," Barrett said. Judging by his tone, he wasn't looking forward to that. Or so she thought, but then he added, "I'll be there for this baby." He kept his attention on the road as he drove out of town. "I'll be there for *you*."

It was a good thing she was sitting because that robbed her of some breath. Those were definitely words she hadn't expected Barrett to say. And maybe he didn't want to say them. He could be looking at all of this as one giant obligation, just as he had when he'd stepped up to raise his brothers after his father's suicide. His grandfather had helped with that, of course, but Barrett had done more than his fair share of parenting.

Della wanted to give him an out. She wanted to tell him that he wouldn't have to get emotionally invested the way he had with Daniel and Leo. But she was afraid that anything she said right now would just hit some very raw nerves. It was best that she give him some time. As much time as they could manage, anyway, considering that in about six months they'd be parents.

"Hell," Barrett muttered, getting her complete attention when he drew his gun.

Della automatically did the same, and just ahead on the road, she spotted the black SUV. She couldn't be sure it was the same one their attackers had used, but she took out her phone to call in the plates. She wanted an ID on whoever owned the vehicle.

Trying to tamp down the surge of adrenaline, she looked down at her phone. However, she didn't manage to press a number because Barrett cursed again, and he jerked the steering wheel hard to the right. Della got just a glimpse of something in the road. A small black box.

And the blast roared through the cruiser.

BARRETT DIDN'T HAVE time to react other than slamming on his brakes. That might have saved Della and him, though, because instead of being directly on top of the explosive device when it went off, they were still a few yards away from it.

That was bad enough, though.

The front end of the cruiser lifted off the pavement, shaking them like rag dolls, and the airbags bashed into them. Barrett had a hard flash of fear for the baby and her, but he had to shove that out of his mind so he could assess their situation.

And brace himself in case this wasn't the end of the attack.

Beside him, Della batted back the airbag. She also moaned and winced. That caused his heart to slam in his chest, but then he realized she was holding her arm. All the jostling around had likely hurt her stitches. Hell, here she was recovering from the gunshot wound, and she might have other injuries. That reminder replaced some of the shock and fear with anger. Barrett would make sure whoever had done this would pay for it.

"Are you okay?" he asked, shoving aside his own airbag.

"I think so." She sounded dazed, but at least she was coherent. And she'd managed to hang on to her gun. So had Barrett. That was somewhat of a miracle, considering the impact. "You?"

"I'm fine." But he had no idea if that was even true.

Physically, he thought he was okay, but thoughts of worst-case scenarios were flying all over the place.

Because of a thick cloud of smoke and the residue from the airbags, Barrett couldn't see much, but most of the front end of the cruiser was now a mangled heap. Thankfully, though, the damage hadn't extended into the cab of the vehicle. That was something at least.

But it might not last.

There could be a second device nearby. And worse. The person or persons who'd left that bomb or whatever it was on the road could be circling back to try to finish the job they'd started.

Barrett tried to keep watch around them and listen for any sounds of an approaching vehicle or footsteps, but he couldn't hear anything like that. He fired off a quick text to Daniel to request backup. They'd need a bomb squad, too, but Daniel could arrange for that once he was on scene. Right now, Barrett just needed help. And he needed to get Della and him moving.

"The gas in the tank could catch fire," he told her.

Della made a sharp gasp, and, still wincing, she leaned forward, no doubt trying to see the engine. There was still some smoke, hopefully not from a fire and only steam from the radiator, but Barrett couldn't risk them staying put.

Since the cruiser was already on the side of the road, it wasn't that far to the ditch, only a couple of feet, and it was on Della's side. That was both good and bad. It meant she'd be able to get out of the cruiser, but once outside she could be an easy target for gunmen. Barrett had a bad feeling that their attackers weren't just going to drive off and assume they'd done the job of killing Della and him.

Beyond the ditch was flat pasture and a fence. No

trees or shrubs, which meant no place for them to take cover in case they had to shoot. Still, it would have to do until backup could arrive.

While still keeping watch and listening, Barrett leaned over, and he opened Della's door. "I'll get out on this side. You get out on yours," he instructed. "Drop down into the ditch as fast as you can."

Despite her obvious pain, she managed to give him a flat look. "You'll be on the road, right in the possible line of fire."

"Possible," Barrett emphasized. "Right now the biggest risk is for us to be in this vehicle." Again, that could be true, but his every instinct was telling him to move—now.

"I'll get out and cover you," Della insisted. She grabbed her bag, putting it on across her body so her hands would still be free. He nearly told her to leave it behind, but it no doubt held some extra ammo and her phone. Things they might need. "Then, we can get into the ditch together."

It was playing dirty, but Barrett would do whatever it took to get her moving. "Think of the baby," was all he said.

She muttered some profanity that was no doubt aimed at him, but Della did that while getting out of the cruiser. She did just as he'd wanted and practically toppled down into the ditch where hopefully she'd have decent cover.

It wouldn't be enough, though.

He'd need to get them moving down the ditch and away from the cruiser. The need for that became even more urgent when Barrett caught the scent of something he definitely didn't want to smell.

Gasoline.

Hell. It could blow up at any second.

Keeping his gun ready, he got out, using his own door for cover for a couple of seconds while he scanned the road and pastures around them. He spotted the SUV about twenty yards ahead. Not parked there, either. The driver had the vehicle in Reverse and was coming right at them. And that wasn't all. A second man was leaning out the passenger's side window, and he had a gun aimed right at Barrett.

Barrett couldn't stay put in case this thug started shooting in the ditch. Plus, if Della heard shots, she might not stay down. Her cop instincts would kick in, and she'd try to help him. Barrett needed to make sure that didn't happen.

Hoping that the gunman's aim would be off from the movement of the SUV, Barrett left his door open, and while keeping it between the gunman and him, he ran to the back of the cruiser.

The shot blasted through the air.

Judging from the sound of metal slamming into metal, the bullet had hit the door. Good. It was better than hitting him.

Still moving fast, Barrett dropped down into the ditch that he quickly discovered wasn't anywhere near dry. Because of the heavy rains the night before, there was a good five inches of mud and water. It wouldn't make running easier, but they didn't have a lot of options here. Not with the possibility of the cruiser's gas tank exploding and the gunmen closing in on them.

Another shot came, this one pinging off the back of the cruiser. It hadn't come close to hitting Della or him, and Barrett needed to make sure it stayed that way. He positioned himself on her left side, keeping his head turned so that he'd be able to see the SUV when it came closer.

And then Della and he started running.

"Keep low," he warned her though she was already doing that. Keeping watch, too, but now they were having to look behind them. He wanted to put as much distance as possible between them and the cruiser especially since the smell of gasoline was getting stronger.

More shots came, and Barrett twisted around to see the top of the SUV. He took aim as best he could and fired. It no doubt missed the gunman, but it might cause him to duck back in, which would give Della and him precious seconds to keep running. Barrett added another shot, then another.

Before a bullet came their way.

He cursed because he was too damn close, and he had no choice but to drag Della into the mud and water so they'd have some cover. Thankfully, the ditch was deep enough to keep them partially sheltered, but he heard the slow, steady crawl of the SUV coming closer. Once it reached them, the gunman would be able to pick them off like sitting ducks.

Barrett heard another sound. A welcome one this time. Backup. And Daniel was coming in hot with sirens wailing. No doubt letting Barrett, and their attackers, know that within seconds he'd be there.

More shots came, and Della and he had to duck even deeper into the ditch, until all but the top halves of their bodies were exposed. He tried not to think of how much stress this was putting on Della and the baby. He tried not to think at all except to focus on stopping the person who was sending a hail of bullets at them.

The sirens got louder, and Barrett knew that help was only seconds away. Their attackers obviously knew that as well because there was the squeal of tires on asphalt when the SUV sped away.

Barrett wanted to climb out of the ditch and go after them, but that wasn't smart or safe. Instead, he took hold of Della's arm, lifted her and got her moving again.

He needed to warn Daniel not to get too close to the cruiser, but when Barrett reached for his phone in his pocket, he realized it was soaking wet. Likely ruined. So, he went old school, and the moment Daniel came into view, Barrett started waving his hands in a stay-back gesture.

Daniel's cruiser screeched to a stop about forty feet from them. His brother got out, taking cover behind the door. Scottie did the same on the passenger's side.

"The SUV's getting away," Daniel called out to him.

Yeah, it was, but there wasn't anything Barrett could do about that. However, he could warn Daniel and the deputy. "Get down!" Barrett shouted to them.

It wasn't a second too soon.

Because behind Della and him, the cruiser exploded.

Chapter Twelve

Della hated that she couldn't stop shaking. It was something a cop definitely shouldn't be doing. Plus, it was likely causing Barrett to worry about her even more than he should. She wasn't hurt. Nor was he. But the shock and aftereffects of the attack just wouldn't fade.

She could still hear the sound of those gunshots and the explosion. Still feel the bone-deep terror over her baby being hurt.

Barret had had those same concerns, because the moment he had her back at the sheriff's office, he'd called Dr. Tipton and asked him to come. Barrett hadn't wanted to risk taking her back to the hospital. He hadn't been able to drive her back to the ranch, either, because the CSIs and the bomb squad were on the road between town and the ranch. Della figured that being on that very road, where they'd nearly died, wouldn't help her tangled nerves.

At least she was no longer wearing her wet muddy clothes. Esther Ridley, a deputy who worked for Barrett, had some spare clothes in her locker and lent them to Della. The jeans and cotton shirt were big on her, but at least they were dry, and Della had also managed to clean up some in the bathroom. She'd need a shower to get rid of the smell of the mud and the smoke. However, that could wait.

Barrett had changed, too, borrowing some of Daniel's things, but there were still flecks of debris from the airbag in his dark hair.

"Your blood pressure's actually good," Dr. Tipton told her. "A surprise, considering."

Yes, it was. Practically a miracle. And that seemed to steady her some.

The doctor took off the blood pressure cuff and listened to her heart. "Also good," he concluded several moments later.

Barrett was right there in his office with him, and while he wasn't exactly pacing, that's what he looked as if he wanted to do. That and explode. He definitely wasn't shaking, but the danger had lit an angry fire in him.

"Are you hurting anywhere other than the stitches on your arm?" Dr. Tipton asked.

She shook her head. Actually, that wasn't hurting nearly as much as it had, probably because the doctor had put some kind of numbing cream on it when he'd cleaned it and rebandaged it.

"Does Della need to be admitted to the hospital?" Barrett asked the doctor. There was a boatload of worry in his voice.

"No. Not unless she starts to have any cramping. Then, you'd need to bring her right in."

Cramping as in contractions, which could mean a miscarriage. That caused her stomach to tighten and her nerves to start zinging again.

"Don't worry," the doctor said. He'd obviously seen the fear in her eyes. "The baby is very protected. Everything should be fine."

Della wanted to latch on to that. But she knew nothing would be *fine* until Barrett and she stopped the men who had tried twice to kill them. Barrett obviously felt the same way because while they had been waiting on Dr. Tipton to arrive, he'd made some calls, ordering Lorraine, Rory and Curran to come in immediately for questioning. She wasn't sure they would get answers from any of them, but at least they'd know that Barrett and she weren't going to ease up on this investigation.

The doctor gathered his things and gave Della a pat on her shoulder. "Try to get some rest soon."

She would, but Della had no idea when she could work that in. She might not have a choice about it, though, since soon, very soon, she'd be dealing with an adrenaline crash. If it hit her too hard, she might have to try to take a nap on the ratty sofa in the break room.

Barrett and she thanked Dr. Tipton as he left, and the moment the doctor had shut the door behind him, Barrett eased Della into his arms. There was no heat in his hug. Just the comfort he was obviously trying to give her. Comfort that worked surprisingly well. It might have continued, too, if they hadn't heard the voice out in the squad room.

Alice.

Barrett cursed, easing away from her, and he threw open the door. Alice was making a beeline for them, and Buddy was right behind her.

"I'm sorry, boss," Buddy immediately said. "When Alice heard about the latest attack, she insisted on coming."

"Don't blame Buddy," Alice added. "I told him if I had to, I'd use one of the ranch trucks to get myself here."

Alice certainly didn't look worn down or in pain

now. She looked like a terrified mother, and she went to them, hooking an arm around both Barrett and Della. The contact didn't last, though, because Barrett stepped back.

"You shouldn't have come," he snapped, and Barrett gave Buddy a scolding glance despite Alice's insistence that he not blame the ranch hand.

Alice shook her head. "I had to. I had to see for myself that you were both all right."

"We weren't hurt," Della assured the woman, and that was as positive an explanation as she could manage.

"No." Alice muttered something. A prayer of thanks, Della realized. "But whoever's doing this just won't stop. That's why I have to do something." She paused, her breath gusting as she shifted her gaze to Barrett. "I want you to use me as bait to draw out these gunmen."

Della and Barrett groaned in unison, but Alice just talked right over their protests.

"Hear me out," she went on. "Those men obviously want me. That's why they followed me and tried to run us off the road. They could be planning to take me hostage again. Or kill me," she added in a hoarse whisper before she hiked up her chin. She was no doubt trying to look sturdier than she actually was. "Either way, you can use me to lure them out."

Della wasn't sure exactly what kind of lure Alice was suggesting, but it didn't matter. It was a bad idea. Thankfully, Barrett agreed with Della.

"No way am I putting you out there in the line of fire," he told her. "We'll catch these guys through solid investigation and police work."

Of course, there were no guarantees of catching them, but Della had to believe that would happen. And soon.

Alice opened her mouth, no doubt to continue to plead her case for something that wasn't going to happen, but the sound of hurried footsteps stopped them. The three turned in the direction of those steps, and they spotted Lorraine, who was coming toward them. Correction, she was *storming* toward them. There was fire in her eyes, and she had that anger aimed at Alice.

"You killed Robert!" Lorraine shouted, and she launched herself at Alice, latching on to the woman's hair.

Della was so stunned that it took her a second to react. Not Barrett, though. He jumped right in, using his forearm to push Lorraine away. When that didn't work, when Lorraine continued to fight, he shoved his way in between the women, and he muscled Lorraine away.

The one-sided fight got the attention of the deputies in the squad room. Leo, Daniel and Esther hurried to assist, and it was Esther who helped stop Lorraine from charging at Alice again.

"She killed him!" Lorraine yelled, and she repeated that, her voice getting even louder, while Esther cuffed the woman.

The restraints still didn't stop Lorraine from fighting. She twisted her body, trying to wrench herself out of the cuffs while she shouted obscenities and threats at Alice. Obviously, Lorraine believed Alice had been the one to murder Casto. Or else that's what Lorraine wanted them to think, maybe so that it would take any suspicion of guilt off her.

It didn't.

Maybe Lorraine was a genuine hothead, who was likely capable of murder or hiring a hit. Of course, if this was all for show, then the woman was cold and calculating. Which also meant she could be capable of murder.

"Alice didn't kill Casto," Barrett told Lorraine, though he had to manage that over her continuing shouts. "There's proof," he added.

That caused Lorraine to finally quit fighting and go still, but there was nothing but venom in the glare that she turned on Barrett. "You're saying that because she's your mother."

He huffed. "You know my history with Alice. I'm definitely not doling out any favors to her. I don't need favors, not when I know that someone planted evidence to make her look guilty. Alice is a victim here, just like Casto."

Lorraine seemed to bite off whatever else she'd been about to say, and her forehead bunched a moment. Maybe she was considering that. If so, then she quickly dismissed it. "You're lying," she snapped.

"No reason to lie," Barrett calmly replied. "The evidence backs me up. You, on the other hand, have no evidence to clear your name."

Lorraine practically snapped to attention. "What do you mean by that?"

"I think the comment was obvious." Again, Barrett's voice was unruffled, though Della knew there had to be plenty of emotions just beneath the surface. Lorraine could be the person who wanted them dead. "You had motive to murder your former lover because you were jealous of his relationships with other women. That also means you had motive to set up Alice. Maybe a way of killing two birds with one stone. Or rather one knife."

"I didn't kill him!" Lorraine was back to shouting.

"You have the means to hire muscle to kill," Barrett went on. "You've got the money to pay those men who've been tearing their way through this area. And let's not forget that you were once engaged to LeBeau, who was involved in this neck-deep before someone murdered him. Did you do that, Lorraine? Did you hire LeBeau to do your dirty work and then eliminate him so that he couldn't rat you out?"

If looks could have killed, Lorraine's glare and narrowed eyes would have done just that to Barrett. "I want a lawyer," she snarled through clenched teeth.

"I'll bet you do, because you need one." Barrett turned to Alice. "Do you want to file assault charges against Lorraine?"

Della certainly hadn't forgotten that Alice was standing right there, but Barrett's question caused Della to look at her. Alice was shaken up. Rightfully so. And the woman was way too pale, a reminder that, like Della, she was also recovering from her injuries.

"No," Alice said, her voice quiet. But she did aim a hard stare at Lorraine. "I didn't kill Robert, but if you lay one hand on me again, I will file charges."

That caused Lorraine to start struggling against the restraints again, and when she tried to spit at Alice, Barrett huffed. "Take Lorraine to an interview room," he told Esther. "Once she's cooled off, you can remove the restraints long enough for her to call her lawyer. After he gets here, you can question Lorraine and find out if she has an alibi for this last attack."

Of course, even if Lorraine did have an alibi, it didn't mean she was innocent since she could have hired the gunmen. Still, Della wanted the woman on the hot seat, and an interrogation would do that. With Lorraine's obvious short fuse, she might spill something incriminating.

"I also want Lorraine tested for gunshot residue,"

Barrett added to Esther. "If she personally took care of LeBeau, there might be some GSR still on her hands."

Good point. Something that Della wished they'd thought of earlier when Lorraine had been questioned. Still, GSR could show up even after all this time.

Esther led a cursing Lorraine away, and Barrett stayed quiet until the woman was no longer in earshot. Then, he turned to Daniel and Buddy. "I want the two of you to take Alice back to the ranch. Buddy will stay with her."

"But I want to talk about my idea for bait," Alice insisted.

Barrett gave her a look that could have frozen Hades. "No. Because there'll be no bait. If you truly want to help me and this investigation, then do it by going back to the ranch and staying put. That way, I don't have to split my attention between you and finding a killer."

Even if his words hadn't gotten through to Alice, his cop tone and look must have done the job because she gave a heavy sigh. "All right. But keep me as sort of a backup plan. I'm willing to do whatever it takes to help."

Barrett's jaw muscles stirred in a sign of his unease. "Maybe this will help relieve any guilt you have over what happened to Casto. Someone planted your fingerprints on the knife that killed him. *Planted*," he emphasized.

Alice's breath shuddered, and she pressed her hand to her chest. "So, I'm no longer a suspect?"

Della knew that Barrett could keep the woman on his list of possible suspects, but he nodded. "You're not a suspect. Now go back to the ranch and get some rest. I'll be taking Della there soon to do the same."

Alice muttered a thank-you that obviously wasn't heartfelt. Still, Daniel didn't seem to soften. But then he probably wasn't anywhere close to the point where he could forgive and forget. Ditto for Barrett, though Della figured that being thrown together with Alice like this could break down some barriers.

That's what was happening between Barrett and her anyway.

The bad stuff that was happening was adding to the crumbling barriers. It was hard to stay distant from the father of your child when he was a decent guy and wanted to be part of your life. Well, part of the baby's life anyway. One step at a time. Which suited Della, since she didn't know what steps to take, either.

Once Buddy, Daniel and Alice had left, Della was ready to ask Barrett for a laptop so she could help him go over the lab reports. But before that could happen, the next round of interviews came in.

Curran.

The two men in suits with him were likely lawyers.

"You want me to take this one, and you can deal with Rory when he comes in?" Leo asked, getting up from his desk and coming closer to Barrett.

"What the hell are you trying to pull now?" Curran demanded before Barrett could answer. "This is harassment, and my lawyer will be talking to the DA, the mayor and the governor."

"If you need their phone numbers, let me know," Barrett said. His voice was calm enough, but because Della was arm to arm with him, she felt his muscles tighten. "Call anyone you like, but I'm not backing down. If you've had anything to do with these attacks, I'll find out and put you in a jail cell for a very long time."

Lorraine had been all fiery hot temper, but Della could feel an even greater rage in Curran. Apparently, so could Leo, because he stepped between Curran and Barrett.

"I can do this interview," Leo offered again.

"You think because it's a different Logan doing the talking that I'll come up with something new to say?" Curran snapped. He kept his attention on Barrett. "Well, I won't, because there's nothing new. You can dig all you want, but you'll never find anything on me."

Barrett shrugged, but there was nothing casual about the gesture. The air was practically zinging between Curran and him. "Oh, I'll keep digging," Barrett assured him. "But it's time to bring in the Texas Rangers. I intend to call them today and ask for their help in the money laundering investigation."

Curran pulled back his shoulders, and now there was concern on his face. Maybe the man hadn't thought much of Barrett's cop skills, but he seemed to have some respect for, and perhaps some fear of, the Rangers.

"Are you threatening my client?" the lawyer asked.

Barrett didn't even spare him a glance. "No threat," Barrett said, his eyes still on Curran. "Just the next step in the investigation. The Rangers can put more men and resources on this than I can."

Della knew that Barrett hated to turn over control to the Rangers. That told her just how much he wanted to get Curran and have him pay for his crimes. And this was a solid next step toward doing that.

"The Rangers won't find anything, either," Curran concluded, but instead of sounding smug, there was now a worried edge in his voice. He shook his head as if to clear it. "But if you're turning it over to them, then that'll leave you some time to haul Rory in. I want to file charges against him."

Whatever she'd thought Curran might say, that wasn't it. "Charges for what?" Della asked.

"He tried to blackmail me, that's what."

"Blackmail?" Della challenged.

"Yeah," Curran confirmed. "My guess is Rory's desperate for money to pay off the loan sharks who lent him money."

Barrett huffed as if he might not be buying this. "Rory really tried to get money from you?"

"Damn right. He sugarcoated it, but he said if I'd give him a *loan*, then he'd go to Della and use his friendship with her to convince her to clear my name in these attacks and Casto's murder. I told Rory to go to hell, that I didn't need his help in clearing my name because I wasn't guilty. Not only for Casto but for anything else."

Della let all of that sink in. And it didn't sink in well. She wanted to discount anything Curran said, but if Rory was indeed that desperate, then he might have resorted to attempted blackmail. But it wouldn't have worked. There was no way Della would allow Rory to influence the investigation, and Rory had to know that. She'd never given him even a hint that she'd been willing to bend the law.

Barrett stayed quiet several long moments before he turned to Leo. "Go ahead and take Curran into interview." He didn't add any other specific instructions, but Della knew that Leo would press for Curran's alibi for the latest attack, along with trying to push any other hot buttons he could manage.

"After we're done here, I'll have my lawyers file harassment charges," Curran threatened as Leo led him away.

Della had no doubts that Curran's attorneys would be filing those charges. But they wouldn't stick. The

DA and everyone else in Mercy Ridge knew that Barrett was just doing his job. Plain and simple, Curran had the means, motive and opportunity for the attacks, and that made him a solid suspect.

"You have Rory's number?" Barrett asked her once they were alone.

She nodded and took out her phone that was now in her pocket. Unlike his cell, hers hadn't been ruined in the ditch since it had been in her bag. "You want me to call him?"

"Yeah. Find out why he's not here yet, and if he's going to be long. I want to know if Curran is telling the truth about the blackmail attempt."

Since she wanted to know the same things, Della didn't hesitate. She considered that Rory might not answer, especially if he was already on his way here, but he answered on the first ring.

"Where are you?" Della asked, putting the call on Speaker. "You're supposed to be here for another interview."

"I know." Rory sounded strange. Scared, maybe. "I'm not sure I can make it in today."

"This interview isn't optional," Della reminded him. "Barrett and I have some questions."

"Yes, about the attack. I didn't have anything to do with that, so there's really no reason for me to come in."

"Oh, yes there is," Barrett snarled.

"Barrett," Rory muttered, and that fear level in his voice seemed to go up a significant notch. Or maybe it was just the surprise of his learning that Barrett was listening in. "I swear I don't know anything. I haven't done anything wrong."

"Curran doesn't agree," Barrett fired back. "He's

here now, and he's had some…interesting things to say about you."

There was a long silence. "What did Curran say?" Rory finally asked.

"That you tried to blackmail him," Barrett supplied. "That's why you're coming in, so we can talk about that."

"I didn't blackmail him," Rory practically shouted. "I just asked him for a loan."

"Really?" Della challenged. "A loan coupled with your assurances that you'd come to me and try to sway the investigation."

"No!" This time it was a shout, and Rory repeated the denial until his breath broke in a loud groan. "I just needed the money, and Curran said if he gave it to me that he'd expect more than payment in return."

Della didn't doubt that one bit. This sounded like the truth, something that Curran had fudged to make Rory seem guilty of obstruction of justice and other charges. Of course, that didn't mean Rory was squeaky clean here. Far from it.

"You needed the money to pay off the loan sharks?" Della demanded.

"Yes." Rory answered that darn fast, but then he groaned again. "I'm in serious trouble, Della. Even worse than I was…well, before."

Della latched right on to that last word. "Before?"

Again, Rory took his time answering. "All of this started two years ago. Gambling debts," he added with plenty of disgust in his voice. "I had to borrow money then, too, but I couldn't pay it back. I was in danger of losing my business. Losing everything, including my own life. These thugs don't play nice when it comes to paying back loans."

Two years ago. That settled like a tight knot in her stomach. "You were dealing with this when Francine was still alive?"

The silence dragged on way too long, causing Barrett to snap, "Answer the question."

Rory's response was another loud groan, followed by what sounded like a broken sob. "I begged Francine to give me the money. I told her they'd kill me if I didn't pay them."

"What happened, Rory?" she asked, but Della was almost afraid to hear the answer.

"Francine wouldn't give me a dime," Rory went on a moment later. His voice and breath were broken now. "No matter how much I begged her, she wouldn't budge. She said I had to face up to what I'd done and that she wasn't going to bail me out again."

The knot twisted and tightened. So did the fist that started squeezing her heart.

"God, Rory. Did these loan sharks kill Francine?"

"No." Rory gave another hoarse sob. "No, they didn't kill her." He paused again. "I did."

Chapter Thirteen

Hell. That was Barrett's first response, followed by some much stronger profanity. All this time, for two years, Della and he had been looking for a killer, but they hadn't looked in Francine's own gene pool.

"You killed your sister?" Barrett demanded.

It took some time for Rory to say anything else, but Barrett figured that's because the man was crying. And that told him loads, that the man's confession had been the truth.

A truth that had sucker punched Della.

She had gone sheet-white and looked so wobbly that Barrett took her by the arm and had her sit down. This was no doubt bringing back the grief over losing Francine. Grief likely as fresh and raw as it had been two years ago.

"It was an accident," Rory went on, drawing Barrett's attention back to him. "Francine and I were arguing, and my gun went off. I didn't mean to shoot her. I just went over to her place to try to talk her into giving me some money, that's all. I swear I didn't mean to shoot her."

Barrett huffed when he saw a Texas-size flaw in Rory's explanation. "If you just went there to talk to her, then why'd you have a gun?"

More sobbing. "I always carry a gun, and the argument got so heated between us, I pulled it. I don't know why. Maybe I thought it'd make her realize how desperate I was."

Oh, Barrett figured that Francine had known about her brother's desperation. He also figured that Francine had told Rory a flat-out no about doling out any more cash to him. And that's when Rory had pulled a gun on her. Desperation, however, didn't excuse Rory from squat.

"You shot her when she didn't pony up money for your gambling debts?" Barrett pressed when Rory didn't say anything else for several long moments.

"No. It wasn't like that. I took out the gun, and it just went off."

Della sighed, blinked back tears. "You're a PI," she reminded the man. "You know better than to pull a gun unless you intend to use it."

"It wasn't like that!" This time he shouted it. "It wasn't like that," Rory repeated in a hoarse whisper.

Maybe, but Barrett was fed up with Rory trying to excuse himself for a horrible crime. "If it was an accident, then why didn't you report it?" Barrett snapped.

"Because I was scared, and I wasn't thinking straight. I decided to make it look like somebody had broken in."

Obviously, he'd been thinking straight enough because it *had looked* like a break-in. Rory had put his PI skills to good use to make sure the blame hadn't been put on him.

"Whether or not it was an accident, you have to come into the sheriff's office," Barrett insisted. "I'll need you to tell me what happened—on the record," he emphasized. "Bring a lawyer."

"You'll arrest me?" Rory asked.

Yeah, he would do just that. Even if Rory managed to somehow prove he hadn't intended to kill his sister, there was still the cover-up and obstruction of justice that'd followed, along with giving false statements to the cops when they'd questioned him. However, Barrett didn't want to confirm the arrest because that might cause Rory to go on the run.

"Come in right now," Barrett added, taking the phone from Della so that he could speak directly into it. He didn't want Rory to miss a word.

"I can't do that." This time Rory didn't sob, didn't shout, but there was a lot of emotion in those four words. "Someone's been following me. I suspect it's the same gunmen who tried to kill Della and you. It's not safe for me to be on the roads right now."

What a crock. If Rory had truly thought he was in danger, he would have almost certainly mentioned it earlier in the conversation before the subject of Francine had even come up.

"Come in now, or I'll issue a warrant for your arrest," Barrett told him, but he was talking to the air because Rory had already ended the call.

Cursing, Barrett handed Della back her phone and reached for his own to get that warrant. That's when he remembered his cell had been ruined in the ditch. Adding some profanity, he went to his desk and used the landline to make the call. It took him a couple of minutes to explain to the judge why he wanted it, but during his explanation, he kept his attention on Della.

She was still sitting, still looking stunned. With reason. All this time Francine's killer had been right under her nose.

Once he was finished talking to the judge, Barrett put in a quick requisition for another phone, but until it arrived, he pulled out a burner cell from his desk. Good thing he kept one there for backup, since he'd need it. He put it on the charger and went to Della.

"I'm okay," she assured him, getting to her feet.

She wasn't okay, far from it, and while Barrett didn't like to add worries of the baby to the complicated mix, he did in this case. This was yet more stress that Della just didn't need.

Barrett pulled her into his arms to try to steady her. To try to steady himself, too. And it worked. Sort of. There was certainly some soothing going on, but there was also the crackle of heat. He didn't bother cursing it because he figured it would always be there.

He still had Della against him when Daniel came in through the front door, and he made a beeline for them. A beeline complete with an expression that showed some surprise, and likely some concern, about the embrace. Thankfully, his brother didn't bring it up as Barrett eased away from Della.

"I dropped off Alice and Buddy," Daniel told him. "No signs of a break-in or anything, but I saw Josh, and he said he saw someone down by the back fence of your pasture. He said the guy took off when he spotted him."

Barrett went on instant alert. Josh Jenkins was a part-time ranch hand, one with a good eye. "Did he get a description?"

"Only that it was a man wearing dark clothes."

That put plenty of alarm back in Della's face. "Should we go back there to be with Alice?"

"I told Josh to stay close," Daniel explained before Barrett could answer, "and I'm sending over one of my hands to keep watch."

Those were good security measures, but Barrett figured neither Alice nor Buddy would be relaxing any until he was there. Unfortunately, that meant taking Della back out since he had no intentions of leaving her here.

"When Esther and Leo finish with the interviews, Della and I will head out," Barrett said. Maybe Lorraine and Curran would have given them something they could use to blow this case wide-open.

Maybe with the finger pointing at Rory.

If he could keep killing his sister a secret all this time, there was no telling what else he was capable of hiding. After all, his desperation over his loans was still there. But what motive would Rory have had for orchestrating the attacks and killing Casto? None.

Well, unless Curran had put him up to doing it.

If so, then Curran had thrown Rory under the bus by telling Della and him that Rory had tried to blackmail him.

Barrett's desk phone rang, and he thought maybe it was the judge's office calling with the arrest warrant. It wasn't. When he answered, the person on the other end of the line stayed silent for several moments.

"We need to talk," the person finally said. It was a man, and his voice was low with a growl to it.

"Who is this?" Barrett asked.

Another long pause. "I'm the man who's been trying to kill you. And like I said, we need to talk."

DELLA HADN'T HEARD what the caller said to Barrett, but she immediately noticed the change in him. He sandwiched the phone between his ear and shoulder while he riffled through his desk and came up with a recorder. The moment he flicked it on, he also put the call on speaker.

"You're the man who's been trying to kill Deputy Howell and me?" he asked.

That question sent both Daniel and her closer to the phone, and Della held her breath, waiting. Thankfully, she didn't have to wait long.

"I'm the man *someone hired* to kill you both. Casto, too," the man corrected. "I got nothing personal against the deputy and you."

Well, it sure as heck felt personal to her. Especially with her baby put in danger. That sent a surge of anger through her. She was pretty sure Barrett was feeling that, too, because the muscles in his face had turned to iron.

"Who are you?" Barrett demanded.

"I'd rather not give you my name, not over the phone, but like I said, we need to talk. All of this is getting out of hand, and you came damn close to killing me earlier. This was supposed to be a one and done. You weren't supposed to survive the first attack."

Della hadn't thought the rage inside her could bubble up even more, but it did.

"Who hired you?" Barrett pressed.

"I'll give you that. Well, I'll give you what I can anyway, but like I said, not over the phone. We have to meet."

Barrett made a sound of disgust. "Why, so you can try to kill me again?"

"Nope. I'm offering you the real deal. A chance to put an end to all of this mess. In exchange I want a deal that I figure you can work out with the DA. I don't expect to skate. I figure I'll do some jail time, but it won't be life or a needle in the arm. Jail time for me, and in exchange you'll get the person who's behind this."

Oh, mercy. What a decision. No way did Della want

this snake getting anything less than the death penalty, but she also didn't want the attacks to go on. She wanted—no, she needed—to get on with her life. That was the best chance she had of keeping the baby safe.

"All right," Barrett finally said to the caller. "Let's talk. But FYI, I won't be meeting you out in the sticks or someplace where you can gun me down."

"Okay," he answered. "But I want you to bring Deputy Howell with you."

"No deal." Barrett didn't hesitate. "It's me and you, or this meeting doesn't happen."

Apparently, the man had to think about that because he didn't say anything for a long time. "Just you and me," he agreed. "And it won't be in the sticks. I'll meet you at the Drop In Diner just up the street in ten minutes."

"You're at the diner." Barrett sounded skeptical, but he motioned for Daniel to get moving. No doubt so he could see if the man was actually there.

"I'm nearby, and I'll see you coming. Like I said, make sure you're alone. This isn't a setup. I need to make a deal with you. Come now," the man added, and he ended the call.

Barrett made a quick call to have someone trace the number, though they both knew the guy was almost certainly using a disposable cell that couldn't be traced. Still, it was something they had to rule out.

"This is the number of my phone," Barrett said, scribbling it down on a piece of paper that he handed to her. "Stay put, and I mean it. I'll have backup, but I don't want it to be you."

Della wanted to help him, but she couldn't. Too risky. That also meant it was too risky for Barrett, too.

"You have to be safe. You have to take precautions," she insisted.

"I will," he assured, and as if it were the most natural thing in the world, he brushed a kiss on her mouth. "Text Daniel and tell him to stay out of sight and on this side of the street."

The diner was on the opposite side of Main Street, but that didn't mean that's where the gunman was waiting and watching. In fact, he could be anywhere. He might not even be near Mercy Ridge. Or he could be on the roof of a building that would give him a good shot at taking out Barrett.

"If Esther and Leo finish the interviews, have everyone stay put inside the building," he added.

She wanted to repeat her warning for him to be careful, but she knew he would be. Plus, he was already heading out. Not through the front of the building but out back as Daniel had done.

Della immediately felt the fear wash over her in heavy, fast waves. Oh, God. Barrett had to be all right. He just had to be.

It was too risky for her to go right to the windows, but while keeping her hand over her weapon, Della went to the corner of the squad room. She stayed back, out of the direct line of sight of anyone outside. However, she could see out.

There was a handful of people milling around, but almost immediately she saw them duck into the various businesses that lined Main Street. Daniel or Barrett had likely put out the warning for everyone to get inside. What Della couldn't see was either Daniel or Barrett. She figured that was a good thing, and maybe it meant they were keeping out of the path of a would-be attack.

"What the hell's going on?" she heard Curran bellow from the hall.

Della ignored him, though she did hear Leo explain that there could be a gunman outside. If Curran had been the one to hire the thug, then hearing that might cause him great concern. After all, if this was legit, if the hired gun really did want to deal, then he could possibly ID Curran as his boss.

A few moments later, Leo came to her. He, too, had drawn his weapon and was alone. Apparently, Curran had decided to heed the warning and stay put. But she did hear the man having a muffled conversation either with his lawyers or someone he'd called. Della half listened, hoping to catch something incriminating, but she kept her gaze pinned to Main Street.

The seconds crawled by.

And with each one, Della had to remind herself to tamp down her breathing and steady her heartbeat. Not just because it wouldn't do any good but also because of the added stress it might cause for the baby. Her stress went up a significant notch, though, when she heard the next sound.

A shout.

"Don't!" a man yelled.

And it was quickly followed by something else Della definitely didn't want to hear. A gunshot. Then, another. Not on Main Street. The shots seemed to have come from the back of the sheriff's office.

Now the terror came in a hot sticky wave over her, and her first thought was Barrett. God, had he been shot? She wanted to rush out, to hurry and try to help him, but she could be walking straight into an ambush.

Leo didn't stay put, though. "Keep watch of the front door," he barked out, and he hurried toward the back.

It took every ounce of willpower to stay put. This wasn't busywork, she told herself. She needed to make sure whoever had fired that shot didn't come rushing in and try to take them out. Still, she hated not knowing what was happening.

Della finally released the breath she'd been holding when she caught sight of Barrett and Daniel. Barrett was running toward the back of the building. Right toward the sound of those shots. Daniel rushed in through the front door.

"Barrett's okay," he muttered as he ran past her, heading in the same direction that Leo had taken.

"Stay put," she heard Esther say several moments later.

The deputy was no doubt talking to Lorraine. Maybe the woman would listen because right now, they didn't need anyone else distracting them. Especially a distraction from someone who was a suspect in the attacks.

"Leo texted me to lock the front door," Esther said.

That didn't help steady Della's nerves because it meant Barrett thought there was still danger. And there likely was. It'd been a couple of minutes since Della had heard those shots, but the gunman could still be nearby.

With the front of the building secured, Della followed Esther to the back, past Curran, who scowled at her. Past the interview room where Lorraine was waiting in the doorway. Esther went to the back door just as Daniel opened it.

And Della saw Barrett.

Alive and unharmed, thank God.

But someone else wasn't. She saw the blood. Then, the man sprawled out on the ground. If he wasn't already dead, he soon would be, thanks to the slugs he'd taken in the chest.

Barrett glanced at her, motioning for her to stay back. Della did, but by looking over Esther's shoulder, she could take it all in. Leo, Barrett and Daniel were there— their weapons trained not on the guy on the ground but on another man. He had a bulky build and was wearing dark jeans and a black T-shirt. He was also on his knees, his hands tucked behind his head. Or at least they were until Barrett moved in to cuff the guy.

In the distance, Della heard the wail of an ambulance. Since it was coming from just up the street, it wouldn't take long to get here.

"What happened?" Esther asked.

"These are the two men who tried to kill Della and me," Barrett answered.

"I didn't know my partner was going to show up here," the cuffed man volunteered. He gave a dry sneer. "Guess he didn't like the notion of me trying to cut a deal with the sheriff."

"You shot him?" Esther added to Barrett.

"No." Barrett tipped his head to the other man. "He did."

"Yeah, I did, when he tried to kill me first to shut me up," the guy verified. "And now I'm ready to talk."

Chapter Fourteen

Barrett had Leo and Esther wait with the dead guy while he ushered the gunman inside. He made a quick check on Della. Thank God she wasn't hurt, but she sure as heck could have been when those thugs started shooting. Those bullets had gone way too close to the building.

"Get a crime scene unit out here," Barrett instructed Leo and Esther, though he was certain his brother was already doing that. Leo was on the phone with someone while he continued to keep watch around them. It seemed the danger had passed.

Seemed.

But Barrett didn't want anyone taking any unnecessary chances, especially Della. And that's why he motioned for her to go ahead of them. She did, but the gunman and she still managed to exchange long glances as they made their way up the hall and to an interview room.

There was plenty of anger in Della's eyes, and Barrett was sure it was mirrored in his own. If this fool was truly a hired gun as he claimed, he'd come damn close to killing Della and him not once but twice. Della was still sporting the proof of that—the injury on her arm from their encounter.

They passed Lorraine and Curran on the short walk. Both were standing in the doorways of the two interview rooms. One of which Barrett now needed.

"You two can go," Barrett told Curran and Lorraine. Curran opened his mouth to say something, but Barrett shut him down with a glance. "Leave now," Barrett insisted.

The moment that Curran and his lawyers walked out, Barrett ushered the gunman into one of the rooms. He didn't handle the guy with kid gloves but instead let him drop down into the chair. He'd already taken his gun and had searched him, but Barrett now looked at the ID that was in his wallet.

"Cedric Ezell," Barrett read aloud, and that sent Daniel to the laptop in the corner, no doubt to do a run on the man's background. Barrett was betting he wasn't squeaky clean.

To keep everything legal, Barrett read the man his rights and turned on the recorder. He waited for Ezell to start squawking for a lawyer, but he didn't. That might change though if this *chat* didn't go the way he wanted.

"I'm listening," Barrett said, taking the seat across from Ezell. Della stayed standing, her hard stare drilling into Ezell.

"You gotta take murder off the table," Ezell started. "And that should be easy to do since I didn't kill anybody."

"Really?" Barrett didn't bother to sound as if he believed that.

"Really," Ezell verified. "Donnell did the killings. Donnell Lawler," he provided. "He's the dead guy out back."

Barrett glanced over his shoulder to confirm that

Daniel was running Lawler, too. "So, your partner did the murders, and you stood by and watched?"

Ezell lifted his shoulder. "It's the way things worked out. I was the driver, mostly."

It was the *mostly* that caused Barrett's blood to boil. So did what he saw on the laptop screen when Daniel brought it over. Yeah, both Ezell and Lawler had sheets a mile long. Nothing as serious as murder, but there were plenty of arrests for assaults, including one with a deadly weapon. Both had worked as bouncers and that catchall of "personal security."

"Take murder off the table," Ezell repeated, "and I'll tell you everything you want to know."

It was tempting. Mercy, was it. Barrett wanted answers, bad, but he didn't want this idiot to walk. "Convince me that you didn't kill anyone," Barrett said. That was a start. Maybe if he got the guy talking, he'd spill his guts. "Then, and only then, will I consider a deal."

Barrett could practically see the wheels turning in Ezell's head. How much to say. How much to leave out. This thug would do or say whatever it took to try to save his own hide.

"Somebody hired LeBeau, Donnell and me to do a job," Ezell finally started. "We were supposed to rough up Casto. *Rough him up*," he emphasized. "Not kill him. We had orders to rough up his woman, too. Alice Logan. And then we were told to dump them in the woods outside of town."

Barrett didn't say anything. He just gave Ezell a flat look and made a circling motion with his index finger to indicate he wanted him to keep going.

Ezell dragged in a long breath. "LeBeau went crazy or something. I think he was high. Or maybe needing a fix 'cause he uses sometimes. Anyway, we had Casto all trussed up, but he spit in LeBeau's face. LeBeau grabbed a knife and stabbed him. I swear, he stabbed him right there on the ground. I couldn't believe it. I asked LeBeau if he'd lost his mind, and he came after me. He might have killed me, too, if Donnell hadn't pulled him off me."

Barrett could maybe see things playing out like this. *Maybe.* "Why were you supposed to rough up Casto and Alice?"

"Don't know," Ezell readily answered. "I don't know," he repeated when Barrett glared at him and huffed. "I didn't ask why. I just needed the money. I got a boatload of back child support due, and my ex is hounding me."

Barrett hated to think of this scum having children, but it was a reminder that anyone could father a child. He had, and he didn't have any qualifications to make him a good dad. Something he pushed aside, since he didn't need that distraction in his head right now.

From the corner of his eye, he saw Della shift her position, and she leaned closer to Ezell, putting her fisted hands on the table. "Maybe your dead friend, Donnell, had a theory about why you were hired to do it."

Ezell lifted his shoulder again. "If he did, he didn't say."

Barrett doubted that. The pair had had plenty of time together, and even if they hadn't discussed it before Casto's murder, they sure as heck would have afterward. Too bad Barrett couldn't have been a fly on the wall because he needed to know. Of course, once he had the name of the person who'd paid these goons, then he'd have all the answers he needed.

If Curran was behind this, he could have maybe hoped to use Casto's and Alice's attack to distract Barrett, to get him off the trail of the money laundering investigation. It was just as possible, though, that Casto knew plenty about that illegal operation. And maybe Curran had wanted to teach the man a lesson of some sort.

But there were also Lorraine and Rory to consider.

No fury like a woman scorned in Lorraine's case. And Rory, well, he'd had a secret that he wanted to keep hidden. He'd killed his own sister. So, Ezell and crew could be connected to that.

"What happened after LeBeau killed Casto?" Barrett asked to get the interview moving along again.

"Well, we kind of panicked at first. Then, LeBeau said we oughta set up the woman, Alice. He said everybody would think she'd done it anyway 'cause Casto and she got in a fight or something."

Yes, some might indeed believe Alice had done it. Barrett had strongly considered that possibility. In fact, before he'd cleared her, thanks to the proof of planted fingerprints, she'd been at the top of his suspect list.

"We were all wearing gloves," Ezell went on, "but LeBeau dragged Alice over to Casto's body. She was out like a light then 'cause LeBeau had hit her on the head. And he pressed her fingers on the handle so she'd get the blame."

That meshed with the evidence. Barrett wouldn't mention, though, that the setup had failed when the lab had discovered the planted prints.

"And then what happened?" Barrett pressed.

This time, Ezell didn't pause to think. "We left. Me and Donnell started walking toward his SUV and LeBeau headed toward his. LeBeau wasn't parked near us so we went in opposite directions." But now he hesitated. "Once we were out of earshot of LeBeau, Donnell called the boss and went over what happened. When Donnell hung up, he said he had orders to take care of something with LeBeau. He left, and a while later he came back and told me that LeBeau was dead."

That, too, meshed with the evidence. Of course, it could have been Ezell who'd killed LeBeau, but with Donnell dead, there might not be any proof of it.

"Why'd your boss want LeBeau dead?" Della asked.

Ezell's response was another shoulder shrug. "Donnell didn't say."

No, but Barrett could guess about this part. The boss had been pissed off that his or her orders hadn't been carried out. Instead of a "roughing up," this had turned into a murder, and if Barrett was to believe Ezell's story, then LeBeau was to blame for turning an assault and kidnapping into murder.

"Why go after Sheriff Logan and me?" Della asked. Her voice stayed flat, a cop's voice, but Barrett knew there was plenty of emotion beneath the surface. "Why try to kill us?"

"Donnell said it was orders. I was to drive. He fired the shots. The boss didn't want you and the sheriff digging into stuff. Donnell said he was told it was best if you two were out of commission."

Out of commission. A polite word for dead. And not just their deaths, either, but also their child's.

Barrett had to take a minute to rein in his fury. Fury that he wanted to unleash on this idiot seated across from him. But while that might give him some temporary relief, it wouldn't fix things.

"If what you've told me is true, I might be able to talk the DA into taking murder charges off the table," Barrett finally said. "You'll still do jail time." In fact, he could do a lot of jail time because accessory to murder could carry the same penalty as the crime itself.

Now Barrett was the one who leaned in, and he got right in Ezell's face. "If I find out that anything you've told me is a lie, then there'll be no deal. You'll go down for two counts of murder and multiple counts of attempted murder on two police officers and a civilian."

"I've told you the truth," Ezell insisted. "So, it's a deal?"

"I'll go to bat for you," Barrett assured, and he wondered if Ezell had a clue that a cop could lie during an interview. Barrett wasn't lying, not exactly. He wanted this thug's boss more than the thug. But it'd settle better with him and likely Della, too, if everyone involved in this faced maximum charges.

Ezell stared at him as if trying to suss out if Barrett was trying to pull something over on him. Then, he finally nodded.

"Give me the name of the person who hired you," Barrett demanded. "That'll go a long way toward getting me to really go to bat for you."

Ezell nodded again and dragged in a long breath that it seemed he was going to need. "My boss is Rory Silva."

Even though Barrett had steeled himself up, it still felt like a punch to the gut. Della had been best friends with Rory's sister. She'd grieved with him. Or at least she thought that's what was happening. But it was all a sham, since Rory had been the one to kill Francine. Now, if he was to believe Ezell, Rory was trying to kill them, too.

"There's an arrest warrant in the works for Rory," Barrett told Daniel when his brother got up and took out his phone. "But I'll try to contact him again and try to *coax* him into giving himself up."

"And what about this guy?" Daniel asked. "You want me to book him?"

Barrett went over his options. "Go ahead and put him in lockup." They could hold Ezell for forty-eight hours before charging him with anything. Of course, during that time the man would likely wise up and ask for a lawyer. Still, Barrett had gotten what he wanted from him. "After I've talked with Rory and the DA, we'll settle on the charges."

And those charges for Ezell would be legion. Maybe not murder if Barrett did try going for the deal, but there'd be plenty of other felonies.

While Daniel hauled Ezell away, Barrett took Della to his office. He needed to use his desk phone to try to find Rory, but first he wanted to make sure Della was as steady as she could be. She was putting up a good front, but that didn't stop him from shutting the door and pulling her into his arms. He brushed a chaste kiss on the top of her head, too. It didn't feel exactly chaste to him, but then this was Della.

"Rory," she whispered on a hoarse breath.

Yeah, there was the emotion that he knew would come. Rory had betrayed her. Worse, he was a killer. At least according to Ezell he was. Barrett really needed to talk to Rory to see if what the man said meshed with the statement Ezell had given them.

"But at least now we know who killed Francine," she went on.

Della practically melted into his arms, and Barrett was glad she seemed to find some kind of comfort there. Forty-eight hours ago, she definitely wouldn't have let him do something like this.

She'd have to let him do more, of course. More for her, more for the baby. But that was a topic for another time.

"And with one gunman dead and the other behind bars, this could be the end of the attacks," he reminded her. Barrett wouldn't mention that Rory or whoever had orchestrated this could possibly hire more thugs to try to finish the job.

Della eased back a bit and stared up at him with her intense blue eyes. "You believe Ezell?"

"I want to believe him," Barrett settled for saying, and he would have added more, a reassurance that even if it wasn't the truth, they'd get to the bottom of this soon enough, but the knock at the door stopped him.

Cursing softly, Barrett let go of Della so he could answer it. He expected to see one of his deputies, but it wasn't.

It was Lorraine. And she was alone. Her lawyer wasn't anywhere in sight.

"You're free to go for now," Barrett reminded her.

Lorraine nodded, but then she stepped inside, shutting the door behind her. "I need you to see something. I didn't want to give it to your deputy, so I waited until I could speak to you."

Barrett automatically moved in front of Della when Lorraine reached into her purse. Lorraine noticed his shift, too, and her eyes widened.

"I don't have a gun," she insisted. "And I'm not here to hurt either of you. In fact, I think this will help with your investigation." Lorraine pulled out a USB storage device and handed it to him. "There are documents and files on there that prove Wilbur Curran participated in a money laundering scheme."

Barrett eyed both Lorraine and the USB device with plenty of skepticism. "Really?"

"Really," she verified. "Robert was involved, too, but now that he's dead, that doesn't matter." Her eyes welled up with tears, and she swallowed hard. If Lorraine was faking her grief over Casto, then she was good at it. "There's no reason for me to protect Robert any longer."

Barrett stared at her for a long moment. "Casto and Curran were partners in the money laundering?"

"No, not partners. But Robert let Curran use his real estate business to wash some of the funds. And no, I don't know where Curran got the money. That's not in the files. He just funneled some cash, and Robert kept track of it."

Barrett glanced at Della to see her take on this, but she was obviously as surprised as he was. "Why are you doing this?" Della asked.

Lorraine touched her fingers to her trembling mouth. "Because you believe Curran killed Robert, and if he did do that, use what I've given you to arrest him. Then, find a way to make him pay for killing the man I loved."

Chapter Fifteen

The thoughts were whirling around in Della's mind. So much had happened in the last few hours that it was hard for her to focus. But it was definitely something she had to do, because she had to keep watch as Barrett and she drove back to the ranch.

The hired guns were out of the picture, but that didn't mean there couldn't be others. After all, Rory was still at large, and if he'd truly hired Ezell and his partner, he could hire others. Ditto for Curran. And then there was their third suspect—Lorraine—and what she'd given them.

"Do you believe Lorraine was telling the truth about why she gave us that dirt on Curran?" Della asked Barrett.

Now that they'd had a couple of hours to process what was on the USB and the details Ezell had given them in the interview, Della was hoping his mind was clearer than hers. Like her, though, he was keeping watch as well, and she was certain Daniel was doing the same as he followed behind them in another cruiser.

"The info on the USB looks legit," he answered after a long pause. Though it would be up to the computer geeks at the Ranger lab to determine that. "Maybe she wants to get back at Curran. Maybe she just wants suspicion on someone other than herself."

Yes, that was Della's take, too, and it caused her to let out a weary sigh. It was hard to know the woman's actual motives, but Lorraine had seemed genuinely broken up about Casto's death. Still, that didn't mean she hadn't hired Ezell and the others for a "roughing up" job that got out of hand.

Della breathed a little easier when Barrett took the final turn to his ranch. Ironic, that just hours ago seeing his place had been a source of added stress. But no more. The barrier was no longer there between Barrett and her. Along with the heat from the attraction, there was also, well, a bond between them. A baby could do that.

Could cause other problems, too.

Along with everything else on his plate, Barrett was no doubt dealing with the pregnancy, and that meant soon they were going to have to talk about it.

When Barrett's house came into view, Della got a jolt of fresh adrenaline the moment she spotted the Culver Crossing cruiser. "Jace is here," she said, recognizing the vehicle. "Something must be wrong."

Barrett must have thought so, too, because he motioned for Daniel to wait in his own cruiser while Della and he hurried into the house. They found Jace all right, along with Buddy and Alice. They all appeared to be fine.

"I was just about to call you," Jace told her. "I'm taking Alice back to my place, and I'll bring in a reserve deputy to guard her."

"I thought it was best if I got out from under your feet," Alice quickly added, her comment aimed at Barrett.

Barrett stayed quiet a moment, probably figuring out

the best way to respond. He likely didn't want to say something along the lines of "you're welcome to stay as long as needed." No. Because he was as uncomfortable with her being here as Alice was.

"You've got the manpower to guard her?" Barrett asked Jace.

"I'll make do," Jace assured him. He tipped his head to Della. "You okay?"

She nodded. "But we have a lot of updates on the investigation. Barrett and I just did the report before we left his office, and we copied you on it."

"I was reading it while Alice was getting ready to go. Once Rory's found, maybe things can start getting back to normal."

Yes, and that included her going back to work. Della wasn't sure she was ready for that just yet.

"I can have Daniel follow you to Culver Crossing," Barrett offered.

"Appreciate it," Jace said, and he headed for the door. Buddy did, too, telling Barrett to call him if he needed him.

Alice paused a moment, her gaze lingering on Barrett. "Thank you for everything."

He huffed as if insulted that she'd thank him for doing his job, but then his expression softened just a little. "Stay safe," he muttered. It wasn't exactly warm and fuzzy, but it did seem to be a step toward thawing their relationship.

"Wait here," Barrett told Della, and he went to the cruiser to have a word with Daniel. No doubt to explain that he wanted Daniel to provide some backup on the drive to Culver Crossing. Della was thankful for the extra security measure, but maybe it wouldn't be needed. Maybe the danger was truly over.

Maybe.

When he was finished talking to his brother, Barrett came back to the house, locked the door and reset the security system. He definitely seemed in "let's get to work" mode because he headed straight for the laptop on the kitchen table.

"You should eat and get some rest," he told her, his attention on what he was reading on the screen.

Della got a bottle of water from the fridge, but she didn't want either rest or food right now. She'd eaten just a few hours earlier in Barrett's office when Leo had ordered sandwiches from the diner. And as for rest, that wouldn't happen with her thoughts going a mile a minute. Still, she did want to see if there were any updates on the case, so she went to Barrett and read from over his shoulder. Della instantly saw the reason he muttered some profanity.

Rory was still nowhere to be found.

And Curran had called the sheriff's office to blast Barrett about the so-called evidence Lorraine had given them. Curran hadn't had the number to Barrett's burner cell or he would have no doubt contacted him directly.

"How'd Curran find all of this out so soon?" Della asked. She had a long drink of the water, then set the bottle aside.

"Probably from Lorraine herself. She might have wanted to gloat that she'd given us something to put him away. Curran's lawyer will fight any arrest warrant," he added after a moment.

Of course, he would. No way would he just allow himself to be locked up. And the trouble was, the evidence was questionable. There was no chain of custody on it, which meant there was no way to verify if someone had tampered with the info so it might not hold up in court. Still, unless the info on there was completely false, there was finally some proof that Curran was dirty. That was a start anyway.

"This could make Curran…desperate," Barrett went on. "If he's the one who actually hired Ezell and the others, then this could spur him to make another attempt. Not just to take out Ezell, but us, too."

Yes, Curran could hire more gunmen for that. Then again, maybe Curran and his lawyers would stay busy enough with the legal wrangling so Curran wouldn't have time to put together something like that.

"Eliminating us won't help Curran," Della said. "The Rangers will still go after him."

Barrett nodded but then looked back at her when she made a slight sound of pain as she reached for the water bottle. "You're hurting," he said, getting to his feet. There was plenty of alarm suddenly on his face.

"No. It was just a twinge, that's all."

He gave her a flat look, clearly not buying that, and he glanced down at the bandage. He couldn't see the actual stitches, but the area around the bandage was no longer an angry red color.

Barrett cursed again, probably remembering the attack that'd led to her injury. She hated that he was likely beating himself up about that, and Della reached up to try to smooth away the worry line on his bunched up forehead.

"You really don't have to worry about me," she said.

His expression said otherwise. Barrett's eyes were stormy gray now and nailed to her. And just like that, the moment changed. His worry morphed into something else. Just as intense. But definitely different, and she recognized it, too.

The lust.

He stepped back as if fighting it, but Della didn't want him to gather enough willpower to move away from her. They'd been dealing with this attraction, well, for as long as they'd known each other, and she knew she would feel a heck of lot better in his arms than out of them.

She moved in, came up on her tiptoes and kissed him.

It took a couple of heartbeats, but she felt him lose the battle, and his mouth crush hers. The kiss was hard, almost brutal and in direct contrast to his touch. He slid his arm around her waist and eased her to him with surprising gentleness. A gentleness she wasn't sure she wanted. Barrett was treating her like glass, and she wanted him to treat her like his lover.

Della helped remedy that. She deepened the kiss and pressed her body against his, making sure there was pressure in all the right places. And Barrett reacted all right. There was a low rumble in his throat, and she felt the leash snap on his self-control.

Good.

That was her first thought, but soon she had trouble thinking at all. Her body just reacted. She forgot all about the nightmare they'd been through. Forgot about her injury and that she was pregnant. Instead, she let herself slide right into the heat he was offering.

And he was offering plenty.

The kiss became hungry, and soon it wasn't enough. She wanted more. To touch him. To have him take her as he'd done so many times before. Della started to tell him that but then realized it wasn't necessary.

Without breaking the kiss, Barrett scooped her up in his arms and headed for the bedroom.

BARRETT FIGURED HE should take a moment and re-consider what he was doing. But he didn't want to re-consider. He wanted Della, and a moment or two of thinking about that wasn't going to change things.

Apparently, not for Della, either.

She certainly didn't hesitate when she hooked her good arm around his neck and used the leverage to pull his mouth closer to hers. Not that it could get closer, but she certainly tried.

The ache was already there. The need. And despite everything that had gone on, the fire was even hotter than usual. Maybe because he'd gone so long without her. His body was already urging him on, but he forced himself to be gentle when he eased her down onto the bed.

Della didn't bother with gentle when she caught onto his shirt to get it off him. Figuring it would be better for her arm, Barrett just shoved up her top, pushed down the cups of her bra and kissed her breasts. Those kind of kisses had always revved her up fast, and now was no different.

She arched her body, pushing her hips against his. That revved him, too, and let him know that this was going to be fast. Too fast. But that was the trouble when the need was this strong.

Moving her hand between them, she unzipped him and slid her palm down into his boxers. Barrett hadn't needed anything else to kick up the fire a notch, but that did it. It also let him know that he had to do something about getting them at least partially naked.

He got off her, not easily, because Della was still

touching him, but he finally maneuvered enough to shimmy off her loose jeans and shoes. Her panties came next, but he took a moment to drop some kisses on her stomach. And he tried not to think of the pregnancy.

Barrett failed.

He definitely thought about it. Della must have felt his hesitation because she shook her head and went after his jeans.

"We're doing this," she insisted. "Pregnant women might not get to have multiple cups of coffee, but we can have sex."

For some reason that made him smile. Not for long, though. That's because she managed to shove down his jeans and boxers, and then dragged him back down on top of her. It didn't take much encouragement for that to happen. Barrett was already primed and ready to go.

Despite her hands and mouth urging him on, Barrett went slow. And stayed gentle when he slipped inside her. The sensations nearly robbed him of his breath. Yes, it'd been too long without her.

Della kept up the urging, lifting herself to meet his strokes when he began to move inside her. He knew her body so well. Knew that she was already close to the peak. Part of him wanted to draw out the pleasure, to linger until maybe some of this heat inside him had cooled.

But he couldn't.

Della made a sound of silky pleasure, and she released the grip she had on him to fist her hands in her hair. Her eyelids fluttered down. Her mouth opened. Her face flushed. And she went straight over the edge.

With her body closing around him like a fist, Barrett had no choice but to go with her.

He didn't rush his coming back from the ripples of

pleasure. Barrett kept the intimate contact, though he did put some of his weight on his forearms so that he wouldn't crush her.

"I needed that," she whispered. "Thanks."

She made another sound, a low moan this time, and he knew the drill. Della wasn't much of a postsex cuddler and would soon drift off to sleep. Good. Because she needed the rest. Barrett did, too, but he'd skip it and get some work done once he was sure she was sacked out.

He shifted his position again, dropping down beside her on the bed. She didn't stir, but since she was nearly naked, he lifted the side of the quilt and laid it over her. However, when he went to get off the bed, her good arm came around him, pulling him closer. Apparently, she was in a cuddling mood after all.

Barrett snuggled her against him, her head fitting right into the curve of his neck. It was perfect. A reminder of everything he'd missed when they'd been apart these past two months. But he couldn't help thinking—was this temporary?

Della and he hadn't really resolved anything between them. Yes, the sex had been damn good, but they hadn't talked about the future. About the baby. In a little more than six months, they'd be parents, and while that gave them plenty of time to work out how they were going to handle parenthood, he thought he would need every minute of those months to come to terms with it.

He hoped like the devil that he didn't screw this up.

Della's breathing soon settled into a slow, familiar rhythm. Her muscles relaxed. That should have been his cue to get up and get to work, but he didn't budge. In fact, he closed his own eyes, figuring that a little nap wouldn't hurt.

Barrett wasn't sure how long he'd been asleep, but he woke with a jolt when he heard the sound of ringing. It took him a moment to fight through his hazy mind and determine it was Della's phone—which was somewhere on the floor in the heap of their clothes.

Della stirred, too, muttering something incoherent, but she crawled over him to get to the side of the bed. She reached down, took her phone from her jeans pocket and blinked while she looked at the screen.

"It's Jace," she said.

Since this could be business, Barrett didn't curse, but he did glance at the clock on the bedside table. Then, he did curse. Because his nap had lasted over two hours. Outside, it was already dark.

"Yeah?" Della answered, sounding as groggy as she looked. However, she did remember to put the call on speaker.

"Is Barrett there with you?" Jace immediately asked. "Are you both all right?"

"Yes on both counts." There was a quick shift in Della's posture. She sat up, and she suddenly looked very much like the cop that she was. "Why?"

"Good." Jace muttered some profanity, too. "Because we've had some trouble."

Chapter Sixteen

Trouble.

That was the one word that came through loud and clear, and Della could tell from Jace's tone that whatever had happened was bad. Her relaxed muscles tensed again, and she went on instant alert.

"What happened?" she asked.

"It's Alice." Jace muttered some more profanity. "I dropped her and the reserve deputy off at her house a couple of hours ago and told her to stay put. Apparently, she didn't."

Sweet heaven. That definitely wasn't good. The person who'd hired those gunmen was still out there. Was still a threat.

"Where'd she go?" Barrett snapped. He got up from the bed and started to get dressed. Della did the same.

"I'm not sure. The reserve deputy, Crystal Rankin, said that Alice went to her bedroom to lie down. Crystal thought all was well, but when she went to check on Alice about two hours later, she found a note that Alice had left on her bed. Apparently, someone called Alice and convinced her that both Barrett and you had been taken hostage."

"What?" Barrett snapped, anger and shock in his tone.

"Yeah," Jace verified. "She wrote in the note that she

took some money from her safe to pay a ransom and that she was going to save both of you."

Della wasn't sure whose groan was louder—hers or Barrett's. "Who convinced her to go out?" Barrett pressed.

"Don't know. But Alice said something else in the note. She said she had to save the baby, her grandchild." Jace paused. "Della, are you pregnant?"

How the heck had Alice learned about the baby? Della definitely hadn't wanted to tell him this way, and she couldn't take the time to think of a better response, so she just said, "Yes." Later, though, she'd want to talk to him about it. Would want to ask Alice, too, how she'd known. But for now, they had a more serious problem.

"How long has Alice been gone?" Della asked, not only to get Jace to shift subjects but also because she truly wanted to know.

"About two hours at most, judging from the time she was out of Crystal's sight. I've been trying to call her, but she or someone else turned off her phone."

Della was betting it was the *someone else*. If Alice had believed they were in danger, she would have kept her phone on in case Barrett or she tried to contact the woman.

"I'm at Alice's place now," Jace went on, "but there's no sign of her. She didn't use her car, but it's possible she met this person at the end of the road. That way, Crystal wouldn't have heard anyone pull up. The bedroom window is unlocked so that's probably how she got out."

Yes, that was possible, but this still didn't make sense. "How could someone have convinced Alice that we'd been taken hostage? Better yet, why wouldn't she have called Barrett or me to verify that?"

"Again, I don't know. Maybe she wasn't thinking straight. Maybe this person convinced her that if she called you, it could get you killed."

Della thought about Alice's head injury that'd been serious enough for her to stay in the hospital. That might be playing into all of this. That and the recent psychological trauma she'd experienced. Still, it didn't make sense that she'd fall for something like this.

"I've called in every deputy available," Jace went on. "Barrett, I'm asking you to do the same."

"Of course," Barrett assured him. "But if this is an attempt to get to Della and me, then I figure very soon we'll be getting a call from the kidnapper."

Jace made a sound of agreement. "Let me know when that happens. In the meantime, I'll keep looking for her."

Barrett assured him that he'd do the same, and when Della ended the call, he took out his own phone. However, before he could contact any of his deputies, the landline on the nightstand rang.

Considering that Barrett still didn't have his own cell phone, Della thought someone from his office might try to contact him this way, but with everything else going on, she moved closer to listen when he answered it. What Della heard sent her heart to her knees.

"I'm so sorry," the woman said.

Alice.

"Where are you?" Barrett demanded, and Della heard the emotional punch in his own voice, too.

Alice didn't respond, but there was some mumbling in the background. The woman wasn't alone. "I, uh, can't say," Alice finally muttered. There were more mumblings, but Della couldn't make out the second voice. "You're supposed to come and rescue me. You and Della are supposed to come." Alice made a hoarse sob. "But please don't do it—"

And with that, the call cut off.

Della felt the fear slide through her. She hadn't needed any proof that whatever was happening was a setup to get to Barrett and her, but Alice had just confirmed it. That confirmation might have cost Alice bigtime. Whoever had her probably was going to make her pay for blurting out that warning.

Cursing, Barrett hit redial, and Della heard the ringing. What she didn't hear though was anyone answering it, and with each ring, she could feel the stress rising inside her.

"The kidnapper won't kill her," Della assured him, and she tried to reassure herself, as well. But he or she would hurt her. In fact, the kidnapper might do all sorts of nasty things to get Barrett and her to come out into the open.

Where they'd almost certainly be killed.

When no one answered after nearly a minute, Barrett hung up and hit redial again. Like before, the ringing started. Then stopped. In fact, everything stopped, including the dial tone.

The line was dead.

That definitely didn't help Della tamp down her fear. Since there wasn't any bad weather to disrupt service, someone had almost certainly cut the line, and now they had no way to contact Alice. Of course, the kidnapper would figure out a way to contact Barrett and her. Della was sure of that.

Barrett still had his cell in his hand, and he hit the button to make a call. He frowned when he looked at the screen. "It's dead, too."

Della knew that wasn't a coincidence, and she held

her breath while she checked her own phone. It was also dead.

"Someone's using a jammer," Barrett growled.

Della had heard about such things but didn't know a lot about them. However, what she did know was that the person using the jamming device had to be nearby. This wasn't something that would work from a long distance.

"You think someone set up a jammer here at your place?" Della asked.

Barrett didn't get a chance to answer before they heard something. Something that Della definitely didn't want to hear.

A woman screamed.

BARRETT FORCED HIMSELF to put aside the emotional punch he got from hearing that scream. Forced himself to think through what was happening. But one thing was for certain.

The scream had been close.

Damn close. In fact, he was pretty sure it had come from the vicinity of his own barn. Not good, since the barn was only yards from the house.

Barrett hurried to the window that faced the back of the house, and he peered out through the slats of the blinds. It was pitch-dark outside, not even a sliver of a moon thanks to some clouds, and the exterior lights were off. That in itself wasn't unusual. The lights got turned on only if he or one of his hands had work to do at night. But now Barrett needed those lights to try to figure out what was going on.

"No!" someone shouted.

Barrett still couldn't see anyone, but it helped him

pinpoint the location of the person who'd shouted. Definitely the barn.

"That sounds like Alice," Della said, hurrying to the other side of the window to peer out.

Yeah, it did, though Barrett couldn't be positive. Still, it would make sense for the kidnapper to bring her here. It'd make it easier for him or her to try to get to them.

Barrett needed to make sure that didn't happen.

"Stay back from the window," he warned Della. "I want to check the security system."

Judging from the way Della sucked in her breath, she hadn't realized that the alarm could be affected. It wasn't tied to the landline, but Barrett suspected that it, too, could be jammed.

Thankfully, Della stayed put, but she did ease back a little. However, he had no doubts that she'd continue to keep watch. She'd want to spot the woman who'd yelled and make sure that someone didn't try to get in through the back of the house.

Barrett cursed when he saw no lights on the security panel. It was definitely jammed. However, he did still have electricity and hopefully internet, too. He picked up the laptop, taking it back to the bedroom, and he used it to fire off emails to both his brothers. He filled them in on the situation and requested backup.

Backup with caution.

He'd emphasized that he didn't know what he was dealing with so they were to make a silent approach. Barrett had no idea if Jace, Leo or Daniel would even check their emails, but he hoped like the devil that they did.

"Do you see anything?" Barrett asked Della.

"No, but your barn door's closed." She paused, continued to peer through the blinds.

Yeah, he normally kept it closed at night. That didn't mean, though, that someone hadn't sneaked in there. And that led him to a thought that riled him to the core. Someone had slipped onto his property while he'd been asleep. That damn nap he'd taken could end up costing them.

"You're not going out there," Della said when she glanced at him adjusting his holster and checking his gun.

He'd debated it. Barrett wanted to know what was going on in that barn, and if Alice was in danger, he wanted to do his job and rescue her. But leaving the house meant one of two things. He either had to take Della with him or leave her inside and hope this wasn't a ploy to separate them so the kidnapper could have an easier time picking them off.

"I can give you backup," she reminded him, tapping her own holster that she'd put back on after they'd dressed.

She could. But the cost could be sky-high if anything went wrong. And with the kidnapper already nearby, plenty of things could go wrong.

"We'll wait a few minutes. I sent an email to Daniel and Leo, and if it goes through, I want to give them time to respond."

Della made a sound of agreement and went back to keeping watch. He knew the instant she'd seen something because of the change in her body language. She drew her gun, and Barrett hurried to the window, easing Della behind him.

"Someone opened the barn door just a fraction," Della relayed to him.

He could see that. But what he couldn't tell was if

someone was still in the doorway. Without any lights on, everything was in the shadows.

"We'll have a better angle from the kitchen window," he said, considering that idea. Anyone who wanted to shoot them would have a better angle, too, since there were no blinds on that particular window and it was much larger than the one here in the bedroom. In fact, it spread out across nearly the entire kitchen wall.

"We can stay down," Della suggested.

True, but if they got in a position to see the barn door, then they were also in a position for the kidnapper to see them. Plus, Della and he wouldn't be able to shoot until they were certain Alice wouldn't be in the line of fire. Unless the kidnapper was an idiot, he or she would use Alice as a human shield.

But who was doing this?

Maybe another hired thug? Of course, it could be Rory. He was a PI after all, and if he was desperate enough, he might believe that killing Della and him would stall the investigation. Ditto for Curran. Heck, for Lorraine, too. In other words, Barrett couldn't eliminate any one of them.

"We'll stay down," Barrett verified, and he motioned for them to head to the kitchen.

Along the way, he checked the windows and doors to make sure no one was trying to break in. There were no signs of that, but he'd need to keep his ears honed for any unusual sounds.

Barrett stayed ahead of Della, and he paused in the living room to confirm that all was clear in the kitchen. It was. No one was lurking in there, ready to strike. And he'd been right about having a better angle on the barn. He saw it much better now, including the ajar door.

And the person standing inside.

He couldn't be positive, but he thought it was Alice.

Barrett didn't dare call out to her because he didn't want to give away their position in the house. However, he did move closer, motioning with his hand for Della to stay back. He went to the side of the window, trying to pick through the darkness.

That's when he saw the gun.

Someone had Alice in a choke hold and had a gun pointed at her head. Barrett had suspected things were this bad, but seeing it confirmed it. Too bad he couldn't tell if it was a man or a woman holding Alice, since the person was wearing long sleeves and gloves. Barrett also couldn't determine height since it appeared the person was hunched down, staying completely behind Alice.

He was so focused on watching the two figures that adrenaline and shock speared through him when the phone rang. Again, it was the landline, but he had an extension in the kitchen. Dropping down a little lower, he reached up and took the phone.

"Barrett," Alice said the moment he answered. He peered out the window again and saw the phone. Alice's captor had it gripped in the hand that he or she was using for the choke hold.

"Who has you?" Barrett asked.

Again, Alice didn't answer that, and now that his eyes had adjusted some to the darkness, he could see the grimace on her face. "I'm to tell you that Della and you need to come out. If not, we'll all die."

The kidnapper's plan was for them to all die no matter what. Barrett needed his own plan. One that would buy him some time with the hopes that backup would soon arrive.

"I'll come out," Barrett finally said. "But not Della.

She took some pain meds for the gunshot wound, and they knocked her out."

He heard some whispers, saw Alice shake her head. Then, the choke hold tightened. The gun jammed even harder into her temple.

"You're to bring Della," Alice insisted. "Even if you have to carry her." She shook her head again, wincing, and Barrett also thought she was crying. "Don't come out here!" Alice shouted.

Just as the shot rang out.

DELLA'S BREATH STALLED in her lungs. Oh, God. Had Alice been shot?

She leaned out to get a better look, but Della didn't see anything. The two figures who'd been in the doorway of the barn weren't there. She doubted that was a good thing. Nor was the fact that she didn't hear any other shouts from Alice.

Barrett muttered some profanity, his gaze sweeping over the yard before it came back to her. "I'm going out the front door and will circle around back. I want you to stay put."

She was shaking her head before he even finished. "You need backup. Plus, it won't be any safer for me to be inside than it will to be with you. We need to check on Alice. If she's hurt…"

But Della didn't finish that. Couldn't. She couldn't let herself think the worst. Maybe the kidnapper had just fired a warning shot to keep Alice from trying to shout out to them. After all, whoever had taken her would need to keep her alive if for no other reason than to draw them out of the house.

And that's exactly what was happening.

They were cops, and a civilian was in grave danger.

They had to do their jobs and stop it. Of course, they also had to put aside the emotional part of this, since she doubted even Barrett could forget that it was his mother out there.

"I'll stay behind you," Della added, and she would have continued to try to persuade him if there hadn't been another sound.

Alice screamed again.

And there was a shot.

Both sounds had definitely come from inside the barn, and despite Della not wanting to think the worst, she believed that Alice might be fighting for her life.

Cursing, Barrett went to a closet in the adjoining living room and came back with a Kevlar vest. "I have just one, and you're wearing it," he insisted.

Della hated that he'd be going out there unprotected—while trying to shield her, no doubt—but this was the compromise that would prevent him from having to do this alone.

She set aside her gun to put on the vest. While she did that, Barrett took out two other guns from the cabinet over the fridge. "For backup," he said, tucking his in the waist of his jeans.

Della did the same to the gun he gave her, and as soon as she'd finished, they got moving. Good. She didn't want to wait another second to give Barrett time for second thoughts to settle in.

Barrett unlocked the front door, and he looked around the yard before he stepped out onto the porch. He made another sweep before he motioned for her to follow him. Della did, and she tried to settle her heartbeat drumming in her ears so that she'd be able to hear.

There were no other screams or shots, thank goodness. No sounds of footsteps or anyone approaching, either. Maybe Leo or Daniel would arrive soon to help, but if not, Barrett and she would have to make this work. He had the advantage, after all, of knowing every inch of his own property, and he used that advantage by ducking behind trees and shrubs as they made their way to the backyard.

Barrett stopped when they reached the back of the house and had another look around. They had a clear view of the barn now and the still open door, but there was no sign of Alice and her captor. Unfortunately, the captor might have a clear line of sight of Barrett and her when they crossed the yard to the barn. That's almost certainly why Della felt Barrett's hesitation, and she prayed he didn't turn around and go back.

The next sound stopped any thoughts of that.

There was some movement in the barn. But not ordinary movement. There seemed to be a struggle going on. A fight. One that Alice could be losing. Any of their suspects or a hired thug would be bigger and stronger than Alice. And that was likely why Barrett got them moving again.

Despite those sounds, Barrett didn't make a beeline for the barn. He went to the right, following a line of mountain laurels and a fence. Neither gave them much cover, but it was still better than being out in the open.

As they moved, Della kept watch behind them, hoping they wouldn't be ambushed. But they made it within ten feet of the barn before Barrett pulled to a quick stop. He whispered something, something that she didn't catch, but then she looked on the ground in the direction of where he was pointing.

What the heck?

It appeared to be a small black box, and there was a sound coming from it. Sharp clicks.

"It's a bomb like the one on the road," Barrett warned her. He hooked his arm around her waist and pulled her to the ground on the other side of one of the trees.

The explosion blasted through the air.

It was deafening, and it sent up a spray of debris that rained down on them. Della had no choice but to cover her head and hope that Barrett and she didn't get hurt. Barrett helped make sure that didn't happen—to her anyway. Keeping his gun ready, he crawled over her, shielding her with his body.

She wanted to curse him, to tell him not to risk his life like that, but she couldn't. Because he was thinking of the baby.

The moment the debris stopped falling, Barrett lifted his head, his gaze zooming around, but it didn't stay lifted for long. A shot came their way. The bullet smacked into the ground just a few feet away from them. Barrett covered her again just as a second shot smacked into the tree.

Della felt the raw mix of fear and adrenaline. Her breathing was too fast. Ditto for her pulse. But there was no way to settle her body when it was bracing for a fight. And screaming for her to get to Alice. If the kidnapper was firing at them, then that could mean Alice had been shot.

Or worse.

There were certainly no sounds of the woman now. Nor anything to indicate a struggle. Just the shots. Two more of them before everything went silent.

Della pulled in her breath, waiting and listening, but the seconds crawled by with no other shots. Barrett lifted his head again, glanced around.

"We'll crawl the rest of the way," he whispered. "Once we reach the barn, we'll run to the back and get in that way. Stay behind me, and if the shooter fires again, swear to me that you'll get down."

"I swear," Della said, and it was the truth. She couldn't risk being shot again. Not even while wearing the vest because it only covered her chest area. Even if the shot wasn't fatal, blood loss could cause her to lose the baby.

Barrett nodded. "Use the flashlight on your phone to check the ground," he instructed. "I don't want us stepping on a bomb."

Sweet heaven. She hadn't even considered that possibility, even though the last blast had only been minutes ago. Yes, it was possible that Alice's captor had left booby traps that could kill them.

Della continued to keep watch, but she used her phone to shine a light on the ground. Thankfully, it was mainly dirt that covered the back of the barn so a bomb would have been easy to spot. She didn't see anything. Didn't hear anything, either, which only caused her concerns to spike. It could mean that Alice was dead and that her captor was now lying in wait for Barrett and her.

"Stay low," Barrett whispered to her when they started to move again.

She did, and they hurried from the side to the rear double doors of the barn. Like the front, they were open. Not just ajar, though. Fully open. Almost as if it were an invitation for them to come in.

And be killed.

Barrett paused just outside those open doors, and he glanced around as if trying to figure out the safest way to approach this. He finally motioned for her to get down on the ground.

"All the way down," he muttered when Della crouched. She wanted to insist that he get down, too, but now wasn't the time for an argument. The kidnapper could use the sound of their voices to pinpoint their location. If so, shots could easily go through the barn walls.

Della went belly down on the ground and levered up her torso in case she had to shoot. Barrett stooped, hunkering down, but he also kept his gun aimed and ready.

"Alice?" he called out, his voice shattering the silence.

Della steeled herself up for a gunshot. One that hopefully wouldn't hit them because of their positions.

But nothing.

"Alice?" Barrett repeated, louder this time.

Still nothing. And that's when Della saw something in the dirt. Footprints. They looked recent, and they were leading away from the barn and toward a wooded area to the left of the pasture.

"Hell," Barrett growled. "The kidnapper's getting away."

Chapter Seventeen

Barrett fired glances all around him. He listened, too, but he couldn't see any signs of Alice or the person who'd taken her. And unfortunately, those footprints led into some thick clusters of trees. Beyond that, there was a ranch trail.

Which would make for an easy escape route.

Before Barrett took off in that direction, though, he peered around the edge of the barn door and looked inside. It was too dark so he risked turning on the lights. Part of him half expected to see Alice, maybe sprawled out on the floor. But there was no sign of her. However, there were signs of a struggle.

Hay bales had been toppled over, and the loose hay on the ground had been strewn around. The pitchfork that should have been on the hook mounted on the wall had been tossed in front of one of the stalls. It was possible Alice had tried to use it against her captor during the struggle that Barrett had heard.

"No blood," Della said, and that's when he realized she'd crawled in behind him. She got to her feet, moving clear of the open door, and she looked around.

Yeah, no blood was a good thing. It meant Alice was still alive, but she might not stay that way for long.

"Why would the kidnapper have left with Alice?"

Della muttered, but it sounded as if she was talking to herself.

"Maybe he or she thought it was too risky to stay put," Barrett suggested. "Or maybe the kidnapper's just regrouping to make another go at us."

Della didn't have a chance to give her opinion on that because they heard a sound. Not a gunshot. But another shout. And Barrett was betting it had come from Alice.

"No!" Her voice echoed through the woods.

Doing another quick check of the grounds, Barrett stepped outside and pinpointed where the sound had come from. Definitely in the direction of the ranch trail. It was possible the kidnapper had parked a vehicle there and was now trying to move Alice.

He had a short debate with himself about what to do. Della and he could hurry back to the front of the house and get the cruiser, but it'd take him a while to get to that trail since he'd have to go back up the road. Judging from Alice's scream, she didn't have that kind of time.

"Stay behind me," Barrett reminded Della again.

He took off, not running exactly because he didn't want to kick up the pace too much and force Della to keep up with him. He stayed at a light jog, keeping watch, listening.

There was another shouted, "No," and he was pretty sure there was a struggle going on. Whatever was happening, Alice seemed to be fighting it. Good. The fact that she was alive and still able to try to defend herself might mean that Della and he could get to her in time.

Barrett just hoped the cost wouldn't be too high.

After all, each step they took put them closer to a would-be killer. One that had targeted Della.

"Don't shoot," someone whispered, causing Barrett and Della to come to a quick halt.

Barrett caught onto Della, yanking her behind a tree with him, and he glanced around, looking for the person who'd spoken.

"Don't shoot," the man repeated.

Judging from Della's groan, she recognized the voice. So did Barrett, and it didn't make him lower his guard.

Because it was Rory.

Hell. Was he the one who'd kidnapped Alice? If so, Alice wasn't making any noise now, and Barrett didn't hear anyone moving around. As close as Rory was, he would have definitely heard something.

"Come out with your hands up," Barrett warned him, and he tried to keep his voice as low as possible. If Rory wasn't the kidnapper, then Barrett didn't want Alice's real captor hearing any of this.

"I want to help you," Rory answered. He was whispering as well, and each word came out shaky and hoarse.

"You can help by doing what I just told you. Come out and keep your hands where I can see them."

Behind him, Barrett could feel Della trembling. Could feel her breath gusting. But she also had her gun aimed, ready to take out the man if he was a threat.

Barrett certainly hadn't expected Rory to just surrender. And that's why he was shocked when the man did. Rory stepped out from behind a large oak. He still had his gun gripped in his hand, but he'd lifted his arms over his head.

"Drop your gun," Barrett ordered. "Kick it toward me."

"I need to keep it," Rory argued. "Someone has your mother, and she needs our help."

Considering that Rory had killed his own sister, obstructed justice and then gone on the run, Barrett didn't have a lot of faith in any help the man could give them. Still, Rory was right. Someone did have Alice.

Maybe Rory.

"Drop your gun now," Barrett ordered, and he made sure Rory knew he meant business.

Rory swallowed hard, tossed down his gun and, as instructed, kicked it toward Barrett. He then put his hands back up in the air.

"Did you kidnap Alice?" Barrett came out and asked.

Rory's eyes widened. "No. Of course, not."

"Then, what the hell are you doing out here?"

"I came to talk to you. To try to explain that I'm not responsible for the attacks." His voice broke. "I needed your help."

Maybe, but something about this didn't mesh. "Where's your car?" Barrett demanded.

Rory tipped his head in the direction of the road. "I stopped and parked when I saw Della and you run out of the house and toward the barn. I figured something was wrong."

Barrett wanted to laugh. Yeah, something was definitely wrong. And Rory might be a big part of that.

"I slipped into the trees so I could see what was happening," Rory went on. "I heard someone running. Maybe fighting. Not Della and you. You were still by the barn. This was someone else, and when I went deeper into the woods, I caught a glimpse of your mother."

Everything inside Barrett went still. "If you saw my mother, then you also saw the person who has her."

Rory nodded. "But I couldn't make out who it was. The person was wearing a ski mask or something." Another pause. "He had a gun to your mother's head."

"He?" Della and Barrett questioned in unison.

Rory opened his mouth, closed it and obviously reconsidered. "Maybe it was a man. Like I said, I only got a glimpse."

Too bad that brief look hadn't told them more than they already knew. Someone had Alice. And now they had the added problem of what to do with Rory. Barrett had no intention of trusting the man. For all he knew, Rory had Alice stashed somewhere and was pretending to be an innocent bystander to this mess.

But the next sound Barrett heard had him rethinking that.

A gunshot.

It hadn't been fired directly at them, but he thought the shooter was likely by that ranch trail that was still a good fifty yards away.

"Turn around," he told Rory. Barrett took out a pair of plastic cuffs, whirled Rory around when he didn't listen and restrained the man.

"I can help you," Rory protested.

But he was talking to himself. Barrett scooped up Rory's gun, tucking it in the back waist of his jeans.

"Let's go," he told Della. "You stay put," he added to Rory.

Whether the man would do that was anyone's guess, but Barrett didn't have time to deal with that now. At least Rory wouldn't be able to come up from behind and shoot them. Not with his hands cuffed behind him. He wouldn't be able to put up much of a fight, either.

Just as they'd done when they started their run, Della stayed behind Barrett, and when he glanced over his shoulder, he saw that she was keeping watch, as well. He kept them moving fast, heading toward the sound of that last gunshot. Even though it wasn't that far, it seemed to take a lifetime or two, and with each step, he was reminded of the danger that was no doubt waiting for them.

Barrett stopped when they were only a couple of yards away, and he pulled down one of the low-hanging tree branches so he could try to spot any vehicle.

He did.

There was a black car parked on the trail. The headlights were off, but the engine was running, and the back passenger's side door was open. The light from the car's interior speared through the darkness, allowing Barrett to see.

Alice was on the ground, in a fight with someone dressed all in black. Someone with a gun.

And that someone fired a shot at Alice.

"STOP!" DELLA SHOUTED though she wasn't sure how she'd managed to speak. What she saw had caused her throat muscles to clamp tight.

Della's cop training kicked in, and she took aim at the person who'd fired that shot. But she couldn't shoot back. She didn't have a safe shot, not with Alice in the line of fire. And not with the kidnapper dragging Alice by her hair into the back seat of the vehicle. Alice had stopped struggling, and there was fresh blood on her face, but she seemed to be alive.

Barrett's training must have kicked in, too, because he muscled Della back behind the meager cover of the tree. He joined her there, leaning out so he could see the car. Della did the same from the other side, but she knew Barrett would want her on the ground if the shooter pulled the trigger again.

"Has Alice been shot?" Della muttered, figuring that Barrett wouldn't hear her.

Even if he had, he likely wouldn't have known the answer. The kidnapper shut the door, cutting off the light and making it impossible for them to see inside the vehicle. Della certainly hadn't been able to tell if the person who had Alice was a man or a woman.

"If he or she tries to drive out of here, I'll shoot out the tires," Barrett told her. "That might not stop the car, but it'll slow it down."

True, and then they could hopefully go in pursuit. It wouldn't be easy on foot, but the driver wouldn't have an easier time of it, either. There was no way to turn around on this part of the trail. It wasn't nearly wide enough for that, and trees lined both sides. The driver would have to go in Reverse in the dark.

"We need to talk," Barrett shouted out. "I understand it's me you want. If so, let Alice go."

Nothing.

Well, nothing from the car anyway. But there was a rustling sound behind them that had both Della and Barrett pivoting in that direction.

"It's me," someone said. *Daniel.* "I got your email."

The relief rushed through Della. They had backup. Something they might need before this was over.

Daniel snaked his way through the trees and took cover behind the one that was directly across from them. "Other than Alice, any idea who's inside?" he asked.

"No," Barrett answered. "But I think we're about to find out," he amended when the back window lowered.

Della saw Alice, and yes, the woman was definitely bleeding. There was a thick streak of it making its way down the side of her face. She looked dazed, too, maybe because of another head injury, or it was possible the kidnapper had managed to drug her.

The kidnapper was no longer next to Alice but was

instead in the front seat, behind the steering wheel. A gloved hand was extended over the seat, and the gun was once again pointed at Alice's head. Della heard the driver mutter something. Then, Alice groaned and nodded.

"You need to back off," Alice told them, no doubt repeating the instructions she'd just been given. Her words were slurred. "If you don't, I'll die. We'll all die."

A moment later, the car engine started. And Barrett took aim at the tires.

"Don't," Alice said. Again, it was a repeat of what had come from the driver.

Della wished she could hear the kidnapper's actual voice, and then they'd know better what they were dealing with. It might be easier to negotiate if they knew the person's identity.

"I won't shoot out the tires if you don't try to drive off," Barrett countered. "You obviously came here to talk. So talk, and tell me what the hell you want."

There was another sound behind them, causing Barrett, Daniel and Della to pivot in that direction. It was Leo, and he had latched on to Rory's arm.

"Any chance this clown will be able to help with the negotiations?" Leo asked. He'd obviously heard at least the last bits of conversation.

Rory shook his head. "I don't know who's doing this."

Maybe. But Della wasn't going to buy that until she had some proof. And that's why she tested the waters. "We have Rory Silva," she called out.

More mutterings came from the driver. "So what?" Alice repeated.

That could indeed mean he'd had no part in this, or the kidnapper could be covering for him. Leo must have felt the same way because he pushed Rory into a sitting position on the ground.

"Stay put," Leo warned him.

"Well?" Barrett shouted to the driver. "Since you're not driving off, I expect you to tell me what you want."

There was a short silence, followed by whispered instructions from the kidnapper. Instructions that caused Alice to turn and look at the person. She shook her head as if trying to come out of her dazed state.

"I can't do that," Alice insisted. She was speaking not to them but to her captor. "You'll just have to kill me."

"What does the kidnapper want you to do?" Barrett demanded.

Alice looked at him. "To trade me for you. I won't do that." Alice's voice was still shaky, but there was plenty of determination in her tone and expression before she turned back to the driver. "None of this will help you. It's too late. You need to give yourself up."

It sounded as if Alice knew the identity of her captor. Barrett must have thought so, too, because he called out again. "Who kidnapped you, Alice? Who's doing this?"

The words had no sooner left Barrett's mouth than the driver hit the accelerator, and the black car began to speed away in Reverse. True to his word, Barrett shot at the tires. So did Leo and Daniel, and they hit the two on the side of the vehicle that was facing them. They also took off, running to catch up with the kidnapper.

The shot-out tires definitely didn't stop the car, but obviously the driver was having trouble staying on the narrow trail because he or she clipped a tree with the rear bumper. There was the sound of metal scraping against wood and some splinters flew, but the driver continued.

So did all four cops.

They darted through the trees, using them for cover, while continuing to shoot into the car. The engine this time. They couldn't risk firing into the windshield because Alice could be hit.

One of the bullets must have hit the radiator because steam started to spew from the car. It was enough of a distraction, and it caused the driver to hit another tree. Harder this time, and it ripped off the bumper. It also slowed down the vehicle enough for Barrett to catch up.

"No!" Alice shouted, and she turned in the seat and tried to hit the driver. It wasn't enough to stop the kidnapper from pulling the trigger.

The shot blasted through the driver's window, shattering the glass and sending it spewing.

Barrett ducked and Della prayed it was in time and he hadn't been hit. She couldn't see any blood on him. However, she did see something that sent her heart leaping to her throat.

Lorraine.

The woman was behind the wheel of the car. Her face was tight with rage and desperation.

And she fired another shot at Barrett.

WITH ALL HELL breaking loose, Barrett dived to the ground, and he pulled Della down with him. He tried to keep her behind him, as much out of harm's way as he could manage, but there wasn't any safe place for her.

Not with Lorraine firing shots at them.

Worse, she was maybe shooting at Alice, too, and unlike them, Alice could get hit at point-blank range. Still, he could hear his mother shouting. Could hear the struggle going on in the car.

And Barrett wanted to know why this was happening. He hoped he got the chance to question Lorraine about it, but he figured this had to go back to Casto. If Lorraine had hired LeBeau and the others to rough up Casto and Alice and then things had gotten out of hand, it could have led to murder. It might lead to another one, too, if he didn't do something fast.

"Wait here with Della," Barrett told Daniel.

Della wouldn't like that order, but there was a chance that Lorraine wasn't doing this alone. She could have hired other thugs to help her do whatever it was she was trying to do. Maybe kill anyone involved in the investigation so that she wouldn't be brought to justice?

If that was her motive, then Barrett needed to make sure she failed.

Another shot blasted through the air, and he tried not to think of Lorraine putting Della and therefore the baby in danger. Barrett shut all of that out and focused on getting to the car.

At least the vehicle was no longer moving, thanks to Lorraine. She'd bashed it into a tree, and the now flat tires had gotten wedged in the shallow ditch. Lorraine might still be able to get the car going, but that wasn't going to happen while she was still fighting Alice.

And she was fighting her.

Alice used her tied up hands like a club and swiped at Lorraine, but Lorraine ducked and bashed her gun against Alice's head. Alice groaned in pain and slumped against the seat. She wasn't unconscious, but Alice was clearly dazed. Too bad because as long as Lorraine was focused on Alice, she wouldn't have seen Barrett coming at her.

But she did see him.

Lorraine climbed over the seat, positioning herself behind Alice, and when the woman took aim at him from over Alice's shoulder, Barrett had no choice but to drop to the ground and roll to the side and take cover behind the tree that Lorraine's car had hit.

"I'll kill her. So help me God, I will," Lorraine shouted.

She sounded as if she'd totally lost it. Looked it, too. Obviously, she hadn't counted on things getting this messed up. Maybe she'd thought she could use Alice to draw out Della and him, kill them, and then her life would go back to normal.

Fat chance of that.

Lorraine might get off more shots, but eventually she'd have to reload, and that's when Barrett could charge at her. Or take his own shot. He couldn't do that now, though. Not with Alice directly in front of Lorraine.

"Stay back!" Lorraine shouted when Leo moved closer. "I'm leaving with Alice, and the only way to keep her alive is to put down your guns so I can get out of here."

For Lorraine to drive, she'd have to climb back over the seat. And while doing that, she'd lose her human shield. When she realized that, Barrett was concerned Lorraine might turn this into a suicide mission, along with taking out as many of them as she could.

"How the heck did you convince Alice that you'd taken me hostage?" Barrett asked. He didn't especially care, but he wanted to keep Lorraine focused on his voice. Wanted to keep her talking. That way, maybe Leo could get in a position to take out the woman.

"I recorded our conversations at the sheriff's office," Lorraine admitted. She kept the gun propped on Alice's shoulder, pointed in Barrett's direction, but she could easily turn it and shoot Alice in the head. "Then,

I spliced together sentences using an audio editor app I bought."

Lorraine sounded smug about that accomplishment. Smug and on the verge of losing it. He could see the woman's hand shaking. And bleeding. Barrett noticed that she, too, had a head injury.

From the corner of his eye, he also saw Leo. He was belly down, crawling over the ditch and onto the trail. His plan was no doubt to get to the other side of the car so he could come at Lorraine from behind.

"You obviously need medical attention. How'd you get hurt?" Barrett asked Lorraine. Again, not because he cared, but he needed the sound of his voice to cover up Leo's movement.

"The bitch hit me with a pitchfork," Lorraine spat out, and that must have caused a surge of anger because she bashed her gun against Alice's head again. "She fought like a wildcat to save her *little boy*." Lorraine's voice dripped with a combination of venom and sarcasm on the last two words.

But Barrett wasn't feeling either of those things. It tightened his gut to know that Alice had tried to protect him. And it had put her in the hands of this lunatic.

"You jammed my phone," Barrett called out to Lorraine. "You're also the one who hired Ezell."

He needed to give Leo more time, along with maybe distracting Lorraine so that she wouldn't hit Alice again. Alice was barely conscious now, and she was moaning in pain. It was possible that Lorraine had fractured Alice's skull.

"Of course, I did," Lorraine snapped. "Using the jammer was something that Harris LeBeau taught me way back when. That and where to buy explosives for the bomb I set on the road. I couldn't have you calling for your brothers so I used a jammer," Lorraine snapped. "For all the good it did. You obviously got word to them somehow."

Yeah, he had, and Lorraine was about to come face-to-face with the result of Leo getting the "word." Barrett saw Leo peer into the window behind Lorraine. If his brother was fast enough, Leo could throw open the door, latch on to Lorraine and drag her out of the car before the woman could get off another shot. Especially a shot that could be fatal.

But that didn't happen.

Lorraine must have heard or sensed something because she whirled in Leo's direction, and the woman turned her gun toward him.

"Watch out!" Della shouted, both Daniel and her moving closer.

Barrett moved, too. So did Alice. His mother hit the gun just as Lorraine fired.

The bullet slammed into Alice.

The blood splattered all over Lorraine, all over the car. Barrett didn't want to think about Alice being dead. He needed to do his job and put an end to the danger.

Barrett pushed forward, moving ahead of Della and Daniel. Since Lorraine still had hold of the gun, he charged at her before she could take aim at him.

But she didn't.

With Leo gripped onto her shoulders, Lorraine still managed to turn the gun on herself.

And she pulled the trigger.

Chapter Eighteen

It was chaos. A different kind of chaos than there'd been just minutes earlier when Barrett, his brothers and Della had been trying to stop Lorraine. Lorraine had ended her life but had left plenty of mess to clean up.

The ambulance siren wailed as it came to a stop on the ranch trail, and the EMTs sprang into action. Good. Because Alice needed medical attention ASAP.

Leo had moved Lorraine's lifeless body off Alice, and both Della and he were trying to slow Alice's bleeding from the gunshot wound.

Not to her head, thank God.

That'd been where Lorraine had intended the bullet to go, but the shot instead had slammed into the top of Alice's shoulder. She was losing a lot of blood, and it didn't help that she had the other injuries Lorraine had given her during their struggle. She was conscious—that was something at least—but Barrett could tell from her moans that she was in a lot of pain.

It didn't matter that Alice and he hadn't had the best of relationships. He still hated to see her suffer. Especially because of him. Alice had hit Lorraine's gun to stop him from being shot.

His mother had literally taken a bullet meant for him. No way to dismiss that. No way that it couldn't matter. It did. And Barrett felt a barrier or two lower between Alice and him.

Della climbed out of the back seat of Lorraine's car so the EMTs could have access to Alice. Barrett wasn't far, only a few yards away, and he went to Della not only to try to steady her. To steady himself, too. He pulled Della into his arms and held on. She gave a weary sigh and melted against him.

"You should check out Della, too," Alice insisted. Her words were a little slurred, but that came through clear enough to give Barrett another jolt of fear.

"Are you okay?" he asked, moving Della back so he could look at her. "Were you hit?"

"No," Della answered. "I'm all right." She checked him over, too, no doubt to make sure the same was true for him. Lorraine had fired a lot of shots, and any one of them could have hit his brothers, Della or him.

"The baby," Alice added, and her eyelids fluttered down. "I heard Della and you talking about it. Della needs to be checked because of the baby."

So, that's how Alice had found out. And after one look at Leo and Daniel, Barrett realized that they now knew, too.

"Yeah," Barrett confirmed. "Della's pregnant with my baby." He hadn't meant that to have the edge of a threat, but he didn't want his brothers giving him any grief.

They didn't.

Leo and Daniel exchanged looks of mutual surprise, and then grins. "Figured you and Della had gotten back together," Leo added. "Didn't know you were *this* back together."

Barrett nearly blurted out that the pregnancy wasn't

planned, but that might seem as if he was somehow dismissing it.

He wasn't.

Barrett wasn't sure when it had happened, but this baby had moved to the top of his list of priorities. The baby, along with Della, of course.

"So, what will you do about it?" Leo asked, and he had enough of a grin to make Barrett scowl at him.

"I'll get back to you on that," Barrett grumbled. Because, heck, he wasn't the one in the driver's seat here. The real question was—what was Della going to do about it? Was she going to let him be a big part of her and the baby's life?

"She's lost some blood," one of the medics said, getting Barrett's attention. "We've got her stabilized for now but we need to take her to the hospital."

The other medic hurried back to the ambulance to bring out a gurney. The two immediately started to move Alice onto it. Despite all the jostling around, Alice still managed to make eye contact with him.

"I'm so sorry about all of this," Alice told him. "If I hadn't been so stupid, none of this would have happened."

Barrett shook his head. He could definitely give her an out on this. "Lorraine was desperate. If she hadn't used you, she would have found a way to try to get to us."

And it likely hadn't helped Alice's state of mind to believe that a pregnant Della was in danger. Alice hadn't exactly been mother of the year, but it was obvious that she still had some maternal feelings for her offspring.

"We'll be at the hospital soon," Della assured Alice as the EMTs put the woman into the ambulance.

Alice managed a nod. "You can have yourself checked out, too."

That wasn't a bad idea, and maybe Della wouldn't argue with him about it. He was betting her nerves were as raw as his, and a little reassurance from the doctor could help.

"I'll deal with him," Leo said, hauling Rory to his feet. "My cruiser's parked at your house."

Barrett certainly hadn't forgotten about Francine's brother, but it was the beginning of some "chaos" for Rory, too. Leo would book him on an assortment of charges stemming from Francine's death. But for now, Barrett had one question for the man.

"Did you have anything to do with what Lorraine did tonight?" Barrett demanded.

"No." Rory said it with plenty of conviction, too. "Like I said, I just came over to talk, and I saw Alice getting dragged away. I didn't even know it was Lorraine until after we got out here and she started talking."

Barrett kept a hard stare on the man long enough to see if it would make him squirm from any lies he'd told. But there wasn't any squirming. Maybe Rory truly hadn't had anything to do with Lorraine. Even so, the man would get jail time for the other charges.

So would Curran.

It was ironic that Lorraine had been able to give them the proof that would finally put Curran behind bars. If Lorraine weren't already dead, Curran likely would have wanted to get back at her for that.

"I can wait here for the medical examiner and the crime scene unit," Daniel said as the ambulance began to back out down the trail.

Barrett nodded, thankful for the offer. He really wanted to get Della to the hospital. Apparently, Leo was in a hurry, too, because he headed back through the woods with Rory in tow.

Daniel gave another glance at the ambulance before he turned back to Barrett. "Are you all right about being with Alice at the hospital?"

It was as simple a question as it seemed. A lot of years and bad blood had gone into their feelings for their mother.

Barrett nodded. "I just don't want to hang on to the bad stuff any longer."

Seemingly amused, Daniel flexed his eyebrows when he glanced at Della. "Obviously, this baby and you have had an effect on him."

Della smiled when Daniel did. "Are you all right with being an uncle again?" she asked.

"You bet," Daniel assured her. He leaned over and brushed a kiss on Della's cheek. "Now, put Barrett out of his misery and kiss him. He looks like he's ready to implode or something."

Barrett hoped to hell that wasn't how he looked. He was trying his best to level out so that Della would do the same.

"Come on," Barrett said, slipping his arm around Della to get her moving. It wasn't a long walk back to his house, but they'd have to make their way through the woods again.

Della took a few steps but then stopped. She leaned in and kissed him. At first Barrett thought that maybe she did that because Daniel had brought it up. But when her mouth lingered on his, and she deepened the kiss, Barrett figured out that his brother had had no part in this.

"Better?" Della asked, easing back from him. She ran her tongue over her bottom lip, causing his body to clench. Considering everything they'd just gone through, it was an unexpected reaction.

But definitely a welcome one.

That's why Barrett pulled her back to him and kissed her. He needed to feel the familiar heat. Needed to be reminded that they'd come out of this alive.

He let the kiss linger another moment, until the heat really kicked in and let him know that when it came to Della and him, there was a fine line between a kiss and full-blown foreplay.

He was quickly crossing that line.

That's why Barrett got her walking again, but there was no need for the crazy pace they'd needed to get to Alice in time. And speaking of Alice, that was another reason for him not to go back in for another kiss. If Della and he kept it up, they wouldn't get to the hospital anytime soon.

"How much of a hassle are you going to give me about being examined by the doctor?" he asked.

"None," she readily answered. "I'm positive the doctor won't find anything wrong, but it won't hurt."

No, and it would make them both rest easier. Well, when they actually got rest, that is. Barrett was hoping it wouldn't be too long before that happened. While he was hoping, he added the hope that Alice's injuries wouldn't be that serious, and that way he could get Della off her feet. And that led him to his next question.

"Are you going to give me any hassle about staying at my place for a while?" he asked.

She stopped, looked up at him. "None."

Barrett smiled. He liked the way this conversation was going. "Good. Because I want you in my bed tonight."

Della smiled, too. Obviously, she hadn't gotten the

memo on the fine line between kissing/foreplay because the next kiss she gave him was long, hard and deep. Just the way he liked his kisses from Della. When she pulled back this time, he expected to see the glaze of lust—and it was there. But there was something else.

"I know the timing is off, but tell me how you feel about this baby," she said.

Barrett didn't even have to think about it. "I love him or her." That was the easy part. It was automatic, and the love went bone-deep. The hard part came, though, as well. "The kid deserves better than me for a father."

Della shook her head, smiled a little and got them walking away. "There's no one better than you. I know it. Soon, this baby will know it, too."

Mercy, she had a lot of trust in him, and for some reason, it made Barrett feel as if he could trust himself. He'd been a kid when he'd tried to help his grandfather raise Daniel and Leo. He wasn't one now. And the stakes were sky-high, so he'd have to do whatever it took to love and raise this baby.

Whatever it took to have Della, as well.

Because he was in love with her.

That hit him like a meaty fist and robbed him of some of his breath. He was in love with Della.

When the heck had that happened?

Maybe it'd been when he had come so close to losing her. Of course, it was possible that the love for her had always been there, but he'd just finally got around to admitting it.

Barrett stopped, turning her so he could give her another kiss. He was hoping the heat would work some magic because he needed all the help he could get. When he pulled back, she was a little breathless and still had a trace of a smile on her incredible mouth.

"How much of a hassle are you going to give me if I tell you I'm in love with you?" he asked.

Her smile widened. "None. Because I'm in love with you."

Della laughed—probably because he looked dumbfounded that it hadn't taken any coaxing. Not that he wanted coaxing. He wanted her "none" and everything that went along with it.

Still chuckling, Della slid her arm back around him. "How much of a hassle will you give me if I ask you to marry me?" she said.

Now, this was easy. So was the kiss Barrett gave her before he answered, "None."

* * * * *

THE DECOY

CAROL ERICSON

Prologue

Rule number three. Never leave fingerprints or DNA.

He didn't have to worry about that. He was careful and clean. Besides, he'd much rather do the deed in the comfort of their own homes, among their own possessions. It might give them a bit of solace. He was no monster. He was a…facilitator, a conduit, if you will.

Who wanted to traipse all over LA looking for a dump site with a dead body in your car? You could never tell who was watching. Whether a place had cameras or not. Cameras tracked your every move these days. With a little surveillance, you could take care of any electronic witnesses yourself. That was what he did.

And rape? His stomach lurched. Sex was filthy. He would never leave his bodily fluids inside another person.

The woman beneath him gurgled, and he blinked. Time to get back to business.

As he choked the last bit of life out of Andrea with his gloved hands, he watched the light die from her wide eyes. The force of the power that surged through his body made him hard. He closed his eyes to relish the sensation…just for a few seconds of indulgence.

He would never tell anyone about that part—about the sexual arousal. He didn't know why it happened.

He didn't ask for it. It wasn't his raison d'être. It made him feel slightly ashamed.

He removed his hands from Andrea's neck and flexed his fingers. It took strength to squeeze the life out of someone. He'd forgotten how much. That other time had been so long ago.

He left Andrea in her bed. She'd been there when he'd pounced, and it had really been more of a creep than a pounce. By the time she realized he was in her house, at the foot of her bed, she had zero time to react or escape.

No, actually, she had reacted—a gaping-mouthed silent scream. The wisps of sleep still clinging to her mind, she hadn't been able to process the sight of a strange man in her bedroom.

The mattress huffed when he pushed off the bed, the same sound Andrea had made when he first took her by the throat. He smoothed a gloved hand over the cap covering his head. He wouldn't be leaving any of his hair behind. No prints. No bodily fluids. He'd taken care to avoid neighborhood cameras. He certainly didn't know Andrea.

That wasn't completely true. He brushed a knuckle across her smooth dark skin. He'd stalked her long enough to know her habits, some of her likes and dislikes, a few of her friends. Long enough to know she'd broken up with a boyfriend and lived alone in this small, neat house. That was as close as he'd gotten—as close as he'd wanted to get.

He wrapped some double-sided tape around his hands and patted the covers around Andrea's body. Who knew what he'd dragged into this room on his person? There could be fibers from his clothing, bits of seed or dirt that could be identified from his area. He'd watched enough forensic crime shows to know anything could be analyzed these days.

He studied the minuscule debris on the tape, peeled it from his hands and shoved it into his pocket. He reached into his other pocket and pulled out a playing card.

Hovering over Andrea, he placed the card between her parted lips. Then he snipped off one of her dark curls and dropped it into a plastic bag. Eyeing his handiwork, he sighed. Now he'd have to create a mess. He hated leaving a mess.

The blade of the box cutter winked at him as it caught the light from the lamp next to Andrea's bed. Holding his breath, he sliced the pinkie finger from her left hand.

The souvenir.

Chapter One

Kyra clutched her throat with one hand. "I don't understand. The Copycat Player is dead. I was there. I saw Jordy Lee Cannon die. You found all the evidence you needed at his mother's house. The jewelry, the box cutter, playing cards."

"But no severed fingers." The phone call announcing another homicide had already propelled Jake to his feet. "We got the right guy, Kyra. This is someone else. Slightly different MO."

"Slightly different?" She scrambled to a crouching position, grabbing the handrail of the bridge that crossed the canal to Quinn's house for support to hoist herself up. "Then maybe it's not a copycat of the...er... Copycat."

Shaking his head, Jake grabbed her hand. He hated that she had to go through all this again. They'd just ended the horrific reign of a murderer who'd been mimicking the MO of a killer from twenty years ago—a killer who'd slaughtered Kyra's mother and never been caught. Now she'd have to face the constant reminders from another sick bastard.

"A playing card in the woman's mouth and a severed little finger. This guy's following the same pattern, except he murdered the victim in her home and left her body there."

Jake's muscles tensed as he looked into Kyra's eyes. Her mother had also been murdered in their home while Kyra slept in the bedroom.

Kyra squared her shoulders. "Then the crime scene should be rich with evidence and you'll catch this guy before he does it again. Because he'll do it again. Jordy managed four victims because he strangled them in his car and dumped their bodies. This guy has already made a big mistake."

Blowing out a breath, he tugged on her hand. "I'm heading over there now. I'll walk you back to Quinn's. Can you get a ride home?"

"Of course, but you should come inside and tell Quinn yourself. I'm sure he'd rather hear this from you."

They walked back across the wooden bridge over the canal where Abbot Kinney had tried to re-create Venice in the middle of a Southern California beach town. The charm of the location and evening was spoiled by the news of another homicide. No wonder he couldn't get to second base with Kyra.

After a few bumps in the road, they'd gotten close working together on the case of the Copycat Player. Her position as victims' advocate on that task force and her tragic ties to the original killer, dubbed The Player, had proved invaluable to the investigation.

Jake hesitated at retired detective Roger Quinn's red door. Quinn, who had never solved The Player murders twenty years ago, had taken solace in the fact that they'd stopped The Player's copycat. Now they had to go through it again, and Quinn would be asked to re-live the case that still haunted him.

Kyra stepped through first, and Quinn glanced up

from the flickering blue light of the TV. One look at their expressions, and the lines on Quinn's craggy face seemed to deepen.

"What's wrong with you two?"

Jake held up his phone. "You're not going to believe this, but I just got a call about a homicide with the same MO as The Player—card between the lips and a missing finger."

Quinn's faded blue eyes narrowed. "Oh, I believe it. Seems like The Player has inspired a new generation of killers. It's because I never caught him, never stopped him."

Kyra rushed to Quinn's side and crouched beside his chair. "He killed her in her home. He surely left something behind. They'll get him, just like they got Jordy."

Quinn placed his gnarled hand on Kyra's head and met Jake's eyes. "Hope you haven't dismantled that task force, Detective."

JAKE PULLED UP to the crime scene, where the revolving lights of the emergency vehicles bathed the street in an eerie, familiar glow. He double-parked in front of the modest, well-kept house that would never be the same again and flung open the door of his sedan.

A young man sat on the back of the ambulance, wrapped in a blanket, his head down, legs swinging. Must've discovered the body.

Jake nodded at his partner, Billy Crouch, standing on the porch talking to a uniform. Their division didn't cover this area of the San Fernando Valley, but he and Billy had led the Copycat Player task force and were the go-to guys now every time a playing card and severed finger figured in the crime scene. After Jordy Lee Cannon, he hadn't thought there'd be another.

He took one big step over the yellow tape and strode toward the house. The cheery pot of flowers on top of the air-conditioning unit that jutted from the window made him falter, and he cursed under his breath at the injustice of a life cut short.

His glance took in Billy's casual clothes that still looked runway ready, and he brushed a scuff of dirt from his own jeans. If he'd been home when he'd gotten the call, he would've put on a pair of slacks and an Oxford shirt, at least, but he'd gone casual himself for dinner with Quinn and Kyra. It was supposed to have been a dinner to celebrate the end of the Copycat Player, and now here they were again.

He joined Billy on the porch. "What do we have in there, partner?"

"Young African American woman strangled in her bed. Not much upset. He must've surprised her in her sleep." Billy's mouth flattened into a grimace. "Queen of hearts placed between her lips and left pinkie finger removed."

"Anything else taken? Jordy had been snatching pieces of jewelry from his victims. Anything like that?" Jake pulled a pair of gloves from the black bag over his shoulder and slipped them on.

Billy raised one shoulder. "Too early to tell. Andrea Miles was in bed, pajamas on, makeup off, no jewelry."

Jake crossed the threshold of the house, and his gaze darted around the neat room, framed pictures undisturbed, multicolored pillows propped up against the arms of the couch, a laptop computer charging on a table. "Lived alone?"

"Yeah. Boyfriend moved out recently. He's the one who called in the murder. They were supposed to meet earlier today to sign some paperwork regarding the house, and she missed the meeting."

"This murder didn't happen tonight?" Jake poked his head into the bedroom where Andrea lay on her bed, covers pulled up to her waist. He could see the red face card in her mouth from here. "No sexual assault?"

"Just like the others, and yeah, looks like she's been dead for at least twenty-four hours based on the fixed, dilated pupils, body temperature and lividity." Billy gestured to the patrol officer standing guard over the body. "Can we have the room?"

"Yes, sir." The officer squeezed past them at the door, leaving Billy and Jake alone with the victim.

Jake approached the bed, not touching anything. Billy had already done a preliminary examination of the body, and neither the photographer nor the fingerprint tech had gotten here yet, so he wanted to leave the scene intact for them.

The responding officer had given Billy the lowdown, and Jake continued to pick his partner's brain. "No forced entry?"

"Not that they can see at the windows or doors."

"Boyfriend just moved out. Does he still have a key?"

"He does." Billy jerked a thumb over his shoulder. "That's how he got in to discover Andrea had been murdered. He used his key."

"We'll bring him in for questioning." Jake picked up Andrea's left hand—the one now missing a finger. "I mean, he could've staged this to look like a copycat."

"Anything's possible, man." Billy jerked his head up at the sound of footsteps outside the bedroom door. "You need any more time before we invite the hordes in here?"

"I'll take a look around the rest of the house." Jake

skimmed his hand across the bedspread, his glove sticking in a couple of areas. "Have you spoken to the boyfriend yet?"

"Not really. He was in shock. That's why I sent him to the ambulance." Billy nudged Jake's arm as he studied his fingertips. "What's wrong? Find something?"

Jake whipped out two tags from a plastic bag and stuck them on the bedspread in two spots. "I felt something here and here. It felt sticky. It could be saliva, semen. Make sure these are preserved and tested."

Billy turned to the door and invited the crime scene investigators hovering there into the room. "Do your thing. Jake, I'll hit up the boyfriend. See if he can form a coherent sentence now."

Jake gave up his spot next to the victim to the techs and backed out of the room. He did an about-face in the hallway and entered another bedroom. This one contained a daybed and a small dresser and looked unused—for the guests Andrea would never have.

He checked the window and the screen on the outside and popped his head into the small closet. Could the killer have hidden here waiting for Andrea to come home? Possible, but how'd he get in to ambush her?

He took a few steps across the living room to another bedroom, which had been converted into an office. This room didn't have a closet, just a desk, filing cabinet and a bookshelf. Crouching down, he read the titles—mostly self-help, yoga and exercise books, and a volume of Langston Hughes poetry. Jake swallowed. A dream deferred, indeed.

A cursory check of the window offered him nothing, and he entered the kitchen. He tried the door next to the pantry, and it opened onto a one-car garage where Andrea's compact waited.

He flicked the switch to his right and light flooded the garage. Andrea's organization skills didn't extend to the garage. Although she'd left enough room to pull her car inside, she'd crammed boxes and bikes and snowboards into the remaining spaces.

He took one step down and felt the hood of the car with his hand. He opened the car door and looked for a garage door opener on the visor. Instead, Andrea's new-model car had buttons that could be programmed to open a garage door.

He punched one, and the garage door started its journey along the tracks. Another stab at the button stopped the door's progress and another brought it back down. The garage door wasn't locked, but it would've made a lot of noise opening. Andrea probably would've heard that.

Jake picked up a crumpled receipt on the console and squinted at the date. Andrea had bought a soda and a bag of chips at a gas station convenience store at 8:46 p.m. yesterday. If she had been dead for about twenty-four hours like Billy thought, this must've been her last trip outside.

Resting his hands on the steering wheel, he murmured, "What happened when you got home, Andrea?"

The door to the kitchen swung open, and a cop stuck his head into the garage. "Is that you, Detective Mac?"

Jake waved his hand out the car door. "Checking out the vehicle."

"Okay, medical examiner is here, and Detective Crouch is done talking to the victim's ex."

"Thanks. I'll be there in a minute."

The cop ducked back inside the house and the door slammed shut. Jake dropped the receipt into a plastic bag.

He slid from the car and tried the handle of the door

back to the kitchen. The handle didn't turn, but he was able to push open the door. He ran his finger over the button on the handle, which was in the locked position.

"What are you doing?" Billy stuck his foot against the door to hold it open.

Jake tapped his fingertip against the wad of gum lodged against the lock tab in the door. "This is how the bastard got in…and he left his DNA."

Chapter Two

Kyra propped up the wall in the back of the conference room as Jake and Billy took turns reviewing the evidence in the Andrea Miles homicide. Most of the equipment from the previous task force hadn't even been removed yet.

Despite her role in the takedown of Jordy Lee Cannon, the Copycat Player, she felt her place was still at the back of the room. Jake hadn't told the rest of the task force that her mother, Jennifer Lake, had been one of The Player's victims twenty years ago, and if she continued to keep a low profile, they'd never find out.

She didn't want to be that girl, and had gone to great pains to put the past behind her and forge a new identity. She didn't need the publicity splashed all over the local news and the internet. That notoriety could only lead to disaster for her.

A wad of gum flashed on the slide. Jake said, "I found this crammed in the lock mechanism of the door that leads from Andrea's house to her garage. If you always keep that door locked, chances are you don't check it. You just let the door close. We believe the killer slipped into Andrea's garage when she pulled out, and then he stuffed the gum in the door she'd left open, which her ex said they did a lot. This gave the killer access to the house at night, where he could lie in wait. When she pulled her car out that last time, he slipped in, gained access to the house and hid out, waiting for her to return and go to sleep."

Kyra crossed her arms against the shiver snaking through her body. That meant the killer must've stalked Andrea long enough to learn some of her habits.

"But—" Jake aimed a red laser at the slide on the screen "—if he chewed this gum to soften it up, we have his DNA and maybe even teeth impressions."

Clive Stewart, the fingerprint tech standing next to Kyra, mumbled, "Idiot. He might as well have left a bunch of prints at the scene."

Kyra moved closer to Clive and whispered, "Which he didn't?"

"Not a one."

Jake and Billy took a few more questions before adjourning the meeting, and several members of the task force moved next door to the conference room, which had been repurposed into the task force war room.

The officers were already calling this killer The Player 3.0. It was either that or Copycat 2.0. What was it about The Player's reign of terror that had so fascinated two killers twenty years later?

As she grabbed the back of her chair in the war room, Jake called, "Kyra, I have Andrea's contacts."

She pushed in the chair and wended her way through the other desks to Jake's. "Is her family here?"

"Her parents are coming out from Atlanta, and two of her friends and her ex have requested some assistance in dealing with her murder." He slid a piece of paper toward her with names and phone numbers printed on it. "We questioned the ex-boyfriend this morning. His alibi is solid. He's also shaken to the core. The breakup was Andrea's idea, and he wasn't over her."

"I'll reach out to them." She shoved the piece of paper in her pocket. "Something else?"

Jake drummed his thumbs on the edge of his keyboard. "Matt Dugan left all of his worldly possessions to you. Did you know that?"

"H-he did?" Kyra pulled her sweater around her body.

"His parole officer called to tell me." Jake shrugged. "You were the closest thing he had to family."

"We were two mixed-up kids in the same foster family at the same time. I'd hardly call that family. I'd hardly call someone who stalks and harasses you family, either." She spun around and called over her shoulder, "Not interested in Matt's worldly possessions, whatever they are."

"That's the thing, Kyra. We don't know what they are."

She stopped her forward movement, but didn't turn around to face Jake. During the Copycat Player's killing spree, Matt Dugan had left playing cards at her house and car in an attempt to terrorize her over her mother's murder, as her foster brother was one of the few people who knew her real identity. Matt's actions had prompted Jake to go digging into her background…and he probably would've dug further if Matt hadn't died of a drug overdose.

She cleared her throat. "I can assure you, Matt didn't accumulate much of anything during his stints in prison."

"But before he died, he told me someone had paid him to plant those cards for you. Maybe that info is among his effects. Maybe we'll find something, something that will connect that person to Jordy or this current killer."

She turned slowly, still clutching her sweater. "Why would you even think that? Matt was a scammer. He was yanking your chain to up his price for information."

"If there's a chance that there's a clue among Matt's stuff, wouldn't you want to find it if it stops one more murder?" Jake's hazel eyes seemed to probe her soul—he knew where to hit her.

"Of course. I just think you're putting too much faith in a master manipulator. Even this—" she flung out her hand "—leaving his junk to me is a last jab to get under my skin."

He held out an envelope in the space between them. "I got this from his parole officer. It's Matt's handwritten will and a key to his apartment. His roommate still lives there."

"Lucky me." She snatched the envelope from Jake with a hand she hoped he hadn't noticed was trembling. When would she ever get Matt out of her life?

An hour later, she was on her way to Jeremy Bevin's place to discuss his feelings about his murdered ex-girlfriend. As a therapist and victims' rights advocate, she'd worked closely with the LAPD in the past on homicide cases. She had a unique perspective to bring to the table, even though only Jake knew about that.

She'd been eight years old when her mother, Jennifer Lake, had been murdered by The Player twenty years ago. That case had never been solved, despite Detective Roger Quinn's best efforts. Quinn and his wife had wanted to adopt her, but Quinn's alcoholism and probably his age at the time had quashed those plans.

She pulled across the street from Jeremy's apartment and stepped out of the car. She tilted up her nose and sniffed. Despite the sunshine and warmth, fall had crept out from beneath the blanket of oppressive heat that often characterized late summers in LA. Only a true Angeleno could discern the differences between the sunny, blue skies of summer and the sunny, bluer skies of fall. The quality of the air had a slight lilt to it instead of the stillness of waiting. The feel of the sun on her shoulders was more like a light scarf than a beach towel.

Kyra walked across the street and planted herself in front of the heavy security door of the apartment complex. She trailed her finger down the row of buttons with names neatly typed out beside them and located Jeremy's apartment number. She drilled her thumb against the button, and the lock on the door clicked without a peep from the intercom. He *was* expecting her, but she thought he would have been a little more careful after his ex-girlfriend had just been murdered.

She heaved open the door and stepped onto the cool tile floor. Veering around a group of people carrying bags of groceries, Kyra headed for the elevator. In the style of the sprawling San Fernando Valley, this apartment building didn't have many floors. She rode the elevator to the top and got off on the fourth floor, where the front doors to the units were all tucked into alcoves off the main hallway.

Before she reached Jeremy's door, she heard a click and a rustle, and a young bearded man stepped into the hallway. "You're Ms. Chase?"

"Yes. You can call me Kyra. Can I call you Jeremy?" She took his outstretched hand and gave it a squeeze.

"Yeah, Jeremy's fine." He widened the door for her, and she walked into his bare apartment. He hadn't bothered to put pictures on the wall yet or even unpack boxes, which were stacked in a corner. Hadn't he and Andrea broken up a few months ago?

"Have a seat." He waved in the general direction of two chairs, both facing a flat-screen TV, a small table in front littered with to-go boxes, chip bags and video game controllers.

She'd seen pictures of Andrea's tidy house. Maybe she'd kicked her boyfriend out for reasons of cleanliness, or maybe these were signs of his depression.

She sat in one of the chairs and placed her purse at her feet, gun pouch outward, not that she needed her weapon for a discussion with Jeremy, the jilted boyfriend.

"Do you want something to drink? I got soda in a can or bottled water."

"A soda would be great, thanks." She always wanted her clients to feel she was comfortable so that they could take the cue from her.

Jeremy banged around the kitchen and returned with two cans—a soda for her and a beer for himself. He handed her the drink and cracked the tab on his own.

"You don't mind if I have a beer, do you? I figure that's one of the advantages to having a therapist come see you at home."

"Have you been drinking a lot of beer?" She took a sip of her soda, didn't see a clear space to set it down and so held it in her hand, her fingers tingling from the cold.

"You mean before or after the…murder?"

"Either, both."

"Both. I started drinking more when Andrea and I split up, and I'm not about to stop now that she's dead." To prove his point, he gulped back a quantity of liquid from the can.

"I'm not here to get you to stop drinking, unless that's what you want. As you know, I'm a victims' rights advocate. I'm here on behalf of the LAPD, and I'm here to help you, if you need it or want it."

"I do." He dragged the back of his hand across his mouth. "I don't mean to be an ass. I just feel so…guilty, you know?"

"That's not uncommon, and I can sit here all day and tell you Andrea's death isn't your fault, but you're still going to feel guilty." She wet her lips again with the drink and set the can at her feet. "Tell me about Andrea and your relationship with her."

Her request opened the floodgates, and Jeremy talked about how he and Andrea had met online a few years ago and had bought the house together nine months ago.

"My friends all thought I was crazy to buy the house with her because we fought a lot, but I always had faith in us." He scratched his beard. "It wasn't even because she was Black and I'm white. Our race wasn't the issue, ever. She just always had a lot more going for her than I did, and she expected me to step it up and I never did."

"Had she moved on to someone else?"

"No. That's why I thought we still had a chance. I was hoping our meeting the other day might lead to something. I was going to prove to her that I wasn't stalking her."

Reaching for her soda can, Kyra almost knocked it over. "Excuse me? Someone was stalking Andrea?"

"I don't know. I think she was making it up."

"Making up what, exactly?"

Jeremy dented one side of his beer can with his thumb. "She accused me of trying to scare her into asking me to move back into the house."

"Scare her how?"

"She asked me if I was following her or watching her."

"Did you tell the police about this?"

Jeremy blinked. "No. I kind of forgot about it, honestly. She made her accusations, and I denied them. It was just another way we went around and around. Do you think...?"

"I think it's important enough to tell the police about it. Maybe the killer was stalking Andrea."

Jeremy slammed a fist into his palm. "If I could get my hands on that guy, I'd kill him. Andrea would've taken me back. I know it."

Kyra doubted Andrea had had any intention of taking Jeremy back, but if he wanted to believe that, she wouldn't dissuade him. Instead, she encouraged him to talk about his feelings of rage and revenge.

They wrapped up their conversation after about an hour. Jeremy had even cleaned off the table while she was there and had traded his beer for water. Progress.

As she left, Kyra handed Jeremy one of Jake's cards. "Make sure you call Detective McAllister and tell him what you told me about Andrea's stalker. It could be really important information."

"I will. Thanks, Kyra." He shoved the card in the back pocket of his jeans. "You know, that house is mine now. She hadn't removed me from the title yet, but I don't think I can ever live there."

Kyra said goodbye and returned to her car. As she wasn't sure Jake's business card would ever make it out of Jeremy's pocket and would probably end up in the washing machine, she called Jake herself.

"How'd the session go with Jeremy Bevin?"

"Interesting." Kyra started the engine of her car. "He said something about Andrea having a stalker. Did you get that from him?"

"Not at all. We asked him if she had a new boyfriend or any enemies, and it was a no to everything."

"Andrea thought Jeremy was stalking her to scare her into letting him move back in."

"That's…drastic."

"Yeah, well, he's kind of a dramatic guy. I wouldn't put it past him, and apparently neither did Andrea. Anyway, I gave him your card just in case he lost the one you gave him and told him to give you a call, but he's a lost soul right now."

"I'll keep on top of it." Jake cleared his throat. "Are you going to check out Matt's apartment?"

"You mean to inspect my inheritance?"

"I'm serious, Kyra. I'd like to see what Matt has among his possessions."

Kyra's heart did a somersault. She wouldn't mind seeing what Matt had in his apartment, either, but she'd prefer to do it alone, away from Jake's curious eyes.

"Okay, I'm already out here in the Valley. It won't take me long to get to Matt's place. You can meet me there." She shifted into Drive and pulled away from the curb before she even ended the call. If Matt had anything incriminating about her past in his stuff, she could snag it before Jake even arrived.

She entered Matt's address in her phone and navigated the streets as it chirped out directions. About twenty minutes later she rolled onto a street of matching run-down apartment complexes. Trash cans between buildings overflowed, and broken toys and discarded furniture created an obstacle course along the sidewalks. She slowed down to scope out a parking space as her tires hit pothole after pothole in the asphalt. Leave Matt to find a neighborhood where his hardened would barely raise an eyebrow.

She parallel parked her car between an old junker and a monstrous late-model SUV with big, shiny rims and blacked-out windows. As she slid from her car, two men lounging on an abandoned sofa at the curb gave her the once-over. She rested her hand on the gun in her purse and walked past them with a long stride.

Matt's building had no security entrance or lobby, just a dirty courtyard that the residents seemed to use for storage. Kyra stepped over a deflated inner tube and climbed the stairs to Matt's unit.

She held her breath as she knocked on the door. Matt had a roommate, but Kyra was in no mood to exchange small talk with another parolee like Matt.

She knocked once more before inserting the key in the dead bolt. It didn't turn. The roommate hadn't bothered to lock the top lock. She shoved the key into the lock on the door handle, turning it at the same time. She bumped the door with her hip and it opened.

"Hello?" All she needed was for the roomie to come at her from the back, but nothing stirred in the apartment.

She sniffed the air, detecting the skunky smell of weed clinging to the drapes and worn upholstery. She yanked back the curtains at the front window, sending a flurry of dust to swirl in the sunbeams.

She wrinkled her nose. The place wasn't as messy as she'd feared. Maybe because Matt hadn't been here for weeks.

Nothing in this room belonged to Matt, so it didn't belong to her. She tripped over a pair of boots on her way to the bedrooms in the back. She poked her head into the first room she came to and dismissed it. Not Matt's—too neat. She crossed the hall to the room with the door shut and pushed it open. Yeah, definitely Matt's.

The bed remained rumpled from Matt's last night there, and piles of clothes dotted the floor as if he'd undressed and let his clothing drop in small heaps where he stood.

She had no intention of cleaning up Matt's mess. If his roommate wanted to trash the clothes or donate them or whatever, he was welcome to them.

She wandered to the battered nightstand next to the unmade double bed. An empty bottle of whiskey lay on its side, pointing to an ashtray with a few cigarette butts and a wad of dried-out gum.

She opened the drawer, and a few batteries rattled around. There was also a box of condoms and a prescription vial for marijuana.

"Anything good in there?"

She whirled around, nearly slamming her fingers in the drawer, to face Jake, framed by the bedroom door. "You scared me. How'd you get in?"

Holding up a key between his fingers, he said, "Matt's parole officer sent two keys. I kept one for myself."

"Of course you did." She opened the nightstand drawer again to finish her inspection. "What did you need me for?"

"You're the rightful heir. I can't just nose around in here by myself." He stepped into the room and kicked at a pile of clothes. "Find anything of importance?"

"You mean like the phone number or instructions from the guy who paid him to plant those cards for me?" She held up the box of condoms and shook it. "Nope. Just these. Need some?"

She fired the box at him, and his right hand shot out and caught it. He squinted at the writing on the box and tossed them onto the bed. "Not my brand."

Heat touched her cheeks, so she buried her nose farther into the drawer. "Nothing much in here. I think it's more likely that Matt was lying to you about getting paid to torment me with the playing cards. He was just scamming to get more money out of you."

"Maybe." Jake crossed the room to a feminine-looking carved dresser, its mirror hidden by the clothing piled on top of it. With one hand, he swept the clothes onto the floor. "Just like a teenage girl, Matt has some photos stuck in his mirror. And you said he was a cold bastard."

"I didn't even notice those." Kyra joined him and hunched over the dresser. She scanned the mostly old pictures and zeroed in on one of a hodgepodge family at the same time Jake jabbed his finger at it.

"Is that one of Matt's foster families? The foster family you shared?"

Kyra snatched the picture from the mirror. "No. Matt's too young in this picture. He was older when we were in the same family."

"Wonder why he kept that one."

"Maybe it was someplace where he was relatively happy." Kyra left the photo on the dresser. "Do you want to check the closet? I'll look through these dresser drawers, but I think we're on a hopeless mission here."

"Maybe, but it seems strange Matt would go through the trouble of leaving a will with you as his beneficiary if he had nothing to leave you."

Jake turned from the dresser, and Kyra let a small breath escape as she slipped the photo into the pocket of her sweater.

"Probably just his way of messing with me." She opened the top drawer of the dresser and scooped her hands through the jumbled boxers and socks. The corner of an envelope poked one of her fingertips and she shook it free of the underwear covering it.

Keeping the envelope in the drawer, she read the printing on the outside—the name and address of a storage facility in Van Nuys. Squishing the envelope, she traced the edges of a key inside.

She dropped the envelope into the pocket that contained the photo and twisted her head over her shoulder. "Any luck in the closet?"

"Not unless you like leather—a lot of it." Jake slid the closet door closed with a bang. "He did have his motorcycle at the shop with him when he died. That's yours, too. It's a nice Harley."

"Do I look like the Harley type?" She poked a finger into her chest.

Tilting his head, he squinted. "Yeah, I could see you cruising Highway 1 with your blond hair streaming behind you, a pair of these leather chaps encasing your thighs."

"Careful." She shook her finger at him even as a little thrill of pleasure zinged through her veins at the look in his eyes. She dusted her hands together. "Well, I guess that's it. If someone did pay Matt to leave me the cards, we're not going to find any evidence of that here."

"I guess not." Jake scratched his chin as he surveyed the bedroom. "Even for a recent parolee, Matt traveled light."

"Don't forget. Before his stays in the joint, Matt was a foster kid. Traveling light is our modus operandi." She adjusted the strap of her purse on her shoulder. "I'm ready to get out of here."

"Thanks for inviting me along."

"Did I have a choice?" She raised her brows and then

swept out of the room. "Maybe you can have Matt's parole officer let his roommate know I'm done here."

"Huh?" Jake emerged from the bedroom, his hand in his jacket pocket. Had he gone back for the condoms?

"I said, Matt's parole officer can tell the roomie he can have Matt's stuff."

"I'll let him know. Now let's get out of here." Jake picked up a prescription medication bottle from the coffee table and shook it. "Matt's roommate probably doesn't mind you coming in here to look around, but he wouldn't be happy to know a cop had been nosing around his place."

As they walked into the apartment's courtyard, Kyra asked, "Did any of Andrea's other friends say anything about a stalker?"

"Not that I know of. We haven't talked to all of them yet."

"And I suppose you don't know if anything's missing from her place."

"Nope." Jake stopped in the middle of the sidewalk between his car and hers.

"What?"

"I always thought it was odd that the Copycat Player took the fingers *and* the jewelry. Most serial killers are satisfied with one trophy."

"And you never found the missing fingers."

Jake shrugged and pulled his car keys from his pocket. "My theory is that he did it to match the MO of The Player, and really didn't care about the fingers."

"I know, but what do you do with a pile of severed fingers?" Kyra hunched her shoulders and clenched her teeth.

"Probably destroyed them or dumped them, but he still had the jewelry. He didn't destroy all the evidence."

He jerked his thumb over his shoulder. "My car's back this way. I'll catch up with you later."

She waved as a warm glow kindled in her heart. When Captain Castillo had invited her to join the serial killer task force a few month ago, Jake hadn't been thrilled. He'd been double-crossed by a therapist before and didn't trust them. Now he wanted to catch up with her.

She clicked the remote on her car and slid behind the wheel. She buzzed down her window and waved her hand outside as Jake's car passed hers.

She watched him turn the next corner. Then she pulled the photo from the pocket of her sweater and studied the unhappy faces of the children clustered around a man and a woman—Buck and Lori Harmon.

Buck Harmon had his hands on the shoulders of a young girl, who clung to the hand of an older girl. Lori Harmon held a bawling baby on her hip, her hand on the head of a scruffy boy with a dirt-smudged face, her fingers digging into his scalp, forcing him to face the camera. Matt hovered at the edge of the group, a scowl twisting across his face.

Kyra's nose stung. She pulled a lighter from her pocket, the final item she'd taken from Matt's apartment—her sad inheritance. Holding the picture out the car window, she flicked the lighter and touched the flame to the corner of the picture. The orange fire raced across the photo, eating up the faces and the memories with it.

She let the mini inferno get close enough to her fingers to feel the singe. Then she dropped the picture to the street and drove away.

Chapter Three

Jake waited until he got back to the station before whipping out the remaining photos that had been tucked in the mirror above Matt's dresser. One was missing—because Kyra had taken it.

He shoved his sunglasses to the top of his head and squinted at the first picture, which must be Matt at around the age of six or seven, alone with a scrawny young woman who looked like a hippie. Mom?

Another picture showed the same child, presumably Matt, with a boy and a girl, sitting in a row on a floral sofa, each holding a book among some Christmas wrapping paper.

He shuffled through the rest and put them in order according to Matt's age in each picture, creating a timeline of his foster families. Kyra had the one that should've been at the end, the photo of the foster family she'd shared with Matt.

There had been four or five kids along with parents in that picture, but he hadn't gotten a good look at the tall blonde girl holding the hand of a younger girl because Kyra had snatched it out of his hand too quickly. It made sense, though. Matt and Kyra were the oldest children in that home, teenagers ready to be released to a world that had already discarded them. Matt had gone one way—drug, crime, prison; Kyra had gone another—college, career, success, thanks to the intervention of Quinn and his wife, Charlotte.

Why would she want to hide that picture from him and lie about it? Jake grunted and stuffed the photos in his bag. He thought he and Kyra had gotten past the deception hurdle of their relationship.

He'd had to do his own snooping to figure out Kyra's mother, Jennifer Lake, had been one of The Player's victims twenty years ago and that Kyra had changed her name and identity when she went to college. He'd understood why she'd kept that from him and the rest of the task force, but why all the mystery surrounding her relationship with her foster brother Matt Dugan?

When Dugan had contacted him, it wasn't just about who had paid him to plant the playing cards for Kyra to find. Dugan had also promised him some dirt on Kyra. He hadn't trusted Dugan, but the man had died of a drug overdose before Jake got to him. Kyra had been there at the time he slipped into unconsciousness.

If Matt and Kyra had engaged in some sexual relationship as Matt had hinted, Jake wouldn't care about that. Hell, they'd been two lonely, misplaced teens at the time. Who could blame them for finding solace in each other's arms? Was that why Kyra had snatched the photo? She didn't want any questions about her time in the foster family with Matt?

Jake grabbed his bag and exited his vehicle. Maybe he should just leave it alone. If he and Kyra got…closer, she'd tell him what she wanted to. Still, how could they get closer if she kept hiding things from him?

His marriage had ended because his wife had been cheating on him, and he'd been too busy with work to notice or care. He didn't want to go overboard in the other direction with Kyra.

He stalked into the Northeast Division and dropped into his chair at his computer. He shuffled through a few messages on his desk, pulling out the one from Andrea's ex. He was following through on Kyra's advice. Sometimes Kyra got more out of witnesses and people of interest than hardened detectives. Captain Castillo had recognized her value and assigned her to the serial killer task force for the Copycat Player. Jake had resisted her presence at first, but had come to recognize her value. The insane chemistry between them hadn't hurt, either. Not that they'd acted on it.

And now? She was hiding something from him again.

His fingers flew across the keyboard to access Matt Dugan's data. He didn't have permission to see Dugan's juvenile records, but that didn't mean he couldn't view his file from the Department of Children and Family Services.

He pulled up the DCFS database and could only get so far. Pushing back from the desk, he crossed his arms. Who did he know in DCFS?

Billy careened into the war room waving a piece of paper. "Hey, partner. We fast-tracked the DNA test on the gum and we have a match."

Jake smacked his desk. "I knew he'd made a mistake. Is it some felon matched in CODIS?"

"Uh, no." Billy parked himself in front of Jake and held out the paper. "It's Jeremy Bevin's, Andrea's ex."

Jake slumped as if someone had just stuck a needle in him and popped him. "Jeremy? He has an alibi, and are you telling me he copied a serial killer's MO to kill his girlfriend?"

"It happens." Billy lifted one stylishly clad shoulder. "And his alibi is his good friend who was helping him set up stuff in his new place. Could be covering for him."

Jake rubbed his eyes. "Probably not, but let's get the footage from his apartment building or street to verify. I need to talk to him, anyway. Let's bring him in."

An hour later, they had Jeremy sweating bullets in an interrogation room while Billy reviewed the security footage from Jeremy's apartment building on the night Andrea was murdered.

The video showed Jeremy and his friend carrying some boxes into the building, leaving and returning with more boxes, a pizza and a six-pack. They didn't leave again that night. The next morning the friend took off and Jeremy left later, presumably for his meeting with Andrea, which never happened.

Billy clicked his mouse to end the tape. Jake, who'd been hunched over Billy's shoulder, straightened up and said, "Alibi is solid."

"Then how the hell did his gum get wedged into that lock?"

"That's what we're going to find out right now." He crooked his finger at Billy and the two of them went downstairs to the interrogation room.

Jeremy jerked his head up when they walked into the room. "Wh-what's going on? Why am I in here?"

Jake yanked out a chair while Billy took up a position in the corner, folding his arms. "I thought you had something to tell me."

"Well, I do, but—" Jeremy's gaze jumped to Billy in the corner, whose smile seemed downright sinister "—why did you stick me in here?"

"We had to check out your alibi, Jeremy." Jake splayed his hands on the metal desk, his thumbs meeting.

"I thought you already called George, and he verified it."

"We did, but someone used chewing gum to muck up a lock so the door from the house to the garage wouldn't lock. We checked the gum for DNA, and it matched the sample we took from you when we first questioned you."

Jake studied Jeremy's face, which blanched first and then heated to a bright red. "Mine? My gum? I wouldn't need to do that. I still have my key."

"Could've done it to throw us off." Jake held up his hands. "But we know you didn't because we looked at the surveillance video from your apartment building. Your alibi checks out."

"Whew." Jeremy wiped his brow and then sat up, shoulders straight. "I mean, of course it did. I told you, I'd never hurt Andrea. I loved her. Still love her."

"The question is, when were you last chewing gum at Andrea's?"

"I *am* a gum chewer." He reached into his pocket and flipped a pack of sugarless gum onto the table. "I'm a former smoker. Gave it up for Andrea."

Billy made an impatient move in the corner. "Okay, we know how much you loved her. Now answer the question. When were you last chewing gum at that house, and do you throw it in the trash or spit it on the ground? And, no, we're not going to arrest you if you admit you spit it on the ground."

"Sometimes I spit it in the gutter. I figure people are less likely to step on it there." Jeremy's fingers nervously fiddled with the pack of gum. "Before I went to

Andrea's and found her…body, I was there a few days before that to pick up some boxes from the garage."

Jake gave a sidelong glance to Billy. Was he thinking the same thing? Was the killer watching Jeremy at that point and specifically used Jeremy's gum to implicate him?

They had to collect more video from the area for different times.

Jake nailed down the day and time of that visit, as close as Jeremy remembered, and he sat back in his chair. "Ms. Chase indicated that you told her about a stalker Andrea had?"

Jeremy wiped a hand across his brow as the questioning turned away from him and his visits to Andrea's house. "Yeah, Andrea accused me of following her, but it wasn't me. She didn't get into it that much. Told me to stop following her and coming by the house uninvited. When I denied it, she dropped it. I don't know if she believed me or not."

They probed him for more info, but he clearly didn't know anything else.

Jake scooted back his chair. "You're free to go, Jeremy. If you remember anything else, give me a call, especially if you recall seeing anyone hanging around Andrea's house or neighborhood."

Jeremy stood up so hastily he had to grab the chair before it fell over. "That guy, the one who killed Andrea… He saw me spit out that gum and picked it up to fix the lock and frame me, didn't he?"

"We can't know for sure." Billy pushed off the wall he'd been propping up the entire interview. "But we think this guy was watching Andrea long before he killed her."

KYRA GLANCED UP as Jake, Billy and Jeremy filed out of an interrogation room. They all wore grim expressions, and Jeremy looked a little pale around the lips.

Clutching files to her chest, she raised her eyebrows at Jake as he met her eyes. He gave a quick shake of his head.

She followed the two detectives up the stairs while Jeremy peeled off and headed for the exit. She quickened her stride to catch up to Jake as he entered the task force conference room, which they'd reassembled in record time after Andrea's murder.

"Could Jeremy tell you anything more about the stalker?" She tagged along behind Jake as he went to his desk. He slammed down the lid of his laptop, but not before she saw the familiar logo of the LA County Department of Children and Family Services.

She tapped the lid of the computer with an unsteady finger. "Andrea didn't have a child, did she?"

"No, that's another case." Jake dropped into his chair and swiveled it around to face her. "Take Billy's chair. He's on his way out."

She sat across from Jake, their knees almost touching. "What did you find out from Jeremy?"

Bending his head toward hers, he said, "I don't know if you heard yet, but the DNA on that gum was Jeremy's."

She sucked in a quick breath. "No."

"Doesn't mean much. We verified his alibi, and when we questioned him, he said he chewed gum and had probably spit some out around Andrea's house a few days before her murder."

"So, the killer picked up Jeremy's gum to literally gum up the lock." She raised a hand to her throat. "Do you think the killer knew it was Jeremy's gum?"

"Too much of a coincidence if he didn't. He could've used putty or anything else. He used gum with Jeremy's DNA."

"That means Andrea's fears of a stalker were probably right on. This guy's been watching her—and Jeremy. Maybe Andrea brushed it off, thinking it was Jeremy and she didn't have to worry."

Jake's lips twisted. "She was wrong."

"Did her friends or family say anything about her concerns?"

"We're not done interviewing her friends." He grabbed a cup of coffee and drained it. "Have you been in touch with the family yet? Are they coming out from Atlanta?"

"I have their contact info, but I haven't spoken to them. I sent them an email detailing my services, so I'm going to leave the ball in their court for now." She rose from Billy's chair, cognizant of a few looks being thrown their way.

It wasn't like she and Jake were dating or anything. That dinner at Quinn's house after the Copycat Player case ended didn't count. Hell, they hadn't even shared their first kiss…yet.

Jake formed his fingers into a gun and pointed it at her. "Let me know what you want to do with Matt's Harley."

"You seem extremely interested in that bike. You want it?"

"That seems…wrong, but I'll think about it."

She lifted and dropped her shoulders, and spun around to march back to her own desk in the corner. Maybe the Miles family had responded to her email. Or maybe they were too devastated to function.

She pulled up her chair to the desk and clicked on the

email icon at the bottom of her screen. Nothing from the Miles family. She scanned through a couple of messages and clicked on one with an attachment from an unknown sender.

She squinted at the attachment, which appeared as a thumbnail, and her pulse ratcheted up several notches. It was a photo with a familiar configuration.

Her hand shook as she moved the mouse over the attachment. Holding her breath, she clicked on it. The photo she'd just burned in the street now filled her computer screen—with one difference.

Someone had placed a large black *X* over the face of Buck Harmon.

Chapter Four

With her heart thundering in her chest and echoing in her ears, Kyra closed the attachment. She scanned the body of the email, which was blank, and the email address. The message had come from one of the free email providers with a display name of LAPREY.

What did that mean? LA prey? Was she supposed to be prey? She felt like it. Twisting her head over her shoulder, she swallowed the lump in her throat that threatened to turn into a howl.

She caught Jake's eye and gave him a weak smile. She couldn't blame this prank on Matt. Had her foster brother been telling Jake the truth when he said that someone had paid him to taunt her with those cards? If so, was someone else being paid to send her threatening emails?

Was it a threat? Blackmail? If it was blackmail, she didn't know what anyone would want from her. She didn't have any money. No influence. No power.

She dropped her chin to her chest. In fact, she hadn't felt this powerless in a long time.

A touch on her shoulder had her jumping out of her seat.

"Whoa." Jake stepped back. "Sorry I startled you. Are you all right?"

And just like he'd done before with his laptop, she snapped her lid shut. "I'm fine. You scared me."

His brows furrowed over his nose. "I meant a few minutes ago when you looked at me across the room. I thought you were sending me an SOS signal."

"Really?" She snorted. "I think you're just over here checking on that Harley. What do you think I could get for it?"

"Probably twenty grand." He balanced one hip on the corner of her desk. "That's not why I crossed the room."

She flipped her hair over her shoulder. Had she really been sending out an SOS? "I'm okay, just stressed like everyone else in this room."

"Do you want to meet me at Quinn's tonight? I'd like to update him on this murder, get his thoughts. I can pick up dinner or even cook for everyone."

Did he feel safe with her only in the presence of Quinn? What did he think would happen if they were alone together? She could think of several things she'd like to do with him in private.

She coughed. "Cook? Quinn wouldn't expect that, and neither would I. You can order in—just no Chinese. Too much sodium for him."

"He's lucky to have you."

"Ah." She raised one finger. "I'm the lucky one."

"Is that a yes, then? You, me, Quinn, dinner at his place at seven thirty. You can set that up?" With his last syllable, he kept his lips pressed together as if holding his breath.

That sounded…romantic. She pasted on a bright smile. "I'll give him a call. I haven't spoken to him since we left his place the other night when you got the news about Andrea."

"Great." He rapped his knuckles on her desk. "I'll see you at seven thirty…at Quinn's."

He had added that last part hastily when his partner walked by, bumping Jake's shoulder.

The two of them, heads together, walked to their desks, and Kyra returned to her computer and the problem in front of her.

She eased up the lid on her laptop and opened the message. She clicked on the email address and sucked her bottom lip between her teeth as she studied the properties, which told her nothing. She needed to pick the brain of a computer geek to find out who'd sent this message.

Her gaze darted around the room, bustling with phone calls, mini conferences and conversations around the whiteboards, and settled on Brandon Nguyen, the LAPD's tech guy. Just like she'd done with Clive Stewart, the fingerprint tech, she might be able to get Brandon to do a little favor for her—off the radar.

As she watched Brandon, he dropped to the floor, to check some cables, no doubt. She kept her eye on him until he popped up again, brushing the knees of his jeans. He waved a cable in the air and left the war room.

Hastily Kyra jumped from her chair and followed him into the hallway, where she saw Brandon veer into the lunchroom. Perfect.

She walked in on him studying the snack machine. Holding up a dollar bill, she said, "It's on me if I can ask you a question about something."

"Not necessary." He threaded his own money into the machine and punched a couple of buttons. "You can ask me anything, free of charge. That's what I'm here for."

"It's not something related to the case, though, and it is something I'd prefer to keep hush-hush." She sidled up next to him in front of the snack machine and fed her bill into the slot.

Brandon glanced over his shoulder as if she'd just asked him to spill government secrets. He might be a harder nut to crack than Clive had been with the fingerprints. "Um, I guess I can help out, as long as it's not something illegal, you know, like accessing classified information."

She giggled as she selected a granola bar from the rows of junk food. "Of course not. I got an email from an unknown email address, and I'd like to find out where it came from. It's regarding a patient of mine."

That was not a lie. She was her own patient—had been under her own care for years.

His face cleared, and he skimmed a hand through his black hair. "I can help with that. I have some other work to do right now, though."

"Oh, I didn't mean right this minute. Hit me up when you're free. I should be in the war room for most of the afternoon." She retrieved her granola bar from the tray and pointed it at him. "Thanks a bunch."

Two things being in foster care had taught her was how to be adaptable and agreeable. She could be anyone's best friend in the blink of an eye.

She took her seat in the conference room once again, keeping one eye on the clock and one eye on Jake. She didn't want him to see Brandon working with her because he'd ask questions, and she didn't want to lie to him any more than she had to.

She did place a call to Quinn, who was only too happy to have company tonight, especially if it involved a lowdown on the new case. Quinn might be retired, but he still took a keen interest in all things LAPD Homicide.

Finally Jake and Billy grabbed their jackets in unison and made for the door. Jake made a detour at her desk. "Everything set with Quinn?"

"It is." She wagged her finger between him and Billy, who was waiting at the door. "Where are you two off to?"

"If Andrea had a stalker, and it looks like she did, we're going to check for more cameras in that area. Maybe one of the neighbors caught the guy lurking around earlier."

"I hope so. Good luck." She wiggled her fingers in the air. "'Bye, Billy."

Billy gave her a big grin. She held a special place in his affections after facilitating an introduction between him and her friend Megan Wright, a TV reporter for KTOP. As far as she knew, they were still dating but keeping it light. She wished she could say the same for her and Jake. Did having dinner at Quinn's house talking serial killers count as a date?

About thirty minutes after Jake and Billy left, Brandon approached her, eyebrows raised. "I have some time right now before I leave."

"Great." She scooted her chair over while wheeling another in front of her computer. "Have a seat."

As Brandon adjusted the height of the chair, Kyra reached across him and brought up the email. Although he could probably tell the attachment was a picture from the thumbnail, he wouldn't be able to make out the faces. Wouldn't mean anything to him, anyway.

"This is the message, and that's the email—laprey at newmail dot com."

Brandon brushed some straight bangs from his eyes. "That name mean anything to you?"

"Nope." She wouldn't give him her theory about being prey in LA. "Can you track the IP address, or whatever?"

Brandon clicked around the screen with a speed she couldn't hope to follow. "There are a few things I can do. Can I forward this to myself?"

"Without the attachment. It's confidential."

"Sure, sure." He clicked the button to forward the message, and with his mouse he circled the prompt that asked if he wanted to include the attachment. He clicked No. "I need to perform a few functions on this message with programs you don't have on your laptop."

"Understood. Thank you, so much. Coffee, lunch, those disgusting flaming hot things you like from the vending machine…" She jerked her thumb at her chest. "I'm your girl."

Brandon nodded as he walked the chair back to its rightful place. "I'll remember that."

When he left, Kyra packed up her work and tossed the granola bar in her desk drawer. She'd get to the bottom of this one way or another.

Matt had died of a drug overdose before he could tell Jake who'd paid him to leave the playing cards for her—before he could tell Jake any of her secrets. Who else besides Matt and Quinn knew those secrets? Matt could've told someone before he died, someone ready and willing to pick up where Matt left off. But why? She understood Matt's motivation. He'd been obsessed with her and didn't know whether to love her or hate her half the time. Why would some random person be interested in tormenting her about her past, and why would these events coincide with copycats taking up where The Player had left off?

Maybe Matt told someone she had money. She shrugged her ponytail from her shoulder. "Yeah, good luck with that."

"With what?"

She glanced up, meeting Captain Castillo's dark, intelligent eyes. She had to be careful around all these detectives.

"Ugh, you caught me talking to myself."

"I hope that doesn't mean you need therapy." Castillo winked.

"Any therapist will tell you we all need therapy."

"Just thought I'd drop by to see how you're doing. Everything going okay with... Jake?" Castillo looked down as he ran a hand over his tie.

Her pulse jumped and she schooled her face. "Why do you ask? Has he been complaining about me?"

"Not at all. From the looks of things, he appreciates your work with the task force. I mean, you practically caught the Copycat Player single-handedly, didn't you?"

Her cheeks burned. "You mean by almost becoming one of his victims until Jake rescued me? I hope you don't... I h-hope nobody thinks I believe I'm responsible for his apprehension. I hope Jake doesn't think that."

"Never mentioned it to me. I was joking about the rest. Nobody thinks that." Castillo clenched his hands in front of him, and she waited expectantly.

What did he really want?

"Anyway, everything's going great. The team is as welcoming as ever..." She let her voice trail off and pushed back from her desk.

"Do you still see Quinn?"

"I was good friends with his wife. I see him often." She cocked her head and waited. Did he have a message for Quinn?

"Good to hear someone's keeping track of him." Castillo dabbed at a dried spot of coffee on his yellow shirtfront. "Sorry to keep you."

"No problem. Thanks for checking in. I appreciate your recommendation to the first task force."

He leveled a finger at her. "What you do adds value to an investigation. I firmly believe that."

"Thanks, Captain."

She waited until he had left the room, after chatting with a couple of the officers, and then released a long breath. That was weird. Had he heard something bad about her? Did he want to check on her ties with Quinn before lowering the hammer on her?

If he did, she'd find out later. Right now she had one patient to see before meeting Jake at Quinn's, and she didn't want to leave those two alone together for too long.

JAKE HELD UP the bags of food on his way to Quinn's kitchen. "Hope you like Mediterranean—chicken skewers, rice, hummus. Kyra told me to hold off on the Chinese because of the sodium."

Quinn shook his head. "Damn, that girl treats me like an invalid. You want a beer before she gets here and gives me the evil eye?"

Jake swung the bags onto the counter. "As long as she's not going to transfer that evil eye to me for encouraging you."

Quinn held on to the edge of the counter. "Hell, we're two grown men, LAPD homicide detectives, stared down the baddest of the bad. We're gonna let some slip of a blonde control us?"

Jake stopped fussing with the bags and cocked one eyebrow. "Really?"

"You're right. Let's have those drinks before she gets here."

Chuckling, Jake plunged into the fridge and emerged with two cold ones. He twisted off both lids and slid a bottle across to Quinn.

Quinn raised his beer. "To that slip of a blonde."

"I'll drink to that." Jake tapped the neck of his bottle with Quinn's and took a long gulp. Not that he was trying to get Quinn drunk or anything before Kyra got here, but it might be interesting to talk to the old detective without her hovering, and a couple of beers could facilitate that conversation.

As the two detectives faced each other across the counter, Jake told Quinn about Andrea's murder.

"The playing card was between the lips, and the pinkie finger was missing. We're not sure if any other trophy was taken. Andrea was in bed sleeping when he made his move, so presumably no jewelry. Her ex-boyfriend didn't indicate she slept with jewelry on."

"He's striking out on his own." Quinn scraped the blue foil label from the damp bottle with his fingernail.

"What do you mean?" Jake always felt like a novice sitting at the feet of a master when talking to Detective Roger Quinn—yet Quinn had not solved the case of The Player. Jake didn't know how that would feel. He had a perfect record with every homicide he'd worked.

Must be hell.

"The Copycat Player followed The Player's MO up to a point. The Player never took jewelry and the Copycat decided he would. Now, this guy is following The Player, and not the Copycat. He wants to be his own man in some regards."

"Then why follow him at all?"

Quinn rolled a shoulder. "Notoriety? I don't know. You're the hotshot detective now. You figure it out."

"I plan to. Computer Forensics is still going through Cannon's stuff to see where he got his ideas. They're searching to find out if he was reading up on The Player's case, but even if he was, he wouldn't have learned about the missing fingers from any news stories. You guys kept a tight lid on that."

"And yet here we have another killer who knows about it. I guess the lid wasn't that tight." Quinn spread his hands on the counter, his fingers like misshapen twigs against the tile. "Or word got out. It does."

"This guy was stalking Andrea, murdered her in her home, just like a few of The Player's killings." Jake took a swig of beer. "Interesting how the first copycat, Cannon, chose to kill the victims in his car and dump their bodies, like The Player's first few victims, and now this guy is killing in their homes, like The Player's next few victims. These guys really know their serial killer lore, don't they?"

"Sick bastards." Quinn shoved aside the glittering pile of foil he'd peeled from the bottle. "I'd better get rid of this evidence before Kyra gets here."

Jake drummed his fingers on the counter. "Kyra's mother was murdered in her house, wasn't she?"

Quinn's hands froze in midsweep. "She was. Rented a small house in Hollywood."

"And Kyra was home."

"She was home—sound asleep. Never woke up. The killer probably didn't even know she was there."

Jake doubted that. If The Player had stalked Jennifer Lake, just like Andrea had been stalked, he would've known about a child. He wasn't that careless. Still, he'd be damned if he'd correct the old detective. That would be close to sacrilege. He clamped his lips shut.

Quinn pointed to a cupboard to the right of Jake's head. "Why don't we surprise Kyra tonight and set the table."

"I can do that." Jake pivoted to his right and opened the cupboard door. He grabbed a stack of three plates. "What was Kyra like when you first met her?"

"Traumatized. She'd lost her mother, her world. Jennifer Lake maybe didn't make all the right choices as a mother, but she loved her daughter. Kyra cried for her often." Quinn's faded blue eyes shimmered with the memory.

"And after?" Jake skirted around Quinn's sagging body and put a plate on each of the three place mats on the table. "What was she like when the shock...wore off?"

"I don't know that it ever did." Quinn took his turn in the kitchen and gathered silverware and napkins. "The murder affected her, of course. As a child, she was tough and unafraid, sassy, assertive. Then she learned to submerge all that beneath a sheet of ice—her layer of protection."

"Yeah, I'm familiar with that ice."

Quinn poked him in the arm with a fork. "Keep trying, boy—there's a vibrant, caring woman beneath that veneer."

"You love her like a daughter, don't you?" Jake rubbed his arm where the tines had pricked him.

"I do, even though she was never officially ours. I blame myself for that. If it hadn't been for my abuse of the booze at that time, we might've gotten her."

"Maybe that played a role, but your age and the fact that you were the detective on her mother's murder case probably also had something to do with it. Shouldn't blame yourself."

"But that's what we fathers do, isn't it?"

Jake's eyebrows shot up. "You know I'm a father?"

Quinn nudged his arm with his pointy elbow. "You didn't think I'd let my girl fall for someone without doing my own investigating, do you?"

Chapter Five

Kyra banged on Quinn's door louder than she intended after seeing Jake's sedan parked illegally on the street and discovering the front door was locked. So, he had beaten her there and then locked her out.

"Hello, it's me."

As she scrabbled in the bottom of her purse for the key to Quinn's house, the door flew open and Jake filled the frame like he owned the place.

"It's about time." He swept his arm to the side to gesture her through the door as if she hadn't been here a hundred times before.

Bustling into the house, she said, "About time? I'm right on time. You're early."

She tripped to a stop as she took in the table, set for three, a vase of flowers pulled from Quinn's front yard in the center.

It looked a little bit more like a date in here than to-go containers balanced on their laps in the living room as they discussed serial killers. She approved. "Nice."

"We were just talking about… Andrea." Quinn pulled out a chair at the table and waved her into it.

Kyra shifted a quick glance from Quinn to Jake, suppressing a comment with a pursing of his lips.

Jake nodded, instead. "Getting him up to speed."

"Any insight, Quinn?" Kyra took the proffered chair, nose in the air sniffing the spicy aroma of the food steaming on her plate.

"Just that he's still mimicking The Player with the stalking of a victim and killing her in her home."

"Just like my mom." Kyra sniffed and it wasn't the food.

Quinn joined her at the table and squeezed her hand. "Just like Jennifer."

Jake put a beer in front of each of them, along with a basket of pita bread. "Quinn thinks this guy probably took a trophy from Andrea, even though we haven't found what it could be yet."

"You mean in addition to the severed finger?" Kyra ran a thumb down her bottle of beer without taking a sip. "Just because the Copycat Player did? You think it's jewelry again?"

"The way Quinn explained it to me is that the killer would want a trophy for himself, just like the Copycat Player took the jewelry. That was for him."

"And the finger was for...?" She jabbed at a piece of lettuce on her plate, skewering a small crumble of feta cheese with it.

"For the...game." Quinn took a small sip of his beer, and Kyra knew it wasn't his first. His first drink always resembled that of a man slaking his thirst after a long drought. She and his doctor always cautioned him about the wisdom of an alcoholic testing himself every day with just one or two beers.

"You think the killers are playing some kind of game? Wait." She suspended her fork halfway to her mouth, and the cheese rolled off and fell to her plate.

"Do you think Jordy Cannon and Andrea's killer are or were in touch somehow?"

Jake dropped his fork with a clatter. "Is that what you think, Quinn? Is that what you meant by taking his own trophy?"

"Think about it." As if he were taking tea with the queen, he held up his own pinkie finger from the hand wrapped around his bottle. "These killers leave the playing card and then cut off the fingers because they're following the game plan of The Player, twenty years ago. But what do *they* get out of it? The Player had his own sick reasons for severing the fingers and taking them as trophies—reasons we never sorted out. Jordy and this guy don't have those same compulsions, but they're following the same playbook. That's not a coincidence. They know each other, or are part of some sick club."

"They do have different compulsions." Jake scooped up a glob of chicken and rice with a triangle of pita bread and shoved it in his mouth, his appetite clearly not inhibited by the talk of killers and their trophies.

Why would it be? He ate this stuff for breakfast and she, unfortunately, snacked on it.

Quinn shrugged. "Different compulsions, different trophies, different victims."

"But the same MO, copied from The Player. Why would they know each other? The Player's MO is available to anyone with a computer and internet access." She grabbed her bottle. Maybe she needed the booze after all.

"Except the detail about the severed finger is not on the internet. It was kept out of the news." Jake's hazel eyes glowed green around the edges of his irises, as if the ideas behind those eyes were sparking like electrical circuits.

"Quinn, and even you, said those details had a way of leaking out."

"To two different people who both happen to be killers?" Jake planted his elbows on either side of his plate, his appetite on hold.

"If you're buying into Quinn's theory that these killers know each other, you'd better start looking more closely into Jordy's friends."

"That's just it." Taking a swig of beer, Jake settled back in his chair. "Jordy Lee Cannon had no friends."

Quinn steepled his fingers, their crookedness making for a dilapidated church spire. "What's a friend these days? People fall in love online without ever meeting each other in person. I've seen those shows."

Kyra let her mouth drop open in mock outrage. "You watch reality TV dating shows?"

Quinn chuckled. "Only while channel surfing."

"Quinn's right. I'm going to order the full forensics report on Jordy's computer." Jake raised his bottle to Quinn. "I knew it was a good idea coming here."

They finished their dinner in a more normal fashion—discussing the Dodgers' chances of making it to the World Series next month and wondering if they'd have another blast of heat and high winds before SoCal settled down to cooler fall temps.

Kyra offered to clean the kitchen, knowing she could get it done faster than Jake and with the key to Matt's storage container burning a hole in her purse. She had to get out there before Matt's parole officer or roommate or even Jake. She didn't put it past him to get more info from the parole officer and not share it with her. Just like she had no intention of sharing this with Jake.

"Do you two want to take a walk on the canals? I can run the dishwasher, Kyra, and I promise I won't crack open another beer."

She emerged from the kitchen and patted Quinn on the arm, her heart softening. She got it. He wanted to play matchmaker just like on those reality TV shows he claimed not to watch.

Another time and she'd jump at the chance to cozy up to Jake while walking the bridges of Venice, but tonight she had a mission.

"I'm down for that. I could use some fresh air." Jake rose from his chair and stretched, his sage-green T-shirt clinging to the shifting muscles of his chest, giving her a tantalizing look at what she was turning down.

"You know, I'd like that, but I have some work waiting for me at home." She twisted her lips, not even feigning the regret. "Patient files."

Jake shoved his hands in the pockets of his jeans, his eyes narrowing to slits, giving her the same look as her stray cat when she shooed it outside.

"I've got farther to travel than you, so I'll hit the road." He grasped Quinn's hand. "Thanks for the insight, sir."

"Thanks for the food…and the beer." Quinn winked.

Kyra waved a dish towel at them. "You guys don't fool me one bit. I know you had a beer before I got here."

"Busted." Jake grabbed his weapon and slung the holster over his shoulder, looking like a gunslinger from the Old West—all steely-eyed determination and set jaw.

He didn't look happy that she'd shut him down. He'd be even less happy if he knew why.

Raising his hand, Jake said, "Good night, you two."

The door shut, and an unaccustomed silence hung between her and Quinn for several seconds.

Quinn broke it with a cough. "He's a good guy, Kyra, and he already knows about your mother. No need to shy away like you usually do."

"It's not that. I really do have work to do. Besides, the last stroll we had around the canals ended with a phone call about a dead body."

"Superstitious?"

"Perhaps, and I know he's a good guy. Maybe that's why it's best we don't go down this road. You know he has an ex-wife."

"And a daughter, so why are you selling yourself short? You deserve someone in your life, Kyra. Someone good."

"Do I?" She stooped to kiss him on the cheek. "I have to run. Don't fall asleep in your chair."

Back in her car, she picked up her phone, punched in the address of Matt's storage facility and took off. Forty minutes later, she pulled up to the closed gate. The card in the envelope must be for after-hours access, and Kyra let out a breath as she shoved the card in the slot and the gate rolled open.

Matt had even written the number of the storage unit on the envelope. He must've been expecting a return visit to the slammer to rent this space.

Following the signs posted at each corner, she navigated to Matt's unit, nestled along a row of the smaller containers. These had silver rolltop doors with a keyhole on the right-hand panel on the outside.

She parked perpendicular to the door of the unit and scrambled from the car, her heart tapping out a staccato beat. She'd left her headlights on to augment the yellow light that spilled from a bulb every four containers.

With unsteady hands, she inserted the key in the lock and clicked it to the right. The door rattled as if to say, *Come on in. I've been waiting for you.*

She bent over, grasped the handle and yanked up, a muscle in her back jumping in protest. The door squealed as she raised it, and she held her breath, expecting some sort of sick joke from Matt to pop out at her. The only joke was that the unit didn't have lighting, but she did have her cell phone.

Standing at the entrance, panting slightly, she scanned the contents of the storage unit with the beam of light from her phone, her gaze tripping over boxes, a few old suitcases and motorcycle parts. If he had anything in here about payment from someone to leave cards for her or anything like that, she'd turn it over to Jake, but she doubted Matt would've stored something so recent. These looked like the past, not the present.

She took a tentative step into the space and sneezed. Did he have more photos in those boxes? Who knew Matt Dugan had been so sentimental about his messed-up foster families?

She practically stumbled over the first row of boxes and dropped into a crouch. She lifted the lid from one of the boxes and shone her light inside, picking out a mass of papers.

She shuffled through the drawings and sketches, her heart lodged in her throat. She'd forgotten about Matt's artistic talent, which had been submerged beneath his fear and resentment and hate. She'd had those same feelings being shuffled among families who'd regarded her with a mixture of pity, horror and greed.

She capped the box and plunged into the next one. This one contained a sort of jumbled filing system with

Matt's court dates and releases, and communications with his court-appointed attorneys.

She picked her way through some bike parts, probably stolen, and settled in front of another couple of boxes. She tipped the lid off the first one, which contained more items Matt had probably stolen from the garage. Kyra choked on the oily fumes that rose from the rags wrapped around gadgets and parts that must have been of some use on a motorcycle at one point. She felt behind a greasy carburetor where the box lid had fallen, and then froze as she read the black-scrawled label on the box next to this one. *Mimi Lake.* Her nickname when she was a child, her real last name, the last name tied to a murdered woman.

With dread thrumming through her veins, she tipped up the lid of the box bearing her name. Her hands clawed through the newspaper clippings and candid photos of her long after she'd become Kyra Chase. Her stomach heaved and she pressed a fist against her mouth. Why?

A metal scraping sound at the door of the storage unit caused her to spin on her heels and topple to the side. She frantically reached for the gun tucked in the purse that was slung around her body.

"Did you find what you were looking for?"

Jake's voice reverberated in the metal container.

Desperation and rage had her reaching past her gun for another item in her purse. Without thinking, she flicked the lighter and dropped it on top of the open box. Fueled by the old paper, the flames shot up past the rim of the box, the heat instant on her cheeks.

"Look out!" Jake shouted from the entrance and took a step into the unit.

As Kyra scrambled to her feet, the fire jumped into the second box—the one full of oily rags.

The explosion threw her off her feet.

Chapter Six

The boom reverberated in Jake's ears, bouncing off the metal walls of the storage unit. He stumbled back from the searing heat that blasted his face. The flames raced to the ceiling of the storage unit, and black smoke billowed toward him in a noxious cloud.

The explosion had thrown Kyra away from the fire. She was crabbing backward to escape it, but the flames chased her, licking at her shoes.

Jake lunged forward and grabbed Kyra under the arms. He yanked her once, her legs flying off the ground, and then he dragged her out of the container to the cool air and her car.

Her car. If the fire reached her car, that explosion in the storage unit would seem like a firecracker in comparison.

Smoke abrading his throat, he choked out, "The keys."

In an equally strangled voice, she answered, "In the ignition."

He gave her a hard shove. "Get away and call 911."

He watched her stumble away before jumping into the car and cranking on the engine. He threw it into gear and stomped on the accelerator. The car leaped backward, and he propelled it away from the blazing storage unit.

As he exited the vehicle, he heard sirens. He swiveled his head, the smoke stinging his eyes and invading his nostrils, but he couldn't see Kyra. His head jerked back to the unit, now belching orange flames and black smoke in some kind of Halloween extravaganza.

She hadn't foolishly gone back inside to save something, had she?

He had taken one step in the direction of the inferno when someone grabbed his arm.

"Where are you going?" Kyra stared at him through soot-ringed eyes that a Goth teen princess would envy.

Before he had a chance to sheepishly admit that he was going back for her, fire engines blared their warning, and he and Kyra moved out of the way.

She held up a card. "I was going to let them through the gate, but the owner had already gotten a fire warning and remotely released the gates for the fire trucks."

Jake peered back at the fire being fueled by Matt Dugan's only earthly possessions. "The corrugated metal should keep the fire from spreading to other units."

"I hope so." She shoved back strands of hair from her loosened ponytail, smearing more soot across her face.

Turning his back on the busy firefighters, Jake took her by the shoulders, and she swayed toward him. "Are you all right? I smelled gasoline as soon as I walked in there, but never expected a fire or an explosion."

"I'm all right, but I think my—" she looked down and held up one foot "—shoes melted or something."

He rubbed her arms. "If all you lost was a pair of shoes, this is your lucky day. What happened in there?"

"It was that box of rags." She shivered despite the

warmth emanating from the fire and the cinders wafting through the air like fireflies.

Jake quirked his eyebrows. "Matt kept greasy rags in his storage unit for safekeeping?"

"The rags were wrapped around parts, motorcycle parts. I don't know if the coverings started out clean, and gasoline and oil leaked onto them, or if Matt used purposely dirty rags to bundle the parts. I tipped the lid off the box to have a look inside, and it fell behind a carburetor or something, so I didn't put it back on right away, and the fumes escaped."

"And the fire just started automatically? You don't think he had something rigged up, do you?" His hands convulsively tightened on her arms.

"No, that was completely on me." She tapped her chest. "I did the stupidest thing imaginable. The light on my phone stopped working for some reason, and I was in the middle of going through the contents of another box. I—I had a lighter in my purse that I had picked up from Matt's apartment, and I flicked it on to see. I completely forgot about what was in the other box and how the fumes alone could ignite a fire."

"You used a lighter in a storage container with combustible auto parts?" Jake shook his head, trying to figure that one out. Sometimes smart people had no common sense.

"Stupid, I know." She wiped her hands along her grimy slacks. "Thanks for getting me out of there. I'm not sure I would've made it in time."

"I don't know." He slung an arm around her shoulders and pulled her close, because if she didn't welcome a hug after that escape, when would she? "That's the fastest I've ever seen anyone move backward in my life."

"Are you two okay?" A firefighter, his equipment squeaking, approached them.

"We're fine." Jake held out his hands. "Just a little singed hair and a few lungfuls of smoke."

"At least drink some water to soothe your throat. How'd that fire start?"

Kyra repeated her absurd story, which sounded even more ridiculous out loud in front of an incredulous firefighter.

He clicked his tongue. "Extremely dangerous. Is it you who stored those parts like that?"

"Me?" Jake pointed to himself. "No, sir. The contents of that container belonged to Ms. Chase's foster brother, now deceased."

"He didn't get the insurance. He didn't get the insurance." A small man with tufts of dark hair growing out of the side of his head scurried forward, waving papers. "That's Matt Dugan's unit, right? Number 556?"

"That's right. He passed away and left the contents—or what's left of them—to me." Kyra glanced at Jake quickly before returning her gaze to the storage facility's owner.

This was the first time Jake had heard of Matt's storage unit. Why hadn't Kyra told him? Instead, she'd hightailed it out of Quinn's place so fast he'd known something was up. Of course, her hasty departure could've meant she didn't want to spend time with him, but more than ego told him that wasn't the case.

He didn't want to get into that now. Her smoke-blackened face and glassy eyes told him not to go there…yet.

The owner took a wheezy breath. "I just want to let you know Mr. Dugan didn't have insurance on the unit. He declined it. I have the paperwork right here."

"That's okay, Mr.…?"

"Pargarian. Zev Pargarian."

"Mr. Pargarian. He really didn't have anything of value in there, anyway, unless you're into old motorcycle parts, I guess. And those are probably hot…stolen."

The firefighters had done their job, and Matt's unit crouched in its row, a smoking hulk of charred metal.

As the firefighters began to pack up their gear, the captain emerged from the ruins of Matt's life, carrying a box. "We were able to salvage one item. This box was near the door and untouched when we arrived, so we moved it out of the way."

Standing beside him, Kyra stiffened and her body vibrated like a plucked violin string. "You saved a box?"

The captain placed it on the ground between Jake and Kyra, and she dropped her head to read the scribbling on the box's lid. Her body sagged. "I already went through that one. It's nothing but some papers and receipts. You can leave it, and Mr. Pargarian can trash it with the rest of the stuff when he does cleanup."

The captain shrugged in his giant moon suit and hauled the box back to the wreckage of the unit.

Jake opened his mouth and Kyra spun on him, holding out her hand. "I know you have questions, Jake. I have some for you, too, but can we save them until tomorrow? I'm exhausted and I want to drink some water or tea like the firefighter suggested. I'm hoping to salvage these slacks, too."

"Fair enough. You've had a shock. Can you drive home okay?"

"I'm fine. Thanks again for dragging me out of there." Her voice hitched, and she covered her mouth with her hand.

Was it an act to get out of explaining why she hadn't told him about the storage unit and crept off to investigate it on her own? Not that she didn't have every right to do that, as it belonged to her.

"I'm just glad I was there in time to help." He rubbed her back as he walked her to her car. "Take it easy, and drive carefully. I'll talk to you tomorrow."

He waved at her car as she drove away. The fire engines followed her out. Jake had left his own car on the street and had hopped the fence after following Kyra here. She'd never suspected a tail.

Jake wandered back to the debris from the fire and kicked a few of the auto parts, misshapen metal still smoldering. His gaze landed on the box Kyra had dismissed.

Had she really gotten a good look inside with the light from her cell phone? Maybe they were each looking for something different.

Bending at the knees, he hoisted the box into his arms and straightened to his full height. He could carry this without breaking a sweat.

He hugged the box to his chest as he swung by the front office. When Jake tapped on the door, Pargarian looked up from his desk and waved him in.

Jake dropped the box at his feet and pushed open the door that thousands of grimy hands had pushed before. He poked his head in the office and the scent of pine tickled his nose. "Can I ask you a couple of questions?"

Pargarian raised his bushy brows. "It's late and you burned down one of my units."

Jake took his badge from his pocket and flashed it. "Just a few questions. I won't take long, and technically Ms. Chase burned that baby down."

Pargarian plucked several tissues from a box and blew his nose while gesturing with his other hand for Jake to enter.

"Can you tell me the last time Matt Dugan visited his unit?"

"That's all?" Pargarian crumpled the tissues and dropped them in a wastebasket. Rubbing his hands together, he said, "I can tell you that."

Jake parked in front of the little man's desk as he tapped away on a keyboard. He leaned close to the screen and said, "Two months ago. The last time he entered the facility was just under two months ago."

Jake whistled. The papers in the box might not be so old after all.

Pargarian sat with his hands poised over the keys, looking like an incongruous receptionist. "Anything else? That was one question."

Jake jerked a thumb over his shoulder. "Not a question really. Just wanted to let you know I'm taking the one intact box from the fire. Ms. Chase didn't want it, but I'd like to have a look."

"She doesn't want it, and you're the cop. One less item for me to clean up."

Pargarian allowed him to walk out the front door of the office to exit the facility, and Jake hiked to his car, his arms wrapped around the box.

The whole event might turn into nothing at all, except for one thing. After they escaped the fire, Jake had watched Kyra take her phone from her purse and turn off the flashlight.

Either that flashlight came back on its own, or...she was lying and had set fire to the storage unit on purpose.

KYRA PEELED HER sooty slacks from her legs and tossed them in the corner of the bathroom. She didn't want to put them in the hamper with the rest of her dirty clothes and have everything smell like she'd been cleaning chimneys.

She hunched forward, her hands planted on the chipped tile of her vanity, and stared at her black-ringed eyes. She resembled some crazy raccoon, a feral creature who had acted out of instinct and fear.

While she hadn't realized setting the box of papers on fire would result in an explosion that could've killed her and Jake, it was a foolish, thoughtless act born of fear and desperation. She could've simply told Jake the boxes contained nothing of importance, hauled them away to her own place and set fire to the contents in a more reasonable way.

A laugh exploded from her chest, her smile a white gash across her black face. Reasonable? When had it become reasonable to set fire to papers? When had it become reasonable for acquaintances, coworkers, to follow you around the city and sneak up on you? She had a much better excuse for being at the storage unit alone than Jake had for creeping up on her there.

Although if he hadn't been playing detective, she might be part of Mr. Pargarian's cleanup about now. Jake had dragged her out of the unit when he could've turned and run. Everyone else in her life had always turned and run—everyone except Quinn and Charlotte. But Jake hadn't exactly been running toward *her*. He'd been running toward the storage unit.

Coughing more soot from her lungs, she shimmied out of her underwear and bra. She added them to the heap of smoky clothes and whipped the mermaid-dotted shower curtain across the rod with a jangle. Cranking on the faucet, she stepped into the tub that doubled as a shower. Although everything in this apartment screamed 1980s, she'd be a fool to move and give up the rent control.

The warm water coursed over her head and down her face. She washed her hair and lathered up a sponge to scrub her body clean of the ashes and the smell of burnt hair.

After the shower, she dried her hair, slipped into a pair of gray sweats and a camisole, and bundled her clothes to take them to the laundry room later. She gargled with warm water and boiled a cup of hot water in the microwave.

As she curled up in front of the TV, swirling the tea bag around in the cup, the doorbell rang. Startled, she lost her grip on the tea bag and the little square of paper at the end floated to the top of the steaming liquid. She eyed her purse with her weapon still tucked in the side pocket. Who the hell was paying a visit at this time of night?

"Kyra, it's Jake."

She swallowed against her raw throat and walked to the front door. Hadn't they agreed to leave things for tomorrow? Lying got harder for her at the end of the day, harder when she'd shed her armor. Getting harder with Jake.

She twisted the dead bolt and cracked open the door as if she expected the Boston Strangler…or The Player. Instead, Jake stood there with an uncertain smile on his handsome face and the box from Matt's unit in his arms. It wasn't *the* box, though.

She cleared her throat. "Is something wrong?"

"Gah." He grabbed his own throat. "I'm clearing my throat every five minutes. I found out something from Mr. Pargarian after you left, and I wanted to share it with you."

She blinked. He'd gone sleuthing behind her back?

Widening the door, she said, "You rescued that box of old papers? C'mon in."

He squeezed through, encased in the odor of the fire, hugging that damned box like it contained his last possessions on earth instead of Matt's.

"You smell." She pinched her nose. "I told you I went through that box. It contains some legal paperwork, receipts, nothing of importance."

"Maybe not." He tipped his chin toward the living room. "Can I set this down on the coffee table?"

"If you must." She wrinkled her nose.

"I know. I'm sorry. You smell like…roses." His face reddened as if he faced another fire. "Obviously, I came straight from the storage unit."

"I figured that." She crossed her arms over the thin white camisole, squishing down her braless breasts.

The previous and only time Jake had been in her apartment was when he had marched over here to confront her about being the daughter of one of The Player's victims. Now he was here to do what? Confront her about sneaking off to Matt's storage unit without telling him about it? She needed to do some confronting of her own.

She wedged her hands on her hips and thrust out her chest—to hell with her braless status. "I had every right to check out Matt's container on my own. I needed to do that by myself, and I don't appreciate that you tagged along."

He held up a pair of grimy hands. "I know. I could see something was off when you left Quinn's, and it's just the natural detective in me to want to find out the reason."

Her snort turned into a smile, and Jake jumped on it.

"Good excuse, huh?"

"It's just that—" she ran a hand through her loose hair "—Quinn always used to tell me that when I'd find him snooping through my things."

"Then I'm in good company." He started to sit down on her couch, and she waved her arms.

"I don't know if you've looked in the mirror, but you really are a mess. That T-shirt looks as if it's been used to fan a barbecue. I'd rather not have it on my couch."

"Sorry." Jake caught himself and tripped forward. "I can stand."

"Give it to me." She thrust out her hand. "I was just about to put my own clothes in the wash. I can add your T-shirt to the load."

He planted his hands against the thighs of his jeans. "As long as you don't take my jeans, too."

Tilting her head, she said, "They're not as bad as the shirt. I'm surprised you had time to go home after work before going to Quinn's. You were even there early."

"Sometimes I keep a change of clothes in my locker at the station." He grabbed the hem of his T-shirt and pulled it over his head, and Kyra completely forgot what he'd just said.

She swallowed against her scratchy throat as she drank in Jake's hard slabs of muscle shifting across his chest, and the tighter washboard pattern that stamped his abs. She'd seen him in casual clothes before, so she knew he hid something…alluring beneath his button-up shirts and ties, but she hadn't realized he was sex on a stick, or rather a branch, a trunk.

"You have someplace you want me to put this?"

"Put what?" Her heavy eyes, sated with the pure masculinity of his body, slowly tracked to his face.

He waved the shirt in his hand like a white flag.

"This T-shirt. Do you think it'll be done before I leave? I'd rather not drive home in my work car shirtless."

Home? She wasn't sure she wanted him to go home… ever.

"Yeah, yeah, I'll take it and dump it in with my stuff. The wash shouldn't take more than forty minutes, and the drying will be quick with just a few things in the dryer." She grabbed the shirt from his hand, careful to avoid the touch of his fingers. She'd almost been burned once tonight. She didn't need a scorching now.

Holding the shirt away from her body, she turned and looked back over her shoulder. "While I get our things in the laundry, you can wash up in the bathroom. I don't know what you used to clean your face after the fire, but it was largely ineffective. Then I'll get you some tea and honey for your throat and you can tell me what's so important about that box of junk."

"This way?" He pointed toward her bedroom door.

"There's a bathroom to your right." She didn't need the guy wandering through her bedroom, close to her bed.

She emptied the hamper in her bathroom and dumped the soot-stained clothes inside. Then she marched across the small courtyard to the laundry room and shoved everything into a washing machine.

When she returned to the apartment, she glanced briefly at Jake, hoping he hadn't removed any more of his clothing. With his jeans on below his bare torso, he perched on the edge of her couch, the lid now off the box and his hands plunged inside.

When would she finally get Matt out of her life for good? She banged around in the kitchen and held up a cup. "I'm going to make you some tea. One of the firefighters suggested tea and honey for the throat. Do you also want some water?"

He glanced up, his dark brows a V over his nose, both hands clutching pieces of paper. "Yeah, some water would be great."

She filled up a glass of water for him and took it and her own teacup back into the living room. "What's so important about that box?"

"Besides the fact it's the only surviving item from Matt's storage container?" He took the glass from her hand and glugged down half the water, his eyes watering. "I needed that."

"I'll give you more once you start talking." She took a sip of tea, watching him through the steam.

He scooped up a handful of papers and waved it at her. "I don't know if you noticed when you looked in here the first time, but these are not all old. Pargarian told me that Matt had last been to the unit a couple of months ago—so, while the Copycat Player was still active and you were getting those playing cards."

"Okay." She hadn't noticed any dates. She'd been looking for more pictures and…evidence. "What's in there?"

"Like you said—legal papers, receipts, notes. But they're recent, from the time Matt was actively stalking you."

She shivered and cupped her tea. Judging from some of those photos in the box she'd torched, there hadn't been a time when Matt wasn't stalking her. "I'm not sure what you hope to find in there, Detective, but I'm willing to help you."

"Glad to hear that." He downed his water and held out his glass for more.

His tea had finished steeping, so she returned with

his water in one hand and tea in the other. "After you rehydrate, you really should sip the tea. It helps."

"I will." He grabbed the edges of the box and tipped it over on the coffee table. Stacks of clipped and stapled papers fell out, along with slips and scraps of paper.

She grabbed the ones bunched together and squinted at the embossed blue letterhead for an attorney's office. "I think we can sort these into Matt's legal documents, right?"

"You start that pile, and I'll fish out all the receipts. Who knows? They may be telling."

She'd figured Jake had used the box as an excuse to come over here and grill her about why she'd kept the storage facility a secret from him, but he barely touched on that and seemed to think they'd find something in this mess to support Matt's claim that someone had paid him to plant those cards near her apartment and car.

She had her doubts. Matt wasn't that organized. Most of his illegal dealings he kept in his brain, away from the prying eyes of the cops. Nobody could get into Matt's brain—at least not for free.

She stacked the documents in a neat pile detailing a very messy life.

She smoothed her hand over the stack. "Any luck?"

Jake looked up from the three piles he'd set up on the table. "No, but he has some purchases here I think his parole office would've been interested in knowing about."

"This is just wishful thinking. Even if you could find something that proved Matt took payment from someone to torment me with those cards, how would that help your case? Jordy is dead and gone."

"I feel it here." Jake pounded his bare chest with his fist. "It's an instinct. Ask Quinn."

"I've heard plenty about Quinn's instincts over the years. They didn't always pan out." She rose from her place on the floor across the coffee table from Jake. "More tea? Water?"

"The tea felt good on my throat, but I'll have some more water. Do you think the clothes can be switched to the dryer?"

"Probably close." She grabbed his glass and cup. "I'll check."

He curled his fingers around her wrist. "Do you take your piece with you when you go to the laundry room at night?"

"I don't usually do my laundry at night. I was going to save those sooty clothes for tomorrow."

Releasing her arm, he pushed off the couch, and a few of Matt's scraps showered to the floor. "Then let me go. Do you have any dryer sheets?"

"I already put one in the dryer next to the washer I used. Just load and go." She jingled a basket of coins on her way into the kitchen. "A quarter for ten minutes. You can probably get away with thirty. It's light stuff."

"I think I've got some change." He patted the front pocket of his jeans on his way out the door.

As she rinsed the two teacups, she mused on how great it was to have a half-naked man in her place doing laundry. She didn't know about his instincts, but she'd felt that he wanted to be close to her and just maybe it didn't have anything to do with Matt's bits of paper.

Jake yelled from the front door. "Hey, there's a mangy cat here trying to get in your apartment."

She leaned into the small foyer from the kitchen. "Keep him there. I'll bring him some milk and food."

She splashed a little milk into a bowl and took a box of kibble from the cupboard.

Jake widened the door for her, and the cat was threaded around his ankles. "I'm afraid to move."

"Good idea." She squeezed past him, and his bicep brushed the front of her camisole, giving her tingles in all the right places. She crouched, set down the milk and shook the dry food into the bowl already across from her door.

"You're an advocate for pets as well as people." Stepping back, he held the door open for her, giving her a wide berth.

Had he felt the electricity between them, too?

"Just this guy. The neighbors already hate me for encouraging him." She slipped back into the kitchen to get Jake more water.

He took up his position on the couch again, placing his glass on the end table. Rubbing his hands together, he said, "We're halfway through the box. I know Matt isn't going to disappoint."

"You don't know Matt." Before she sat, she reached across the table to grab the pieces of paper that had fallen to the floor. Jake had gotten the same idea at the same time, and they bumped heads.

"Ouch." She drew back, rubbing her forehead.

"Sorry." He reached across the coffee table and smoothed his thumb down her cheek. "You've had a rough night."

She parted her lips, unable to form one word. The rough pad of his finger felt like magic, soothing away any doubts she had about him. Her breath came out in short spurts, and her eyelashes fluttered as if she faced that inferno again and couldn't stare into the heat.

His thumb moved from her face to her bottom lip, which throbbed under his touch.

"You know—" his voice roughened as if he'd never

had that tea "—we've never even kissed. I've thought about that a lot, wondered what your lips would taste like."

"And what did you come up with?" Her voice came out breathy like a bad actress in a B movie.

"Ice." His warm breath caressed her cheek, and she didn't even mind that it smelled slightly of charcoal. "A cool, cherry Popsicle."

"I think I'm going to disappoint you."

"Never." He slanted his mouth over hers and touched her lips in a light kiss. Then he deepened the kiss, caressing her lips with his own, his tongue probing in gentle exploration.

Her awkward position hunching over the coffee table caused her to start listing to the side, so she curled an arm around Jake's neck to steady herself.

He took that as a definite yes and cinched his hands around her waist, pulling her toward him in another awkward scramble over the coffee table with Matt's life between them. That was no deterrent. She'd been waiting so long for the kiss that she could easily scale a coffee table.

Digging her fingers into Jake's broad shoulders, Kyra stepped over the table and fell against him. They toppled sideways onto the couch, and Jake, in a feat of grace and talent, never broke the connection of their kiss.

He moved his lips against hers. "Better to have you on my side."

As he rolled her onto her back, she splayed her hands across the hard planes of his chest. The man was solid in every way, and she wanted him on her side. She did.

He wedged his finger under her chin, tipping back her head. His kisses moved from scorching her lips to her jawline and then her neck.

Her head fell to the side as his tongue found the depression at the base of her throat. Her lashes fluttered open, and her clouded gaze swept the mess scattered across the table. She didn't want to think about Matt now. She didn't want to think about anything other than the sensations soaking her nerve endings.

Then a scribbled word jumped out at her from one of the scraps of paper. She blinked and narrowed her eyes, even as Jake murmured a question in her ear, the low, throaty sound of an invitation.

She lifted her head, and her heart slammed against her chest as she made out the words: *laprey.*

Chapter Seven

Jake repeated the urgent question that had just left his lips, one hand splayed on the smooth skin of her stomach, his fingers inches from her right breast. "Do you want me to continue?"

Her body stiffened beneath his, and then her back arched, one leg slipping off the side of the couch. "Oh, my God."

He snatched his hand away from her warm belly. "I'm sorry."

She wriggled beneath him as if to dislodge him, and he sprang up and sat back on his heels.

Free of him, she scrambled from the couch, banging her shin on the coffee table and taking a few staggering steps like a boozer on a bender. Had he misread every sign from her?

"I'm sorry, Kyra. I thought…" He spread his hands, his naked torso making him feel exposed and clumsy.

Her fingers crept into her loose blond hair, and she shook her head back and forth. "You thought right. You did nothing wrong, Jake. It's me. I thought I was ready for something like this, and I'm just not."

Her words socked him in the gut, and he escaped from the soft couch that seemed to mock him now. "Yeah, sorry. I got carried away by the excitement of the evening. For a minute, I started believing I was the white knight who came to your rescue. My daughter keeps reminding me that girls don't need rescuing."

He was babbling like an idiot, and she looked as if she'd seen a ghost. His seduction techniques must've gotten really rusty in the years since his divorce.

"I'm sorry I intruded on your space. I'm sorry I came here unannounced."

She sliced her hand through the air. "Stop apologizing. I was all on board until… I wasn't."

"Okay. I'll get my shirt from the dryer and get out of your hair." His gaze wandered over her shiny tresses, free from the constricting ponytail for once. He'd been looking forward to running his own hands through those silky locks.

As he made a beeline for the front door, she called his name; he pretended not to hear. He was surprised he heard anything over the roaring in his ears. What an idiot. The woman was as cold as ice. She'd shown him that over and over. Shown him she couldn't be trusted.

He grabbed the hamper by the front door and stalked to the laundry room, feeling as if the fire from the storage facility had followed him. She'd lied to him tonight about going to the facility and then lied about the light on her phone dying. How many red flags did a man need?

He'd missed all the red flags his wife had been throwing about her affair, too. Maybe he was colorblind.

The dryer still had six minutes on the timer, but he stabbed the Cancel button anyway. He gritted his teeth as he watched the clothes flop around behind the glass door, mimicking his thoughts. He didn't even wait until

the spinning stopped before he yanked open the door
and thrust his hand into the warm drum.

He bunched the clothes in his fist and tossed them
into the basket. He plucked his shirt from the pile and
pulled it over his head. He'd be damned if he'd go back
into that apartment half-naked, vulnerable.

Holding the hamper in front of him, he trudged back
to her place. The green-eyed cat gave him a knowing
look. "You know how it feels to be kicked out, too,
don't you, buddy?"

He pushed through the door without even shutting
it behind him and dropped the plastic hamper on the
floor. "They're dry enough."

"Were you talking to someone out there?"

"The cat."

She had her hands in the pockets of her gray sweats,
one bare foot on top of the other. "I'm sorry, Jake."

"Now we're both apologizing." He tugged on the
hem of his shirt and smoothed out a wrinkle from the
front. "Forget it. We both made a mistake."

Her eyes widened for a second, and the luscious lips
that had been his for such a short time trembled. "I…"

Pointing over her shoulder, he said, "I'm just gonna
grab that stuff, if you don't mind. You said you didn't
want the box."

"Oh, no, you can have it." She swept her arm to the
side in a magnanimous gesture that seemed to promise
the world instead of a box of junk. *You can't have me,
but you're welcome to that crap.*

He walked past her, his back stiff. He placed the
empty box on the floor at the edge of the table and swept
everything inside it, destroying his careful sorting. It
didn't matter. He had to get out of here.

He stopped at the door and glanced over his shoulder. "If your cough gets worse, see a doctor."

"You, too."

He raised his hand and escaped into the cool night, or maybe it just felt cool because of the heat bubbling inside him.

The cat flicked his tail and blinked. Jake growled at him. "Good luck."

WHEN JAKE SLAMMED the door, it seemed to shake the whole apartment—seemed to shake her to her bones. She dashed at the tear trailing down her cheek and withdrew the crumpled piece of paper from her pocket.

She didn't have time right now to regret her abrupt dismissal of Jake. She could've pretended. She could've put the paper's words, which matched the email address on the message, out of her head and made love to Jake. Matched him kiss for kiss. Still, if she was going to be with Jake, she wanted to give him her full attention. Now she might never have the chance at all.

She shook her head and smoothed the scrap of paper in her palm, reading it out loud. "'LA Prey' or 'La Prey.'"

What did it mean? Was it some Spanish word she didn't know? Didn't look Spanish. Or French. Could it be someone's name? Nobody would use their real name to send a threat to her.

But now she held a link in her hand that there was a connection between the cards left for her during Jordy Cannon's murder spree and the email sent to her after the murder of Andrea Miles. Matt had contact with La Prey. He was probably the one paying Matt to leave the playing cards. Now, with Matt gone, La Prey had taken on the job of tormenting her himself. Why?

She picked up Jake's glass from the end table with a stab of guilt piercing her heart. This was what Jake had been looking for—a strong suggestion that someone had paid Matt to plant the cards—and she'd hidden it from him. She'd done more than that to him, something she didn't want to examine right now.

Jake was wrong to believe her issues had anything to do with Jordy Lee Cannon's crimes or Andrea's murder. Finding out who was harassing her wasn't going to lead to Andrea's killer, and Jake had already dealt with Jordy.

Maybe Matt had been the one who was paying La Prey, not the other way around. Matt had that picture of the foster family in his possession. He could've scanned it and sent it to La Prey to send on to her. Maybe Matt had already paid this guy to keep up the reign of terror against her. Maybe Matt's lackey didn't even know his benefactor was dead.

She put the cups in the dishwasher and picked up the hamper on the way to her bedroom. She plunged her hand into the warm, slightly damp clothes and dropped to the edge of the bed. Jake couldn't even wait for his T-shirt to dry—and she didn't blame him.

Why couldn't she just come clean with him…about everything? She fell back on the bed, her legs dangling over the side. And see *that* look in his eyes?

Was it worse than the look she'd witnessed tonight? Hurt? Confusion?

She rolled to her side, curling her legs to her chest. She needed to talk to someone. She needed her mom.

THE NEXT MORNING, Jake stumbled into the station, bleary-eyed and still hacking up black gunk. He'd inhaled more of that smoke than he'd thought—had made him go temporarily insane, too. From now on, Kyra Chase could stay in her corner and he'd stay in his.

He plopped into his chair and stared at his blank computer monitor. But, as long as he was in his corner, he had some work to do. He yanked open his top desk drawer and fished around for loose business cards, plucking them out one by one. He needed a better filing system.

A punch to his arm interrupted his task.

"What are you doing in there, searching for old lottery tickets?"

Jake jerked his head up at Billy and snapped his fingers in his face. "Weren't you dating someone from DCFS last year during one of your breaks with Simone?"

"Yes, I was." Billy rolled his eyes to the ceiling, finger on his chin. "Tara Liu."

"Did it end well?" Jake tapped a stack of business cards on his desk, holding his breath. You never knew with Billy.

"Yeah, yeah. Tara's a great girl. Bad timing all around." Billy folded his arms. "You need a favor?"

"Do you think Tara would be game?"

Billy winked. "She was game for a lot."

"Okay, I don't need to hear about it." Jake formed his fingers into a cross. "Do you think she'd help me out with something not by the book, as long as it wasn't hurting anyone?"

"As long as it doesn't hurt those kids. She's fiercely protective of the children in the system."

"This is old news, before her time. Do you have her direct number, and can I drop your name?" Jake swept the cards back into his drawer and slammed it. "Will she remember your name?"

"Really?" Billy tugged on the lapels of his expensive jacket.

"Okay, Romeo. Get me her number."

Billy pulled out his cell phone and tapped the screen. "I'll send it to you."

Seconds later, Jake's phone signaled a new message and he retrieved Tara Liu's number from Billy's text. He tipped the phone at Billy, who was slipping out of his jacket and taking the desk next to him. "Thanks."

Jake pushed the chair back, hand curled around his phone, and made for the door. He didn't need the whole task force listening in on every thread he decided to pursue—and he believed Matt Dugan's past was linked to these copycats.

He nearly plowed into Kyra at the entrance to the war room. "Whoa, sorry. How's your throat?"

"Still a little scratchy. Yours?"

"Same." He brushed past her, the phone digging into his sweaty palm. Without a backward glance, he took the stairs down to the first floor and burst out into the sunshine. He got behind the wheel of his Crown Vic and called Tara Liu.

Her impersonal voice-mail message greeted him. In her line of work, she probably didn't answer calls from unknown numbers, so he'd expected this.

"Tara, this is Detective Jake McAllister, LAPD Robbery-Homicide. I got your number from my partner, Billy Crouch. I have a favor to ask you…off the record."

She might not return his call due to that tagline, but he wanted to be up-front. He hated the gradual wheedling of favors from people, the groveling and begging. He liked to state his case and know right away if it was a go.

He dragged a sheet of paper from his pants pocket

containing information about Matt Dugan's time in the system and smoothed it out on his thigh.

The phone rattled in his cup holder, and he grabbed it, seeing Tara's number on the display. "McAllister."

"Detective, this is Tara Liu with DCFS returning your call."

"Thanks for the speedy response, Tara, and you can call me Jake."

"Not J-Mac?"

"If you want. I take it Billy told you some stories about me—all false, I'm sure."

Her laugh trilled over the line. "How is Billy? Back with his wife?"

Jake swallowed, not wanting to get caught up in Billy's tangled romantic web. "On and off. You know."

"I *do* know." She cleared her throat in a way that marked a delineation between social and business. "What can I help you with? Are you and Billy on the Andrea Miles case?"

"We are. We re-formed the task force and are treating this like a possible serial."

She sucked in a breath. "You want my help with that?"

"It is related." He thought so, anyway. He didn't have to give her all the details. Her voice indicated she'd be eager to help with a serial killer case.

"I can help you off the record, but not if it puts any of my kids at risk. Is that understood?"

"Yes, ma'am." He folded the corner of the paper in his lap and took a deep breath. "I'm looking for information about a person who left the system about ten years ago. You weren't with the department then, were you?"

"Just a grad student in social work, but I can access the records. What are you looking for?"

"Primarily the names of his foster families while he was in the system, when he was a teen. I don't need the whole history."

During the silence on the other end of the line, Jake chewed on his bottom lip.

"The families are supposed to have anonymity." Tara clicked her tongue. "But you are a cop, and you're working a case. I can get you that info on your subject, and it doesn't even have to be under the radar. I wouldn't be doing anything sneaky."

"I don't want to have to go through regular channels, Tara. I don't want to do the paperwork or have to come up with a subpoena. Are you down with that?"

Her answer came almost immediately. "I don't know why, but I know enough from dating Billy that you guys do things off the record for a reason."

Jake gave a silent thanks to his partner and let out a quiet breath through his nostrils. He didn't want to let on to Tara that he'd been holding it. "Thanks. I'll be in your debt, so if you ever need anything, don't hesitate to ask."

"Ooh, I like the sound of that—not that Billy isn't already in my debt, but to have two LAPD homicide detectives at my beck and call is delicious." Again, the clearing of the throat to return to business. "What's the name of this person?"

Jake crumpled the piece of paper with Matt's info on it. He didn't owe anything to Kyra. If she was going to play games with him, he'd play.

"The name of the person is Lake. Marilyn Lake."

"Oh, I thought you were going to give me a male name."

So did I.

He answered, "Did you? You must've misunderstood or I misspoke. This is a girl I'm tracking."

"Marilyn Lake. Left the system about ten years ago?"

"Yes."

"Middle name?"

"Monroe, if you can believe that, and her nickname was Mimi."

"I don't laugh at anyone's names. My name is Tara Scarlett, and I'm Chinese." She shuffled some papers, or maybe that was chewing. "I will look into Marilyn Monroe Lake, and I'll get back to you later today if I have the time. Is there a deadline on this?"

"Today would be great if you can get to it, but there's no urgency."

When the call ended, Jake sat in his car cupping his phone in his hands. The conversation with Tara had left a bad taste in his mouth, and he had to work hard to convince himself he wasn't doing this as revenge for getting shut down by Kyra.

Kyra was keeping something from him that he believed could help in this investigation. He had to trust that she didn't think her information was relevant. He couldn't see her allowing a killer to roam free if she really thought she had a way to stop him.

Nonetheless, she wasn't a detective.

He'd been planning to ask Tara to research Matt, but if Matt and Kyra had shared the same foster family at one point, he might as well start with Kyra's background—and that picture she took from Matt's dresser mirror.

Jake swung one leg out of the car and planted it on the ground. Though his phone had been going off while he'd been on the line with Tara, he didn't plan on making this car his permanent office. He'd return the calls when he got back to his desk.

As he got out of the car, Billy rushed toward him, pointing a finger at his chest. "You're already in position, so you can drive."

Jake's pulse jumped. "Drive where?"

"There's been another homicide. Our killer just gave us another chance to catch him."

Chapter Eight

Jake peeled off his gloves and shoved them into the pocket of his jacket. He flipped his sunglasses over his eyes and peered at Billy pacing the sidewalk in front of Crystal Monroe's house, occasionally shouting instructions at some poor cop who got into his line of sight. His partner needed to talk to Kyra.

Jake pulled back his shoulders and strode toward Billy. "I think we can let the CSI guys do their thing, Cool Breeze."

Billy's nickname had never fit him less.

He ran a hand through his short Afro, a muscle ticking wildly at the corner of his mouth. "Coroner's van isn't here yet. We could've missed something. I need to take another look at her, one more look at her hair."

Jake grabbed Billy's sleeve as he turned toward the house. "That's Crystal Monroe, brother. She's not Sabrina, any more than Andrea was."

"But her hair, Jake." Billy's dark, liquid eyes pleaded with him. "There's something about her hair."

Jake released Billy's arm and patted it, while swiveling his head around. Nobody needed to see Billy falling apart at the scene of a homicide.

"Sure, man. Let's have another look at her hair." He wiggled his fingers into another pair of gloves as he followed Billy back into the house and then the bedroom, where the body of Crystal lay tucked up in her bed.

Poking his head into the room, Jake said, "Can I get you ladies and gents to clear out for a minute? One more thing we need to check on the body."

The crime scene techs grumbled as they packed away their equipment, and Clive, who was just about to dust for prints on the closet door, raised his eyebrows at Jake.

Jake gave Clive a slight shrug and pulled the door closed after him. "Billy, you need to get it together. This is his second African American victim, but it doesn't mean he's specifically targeting Black women, and they have nothing to do with…"

Billy raised a hand. "Sabrina used to do her hair like this sometimes, but Crystal's looks uneven."

Jake turned his gaze to the pretty young woman with her curly hair dancing on her shoulders, the queen of diamonds between her lips and a stain on her yellow bedspread where her left hand lay, bereft of its pinkie finger.

"Okay, Billy, check out her hair. Do your thing."

Billy reached out a trembling hand and took a lock of Crystal's hair between his gloved fingers. He pulled it out straight to its full length. Keeping the hair extended, he repeated the process with the other side like a hairdresser checking for symmetry. It didn't reach as far as the other lock of hair.

Billy twisted his head over his shoulder, a triumphant light in his eyes, a lift to the corner of his mouth. He whispered, "He took it. He snipped off some of her hair to keep for himself."

And bam—Billy had discovered the personal trophy for this killer, the one Quinn insisted had to exist to give the murders meaning beyond the copycat aspect.

"Good job." Jake thumped Billy on the back. "Now let's allow the techs back in here before they riot."

As they walked to the car, Billy's shoulders started to slump, and he was almost doubled over by the time Jake stuffed him into the passenger seat. He turned to Billy.

"These women have nothing to do with your sister, Billy. Sabrina is not going to all of a sudden turn up a victim of this killer."

"Maybe not *this* killer." Billy slammed his fist against the dashboard. "I'm sorry, Jake. I don't know what came over me when I saw Crystal dead and realized we had a second Black victim. It's not that it's any more horrendous because this killer is targeting African American females. That's not what has me upset."

Jake clapped Billy on the shoulder. "I know that. You're thinking about Sabrina. You're seeing your sister in these victims. It's bringing back her disappearance all over again."

Billy covered his eyes briefly. "Did I make a fool of myself back there?"

"I don't think anyone other than me noticed you weren't being Cool Breeze. However—" Jake started the engine "—we do have a therapist on the task force. Take advantage of that. Kyra's here to help not just the victims' families but the cops on the task force."

"Is she helping you?" Billy's sly smile indicated he was coming back to himself.

"I think we're probably better off as colleagues."

"If you say so." Billy grabbed the door handle.

"Where are you going?" Jake asked.

"We have to finish canvassing the neighborhood. I'm sure there are more than a few cameras around. No visible signs of break-in, victim murdered in bed. He was lying in wait for her, just like with Andrea. He knew her habits, knew she lived alone. He must've been stalking her."

"Are you all right? I can do it. You can take the car back to the station, and I'll catch a ride with one of the patrol units."

"Really?" Billy tipped his sunglasses to the edge of his nose. "We all know I'm the charming one. How are you going to get those neighbors to talk?"

Jake swallowed the lump in his throat. "Good to have you back."

He and Billy spent the next two hours going door-to-door, viewing and, in some cases, taking video footage from home security systems.

If Crystal had a stalker, they were going to find him.

JAKE AND BILLY burst into the task force war room, their shoulders thrust back in confidence, their heads held high with bravado. Her heart flipped. Had they found something?

Would Jake mention anything outside the task force briefing? He hadn't bothered to tell her there had been another murder. She'd found out just like everyone else at the station.

Her jaw hardened. If she'd put out last night for Jake, would she still be in his cozy confidence?

Her eyes stung, and she blinked. That wasn't fair to Jake. He'd been reading all her signs correctly until she saw that slip of paper. Now he wanted to get things back on a professional level to protect himself. She got that.

She shoved away from her desk and marched up to the two detectives. "You guys look like you found something."

"We think he stalked this victim, too." Billy's gaze darted from Jake's face to hers. "We're going to compare some of the cars coming and going in Crystal's neighborhood to the ones in Andrea's neighborhood."

"I can start that." Jake shoved Billy toward Kyra. "Why don't you take our resident therapist out for lunch."

"Me?" Kyra poked a finger at her chest. "Things not going well with Megan? You need another setup?"

"Ooh, savage." Billy clutched his chest and fake-stumbled back. "Actually, I'd like to…get a few things off my chest, and Jake suggested I talk to you."

He did? Her skin tingled. She must not be completely on his blacklist.

"Then lunch it is. Come get me when you're ready. I'm going to reach out to Crystal's family." She sauntered back to her desk, and twenty minutes later Billy approached her, his usual swagger subdued.

"I'll drive, and I have a place in mind, if that's okay."

"Lead the way." She grabbed her sweater and purse from the back of her chair. Even in a mood, Billy displayed his chivalry by stopping at the door and sweeping her through with his arm.

He led her to his sedan, and twenty minutes later they were seated in a booth in a dark Italian restaurant more suited to an illicit afternoon affair than a conversation about murder…although Kyra had a feeling they weren't here to discuss the Copycat Player case, at least not directly.

Billy got down to business after they both ordered chopped salads and iced teas. Hunching over the table, elbows planted on either side of the basket of garlic bread, Billy rested his chin on his folded hands. "I had a…a kind of breakdown this morning at Crystal's murder scene."

She schooled her face into a smooth palette. Billy

had been around the homicide block several times, and a strangulation did not usually present the most gruesome of murder scenes. Had he hit a wall this time?

As the thoughts careened through her brain, pinging off each other, she simply said, "Go on."

"Crystal was a young African American woman, like Andrea Miles. And like I told Jake, the fact that the victims are Black or that this killer may be targeting Black women doesn't make it worse because I'm also Black." He ran a hand over his mouth. "But it does make it worse for me because my sister Sabrina disappeared five years ago."

"I'm sorry."

"Poof." He snapped his fingers. "She was gone without a trace. Took her keys, her phone, her car and then disappeared off the face of the earth."

Although Kyra had many questions about Sabrina's disappearance, that was not why they were here. "Seeing these murdered women makes you think about Sabrina."

"Yes, and it's crazy because neither of them particularly looked like my sister and Sabrina wasn't assaulted or taken from her home. Her car, with her purse, her turned-off phone, her keys, was found abandoned at a store near the airport. No sign of foul play. So, it's not like I believe Sabrina could've been a victim of this same killer five years ago. It's just seeing these lifeless women reminds me of my sister."

"Did you have the same feelings of panic when you saw Andrea's body, too, or just today?"

"I felt—" he picked up a piece of garlic bread with his long fingers and ripped it apart "—strange when I saw Andrea's body. Sad. I mean—don't get me wrong—we always feel sad, bad, upset for the victims. We're human, but we have a job to do there, and I've always been able to do that job dispassionately because that's the best way to respond to get justice for these victims."

She nodded, and he dropped the mangled bread on his plate. "I don't know why I'm telling you that. You're good friends with Roger Quinn, one of the most legendary detectives LAPD has ever seen. I'm sure you know how we operate."

"I want to know how *you* operate." She tipped her head at the approaching waiter, who seemed well versed in discretion.

"Not like this." Billy stabbed at his salad, spearing a pepperoncini. "How do you think I got my nickname?"

She cocked her head, taking in his tailored shirt, a pale yellow she was pretty sure only he could pull off with the turquoise tie. "Jake assured me it was your sartorial splendor."

Billy's familiar grin broke for the first time since she had seen him at the station. "That's part of it, but I tend to keep a cool head during investigations. J-Mac is the hothead, but then you already know that."

"We're here to talk about you." She poked around her salad. "Why do you think you started losing your… cool over Andrea's murder?"

He set down his fork and gazed into his tea. "Maybe it's the time of year. Summer to fall. There's always a stillness to the air in LA about now. Do you feel it? It was like this when Sabrina went missing."

She did feel it. The Player had murdered her mother about the same time of year. In fact, that anniversary was approaching.

Nodding, her mouth full, Kyra allowed Billy to set up the scene. She'd prefer he discuss his feelings, but he was a detective and narrative trumped feelings. He recited the events with no emotion, as if they'd been running through his head on a constant loop. They probably had been.

"Sabrina was the youngest of my three sisters, sort of an afterthought. She was just twenty when she disappeared." His hand fisted around his fork. "It's not even classified as a homicide, even after all these years, because there was no evidence she didn't leave voluntarily. I knew she hadn't, though. She wouldn't. She was in school, working, had a social life."

Kyra asked, "You were a detective at that time?"

"Yeah, that's the crazy part. It was my job, and I couldn't find her."

"Did she disappear in the Northeast Division?"

He swallowed. "No. She was living in Riverside at the time."

"So, finding her really wasn't your job, was it?" She swirled the ice in her glass with a straw. "But finding this second copycat, the one who murdered these two African American women, *is* your job."

"We have to get him, Kyra. We can't let him get away with this. Those families need justice. Hell, all families need justice. Those women need justice...and so does Sabrina."

"You've brought justice to a lot of families, Billy, yet all that can't make up for your failure to find Sabrina."

He choked on a leaf of lettuce and covered the lower half of his face with a napkin. "You just told me it's not my fault, not my failure."

"You don't believe that."

"I don't." He crumpled the napkin on the table, keeping it in his hand. "Do you think if we catch this guy, I can forgive myself? Maybe come to believe Sabrina's disappearance isn't my fault?"

"I don't know, Billy." Had she ever forgiven herself for sleeping through her mother's murder? The cops never caught The Player. Quinn couldn't catch him. Her mother never got justice.

She sipped her iced tea and met Billy's anxious expression over her straw. "Tell me how you felt when you saw Crystal's body in that bed."

JAKE UNWRAPPED HIS Italian sub and took a bite. As he mopped the oil dribbling down his chin, he glanced toward Kyra's corner desk. She and Billy had been gone for over an hour. If anyone could help his partner, Kyra could.

Jake had tried to do some digging on his own into Sabrina's disappearance and kept coming up against a brick wall. Her car, purse and phone had been found in a big-box store parking lot, out of the camera's sight. There had been no sign of a struggle, but Sabrina had never used a debit or credit card again.

She'd dropped off the face of the earth. The original detectives on the case had few leads—no boyfriend, no ex-husband, no jealous women, not even a possible serial killer operating in the area of Riverside at the time.

Didn't mean there wasn't one. Didn't mean some guy wasn't traveling from state to state snatching women. Not all serial killers had a hunting ground or even an MO or signature.

The Player had changed up his MO from dumping his victims to strangling them in their homes to murdering them in their cars and leaving them. Serial killers could change their MOs but rarely changed their signatures. The Player's signature had been the card in the mouth and the missing finger.

And his disciples were copying his signature. Why? Why now? Disciples?

His cell phone rang and his heart thumped when he saw Tara Liu's number. She worked fast. It wasn't even the end of the day.

He got up from his desk and meandered to the window. "Hey, Tara. What did you find?"

"I found something quite interesting, Jake."

A soft rustle filled the pause and he couldn't stand it a second longer. "What?"

"I found nothing at all for Marilyn—Mimi—Lake."

"That's not possible. I know she was in the system."

"Oh, she's in the system, all right. I just can't access any of her files."

"What does that mean?"

"Marilyn Lake's DCFS files are on permanent lockdown. I don't think the Pope himself could get in there."

Chapter Nine

"Next time it's on me."

Jake's head jerked up at the sound of Kyra's voice floating across the room. He turned to the side and practically whispered into the phone. "Tara, do me one more favor. Check Matt Dugan's records for about the same time. Gotta go. Thanks."

Jake ended the call as Billy sauntered to the desk next to his. His partner shrugged out of his jacket and hung it over the back of his chair. He sat forward on the chair so as not to wrinkle his threads and peered over the top of his monitor.

Watching Kyra talk to Brandon, their tech guy, Billy spoke out of the side of his mouth. "That was a good call, man. Spilling my guts to Kyra helped. I promise I'm not going to fall apart at the next crime scene, regardless of whether or not the victim looks like my sister."

"Nothing to be ashamed about, Billy." With Kyra in his sights, Jake narrowed his eyes. "Did she do some voodoo on you? Hypnotize you? Put you into a trance?"

Billy cocked his head. "No, man. We just talked. In fact, she didn't say much at all. I know you don't put much stock in therapy, but there's something about it that helps."

"I'm glad. That's why I suggested it." Jake smacked his hand on the desk. "Now that she shrunk your head, we can get back to it."

"Did you go through the footage from the security cameras around the neighborhood?" Billy scooted his chair closer to Jake's desk and stared at the frozen video on Jake's computer screen.

Jake jabbed his fingers at the screen, circling a dark SUV. "We've already started identifying some of the cars that have repeat appearances on the block, and we've ruled out several as belonging to Crystal's neighbors. We also haven't noticed any vehicles that were present near both Andrea's and Crystal's houses."

Billy scratched his chin. "He could've driven two different cars. He's gotta know we're sitting here scanning security systems."

"Oh, he knows, all right." Jake shifted his mouse around and clicked on a couple of different icons on his display. "One security system on the block has been on the fritz the past few weeks. Guess which one."

"The one across the street from Crystal's. The one that would've had a clear view of her garage."

Jake snapped his fingers and pointed at Billy. "Bingo."

Billy whistled through his teeth. "The killer disabled it?"

"Most likely, isn't it? I mean, are we really supposed to believe that the most crucial camera is the one that's out?"

"What about in Andrea's neighborhood? Same thing?" Billy's dark eyes shone with curiosity and excitement, and Jake silently thanked Kyra for bringing his partner back, even though her own life remained shrouded in mystery.

"Perfect timing on that question. I was just about to look at some files Brandon sent me right before you and Kyra came back. Some of the homeowners on Andrea's block weren't around when the guys stopped by to collect video. They did another sweep, and Brandon sent me the results."

As Jake selected the different files, Billy hung over the keyboard, his breath coming in quick spurts. Jake waved the air in front of Billy's face. "Dude, lay off the garlic for lunch."

Grinning, Billy nodded toward Kyra, still in deep discussion with Brandon. "Then you'd better not kiss Ms. Chase over there. She ate the same thing I did for lunch."

Kiss Kyra? He'd be lucky if he got even that from her after she'd stopped his advances cold. And if she found out he was digging into her past, it would probably be game over.

"Okay, I'll remember that. In the meantime—" he flipped his hand in Billy's face "—back off."

Billy repositioned himself until he launched forward, bathing the air in enough garlic to ward off a bunch of vampires. He poked his finger at one of the files. "That's the address across from Andrea's house."

Jake opened the file, and they both slumped back in their chairs. Jake announced the bad news for both of them. "No security system at that house."

Billy said, "The next file must be the house next to it, but still across and in view of Andrea's garage."

Jake double clicked on the next file and choked when it opened.

This time Billy did the honors. "Damn, a security system that's been disabled for a few weeks. I know these things have issues—God knows we've had our problems with store and gas station footage—but what are the chances that security systems in two different locations, just where we need them, are down?"

"Without someone tinkering with the cameras, I'd say chances are pretty low." Jake crossed his hands behind his head and laced his fingers. "Our guy's not stupid. He's aware of the technology and he's savvy enough to disable it."

Billy drummed his long fingers on the desk. "Savvy enough to disable it and avoid it. We're not going to see his car on Andrea's or Crystal's streets. But we might..."

And like a good partner, Jake finished Billy's thought. "See it on another street. He may have crept into their neighborhoods on foot to avoid detection, but he had to have gotten there somehow. He wouldn't use public transportation with all the cameras and witnesses."

"I will set up a canvassing of the surrounding streets and see if we can pull some more video." Billy pushed back his chair.

"Brush your teeth first, seriously." Jake's phone buzzed on his desk, and his nosy partner glanced at the display.

"You reached Tara, huh?" Billy winked. "Give her my regards."

"Excuse me."

Jake nearly jumped out of his chair at the sound of Kyra's voice. She glided around here too silently for his liking. He nervously covered his buzzing phone with his hand.

"I'm sorry. You can get that." She pointed to the phone he was foolishly trying to hide.

"I'll call back." He raised his eyebrows and pasted on a fake pleasant smile—or at least he thought it was pleasant. He usually didn't do pleasant. "What can I help you with?"

What can I help you with? That sounded fake as hell.

She tilted her head slightly, her blond ponytail slipping over her shoulder. She'd had her hair loose the other night, and his fingers tingled with the memory of weaving them through her silky strands.

A rosy pink edged into her cheeks, but her blue eyes had a steely look. "Sorry to interrupt. I just wanted to let you know that the victims' advocacy group I'm working with is sending a car to the airport to meet Andrea's parents. I'm going to be there."

"Thanks for letting me know." Jake slid his hand from his phone and turned it facedown on his desk. "Those poor people."

"If they let slip any pertinent information about Andrea, I'll let you know so you can bring it up when you question them."

"Thanks, Kyra...and thanks." He jerked his thumb at Billy, now on the phone organizing the video collection effort around the two victims' homes.

"He'll be fine, but he needs to find his sister. Now I'll let you get back to your call." She drilled her index finger into the back of his phone and then spun around.

He released a long breath and scooped up the phone once Kyra had left the war room. Turning his back on Billy, he called Tara. "You have something for me on Matt Dugan already?"

"He was easier and I was already in the database, but don't get too excited."

Jake's leg started bouncing beneath the desk. "His files are locked down, too?"

"Not quite. I can see when he entered the system and his first several foster homes, but his record goes dark at about the time you're requesting. In other words, I can't access information about his final foster family before he was released from the system."

"Because it was Kyra's family."

"What?"

"Never mind. Thanks for your help, Tara. I owe you one, and I mean it."

"Don't you worry. I'll collect someday when you least expect it."

Jake ended the call and stared at Kyra's empty desk. Why were her and Matt's DCFS files hush-hush? He doubted the Pope had anything to do with the lockdown, but Kyra had some powerful people in her corner.

If the blackout was for her benefit... Maybe he'd had it all wrong. Maybe Kyra didn't even know about the secrecy of her DCFS files.

He had no intention of stopping here. What kind of detective would he be if he did? His gaze surveyed the room and locked onto Captain Castillo. If Kyra had powerful allies, Jake would start with one up close and personal.

KYRA STOOD BESIDE her car, pretending to look at her phone, keeping one eye on Billy's Crown Vic. If he was going to check out the cameras in the vicinity near the victims' homes, he'd have to take a trip out there—and she'd wait for him for however long it took.

It didn't take long.

With his tailored jacket draped over one arm, Billy strode to his car, his step faltering when he saw her.

She waved and called out, "Getting some directions. On your way to check out security systems?"

He drew closer and answered, "I am. That SOB had

to get to those houses some way, even if he did jump over a few fences to conceal his arrival."

She clicked her remote and turned suddenly as if she'd just thought of something. "Do I have to worry about Tara?"

"Huh?" Billy tilted his head down and peered at her over the top of his designer sunglasses.

"Tara, the woman calling Jake." She dropped her head and scuffed the toe of her shoe against her tire. "Is she my rival?"

Billy threw his head back and laughed. "An emphatic no on that one. Jake barely has time to handle one woman, let alone two. You're in the clear."

"Whew." She flicked her fingers across the nonexistent sweat on her forehead. "You said you knew Tara. Just a work thing?"

"Someone I dated at DCFS. Jake was looking for a favor." Starting for his car, Billy called over his shoulder, "I'll let him know you were worried. He'd be flattered."

"Oh, God. Please don't embarrass me. I'll look like a jealous idiot."

Billy lifted his hand, threw open his car door and got inside.

She sure hoped that was a sign of agreement. If Billy mentioned this conversation to Jake, he'd know that she knew he was looking into her background. It had to be that...didn't it?

She dropped behind the wheel of her own car and clutched it with both hands. Maybe she was being paranoid. Detectives often worked with DCFS. Why wouldn't Jake want a favor from one of the caseworkers?

Why should he hide his phone from her? Not that she hadn't been known to get nosy and try to see who was texting him. If she hadn't been snooping, she never would've learned about his meeting with Matt.

Why did he have to go behind her back? She bit the inside of her mouth, drawing blood. He went behind her back because she lied to him at every turn—and at every turn he met her at the pass.

Sighing, she cranked on the engine of her car. Although she'd been deceiving people all her life, she'd never tried it on a detective before. Quinn knew all her secrets. Hell, Quinn knew her secrets better than she did.

Quinn had told her to trust Jake, tell him everything. Easy for Quinn to say. She could do no wrong in Quinn's eyes. Ever since he'd rescued her, covered in her own mother's blood, stiff with shock and fear, he'd protected her. She walked on water, as far as Quinn was concerned; Jake had different standards.

Jake's wife had cheated on him, and as much as he blamed himself for her infidelity, he would never be able to trust a woman whose whole life was one big deception—a woman like her.

She flexed her fingers on the steering wheel of the car and set out to meet the other victims' rights advocate who'd be meeting Andrea's parents at the airport with her. Her breathing had returned to normal and her heart beat in her chest at a steady pace.

She didn't like that Jake was possibly snooping around in her background, but she knew he wouldn't find what he was looking for.

Her DCFS files were protected more securely than the gold in Fort Knox.

JAKE HUNG ON Castillo's door frame. "Can I talk to you for a minute, Captain?"

The captain glanced up, a quick look of irritation on his haggard face. By Castillo's appearance, you'd think he was the one in charge of a task force for a serial killer who'd just claimed his second victim.

Castillo recovered quickly. "Sure, sure. Sit down. I heard Cool Breeze is out there casting a wider net for security footage. Good idea."

Jake closed the door behind him and sat in one of the chairs facing Castillo's neat desk, his gaze tracking across the family pictures behind Castillo's head—soccer games, ballet recitals, vacations to Yellowstone. He'd missed out on all that with his own daughter.

"We discovered two cameras facing the victims' houses that weren't working in the crucial weeks leading up to their murders. We think he disabled them somehow."

Castillo tapped his pen on the desk blotter. "It doesn't sound like we're dealing with a stupid killer here, does it? Jordy Lee Cannon made the mistake of having prior contact with his victims. This guy seems to be choosing his randomly—unless he's zeroing in on African American women. You think the killer could be Black? Rare for a serial killer."

"It is, although not unheard-of. We did have the Grim Sleeper, who operated for years."

"How's Billy holding up?"

Jake's eyes popped open for a split second. Had the uniforms been talking? "He's great, good. Sharp as ever."

"Okay." A smile hovered at Castillo's lips. He knew Jake would never betray his partner. "You had a question about the task force? Need more people?"

"I had a question about Kyra Chase."

Castillo's eyes blinked rapidly. His hands rearranged

items on his desk as if mimicking the sorting going on in his brain. "I thought you were happy with her help on the Copycat Player task force. Is there a problem now? You have to let go of that incident with Lizbeth Kruger, Jake."

Jake's blood percolated as he sliced his hand through the air. "It has nothing to do with that, and I'm not ever going to get over that betrayal, but I've put it behind me."

"Then what about Kyra?"

"I, uh, stumbled across her files in DCFS." Jake rubbed out a spot on the edge of Castillo's desk with the pad of his thumb. "They're blocked, blacked-out, whatever you want to call it."

Castillo's dark eyebrows, where the salt hadn't invaded the pepper yet, jumped, and a look Jake couldn't identify spasmed across his face. "Why would you be looking into Kyra's foster system files?"

"I wasn't specifically looking into them." The lie slid from his mouth even as he knew that Castillo knew he was lying. "Just stumbled across. I was surprised they were locked down. Did Detective Quinn order that?"

Castillo spread his hands. "I have no idea. Didn't know they were dark, wouldn't know why they were dark, and, frankly, I don't care. I've heard some rumors that you and Kyra are…close. If you're using department resources to conduct your own background investigation on a romantic interest, I don't have to tell you how that looks—even if you are J-Mac, the hotshot homicide detective. Got it? Stop looking."

Jake's hands curled into fists on his knees. He didn't like Castillo's tone or his implications, but the captain wasn't wrong. He splayed his fingers and took a deep breath. He'd come a long way in his anger-management techniques.

"Understood. That's not the reason, by the way, but understood anyway. It has more to do with her foster brother Matt Dugan. I'll back off."

"Dugan has a rap sheet a mile long. All you have to do is look at it to follow the course of his sorry life." Castillo placed his hand on the receiver of his phone. "If there's nothing else, McAllister, I have a few calls to make before I leave today."

"Thanks for your time, Captain." Jake heaved himself out of the comfortable chair and shut Castillo's door behind him…very softly. Didn't want to give the guy the wrong impression.

Why the hell was Castillo so adamant about Jake keeping his hands off Kyra's files? Was the captain somehow involved in the masking?

By the time Jake returned to the task force conference room, most of his team members had left for the day. He sat heavily at his desk and rubbed his eyes.

Although he should just leave Kyra to her secrets, he couldn't shake the feeling that Kyra's past was somehow linked to these copycat killings. The obvious flag for his hunch was that her mother had been one of The Player's victims twenty years ago. As well, the lead homicide investigator on the case had taken Kyra under his wing. To the point where he'd ordered her DCFS record sealed?

Jake would bet on that. No use asking the old detective about it. Quinn's loyalty toward Kyra ran deep and wide. He'd never betray her secrets.

Jake rubbed his chin. Even if that betrayal meant catching a serial killer? But did it? What proof did he have that Kyra's background, other than the murder of her mother, had anything to do with the current rash of killings?

He grunted softly to himself. Maybe he should just be honest with himself and admit that he wanted to learn everything there was to know about Kyra Chase because he wanted… Kyra Chase.

He felt an undeniable connection and attraction to her despite the secrets that had erected a barrier between them. The roadblock wasn't just on his side, either. After his marriage crashed and burned, he vowed to never get into a relationship with a woman he couldn't trust.

Still, Kyra had her own reasons for holding him at arm's length. She didn't trust him, either, or at least she didn't trust him with her secrets.

Maybe she was right. Despite the strong chemistry between them, they weren't meant to be. Even if the attraction was good enough for a roll in the sheets a few times, at this point in his life he wanted more than that. He had a daughter he hardly knew. He wanted to establish some kind of home life here in LA, an environment where Fiona could visit more frequently.

He logged off his computer and shoved it into his case, along with files and notes on Andrea and Crystal. A folder fell on the floor, spilling its contents, and he looked into the dead eyes of Andrea Miles.

As he shoved the photo back into the folder, he muttered to himself, "Great environment for Fiona."

He slung his bag over his shoulder and swept his phone off the desk. It buzzed in his hand, indicating a text message. Maybe Billy had already gotten a line on some video.

Cupping the phone in his hand, he glanced at the display—unknown number, not uncommon for his work phone. He perched on the edge of his desk and opened the text: Buck and Lori Harmon are the names you're looking for.

Jake cocked his head and reread the message. Was he looking for names? He texted back: Who is this?

The message showed that it was delivered. He stared at his phone for two minutes. Then he called back the number. It went straight to a recording informing him that there was no voice mail for the number.

Someone wanted to remain anonymous. He'd never heard of Buck or Lori Harmon and didn't know he was looking for them.

One of the officers they'd brought onto the task force to help survey video called from across the room. "J-Mac, I'm out for the duration. You're the last man standing. You wanna lock up, or are you on your way out now?"

Blinking, Jake scanned the empty room and then glanced at the names in the text. He swung his bag onto his desk and pulled out his laptop. "I have a few more things to check. I'll close up shop on my way out."

The officer waved and left the door open.

Jake fired up his laptop again, his fingers tingling, eager to attack the keyboard. Should he look up the name in the criminal database or just in a search engine? Could this be the first big break in their case?

He started with a search engine and typed in the names. Texts and links spewed over the screen, and he clicked on the first one.

The article headline said it all, and he read it aloud to the empty room. "'Buck Harmon, Foster Father, Brutally Killed by Foster Child.'"

As soon as he read that the foster child who had murdered Buck was a sixteen-year-old female whose name was not being released because she was a juvenile, he didn't have to read any more. He knew her identity.

It was Marilyn Monroe Lake. Kyra Chase was a killer.

Chapter Ten

After the emotional meeting with Andrea's parents, Kyra stepped into the hushed atmosphere of the Santa Monica Public Library and inhaled the scent of musty pages that permeated the air despite the electronic age of digital everything. The public libraries had always been her refuge, and that comforting smell still brought her peace even though her mission today filled her with anxiety.

Brandon Nguyen was able to trace the IP address behind the email from "La Prey," as she'd decided to call him, and that IP address led to this library.

The fact that this was her local library, the one closest to her apartment, filled her with a kind of shivery dread.

Someone who knew about her past had been in this library sending an email to her work address, taunting her, threatening her, trying to frighten her. She didn't know what she hoped to find here. The phantom emailer was long gone. The librarian was not going to hand over any library records or CCTV video to her.

However, the librarian might hand it over to the police, specifically a homicide detective investigating a serial killer.

Kyra wandered to the row of computers where the

silence had been invaded by clicking keys and the soft giggles of high school students pretending to do homework. She trailed her hand across the keyboards of three unoccupied computers.

An old homeless woman on the last computer in the row looked up. "Psst."

Kyra raised her eyebrows and met a pair of lively dark eyes set in a leathery face besieged by lines running every which way. "Me?"

"Yeah, you." The woman drew herself up in the chair, pinning her sagging shoulders to the back. "You need to see the reference librarian to use the computers."

"Thanks for the tip." Kyra's gaze darted to the monitor in front of the woman, ablaze with pictures of gaunt models displaying haute couture, then dropped to the baggy gray Santa Monica College sweatshirt covering the woman's form like a sack and what looked like men's black slacks folded up at the ankle to reveal a dirty pair of sneakers with a hole in the toe.

Kyra's nose stung. "C-can I pay you for that advice?"

The woman's eyes lit up. "Well, that's what I'm here for. I'm the information desk…when I'm not designing clothes."

Two girls at the high school study table behind the computers sniggered and snorted. Kyra whipped her head around and gave the girls a hard stare.

The grins died on their lip-glossed mouths, and they hunched over their laptops.

Kyra reached into her purse and pulled a twenty out of her wallet. She slid it beneath the woman's keyboard. "Will that be enough?"

The homeless woman snatched it, and the bill disappeared among the folds of her clothes. "That will do."

"Do you come here every day and, um…work?"

The woman nodded.

"I suppose there are a lot of people using these computers over the course of a day."

"All the famous designers work here." The woman brushed a hand down the front of her sweatshirt, and Kyra knew she wasn't going to get anything coherent out of her.

"Everything okay?" A librarian, twirling a pair of glasses between her fingers, glanced between Kyra and the homeless lady.

"I think she wants to check out a computer, Inez." The woman turned back to her own screen, dismissing both of them.

"Thanks, Yolanda." The librarian, Inez, smiled at Kyra. "Is that right?"

"No, but I do want to talk to you about the computers."

Inez gestured with her glasses. "Follow me."

The librarian scooted behind the reference counter and faced Kyra across the smooth surface littered with flyers and cards. Inez had put her glasses back on, making her look more formidable.

Kyra put on her best therapist's smile—soothing, nonthreatening, understanding.

"I have a—" Kyra glanced over her shoulder and hunched toward Inez "—bit of a stalking problem."

"Oh, no." Inez pressed three fingers against her rather pale lips.

"Someone has been sending me unwanted emails from a bogus email address. I had a friend of mine who's in IT track down the IP address of the sender, and it came back to one of your computers here in the library." Kyra swept her arm behind her as if to indict the entire library in this stalker's crime.

"That's terrible." Inez's fingers trailed from her lips to her throat, and if she had pearls, she'd be clutching them. "You don't think Yolanda is responsible, do you?"

"Oh, no, no. I sort of have an idea who it is, and I'd like to catch him in the act. You know, have some proof to wave in his face." Kyra folded her hands on the counter on top of a stack of flyers announcing a story time.

"That's terrible. I had a stalker once." Inez slid her glasses to the tip of her nose and whispered, "My ex-husband."

Pursing her lips, Kyra shook her head. "Even when you know who it is, it can be frightening. Sometimes *because* you know who it is, it's even more frightening."

"I agree." Inez readjusted her glasses, which magnified her eyes. She waited quietly.

This was where being a cop came in handy. Kyra said, "I know this is an unusual request, but is there any way you can look at your records and let me know who was at a computer on a particular day at a particular time? Video footage would be even better."

Inez blinked. "I'm sorry. I can't do that."

"All I need is a peek." Kyra crossed her finger over her heart. "I swear, I won't tell anyone. I'm at my wit's end."

"I understand, but it's against our policy. Perhaps if you filed a report with the police. I could release that information to an officer."

"That's the thing." Kyra pressed her palms together and rested her fingers against her chin, silently apologizing to every cop she knew—even Jake. "I think my stalker *is* a cop, which makes things tricky."

"It certainly does. Santa Monica PD?"

Kyra nodded vigorously, hoping she'd never need the assistance of anyone at the SMPD.

"I'm sorry. I just can't." The eyes behind the glasses brightened. "Maybe you could do a stakeout. If he's coming at the same time every day, you could sleuth among the stacks and surprise him."

Kyra stifled a chuckle by smacking her hand over her mouth. When she'd arranged her features into a more fitting expression, she peeled her hand away from her mouth and said, "I might just do that, Inez. Thanks for your time, anyway."

Inez called after her back. "I'll keep my eyes open."

Several library patrons shushed the librarian, and Kyra waved a hand in the air. When she landed outside, she huffed out a breath. She'd known it was a long shot.

If she'd had Jake by her side, getting that information would've been a piece of cake. She could've had him by her side if she'd come clean about her past. She could have shown him the picture of the Harmons and told him why it was a threat to her, and in the very act of telling him, she'd remove the threat.

She'd kept that dark period of her past a secret from everyone, especially guys she was dating. While not wanting to scare anyone off, she'd been scaring men off for years with her secretive nature.

She didn't want to scare off this one.

Striding to her car, she snatched her phone from her purse and called Quinn. "I'm out and about. Do you want me to pick up some food and head over?"

"I was just going to heat up meat loaf. I'll do enough for two." He paused. "Are you all right?"

"Why do you ask?"

"Something in your voice, Mimi."

"I'll be right over."

She drove the short distance from Santa Monica to Venice down traffic-heavy Lincoln. Turning onto the street that led to the canals dropped her into a different world. Most likely Quinn wouldn't have been able to afford a house on the canals, blocks from Venice Beach, on his detective's salary, but his wife, Charlotte, had been a bestselling author of thrillers and mysteries and had sunk most of her money into their beach cottage, creating an oasis for Quinn away from the grit and grime of his job.

Jake had the same type of getaway with his home in the Hollywood Hills. His creative endeavors on two screenplays had allowed him to buy his own refuge from the job.

Kyra crossed the wooden bridge over the canal and knocked on Quinn's red door. Just as she was about to use her key, he answered.

Stepping over the threshold, she sniffed the air. "Smells yummy in here. Is this meat loaf another contribution from Rose?"

"It is. She's a damned good cook."

"Yeah, she's got something cooking for you, all right." Kyra opened her mouth and winked one eye in an exaggerated fashion.

Quinn poked her in the back. "Go on. At least one of my acquaintances has some home-cooking skills."

"Hey, I'm very good at picking up the phone and ordering." She breezed past Quinn into the kitchen. "You have any beers?"

"Now you're encouraging me to drink? You're usually trying to hide them from me." He sat on a stool at the counter that separated the kitchen from the living room. "Bad day?"

She popped her head out of the fridge, clutching two cold ones in her hands. "Bad, scary, frustrating."

His bushy brows rose to his gray hair. "Scary? You're okay?"

"I'm fine." She twisted the caps from the bottles and shoved a beer across the counter to Quinn's hands, gnarled by arthritis but still able to grip a gun. "I suppose I should start at the beginning."

Taking a sip of beer, he squinted at her through one eye. "I know the beginning, Kyra."

"Sometime after that—" she chugged down some of her drink and wiped the back of her hand across the suds on her lips "—Matt Dugan decided it was a good idea to leave me his worldly possessions."

"That Harley? I'd take that off your hands if I could ride it."

"That bike's getting a new home. Anyway, Matt's parole officer told Jake about my inheritance, and Jake asked if he could come with me to Matt's apartment. He thinks Matt might have been in touch with Jordy, the first copycat killer, because of the playing cards he was leaving me."

"Is Jake wrong?" Quinn folded his hands around the damp bottle.

"I'm not sure." She then told Quinn about the search of Matt's room and the picture of the Harmons she'd taken from his dresser. "Jake saw the picture before I snatched it, but I'm not sure he made any connection to me."

"You're keeping things from him again." Quinn dragged his fingernail through the foil label on the bottle.

"It got worse." She drank more beer for confidence and relayed the rest of the story about the key to Matt's storage container and how she'd set the whole thing on fire to keep Jake from seeing the newspaper clippings and pictures of her Matt had saved.

Quinn set the bottle down on the ceramic tile so hard she thought he'd cracked it. "Kyra, you could've killed yourself and Jake. What the hell were you thinking?"

"I didn't think the whole place would turn into a fireball."

"Did Jake suspect you?"

"I don't know." She lifted and dropped her shoulders. Would he have attempted to make love to her if he thought she'd knowingly torched a storage container with both of them in it? She tapped her finger along her buzzing bottom lip. Maybe.

"Now you want to tell him what you did."

She held up her hand. "Wait. It gets worse. I haven't even told you about the email yet."

"You'd better slow down." He jabbed a crooked finger at her half-empty beer bottle cradled possessively between her hands. "Or you won't be coherent enough to tell me anything."

"When I was at the station, someone sent me an email and attached that same picture of the Harmons."

"Can't blame Matt for that one. The man's dead." Quinn scratched his grizzled chin.

"I realize that, thanks. I did ask our IT guy to trace the IP address, and it came back to the library in Santa Monica. Obviously, it's someone who wants to hide his identity."

"It could be the same person who hired Matt to harass you. Now that Matt's gone, this person has to do his own dirty work."

"I'm pretty sure that's the case. I haven't told you the rest of the storage unit story."

"There's more? It's not enough you set it on fire. Did you blow it up, too?"

"No, but Jake rescued one of the boxes from the unit that didn't burn. I didn't care if he had that box because I'd already checked it out, and as far as I could tell, it contained a bunch of scrap paper and receipts." She took a tiny sip of beer, watching Quinn over the bottle.

"Let me guess. It has more pictures in it."

"Wrong, but when Jake and I were going through the box at my place…"

She stopped when Quinn quirked his eyebrows up and down. "You invited Jake to your apartment?"

"He just showed up with the box." She flicked her fingers in the air. "As I was saying, when we were going through the box, I saw a scrap of paper with the same name as the one in the email address."

She didn't intend to tell Quinn she'd seen that piece of paper while in the throes of passion in Jake's arms. Quinn was a father figure to her, and you just didn't tell your dad stuff like that—even though he would've approved wholeheartedly.

"There's your connection. Unusual name?" Quinn cocked his head.

"Yeah—La Prey. That was in the email address with the picture attachment, and that name was printed on a piece of paper in Matt's storage unit."

"La Prey? What does that mean?" Quinn slid from the stool. "I'd better get the meat loaf out of the oven."

"I have no idea. It could also be LA Prey, like Los Angeles prey, like I'm his prey." She grabbed plates from the cupboard, feeling lighter already. It always helped to confess her sins to Quinn. He never judged her.

"Mashed potatoes are in the microwave. I didn't want to overheat those."

They suspended discussion of Kyra's crimes and misdemeanors while they bustled around the kitchen, grabbing dishes and food to lay out on the kitchen table by the sliding doors.

When the table was set, Quinn pulled out her chair for her.

She smiled her thanks and said, "Ever since Jake came over here, set the table for dinner and even put a vase of flowers in the center, eating on the couch in front of the TV isn't good enough for you."

"It was nice." He patted her hand as he sat down. "This is nice. Why waste that view off the patio."

She glanced through the glass doors at the moonlit water as it lapped against the rocks that formed the borders for the canals. "You're right. It's beautiful. Charlotte loved this house."

"And you. Charlotte loved you." Quinn's blue eyes watered. "You should've been ours. If I hadn't had that drinking problem, DCFS would've given you to us."

"It was more than that and you know it, Quinn."

"They thought we were too old." He made a spitting noise with his tongue. "Nonsense."

"It wasn't just that, either. Looking back now in my position as a therapist, the social workers probably didn't think it was a good idea for a homicide detective and his wife to adopt a girl he'd rescued from the bloody scene of her mother's murder."

"Why not?" Quinn pounded the handle of his fork on the table. "Who better? I knew what you'd been through. I was in the best position to protect you."

"And you did anyway." She dug into her meat loaf and smacked her lips. "You're right. Rose is a hell of a cook."

Quinn knew she'd never allow him to blame himself

for her time in the foster care system. He and Charlotte did everything they could to help and protect her.

With the subject thoroughly changed, Quinn returned to their previous one. "I take it you already went to the library to nose around, and they wouldn't tell you anything."

"Exactly." She scooped up a mound of potatoes and studied it on her fork, wondering how Rose got the potatoes so fluffy.

"I know who could've helped with that if you'd told him." Quinn swirled the last sip of beer in his bottle and then downed it, daring her to disagree with him.

She couldn't. "Believe me, I wished more than once for Jake at my side."

Quinn shoved his plate away and pointed at the kitchen counter next to the landline phone he still had plugged into the wall. "Hand me a piece of paper and the pen by the phone."

Kyra hopped up from her chair, taking their plates with her. After she'd placed them in the sink, she retrieved a memo pad and pen from the counter. She smacked them down in front of Quinn and took her seat, scooting it closer to his.

He tested the pen with a blue scribble in the upper-right corner of the pad of paper. "Okay, Matt planted playing cards for you during the first copycat killer spree. He hinted to Jake that someone had paid him to do it. Matt dies of a drug overdose before spilling the beans."

Despite the way Quinn clutched the pen, his writing was neat and sure as he marked down each point.

"Then Matt leaves you everything he has, including pictures from your foster care with the Harmons. You destroy one of those pictures and someone named

La Prey sends you the same pic as an attachment to an email." He glanced up, his blue eyes clear and bright. "How am I doing?"

She gave him a thumbs-up. "So far, so good."

"You then discover a piece of paper with that same unusual name among Matt's things, indicating a connection between Matt, the playing cards, the email and the pictures."

She planted her elbows on the table and said, "I didn't want to believe it, but it sounds like this La Prey person did pay Matt to plant the cards and maybe intended to use him for other...pranks. When Matt died, La Prey picked up the mantle and carried on by himself. But why? And what does any of this have to do with the copycat killers?"

"We need to find La Prey." Quinn shook a finger at her. "You need to tell Jake everything—yes, even why you got rid of that picture of the Harmons. He can help you. I have a good feeling about that guy, and not just because he's an LAPD homicide detective."

"What if he...?" Kyra sawed her bottom lip, the memory of Jake's kisses tingling.

Quinn smacked the table between them. "Stop right there. If he can't understand why you did what you did, he's not the man I thought he was, and he's not worthy of you. Your deception is a different matter."

"What does that mean?"

"I mean, young lady, when you constantly lie to people, you erode their trust in you. Jake may be able to forgive you for your actions—he might have a harder time forgiving your deception."

Quinn's words pained her heart, and she tapped her chest. "It's even worse. His wife cheated on him with a coworker."

"Then you face the consequences, but you tell him the truth—if not for your relationship with him, then for the case. You're withholding important information."

"I know you're right." She stabbed a finger at his list of events. "Put down 'Kyra comes clean' in your bullet points there."

He waved the memo pad in the air. "I'm not done yet. I'm interested in this name, La Prey. Is that how Matt wrote it down, as two words with a space between them?"

"No, I just say it that way for convenience. Matt and the email address had it all run together as one word—*laprey.* Here, I'll show you." She took the notepad from his hand and picked up the pen. She carefully printed out the name and turned the pad toward Quinn.

He studied the pad for several seconds and then held out his hand for the pen. Clutching the pen, he hunched over the paper, poking at each letter. Then he wrote something beneath it and looked up at Kyra, the lines on his face etched even deeper than usual.

She caught her breath. "What's wrong?"

"*Laprey* is an anagram. It's not only advisable that you tell Jake what's going on—it's imperative."

He shoved the paper toward her, and with her heart galloping in her chest, she read the rearranged letters —*player.*

Chapter Eleven

Jake pushed the computer from his lap, putting distance between himself and the seamy story of a foster parent abusing his charges and the one foster kid in his charge who fought back—stabbing Buck Harmon to death.

He had no doubt the unnamed teen was Kyra Chase.

He rubbed his eyes and then trained them on the view from his window, a sheet of glass that took up the whole wall, bringing the glittering lights of the city into his home. You'd think he'd want to get away from the city, with its evil and darkness, but from up here it looked…enchanted. When he was in this house, looking down at the lights, he could remember all the good, all the decent people.

His gaze wandered to his open laptop, and his blood pounded in his temples as he studied the smug face of Buck Harmon. He knew some foster parents did it for the money; he also knew so many more who did it from the goodness of their hearts. He saw those people when he looked down from his perch in the Hollywood Hills.

The headlights of a car moved across the window as it pulled into his driveway. He pushed up from the couch and peered outside at Kyra's compact stopping behind his car.

The knots in his gut that had been unraveling tightened. Why was she here? What was he going to say to her? If he admitted he knew about her past, she'd accuse him of snooping. If he pretended he knew nothing, she'd sense something was off. Billy was right—Kyra knew people. She'd gone into the right field.

Before he had time to decide how to play it, his doorbell rang. He practically dragged his feet to answer it, when normally he'd be jumping out of his skin at a visit from Kyra.

He swung open the door, and he didn't even get a chance to say hello. She charged past him, her blond hair loose and messy, her eyes glassy and bright.

She took several steps into the room and then spun around, throwing her hands in front of her as if offering him something that wasn't there.

"I have something to tell you—several things to tell you."

He nodded, his jaw seemingly locked in place.

"That picture you saw in Matt's mirror, the one of the family? That was our foster family, the one Matt and I shared. The parents were Buck and Lori Harmon, and I killed Buck Harmon when I was sixteen. Stabbed him."

She seemed to run out of steam, and he gaped at her like an idiot. She took his silence as encouragement, and she wound herself up again, throwing back her shoulders and pacing to the window.

"I'm not proud of what I did, but he deserved it. When I was living with the Harmons, I discovered that Buck was molesting the younger girls. I tried to tell my caseworker at DCFS, but she didn't believe me, and the girls all denied it—because they were scared. Even Quinn couldn't help. The social worker wouldn't even move me out of the home, not that I really wanted to leave the younger girls. The Harmons were the only ones willing to take...troubled teens.

"I tried to protect the girls. I—I told Buck he could have me instead if he left them alone. Do you know what he said?" She twisted her head over her shoulder to meet his eyes.

Jake's stomach turned, but he said quietly, "No."

"He told me I was too old." She snorted, which turned into a sob. "He liked them young and fresh, wasn't interested after they hit puberty."

Jake's hands curled into fists, and he felt like smashing them through the plate-glass window. "You took out the trash."

She turned toward him and flattened her hands against the window, her blue eyes wide, the lights of the city still reflected in their depths. "It was self-defense. One night when he came for one of the girls, I was there to stop him. He smacked me across the face and brandished a knife. Told me he'd kill Sophie if I didn't watch him defile her and take pictures for him, and then he'd kill me."

Although Jake wanted to reach for her, he knew better. He stuffed his hands in the pockets of his jeans and froze in the middle of the room. The news stories had confirmed the killing was in self-defense without going into this level of rancid detail.

"Something snapped inside me." She formed a cross over her chest with both hands. "When he held the knife to Sophie's throat, I went for him. Used a few tricks I'd learned from Quinn and was able to disarm him. Didn't hurt that Buck was on his third six-pack. I got the knife from him, but he didn't stop. He laughed. Then he punched me in the stomach and lunged for Sophie. I lunged for him."

Her voice hitched at the end, and he couldn't hold back any longer. He launched toward her and wrapped his arms around her stiff body. A tremble rolled through her frame, and he stroked his hand down her back.

She spoke into his shoulder, her voice muffled. "There was so much blood. Sophie screamed and woke up the entire household. Buck's wife, Lori, knew about the abuse, and she didn't do anything to stop it. She didn't do anything to help Buck at the end, either."

"She called the police?"

"I did." She broke from his embrace and stepped back, her eyes searching his face. "Lori didn't make a move to do anything. The younger kids were hysterical. Matt wasn't home. I was in shock, but I knew what I had to do."

"Did the police arrest you?"

She ran a hand through her tangled hair. "They took me into custody and they read me my rights, but they didn't handcuff me. I told them to call Quinn and Charlotte. They were with me when the cops questioned me."

"That must've been…traumatic." She'd wandered away from him, not needing or wanting his comfort. He licked his lips. "I—I understand why you wouldn't want to tell people about what happened, but I'm glad you told me."

She'd stopped at the edge of the couch, and her back straightened as if a rod had replaced her spine. Cranking her head toward him, she said, "Looks like I didn't have to tell you. You already discovered everything on your own."

His heart stopped for a second and resumed pounding at a furious pace, the blood pulsing against his ears. His gaze shifted past her to the open laptop on the couch, Buck Harmon smirking at him from the screen.

He lowered his voice. "I did find out about the Harmons."

Holding his breath, he watched the emotions arch across her face and braced for an explosion.

Kyra's shoulders sagged and she dropped to the arm of the couch, her feet spread apart and her knees pinned together, looking like a chastised schoolgirl. Not what he expected from her.

He kept his breath pent up, his muscles rigid—just in case.

"I don't blame you." She raised her eyes to his face, her cheeks pale. "Your instincts were right."

He released a long breath through his teeth, which came out as a whistle. "What do you mean?"

"I had a beer at Quinn's, and I could use another."

He sprang into action, heading for the kitchen. He grabbed two beers from the fridge and pointed one at the couch. "Sit down. Glass?"

"Glass? I'm ready to mainline it."

A grin cracked his stiff face, and he twisted off the caps. He joined her on the couch, shutting his laptop with a snap on Harmon's smug face and putting it on the coffee table.

"I'm all ears."

"You've been all ears since I got here. Feel free to jump in at any time." She cleared her throat, swigged some beer and told him about the email she'd received at work with the Harmon family picture as an attachment.

"It obviously didn't come from Matt Dugan." Jake snapped his fingers. "Is that why you were in deep discussion with Brandon Nguyen? You were trying to find out where the email came from?"

"The Santa Monica Public Library, but I'll get to that in a minute." She dropped her lashes. "First, I need to tell you why I, uh, went cold last night in the middle of…everything."

Jake choked on his beer and it foamed from his nostrils. When Kyra opened up, she really went all out. "I thought you just weren't feeling it with me."

"Yeah, right." Color washed into her cheeks and she took another sip of beer. "It's because I saw a piece of paper among Matt's things with the same name as that email."

"La Prey?" Jake furrowed his brow. The name that made no sense. "You didn't tell me about it because you'd have to have told me about the email and the picture."

She laced her fingers around the bottle. "Yeah. Sorry."

She didn't have to apologize for wanting to keep that bit of her past hidden. How much trauma could one girl take?

He coughed. "You have the email, the picture and the connection to Matt. Did you have any luck at the library?"

"What do you think?"

"I think the librarian told you to pound sand."

"Exactly."

"I can help you with that."

"Exactly."

"This laprey probably did pay Matt to plant the cards during the killing spree of the copycat, and now he's taunting you with that picture of the Harmons during this second wave of copycat murders. He could be connected to the killers, Kyra."

"There's more, Jake. Even with all that info, I was

telling myself that Matt's involvement and even La Prey's involvement had nothing to do with the serial killers. I was still planning to keep all of this from you…until tonight."

"What happened tonight?" He hunched forward slightly, watching her lips, not wanting to miss one word that fell from them. Quinn must've convinced her to come clean.

"I was going through everything with Quinn, and he started writing out the events on a piece of paper. When it came to La Prey, he wrote it out as it appeared on the email address and Matt's scribbling. Here, I'll show you." She ripped off a piece of paper from a notebook on his desk and grabbed a pen. She printed out the letters on the paper and shoved it in front of him on the table.

He looked at the word for just a second. She didn't have to tell him why she was here tonight confessing everything. His gaze flew to her face. "La Prey is an anagram for *player*."

IT HAD TAKEN Jake less time than Quinn to see what was right in front of their faces. She'd been the only one to miss it. Had Matt missed it? Matt had a lot of issues, but he was no killer. He wouldn't help one, either.

Kyra crumpled the paper in her fist. "I was so fixated on the LA part, I couldn't see past it. I mean, it can't *be* him…can it? It's just someone using the name to terrorize me for some reason."

Jake tapped one finger on his knee, his hazel eyes dark and flat. "Who else knows your identity besides me, Quinn and Matt?"

"I don't know." She pressed a hand against her midsection to still the butterflies that kicked up every time she thought about this. "There were people at the time who knew, of course. The cops, the social workers. If you noticed, the news stories about Buck's…death didn't mention that the foster child who did the dirty work was the daughter of a homicide victim. That would've been a juicy story, but the press didn't run with it. Still, I'm guessing some of the cops knew. That's why they were so sympathetic."

"Captain Castillo?"

She blinked at him. "He was around, so maybe. I wasn't taken to your division. It was LAPD jurisdiction, but it was a different station. Why Castillo?"

"Not sure." He picked at the soggy label on his bottle. "I suppose it wouldn't be too difficult for someone involved—social worker, cop, medical worker—to have kept tabs on you through the years and followed your name change. If someone wasn't watching you, Marilyn Monroe Lake could morph into Kyra Leigh Chase without a hitch, but if someone had his or her eye on you, was checking up on you periodically, that name change may not have been so seamless."

The creepiness of someone watching her that closely receded slightly with the realization that he knew her middle name. "We're back to cops again. Why? Why would someone be tracking me like that?"

"Matt Dugan did."

"Matt was obsessed with me."

"What was Matt's response to Buck's death?"

Her cheeks grew warm and she pressed the cool, damp bottle against her face. "He thought it was the raddest thing ever. Kept making excuses as to why he'd never done it himself. Started looking at me a little differently after that."

"Do you think it led to his obsession?"

"Absolutely. He fancied us a modern-day Bonnie and

Clyde going on some crime spree together. Quinn had different ideas. That's when he and Charlotte finally got me for good. DCFS was just happy to get rid of me at that point." She clasped her hands between her knees. "But that's Matt, and Matt's dead. Who else would want to keep tabs on me?"

Jake traced a pattern on the thigh of his jeans with the tip of his finger. Without looking up, he said, "When I confronted you about the playing cards during the first copycat killings, you mentioned that The Player was still out there. Do you still believe that?"

"Well, he is, isn't he? Quinn never caught him. He stopped his killing spree. Nobody ever confessed, no witnesses ever came forward. He must be out there somewhere." Her gaze shifted to the huge window that took up one wall of Jake's living room.

He had no drapes or blinds on the window, but he didn't need them. He was high enough on the hill that nobody could see inside his place. He could see them, but they couldn't see him—sort of a metaphor for his job.

Jake said, "He could be dead."

"Could be. Hope so. But if he is—" Kyra twisted her fingers in her lap "—who's this Player tormenting me?"

"If he isn't, why would he be taunting you now?"

Her stomach flip-flopped. She'd never talked about any of this stuff with anyone other than Quinn. The conversation with Jake stripped her bare—and not in a good way.

Crossing her arms over her chest, she asked, "What do you mean?"

"Stay with me for a minute." He held up one finger, a shred of the beer label hanging off his fingernail. "If

The Player isn't dead and he's behind the playing cards and the email, why? Why would he contact you now?"

"Not sure. Maybe because of the renewed interest in his crimes due to the copycats."

"Okay, I'll go along with that, but does he even know who you are? Does he know about Matt and the Harmons?"

"Good questions." She picked up her beer again, less eager to down the remaining sips now that it had done its job of taking off the edge while she'd come clean to Jake. "I asked Quinn about that, and he's always been pretty vague. The news reports at the time did mention that Jennifer Lake's daughter had been asleep in the house during her mother's murder and that she had discovered the body. That's all true."

"The accounts I read never mentioned your name, showed your picture or gave any details about your fate. For all anyone knew, you could've left the state with grandparents or other relatives."

Kyra's throat tightened and she gulped down the rest of the beer after all. "Well, that didn't happen."

"The Player wouldn't have known that. He had no way of tracking you, so he wouldn't know who you were now, especially now with the name change. Maybe that's why…" Jake broke off and rubbed his jaw.

"Why what?" The fluttering continued in her belly, almost as if there was something to be discovered around the corner that she didn't want to know.

"I know Quinn and Charlotte never officially adopted you, but you did go to live with them when you… left the Harmons. When you changed your name, why didn't you take Quinn's last name? Kyra Quinn has a nice ring to it."

"I wanted to. I'd planned on it…" She put her hand

to her throat and met Jake's eyes. "Quinn didn't want me to. I was hurt, but he and Charlotte made up some excuse, which I accepted at the time, and then proved in a thousand different ways it wasn't because they didn't want me. You think Quinn didn't want me to take his name because he didn't want The Player to know who I was."

"I think so." Jake squeezed her hand, which was lying limply in her lap. "Not that he would be looking for you. Why should he? That's what I'm thinking now. Why would The Player, after getting away with several murders, come out of the woodwork now? Just because some sickos decided to copy his demented crimes?"

"Prison. You know better than I do that serial killers stop when they die or are imprisoned. Maybe he's been in jail all this time."

"Still doesn't explain how he found you. Maybe the person taunting you now is just some messed-up acquaintance of Matt's. Matt got drunk or high, told the guy all about you, and he picked it up and ran with it. I'd sure like to talk to him, see if he had any connection to Jordy Cannon. He might even lead us to Andrea's and Crystal's killer." He reached across her to grab her beer bottle. "I'm glad you told me everything."

She nudged the toe of her sandal against the laptop on the coffee table. "Too late. I didn't have to tell you. You found out on your own from Billy's friend at DCFS."

Jake tripped to a stop on his way to the kitchen with the bottles in one hand. "It didn't happen like that."

His voice had dropped, and she twisted on the couch to face him fully. "You don't have to lie. I saw Tara's name on your phone, and I asked Billy about her later—told him I was jealous."

Jake's eyes widened briefly. "I did talk to Tara, but she didn't give me the goods...couldn't. Your file at DCFS is locked down. Matt's, too, for the same time period."

"Oh." She skimmed a hand through her hair. "I have Quinn to thank for that, too."

"I imagine you do." He continued on his way to the large kitchen and edged around the granite island in the center.

She pushed up from the couch and followed him. As he dropped the bottle in the recycling bin, she sat on the chair at the end of the island and planted her elbows on the granite. "How did you find out about the Harmons and what happened there? Did Matt have some paperwork in that box I missed?"

"No." Jake folded his arms and wedged his lower back against the counter.

A muscle twitched at the corner of her mouth. Jake didn't want to tell her. Who was left to betray her? Quinn never would, not even to Jake.

"It—it's okay, Jake. I won't be upset. Quinn made me see that I should've been telling you everything for the sake of the case."

He pushed away from the counter and reached for a shelf on the other side of the kitchen from her. He yanked his phone from the charger and tapped the display.

He placed the phone in front of her and said, "This is how I knew."

Chapter Twelve

Kyra swallowed when she saw the text message calling out the Harmons. "Who sent this?"

"I don't have a clue. I tried texting back. I tried calling the number. It's like the text was sent and the phone turned off." He spun the phone back toward him with one finger. "Unlike you with the email, I haven't had a chance to put a trace on the phone, but my guess?"

She answered for him. "It's a burner."

"Probably stuffed in a trash bin, as we speak. Doesn't mean I can't try. Remember when we thought Jordy had called from a burner phone, and it turned out he'd stolen one from Rachel Blackburn."

"That definitely helped crack the case. Maybe this guy made the same mistake as Jordy." Kyra folded her hands on the smooth granite as if waiting to be schooled by the great detective. "How did this person know you were looking for my foster family?"

Jake tugged on his earlobe. "That's a question I've been avoiding. Who would know?"

Kyra raised her hand and wiggled her fingers, ticking off each one with a name. "Tara, the social worker. Billy, if Tara told him. Matt, who's dead. Quinn, probably. Anyone who overheard you at the station."

"Nobody overheard me."

"That's what you think. I saw the display with Tara's name, and I saw your text exchange with Matt last month. People who are hell-bent on discovering information will find a way."

He swept some nonexistent crumbs from the counter into his palm. "None of those names you mentioned makes sense. If Tara had the Harmons' name, she would've given it to me. Billy wouldn't know or care. As you pointed out, Matt's dead. Quinn wouldn't betray you if I offered him The Player on a silver platter."

"Unless—" she sucked in her bottom lip "—Quinn told you to force me to come clean to you about everything. Quinn has been warning me that the stuff happening to me might be connected to the copycat killers."

"Quinn wouldn't send me an anonymous text from a burner phone, though. He's not that kind of guy. He'd tell you he was going to do it, and then he'd call me directly and tell me."

"You're right." She drummed her fingers on the surface of the island. "It must be La Prey—I mean, the other player. He seemed to know that I'd destroyed the picture of the Harmons I took from Matt's apartment. He knew you were looking into my past."

"He could be making some educated guesses. I was going to meet Matt before he died. Maybe player just assumed I was digging into your past." Jake circled a finger in the air. "He's not some omniscient creature."

"Sure feels like it." She rubbed the goose bumps racing up her arms. "And can I ask you a favor?"

"I figure I owe you a few for snooping into your past."

Wrinkling her nose, she waved her hand. "Forget that, but could you not call this new threat against me The Player? Sounds too much like the old threat against me—or at least my mother. I prefer to think of him as La Prey, sounds almost refined."

"Done. I want to track him down, not just to make him stop torturing you, but to find out why he's so interested in The Player and this current killing spree. He might know these guys."

"You're checking out Jordy Lee Cannon's friends and associates, right?"

"Yeah, though the fact that he's dead doesn't make it easy. If I could've kept him alive, taken him into custody, questioned him…" Jake ground his fist into his palm. "I could've made him talk, give up his secrets and his motivation."

She said in a small voice without looking up, "I'm afraid that's my fault. If I hadn't gone after him myself, he never would've taken me hostage and you wouldn't have had to shoot him."

"We caught him faster because of you. If he had gotten away that night, he might've committed another murder. You may have saved someone's life that night, so don't beat yourself up."

Jake's words gave her a warm glow, and she glanced up at him through her lashes. He hadn't had much of a reaction about Buck Harmon, except to say she'd taken out the trash when she had killed him. That seemed like a typical response from a cop.

Bracing her hands against the cool countertop, she started. "I didn't want to tell you about Buck for the same reason I didn't want to tell you I was the daughter of one of The Player's victims. I know it's a past that has formed me, but I don't want to define who I am today. I can change my identity, but I'll never erase those experiences. I don't necessarily want to erase them. I just don't want to be judged by them, even if that judgment is on my side and takes the form of pity. I don't want people walking around on eggshells in my presence. I'm sorry I lied to you. I'm sorry I hid things from you."

He held up a hand. "It's…understandable."

"When Quinn worked out that anagram, I realized how important it was to tell you everything. Still, it was more than that." She peeled her hand from the counter and ran it along the tail of the tattoo on his left forearm, snaking out of the arm of his T-shirt. "I knew if I ever hoped to have some kind of relationship with you, I'd have to tell you all about my ugly past."

His arm tensed and corded beneath her fingertips. "Do you hope to have some kind of relationship with me?"

His voice, all rough around the edges, sent a thrill to her core, and she dug her fingertips into his flesh. "I do, if I haven't scared you off."

Keeping his arm in her grip, he hunched forward across the island and wedged a finger beneath her chin. "Do I look like the kind of man who scares easily?"

Her lashes fluttered as she took in the strong jaw, set in determination, and the spark in his hazel eyes. She breathed out one word. "No."

Her breath hitched in her throat as he circled the island and planted himself in front of her. He ran one hand through her hair and leaned in for a kiss, slanting his mouth across hers; his lips, slightly chapped, caressed hers, demanding more from her.

For the first time in a long time, she was willing to give more. She'd told Jake more about herself than she'd ever admitted to another man. It was a step, a first step.

She curled her arms around his neck and hopped from the high chair, hanging against him for a few seconds, her toes brushing the wood floor.

His hand slipped from the back of her head and cupped her face as he rained soft kisses on her lips. She sighed against his mouth, her knuckles brushing his prickly jaw.

He fitted his body with hers along every line, so that his erection pressed against her pelvis. She swayed her hips in a sinuous dance to get him even closer.

His breath hot on her cheek, he grabbed her hand and pulled her away from the kitchen. She tripped as he veered course from the stairs that must lead to his bedroom in favor of the living room with its sprawling view of the city. Before she had a second to wonder where he was taking her, his cell phone rang.

She'd never heard that particular ringtone from his phone before. It must've been coming from his private cell—he wouldn't have a song from a boy band on his work phone.

The sound of the ringtone stopped Jake dead in his tracks. He put a finger to her thrumming lips. "I'm so sorry. I have to answer this."

She nodded and almost collapsed on her jelly legs when he released her and returned to the kitchen. He picked up the phone that had been charging next to his work phone.

With his back to her, he answered. "Fiona, what are you doing up so late? Isn't it a school day tomorrow?"

Fiona? Kyra's lips lifted on one side. His daughter.

As Jake launched into a conversation that could only be with an adolescent, Kyra tiptoed to her purse, hitched it over one shoulder and slipped out his front door.

OVER FIONA'S WHINING, Jake heard the soft click of his front door. He twisted his head around, taking in the empty living room and the vacant spot where Kyra had dropped her purse earlier.

He muttered, "Damn."

Fiona interrupted the tirade against her mother and her tyrannical rule, and said, "Dad, you're not supposed to curse in front of me."

"I'm sorry, Fiona. You're right." He sat heavily on the chair Kyra had occupied earlier, her scent, like rosebushes through an open window, still wafting in the air. "You need to listen to your mother and…"

"Brock. My stepfather's name is Brock, Dad."

"I know that." He gave a secret smile into the phone. "When you're with them—"

"Which is most of the time."

His daughter's barbed words pricked him. When had she gotten so…grown-up? "It is, so it's important that you follow their rules."

"Christmas. You said I could come for Christmas break." She heaved a sigh that gushed over the line. "I am not going to Japan with Mom and Brock. I don't want to go to Japan."

"Your mother and I still need to discuss that." Meaning he'd ask and Tess would say no.

"Were you busy when I called? Watcha working on?"

His work was not fit to discuss with a fourteen-year-old girl, even one with a fascination for true crime. Where the hell had she gotten that and why had Tess allowed it? He knew something had gone amiss when Fiona had visited him last year and asked him to take her to Cielo Drive, where the Manson Family had committed their most famous crime.

Who was he kidding? Tess hadn't allowed that. She'd been horrified when Jake told her about Fiona's request, and promptly blamed him.

"I'm working on a case, just like I always am, but I was watching TV when you called and thinking about bed." Well, that last part wasn't too far off the mark. He *had* been thinking about going to bed…with Kyra.

"Boring." Fiona made a disgusted sound. "Just let Mom know I'm for sure coming to your place for Christmas."

"We will continue to discuss it, I promise. Remember, fighting with your mother over everything is not going to help your case."

"All right. Love you, Daddy."

Jake's throat got tight just like it did every time he heard those words from Fiona. God knew what he'd done to deserve them. "Love you, too, Fiona."

When the call ended, he put his phone back on the charger and texted Kyra to let him know when she got home. He didn't know what game was being played, but this guy knew too much about Kyra's past to be ignored.

And before these pranks turned physical, Jake intended to put a stop to them.

THE FOLLOWING MORNING, Jake rolled out of bed with heavy eyes and a fog invading his brain. His single beer the night before hadn't resulted in a hangover. He'd call it a Kyra Chase hangover.

He stepped into the shower and cranked on the water. Two nights in a row, he'd had his plans for seduction waylaid—once at her place, once at his. Maybe next time, they should try for neutral ground.

He scrubbed away most of the residue of disappointment from his body with soap and warm water and got ready for work.

As he drove to the station, he had one thought on his mind…two thoughts—tracking down the phone that had left him the text message about the Harmons, and Kyra.

When he got to the task force conference room at the station, his gaze slid to the side, taking in Kyra's empty desk. She'd texted him when she made it back to her place, not including anything else in her message—no apology, no explanation as to why she bolted.

Kyra must've known it was his daughter on the line. The kid scared her away. She knew he had a daughter, but maybe it was another matter to hear him actually speaking to her. Kyra didn't strike him as the motherly sort, so she just might back away from any relationship that included children.

He shook his head and grabbed the coffee cup that magically appeared on his desk. Nodding thanks to his partner, he said, "Any luck with the footage in the surrounding areas of the crime scenes?"

"We're getting there." Billy picked up his phone. "I have a few more homeowners to contact."

While Billy made his calls, a pinprick of guilt needled the back of Jake's neck. Billy was hard at work on their case, and he was trying to track down a phone that had texted him about Kyra's foster family.

Jake rolled his shoulders, sloughing off the guilt. He couldn't shake the feeling that Kyra's history was inextricably linked to the killings happening recently. To sort out her past could only help him in this investigation.

He ignored the little voice that hammered in his head telling him that sorting out her past would help him protect her, too.

He got on the phone with the tech guys on the task force and gave them the number that had texted him the info about the Harmons. The techies didn't even ask what connection the text had to the case. They assumed anything the task force leader sent over was valid—and they were right.

As soon as he hung up his desk phone, it rang. "McAllister."

"J-Mac, this is Sergeant Montiel downstairs. We just got a call about a dead body, an apparent homicide, in a home in Los Feliz. Has all the earmarks of your guy."

Through narrowed eyes, Jake scanned the activity in the room—people buzzing around like busy bees. In two seconds, he'd be prodding the beehive.

He took down a few details from Montiel, including the address, and stood up. "We have another body."

His words had an instantaneous effect on the room. People dropped what they were doing. Some rushed from the area. Some picked up phones. Some fired up their computers. Everyone had something to do.

Jake clapped Billy on the back. "Let's hit it, Cool Breeze."

Billy rose from his chair and ducked his head. "Victim?"

"She's not African American, so this freak is an equal-opportunity killer."

Grabbing his jacket, Billy said, "Doesn't make me feel any better."

Jake drove to the crime scene with Billy riding shotgun. Jake shot a sidelong glance at his partner, his jaw tight, his shoulders braced for the crime scene. Jake knew Billy cared just as much about this victim as Andrea and Crystal, but he wouldn't have the added torment of thinking about his sister and her fate. Billy was only cool breeze on the surface. Each murder they investigated burned a hole in Billy's soul. He and his partner dealt with the trauma in different ways, and that trauma never went away.

Jake pulled up to the crime scene, which patrol officers had already marked off. The yellow tape wafted in the light breeze, waving them over in a desultory manner. The neighbors formed knots at various locations along the sidewalk, craning their necks to watch the action. He and Billy would be giving them plenty of action in due time.

They strode up to the officer on the perimeter, his arms folded, his sunglasses repelling anyone who wandered too close. They flashed their badges, and Jake said, "Officers inside?"

The patrolman held up two fingers.

When they reached the second officer, stationed at the front door, Billy said, "Are we the first detectives here?"

Officer Nance stepped aside from the front door, which was gaping open. "When my partner and I saw the vic, we didn't waste time with anyone else. We called Sarge immediately to report to the task force."

"Appreciate it, Nance." Billy held out his fist for a bump and Nance complied, reddening to the roots of his ginger hair.

When Jake stepped into the house, the odor of death tickled his nostrils. The air-conditioning emitted a low hum, but the AC wasn't blasting enough to chill a body.

Jake did a half turn. "Any signs of forced entry, Nance?"

"None, sir."

The officer didn't have to tell them the victim was in the bedroom, most likely in her bed. Jake followed Billy down the short hallway where another two officers stood at the entrance to a room.

"We'll take it from here, boys." Billy jerked his thumb over his shoulder. "If you haven't done so already, check all the doors and windows for break-ins. We have a bunch of lookie-loos out there. Start canvassing. We're especially interested in security systems. Anyone who has a camera, let them know we want the video."

The officers fled the room, one of them absolutely green around the gills.

Jake had pulled on his gloves as he walked into the room and approached the bed where a young woman lay neatly against her pillows, staring sightlessly at the ceiling with the queen of spades between her lips. A splotch of blood stained the covers where the woman's hand with the finger severed must be.

Just as in the other two slayings, the bedclothes were neat and orderly, but the killer had to have been on the bed, over the victim, in the position to strangle her.

Billy used a gloved finger to lift the woman's hair from her neck to expose the angry purple marks on her neck. "These crime scenes are almost antiseptic, aren't they?"

"He's a careful guy. That's why he lies in wait—no struggle, less hassle."

"I'm going to check the closet in the second bedroom. We haven't even been able to tell where he's been hiding in the house."

"It's another house without a camera, though. That's one of his criteria."

"What about the rest of his selection process?" Billy's gaze flicked over the dead woman. The officers hadn't given them her name yet. "At first we thought he might be targeting young African American women. This victim doesn't qualify."

"She's young, lives alone, no camera. She lives in a house, not an apartment, and is probably careless in some way about the security of her home. The killer does not want to work hard."

"Probably stalked her like the others to learn her habits." Billy pointed to the door. "I'm going to have a look in the other rooms, garage, too."

Jake flicked back the covers and peered at the bloody stub on the woman's hand. Fingering the woman's long brown locks, he murmured, "Did you take her hair again, freak?"

He was no expert on hairstyles, but strands of hair on the left side of the woman's head did appear shorter than the ones on the right. He'd taken his trophy.

Eyeing the neat covers, Jake patted them with his gloved hands. As he brushed one hand off the edge of the bed, something crinkled beneath his fingers. He turned his hand over and brought it close to his face.

His heart skipped a beat. Stuck to his glove was a piece of tape. At Andrea's house, he'd felt something sticky on the bedspread, and the lab had identified it as the substance on the back of tape. Now he'd found the tape.

"You left something behind this time, freak." He held up the tape to the light streaming through the bedroom window and sucked in a sharp breath.

"Are you ready for us, J-Mac?" Clive Stewart, their fingerprint tech, hovered at the bedroom door with his black case.

Jake looked up with a smile stretching his lips. "You're just in time, Clive. We have a fingerprint."

Chapter Thirteen

Kyra jerked her head up, nostrils flaring. The mood of the task force room had shifted, and a whispered undercurrent swept through the space, almost ruffling papers in its wake. She held her breath until it reached her corner.

She leaned across her desk and whispered to one of the patrol officers tasked with checking home security video. "What happened?"

He raised his eyebrows, his glance shifting from side to side as if the entire room didn't already know. "Copycat 2.0 just messed up. He left a fingerprint."

Kyra wriggled in her seat like a birthday girl at her own party. "That's fantastic news. I hope he's in the system."

For the next hour, she glanced up every time someone walked into the conference room. Finally Jake came striding in with a kick to his step.

She raised her hand, tentatively, not sure if he was mad at her for skipping out on their…encounter last night.

When he nodded at her and winked, she let out a long breath and got back to entering family members for Copycat 2.0's latest victim, Mindy Behr. The task force usually let the press dub the serial killers, and 2.0

had taken off after the murder of Crystal Monroe. She preferred it to the Copycat Player, which had been Jordy Lee Cannon's name and had given her a jolt whenever she heard it.

Despite the noise in the task force headquarters, she got lost in her work, tuning it all out until someone behind her cleared his throat. She twisted her head over her shoulder and knew she'd be looking into Jake's hazel eyes. Her radar seemed to pick up his presence.

She held up a finger, added more data to her file and saved it. "Fingerprint, huh? That's huge."

"Yeah. The guy thought he was pretty clever by using tape to get rid of any hairs or fibers on the bedclothes, but he left a piece of it behind. Clive already lifted it, and we're going to enter it into the database." His lips twisted into a frown, and she couldn't help the little shiver that ran down her back at the thought of those lips on hers.

She blinked. "What's wrong?"

"It's not a perfect print, which might prevent us from getting a clean hit."

"But it's something." She glanced over his head to make sure everyone was too busy to listen. "Are you free for lunch?"

"I am, and I have something to tell you." He rose from his crouch. "Hang on. I have a few more things to do."

"How about I meet you at your car? I...uh, need to hit the restroom anyway."

"I'll be there in ten."

Most of the task force had some idea that she and Jake had more than a working relationship, but she didn't want to highlight that fact. She closed her laptop and stuffed it into her bag. She did make a detour to the ladies' room, but only to check her hair and makeup. If he'd agreed to lunch that easily, he must've already forgiven her for leaving his place last night without a word.

She retouched her lipstick, straightened her skirt and smoothed back her ponytail. Lunch *and* information. She'd hit the jackpot today.

Several minutes later, she waited nonchalantly by his unmarked LAPD sedan, pretending she was looking for something in her purse anytime someone walked by.

Jake put her out of her misery by showing up just a short time after her, his long stride eating up the parking lot between them. He beeped his remote before he reached her, and she slid into the passenger seat.

Scooting behind the wheel, he cocked his head at her. "Big hurry, are we?"

"Is it against the rules or something for us to be… more than coworkers?" She tugged her skirt over her knees.

"Are we?" He started the car and turned down the AC. "Seems to me, forces beyond our control are keeping us apart."

"Yeah, about that." She wrinkled her nose. "I'm sorry I dashed out of there. I knew you were talking to your daughter. I—I remembered her name was Fiona. I didn't want to interrupt or make you feel like you had to rush off the phone with your daughter."

"I get it. The call sort of…spoiled the moment."

She opened her mouth, snapped it shut and started again. "Is everything okay? With your daughter, I mean?"

"She's fine." With his hands resting on the top of the steering wheel, he pointed out the windshield. "Dandelion Café okay with you?"

"Perfect." She kept staring at his profile. That was

the first question she'd asked about his daughter. Did he not want to tell her about Fiona? Wasn't that what people did in relationships? Opened up?

He glanced at her and flexed his fingers on the wheel. "Just regular teenage angst—she's fourteen. She and her mother argue about everything these days."

"That's normal at her age." She tapped her temple. "I know these things. I wrote the book on teenage angst."

"Yeah, but you—" He broke off, a flash of red on his neck.

"You're right. I had it worse than most, but to every teenager, his or her situation always feels like the worst. Does she have a best friend?"

"I, uh…" The flush on his skin deepened. "She's mentioned a few friends. I'm not sure if she considers one a best friend. Does that make me a terrible father?"

"Of course not." She patted his thigh. "Even if you knew the name of her best friend, it might change tomorrow."

Staring out the window, Jake sucked in his cheek. "I messed up. We were too young for kids. I hadn't even been a cop for a year, and Tess was still in law school."

"But you managed and, despite teenage turmoil, Fiona is a happy kid? Well-adjusted?"

"She seems to be whenever I see her. She does well in school, has friends, plays on the high school soccer team and takes guitar lessons. No boys—that I know of."

Kyra rolled her eyes. "If you're anything like Quinn was when I brought any boys around to meet him, those guys are in for it."

"I hope I get that opportunity." Jake's hands tightened on the wheel before he cranked it to the right. "Maybe we can get a table before it's too crowded."

They snagged a table on the patio with ease. Although the Dandelion was no cop hangout, the hostess seemed to have a soft spot for Jake. What woman wouldn't? He exuded such a tough-guy attitude, you just knew he'd take care of you in a jam. His hotness quotient didn't hurt, either.

How had she been able to walk out on him twice? First time had been for *her* sake, second for his. Maybe fate wasn't smiling on them, but she'd revealed so much to him already that she didn't want to give up on him. And when had fate ever stopped her before?

They sat in the shade on the patio and ordered iced teas.

As Kyra shook out her napkin onto her lap, she said, "Tell me about the fingerprint."

"At the first crime scene I picked up some sticky substance on the bedspread, which turned out to be the glue on the back of tape. I figured then he was patting down the bedclothes and the area to pick up any threads or fibers—clever. I noticed the same thing at Crystal's. I checked for it again at today's crime scene and found a bit of tape. When I held it up to the light—bingo—I saw a fingerprint. His hands must've been dirty when he touched the tape—maybe before he put on his gloves."

"Good. He slipped up." She planted an elbow on the table and rested her chin in her palm. "If he's been arrested before, his prints will be on file. Heck, if he has a driver's license in California, he should have a thumbprint with them."

"It's not like we can run it through the Department of Motor Vehicles database, and the DMV doesn't take a full set for a license. All we have is one finger. It would have to be the same fingerprint with the DMV." He shook off the negative attitude when the drinks came and sucked down his tea straight with no sugar. "But it's something. More will come. I'm feeling confident about the security systems in the areas of the victims' houses. He didn't just appear in one spot and disappear. He had to have walked or driven. We'll get him."

Kyra stirred two packets of sweetener in her tea. "Sometimes I wonder how cops ever solved crimes without DNA and CCTV."

"It was a lot harder, for sure. Look at all the cold cases we have. Anyone who committed a crime prior to 1986 and left DNA has to be sweating bullets today. That knock on the door is gonna come."

"Except for The Player," Kyra said softly into her swirling tea.

"The bastard never left his DNA." Jake tapped one finger on the table. "Weird, how neither the Copycat Player nor Copycat 2.0 has left his DNA at the scene. There's almost always a sexual component to a serial killer's motivation, and yet no rapes, no semen, no DNA."

"We know why Jordy didn't feel the urge to rape his victims. He took his sexual aggressions out on hookers after the slayings." She flattened the empty packets of sweetener with her thumb. "I wonder how this guy satisfies that urge."

Glancing to his right, Jake hunched forward. "God, I hope nobody is listening to this conversation."

"Ugh, you're right." She picked up the menu and scanned the salads and sandwiches. "Is that what you wanted to tell me?"

Jake peered at her over the top of his own menu. "The fingerprint? No, I wanted to tell you about the phone that sent me the text about the Harmons."

"Yes?" She clutched the laminated menu so hard, its edges bit into her fingers.

"As I suspected, it was a burner phone and it's already out of service." He tapped his menu against hers. "Sorry to disappoint you, but we sort of knew this person wasn't going to call from a cell that could be traced."

"Because he called you—a cop. But when he contacted me via email, he couldn't do so completely anonymously, could he? Maybe he figured I wouldn't have the resources to track him down at the library."

Jake said, "You do now. I requested a subpoena for the library's video footage for the day and approximate time you received that email. We'll get to have a look at who sat at those public computers in the library and sent you the photo."

"That's fantastic." She clapped her hands together and held them under her chin as if in prayer, but this man had already answered her prayers. "D-do you think you'll get the subpoena?"

"It's related to a serial killer case. Are you kidding? The mayor would be willing to give me the key to the entire city if it would help me bring in another killer." He stopped talking when the waitress came back to take their orders.

As she watched the waitress approach another table, Kyra whispered, "Do you know Mayor Wexler?"

"I've met him a few times. He's close with Chief Sterling. The guy loves his power."

Kyra closed her lips around her straw. She could tell Jake a lot more about Ben Wexler than probably even the chief knew, since Wexler's wife, Monica, was her client. Some secrets she still needed to keep from Jake.

They got through the rest of their lunch without a

word about murder, rape or DNA, but when it came time to pay the bill, Kyra slapped her hand on the check. "This is mine if you clue me in when you get the subpoena. I want to be looking at that library video with you."

"I wouldn't have it any other way, and—" he pinched the corner of the bill between two fingers and tugged "—you don't need to pick up lunch to bribe me."

"It's not a bribe. I invited you." She yanked the bill from his fingers and fished her debit card from her wallet.

He drove her back to the station. She stopped outside the building and waved him on. "You go ahead. I'm going to make a call outside."

"Good idea. Thanks for lunch." He marched into the station without a second glance.

She hadn't fooled him with her phone-call excuse, but he hadn't objected, either. He must agree with her that it was best to keep their relationship outside of work private—not that coworkers on the task force didn't have lunch together. She'd just had lunch with Billy yesterday, but rumors were not already swirling around her and Billy.

A young woman with black hair waved at her across the parking lot and then skipped toward her. "Kyra, right?"

Kyra glanced at the woman's tatted-up arm and blinked at the bright eyes and ready smile. "Rachel? Blackburn, right?"

"That's right. I wasn't sure if you'd remember me."

"Of course I do." Kyra waved her hand up and down the woman's casual slacks and blouse, a pair of black flats on her feet. "I didn't recognize you at first with the…uh, makeover."

The last time she'd seen Rachel, when her phone had been stolen by the Copycat Player to report the location of a body, she'd been sporting multiple piercings, heavy, dark makeup and black combat boots.

"Oh, I still inhabit that other persona, but I just got hired as an LAPD dispatcher. Detective McAllister was true to his word and got me in."

"I'm sure Human Resources was blown away by you and didn't even need McAllister's recommendation." Rachel had impressed both her and Jake with her keen perception and intelligence, so much so that Jake had gotten her hooked up with a job as a dispatcher.

"Thanks, but we both know a recommendation from Detective McAllister is worth a lot." Rachel screwed up her mouth. "With *most* people in the department."

Rachel had already discovered that J-Mac had a reputation with the LAPD and not everyone appreciated his tactics.

"Do you like the job so far?"

"I do. It's great. Hoping to learn all I can, finish my degree and then apply for a sworn position."

"I'm sure you'll make a great cop, Rachel." Kyra pointed to the building. "You going inside?"

The two walked into the station together and split up on the first floor. Jake was already hard at work by the time Kyra made it to her desk. Her sandwich and salad should've made her sleepy, but the discovery of Mindy Behr's body that morning had everyone amped up, and phones rang off the hook and spontaneous discussions broke out across the room. Nobody needed coffee with the energy bouncing off the walls, but gallons of the stuff disappeared anyway.

A few hours into the afternoon, Jake caught her eye across the room and tapped his personal cell phone. Two seconds later her own phone buzzed, and she glanced at the text.

As she read Jake's words, her pulse danced in her throat. The judge had signed off on the subpoena for the video at the Santa Monica Public Library. Jake promised to let her know when he planned to head out there to view it.

She texted him back with a thumbs-up emoji and let him know the library was open until nine o'clock this evening and that she had a client at five.

The rest of the afternoon flew by in a blur. At a few minutes before four o'clock, Kyra packed up her laptop and wedged the case on her chair. She sauntered to the back row of desks where J-Mac and Cool Breeze held court and leaned against Billy's desk.

"Everything go okay at the crime scene today?"

"As okay as that kind of thing can go, and of course we collected the print." Billy slumped in his chair and extended his long legs in front of him. "You know, I think I would've been able to keep it together even if the victim had been an African American female, but this experience has given me new resolve to find my sister."

"Really? Are you going to reopen the case?"

"I don't have the authority to do that, and missing person cases don't fall under robbery-homicide anyway. I do, however, have a line on a PI. I'm going to call him and schedule an appointment. I can't work this job and hold my breath every time we get a call on a young Black female. I need to know. My family needs to know."

"Let me know if I can be of any help, Billy." She dropped a hand to his shoulder and squeezed. "I mean that."

Jake had been trying to ignore their hushed conversation from the desk next to Billy's, but he finally looked up. "Are you calling it a day?"

"I am. I have a client in my Santa Monica office, and then I'm heading home." She hoped Jake got her meaning that she'd be ready to go to the library with him, without blurting it out in front of Billy. It was one thing for Billy to know about their budding relationship, if that was what you could call it, and another to flaunt the fact that she and Jake were working on a sideline to the case.

She could handle just one person at a time finding out that she'd stabbed her foster dad to death.

Jake winked at her. "Have a good session. Is that what you therapists say?"

"No, never. Have a nice evening. I'll see you two tomorrow. Hope you get a hit on that print."

"Ditto." Jake held up his hands, crossing the fingers of both.

Kyra made the drive home toward the coast, antsy to drop by Quinn's house to let him know she'd taken his advice and told Jake about her past. Quinn would also want the details on 2.0's latest murder, but Jake could serve him those details better than she could, detective to detective.

The fact that Quinn approved of and liked Jake thrilled her. If Jake met Quinn's high standards, then she knew she could trust Jake—and she could. Jake hadn't backed away from her when he found out about Buck Harmon; nor had he gotten mad at her for keeping it a secret from him.

Jake came across trauma like hers every day at his job. He'd been a homicide detective for almost ten years. Other people's misery had soaked into his bones by now, and he hadn't reached saturation point yet.

Maybe that was why the murder of those two African American women had hit Billy so hard. He'd been soaking it all in, just like Jake, but those deaths in particular had pushed him to saturation because of his missing sister.

She snorted and pulled into the parking space for her office. She was guilty of analyzing both detectives without even seeing them professionally—not that she could ever take on Jake as a client now, and not that he would ever seek out help.

He'd had an incident with a former coworker of hers, Lizbeth Kruger. Lizbeth had submitted a report to the parole board on a killer Jake had locked up, allowing for his early release. The guy had killed again, and when Jake found out, he went ballistic on Lizbeth at the station. Kyra had missed the fireworks, but Jake's towering rage had earned him a reprimand and mandatory anger-management sessions. She could only imagine how that went.

As a result, Jake had no fondness for therapists, but he seemed to be coming around where she was concerned. That thought put a little smile on her lips that she couldn't erase until she sat down with her client, who had just lost his job and whose wife had left him because of it.

When the fifty-minute session ended, Kyra checked her phone and saw the text from Jake that they had a meeting with one of the librarians at 7:30 p.m. She recorded notes from the session on her laptop, left a note for her office mate, Candace, and drove home.

After she threw together a quick pasta dish, it took her twenty minutes to decide to leave on her work clothes instead of changing into something more casual. Jake would still have his suit on, and she didn't want the librarian to think she didn't have a right to view that footage.

Jake had indicated he'd pick her up, and they'd go to the library together. She'd told him to text her when he was out front and started pacing at 7:05 p.m. Ten minutes later, her doorbell rang.

She squinted through the peephole and sighed at Jake standing there holding Spot. She yanked open the door. "You didn't have to walk all the way up here, and you certainly didn't need to pick up Spot. He's gonna get white cat hair all over your suit."

Jake unceremoniously dumped the cat on the ground and brushed off his slacks. "Little cat hair never hurt anything."

"Your partner would be shocked to hear that. Do you think Billy would ever allow a cat to shed on his suit?"

"Billy has two small children. When he's with his boys, he's a mess. Don't let him fool you." He nudged Spot with his foot as the cat curled his body around Jake's ankles. "And I'm not going to call for you at the curb."

She peered at him through narrowed eyes. "Did you park illegally again? Because I know for a fact there's no parking out there at this time of night."

He cleared his throat. "I may have squeezed in too close to a fire hydrant. Do you want to stand here talking about cat hair, Billy and parking, or do you want to get to the library and find out who play… La Prey is?"

"Let me grab my purse." She eased the door closed to keep Spot out and picked up her purse from the counter. Jake was right. Now that the moment had come to find out who'd been tormenting her, she was dragging her feet. She felt light-headed, as her fright-or-flight response kicked in.

When she opened the door, Jake had Spot in his arms again. "He's just doing that because he wants to be fed."

"Aw, I thought it was because he liked me."

When the door closed with a snap, Spot leaped out of Jake's arms and stalked away with a swish of his tail.

Kyra laughed. "He knows he's out of luck."

Her mouth dry on the short drive to the library, Kyra kept licking her lips and fidgeting with the strap of her purse.

Jake parked his vehicle and shot her a glance. "This is a good thing. It's going to be okay. This will help us get to the bottom of a lot of things, and I'm convinced it's going to shed light on these copycats. Hold on to that idea."

She dropped her chin in a jerky nod. She was less convinced than Jake that whoever was taunting her had knowledge about the copycat killers, but the thought gave her resolve.

Marching into the library next to Jake with a subpoena in his pocket, Kyra drew back her shoulders, feeling a confidence she had lacked the previous time she'd sidled in here with her lies about a stalker.

She just hoped Inez wasn't working the night shift.

When they entered through the glass doors, Jake veered left toward the circulation desk as opposed to the reference desk, and Kyra blew out a tiny breath from between her lips.

She hung back as Jake gave his name, flashed his badge and asked for Renee. Now, *that* was how you got results.

A short woman with chin-length dark hair streaked with gray approached the counter. "Detective McAllister, I'm Renee Shelton. I've been able to cue up the video from the date and time in question. Do you want to come around to the back?"

Jake shook hands with Renee and introduced her to Kyra. They both circled the long counter and met Renee at the end where she pulled open a swinging half door for them to step through.

As she led them to the back, she glanced over her shoulder. "I set up the computer in the office. Do you need me there to work it, or would you prefer to look at it on your own?"

Jake answered, "As long as it's cued up where we need it, I can handle the rest."

Renee ushered them into a small office with a computer set up on a table, two chairs in front of it. "I'll leave you to it, then. Let me know if you need any assistance."

They pulled the chairs up to the computer and Kyra sat on Jake's left, as he placed his hand over the mouse. "This is perfect. The cameras are pointing right at the public computers."

Kyra stared at the familiar setup of the computers, all empty now. She jabbed her finger at the workstations. "Do we know which one it is, specifically?"

"I passed the info you gave me from Brandon to the library, and Renee indicated it's the computer at the end. He should be showing up anytime now."

Kyra watched the flickering images of other people coming and going in the library, even sitting down at the public computers. She sat up when she saw Yolanda, the homeless woman from the day before, sprint toward the computers, her Santa Monica College sweatshirt bunched up around her waist. From the way she was moving, she wasn't as old as Kyra had imagined before. The sun had damaged her skin, aging her beyond her years.

"That woman was there the other day." Kyra sucked in a breath as Yolanda sat at the computer they were watching, her bags over her shoulder, a piece of paper clutched in her hand. "She must leave before La Prey gets there. Maybe he kicked her off that computer."

She hunched forward, her eyes watering as she focused on Yolanda clicking away on the keyboard, most likely bringing up articles on fashion. The minutes ticked by. Kyra's gaze darted to the clock in the upper-right corner of the video, the seconds racing.

Jake sat back in his chair and clasped his hands between his knees.

Kyra shot a glance at him, and he was no longer looking at the video.

She said sharply, "What?"

"That's it, Kyra. That's who sent you the email."

"It can't be." She cranked her head back and forth between the lying computer and Jake's grim face. "I met that woman. She's not all there. Why would she be sending me emails with the Harmon picture?"

"It's obvious, isn't it?"

"Not to me." But it was, and her stomach knotted.

"He paid Yolanda to send that email to cover his tracks. Player played us…again."

Chapter Fourteen

Kyra's cheeks flushed red, hot with anger, and she smacked her hand on the table next to the computer. "No! I met that woman. I talked to her. She couldn't have done it."

"Why? Because she's a little spacey?" Jake grabbed the mouse again and backtracked to the moment Yolanda sat down at the computer. "Look at her hand. She has a piece of paper. Those could've been her instructions."

Kyra sucked in her bottom lip and drummed her fingers on the edge of the keyboard.

"What?" Jake's word had a sharp edge, but from the look on her face, Kyra remembered something.

"When I first met her, she told me she worked at the library and people paid her for information. I gave her a twenty just to talk to her…and because I felt sorry for her." She kicked the table with the toe of her shoe. "Damn, and all this time she knew."

"That's the good news." Jake circled Yolanda's face with his finger. "She's obviously a regular here. We'll find her, talk to her, pay her if necessary and discover who hired her."

Kyra slumped in her seat, her chin dropping to her

chest. She said in a low voice, "I thought tonight was the night. I thought I'd see his face."

"We'll find him." Jake squeezed the back of her neck lightly. "That woman, Yolanda, is not going to have any loyalty to some guy off the street who paid her to send an email."

"She's not going to have any loyalty to us, either, unless I can convince her I'm a supermodel."

"Excuse me?"

"Oh—" she waved her hand in the air "—never mind. It's a long story. How are we going to locate Yolanda?"

Jake gave Kyra a quick, appraising look. She wouldn't have to do much to convince *him* she was a supermodel with her high cheekbones and wide eyes.

He dragged his gaze away from Kyra's perfect features, ended the video and closed out of the program. "You said she's a regular, right?"

"Seemed to be. The reference librarian knew her name, and Yolanda knew the reference librarian."

Jake wheeled his chair back from the desk and said, "We'll ask Renee the name of the reference librarian who usually works at the time you were here, and have her give us a call the next time she sees Yolanda."

"We don't even have to go through all that. The reference librarian who knows Yolanda is named Inez. We can tell Renee to have Inez call us…you."

"That'll work." He placed his hands on the back of her chair, his knuckles skimming her shoulder blades.

Being cooped up in this small space, working closely with Kyra, had put his senses on high alert. Every time she shifted in her chair, he caught a whiff of her rose scent. Every time her fingers accidentally brushed his hand, he felt a quiver down his spine. Despite his attraction to her, he was ready to call it a night—alone.

"What's wrong?"

Kyra had folded her arms and was bouncing her knee up and down. "How did he know that I'd track him to the library? This guy not only used a public computer, he paid someone to do the deed so he wouldn't be caught on camera."

"He's not an amateur." Jake lifted his shoulders. "He knew to contact Matt Dugan, used Matt's knowledge of you to stalk you. He knows you work with the police because he left one of the cards by your car parked outside the station. He knows who you are, Kyra. That's no secret."

She hopped up suddenly. "And we're going to know who he is soon enough."

They exited the room and Jake poked his head into the office next door. "Renee, we're done, but we do have another request."

"Did you find what you were looking for?"

"In a manner of speaking." Jake slid a glance at Kyra. "We'd like to speak to a homeless person who was on the computer. Kyra said that the reference librarian, Inez, knows who she is."

Renee gave them a tight smile. "That doesn't surprise me. Inez would know the regulars on the public computers."

Jake raised his eyebrows hopefully and asked, "Is Inez here tonight?"

"Inez left for the day. If you want to leave your card, I can have her call you."

Kyra rustled in her purse. "I'd like to leave my card with a note for Inez. I met her yesterday, and she'll know what I'm talking about."

"That's fine." Renee held out a pen to Kyra, who continued to rummage in her purse.

"Thanks." Kyra leaned over Renee's desk and printed a note on the back of one of her cards. Before she handed it to Renee, she nudged Jake in the ribs. "Leave one of your cards with mine so she knows it's part of the search warrant and legit."

Jake pulled a card out of his pocket and handed it to Kyra, who held them out to Renee.

"I will leave these for Inez at the reference desk so she can't miss them."

They both thanked Renee and walked out into the night air, now being taken over by a low marine layer rolling in from the Pacific.

Jake stopped under a streetlamp that had just turned on, the moist air carrying a hint of salt and caressing his face. "What was in the note?"

"I told her I needed to speak with Yolanda and to let me know the next time she saw her in the library, or at least let me know the hours Yolanda haunted the public computers." She shook her head, her blue eyes glassy beneath the light. "I'm just not sure how much help Yolanda's going to be. She thinks she's involved with the fashion industry and that she's looking for new styles for the designers."

Jake pressed a hand to his forehead. "Wow. How did The Play… La Prey manage to settle on Yolanda for this task? Seems like he was taking a big risk with her."

Kyra jerked her head up when he almost said The Player again. He'd honor her wishes of calling the guy La Prey in her presence, but that didn't change the fact that he'd used an anagram of the player to ID himself.

She brushed her hair from her face, accustomed to having it drawn into a ponytail. "Yolanda must have her moments of clarity, or maybe she's just really good at following directions."

"We'll find out, one way or the other." Jake turned toward where he'd parked his car, and after a few moments, Kyra followed him.

As he opened the door for her, he grabbed her hand. "Didn't Quinn ever tell you that good investigative work takes time?"

Her lips lifted at one corner. "Quinn also told me to trust you. I should always listen to Quinn."

Jake slammed her door with a full-fledged smile on his face. He owed Quinn a six-pack.

THE NEXT MORNING, Jake walked into the task force war room, dragging his heels. Castillo had already called him to let him know he was going out to Mindy Behr's family home today in San Marino, a ritzy area just south of Pasadena.

Turned out the Behrs were big contributors to Mayor Wexler's campaign. Now the brass would turn up the heat even higher on the task force. The urgency of the investigation shouldn't depend on the victims, but it often turned out that way.

His eyes tracked to Kyra's desk as if it held some magnetic power over him—just like she did—but she hadn't made it in yet. She didn't always report to the station to work. She had clients outside her police work, although he knew she was one of the LAPD-sanctioned therapists. Her name had even cropped up on the list the department had handed to him when they mandated anger-management sessions for him after his blowup at that Lizbeth woman.

He'd opted out of one-on-one therapy and had chosen a group meeting instead. He had to admit the group had helped him, but it was because the group leader, Max Darotta, employed what Jake learned later was behavioral therapy. Max gave the group members actual tools to use. He couldn't have handled sitting there talking about his feelings.

He gave a shiver and hunched his shoulders. It was a good thing he hadn't chosen therapy with Kyra after all. At that time he probably would've hated it and her, and then he wouldn't have been able to date her later.

Not that they'd been on an actual date yet.

He jumped as Billy thumped his back. "Daydreaming, brother?"

"Yeah, daydreaming about when you're going to come up with some video we can actually use."

"Just might be your lucky day." Billy winked and then hunched in closer. "You hear the Behr family is connected?"

"Friends of Wexler's. Castillo called me this morning. I'm taking a jaunt out to San Marino today to talk to them."

Billy crossed one index finger over the other and held them out. "I can't go with you today. Is that all right, or does Castillo expect the both of us?"

"Hate to break it to you, Billy, but your name never came up in the conversation."

"Then you're on your own." Billy skimmed his hand across his short Afro. "This is a PR move for Castillo and Chief Sterling. From what I've heard, Mindy didn't have much contact with her parents. They didn't know her friends, but it didn't stop them from disapproving of them. They're not going to be able to tell you much about Mindy's habits and whether or not she was being stalked."

"I know that, but you're a better PR guy than I am."

"You're the task force lead." Billy drilled his finger into Jake's chest. "They want the top dog."

Jake barked just as his desk phone rang. "McAllister."

"It's Captain Castillo. You're taking Kyra with you to the Behrs."

Jake's heart jumped and then settled to a dull thud. Though he looked forward to any time spent with Kyra, it wasn't common for someone like her to sit in with a detective when he or she was questioning family members. Now he knew Billy was right. This was a PR move.

"You got a problem with that? I thought you two were—" Castillo cleared his throat "—getting along."

Jake hadn't been too pleased with Kyra's appointment when they'd first formed the task force for the Copycat Player. He'd moved past that...way past that.

"No problem at all, Cap. I've watched her work, and she's an asset. I'm just wondering what kind of interview this is going to be. Do the parents have material evidence or insight into their daughter's murder?"

Castillo snapped. "No. Wexler and the chief are calling the shots on this one and the rest of us dance. Is that too hard for you to figure out, J-Mac?"

Jake had held the receiver away from his ear and now rolled his eyes at Billy, who was mouthing something to him.

"No, sir. Not at all. I'll let Kyra know, and we'll be out there this afternoon."

Castillo slammed the phone down before Jake could even pull the receiver from his ear. "What is Castillo's problem these days? He acts like we never ID'd and stopped the Copycat Player last month."

"You know how it goes." Billy raised his eyes to

the ceiling, holding his palms up. "Stuff rolls down-hill. Wexler's on Sterling's backside, who's on Castillo's backside, who's on ours. We just need to find a way to remove a few of those backsides."

"Thanks for the primer on politics." Jake folded his hands behind his head. "Now give me one on handling well-connected families of victims, who are probably going to report back to the chief."

"You don't need me for that. You'll have Kyra with you. She'll have your back, but you know what?" Billy's gaze wandered to Kyra's side of the room. "You might want to watch that one."

Jake's pulse ticked at the side of his mouth. Had Billy discovered something about Kyra's past? "What do you mean?"

"She saw Tara's name on your phone, and then she hit me up later and asked if you were dating Tara. Bro, you don't want no crazy girlfriend. They become crazy *ex*-girlfriends."

Jake let out a breath that turned into a chuckle. He *wished* Kyra was the jealous type. "I think she's okay. Haven't seen her today?"

"No." Billy waved at two cops coming through the door. "We've got video to look at. We got a line on some cars in Andrea's neighborhood, and a few of them look similar to cars in Crystal's neighborhood. We're going to isolate those and get to work on the blocks around Mindy's house."

"Thank God for CCTV." When Billy walked away, Jake picked up his work cell and called Kyra. She answered right away.

Her voice breathless, she asked, "Did Inez from the library call you?"

"Haven't heard from her yet, but it's still early." He paused as Kyra breathed heavily into the phone. "Are you okay?"

"I'm fine. Just finished doing some yoga on my living room floor."

His heart returned to its regular beats per minute, which were higher than normal when talking to Kyra anyway. "The task force has an assignment for you."

"I know. Captain Castillo already called me. I can be at the station in about ninety minutes if that's not too late."

"I'll make sure it's not. I haven't even called the Behrs yet to set a time. Not that I'm complaining, but do you know how this came about? How did they even know we had someone like you on the task force?"

"No clue. Maybe they were asking for additional services? People like that are accustomed to full-service attention—not that I'm saying they don't deserve it at this time."

"Just curious. I'll see you at the station in an hour and a half, then. Good thing I wore one of the suits Billy suggested for me."

"You may not have the sartorial splendor of Billy, but you can definitely fill out a suit."

When they ended the call, Jake had a warm feeling in the pit of his stomach at Kyra's compliment. He really didn't want a jealous woman—he'd seen how deadly that emotion could be—but could puff out his chest a little at Kyra's compliment. If she wanted him for more than his detective's mind, he'd take it.

The warm fuzzies receded as he pondered the puzzle of Kyra Chase. She seemed to have connections he could never quite fathom, and he didn't know why those connections always came with an edge of mystery.

DRAGGING THE ELASTIC band from her hair, Kyra muttered to herself, "Definitely fill out a suit? You are definitely an idiot. Who says things like that?"

She rolled up her yoga mat and shoved it into the hall closet. On the phone with Jake, she'd had an urge to step up her game. He hadn't made any moves last night when they left the library, but then she hadn't exactly been sending out welcoming vibes.

She'd been angry when she discovered La Prey had beat her again. Seeing his image on the library video and identifying him would've put an end to his torment. What did he want from her, anyway? He hadn't demanded money or information or favors. Probably one of those sick crime buffs who spent all his time researching other people's misery and wanted to feel connected to it all. She knew there were internet discussion groups, blogs and message boards devoted to true crime. She'd snuck in on a few of them anonymously. Some comprised amateur sleuths who cared for victims and really did want to help, and others were composed of vicarious thrill-seekers who wanted to feel close to the action. If any of them actually did get close to a violent murder, they'd change their minds really fast and find another hobby.

As she showered, she heard Jake's lingering questions in her head. She had an idea how she'd gotten on the Behrs' radar. Mindy Behr's mother must be friends with Monica Wexler, the mayor's wife. Even if Kyra would never reveal that she saw Monica Wexler on a professional basis, there was nothing stopping Monica from telling her friends about her therapist.

Jake could continue to think she had some Svengali-like powers over the LAPD, or that Quinn's influence somehow stretched to the mayor's office, but she'd never out a client. Everyone had a right to their secrets.

Dressed in a pair of straight-legged beige slacks and a white blouse with a ruffle at the neck, Kyra draped a beige sweater with a white zigzag through it over her shoulders and locked up her apartment.

On her drive to the station, she checked her phone several times for a message or call from Inez. She'd also kept an eye out for Yolanda on her morning walk down to the beach and back, peering at transients on bus stop benches and huddled on the steps of businesses before they opened for the day. Other than a few requests for money and an invitation to go swimming in the ocean, she had come up empty. Yolanda could spend her nights in a shelter and then wander into the library during the day to do her…business.

Kyra eased out a sigh and rolled into the parking lot of the LAPD's Northeast Division. She'd have to leave the finding of Yolanda to Inez.

When she got to the conference room that housed the task force, she stood at the door with her mouth slightly ajar as she watched the activity and heard a buzz of conversation. Grabbing the sleeve of one of the uniforms as he squeezed past her, she said, "Fingerprint?"

"Video."

Kyra wended her way to Jake's desk and planted herself next to it. "You have promising video?"

"A couple of cars from Andrea's neighborhood around the time we figure someone snuck into her garage match a couple of cars in Crystal's neighborhood. We have clear enough footage on Andrea's tape to get some license plates. Billy and his team are scouring the footage in Mindy's neighborhood." Jake grabbed his jacket and grimaced. "And I have to leave the action to hold the hands of Wexler's pals."

"Hey!" Kyra jabbed him in the ribs. "Wexler's pals are also grieving parents. They can't help it if they have the pull to get some extra attention. Anyone in their position would take advantage of that."

"You're right." He put a hand over his heart. "That's why you're going with me."

Herding her out of the room with his hand pressed to the small of her back, Jake pointed at Billy and said, "Keep me posted."

Kyra didn't mind the heads turning at their departure. They had a legitimate reason to be together today.

As Jake took his car north through LA to the Foothill Freeway, they discussed the case, Yolanda and even Billy's canceled meeting with the PI today. Kyra wasn't the only one tiptoeing around their mutual decision last night to head to their own beds, alone.

Whenever the time seemed to be right and their emotions swept them up in a tidal wave, some outside force erected a barrier, or, in the case of the phone call from Jake's daughter, the force was more like an insinuation that floated between them.

Last night the only emotions Kyra could muster were anger and frustration at the wiliness of her adversary, and Jake had seemed tired, defeated. Did he feel as if he had to work too hard at seduction? Would he get tired of the effort?

She focused her gaze outside the window at the banners with roses on them as they followed the same route as the Rose Parade. Tapping the glass, she said, "I always wanted to go to the Rose Parade when I was a kid. Did you ever go?"

He snorted. "My old man would've never taken us

to anything like that, but I've been a few times as an adult with Fiona. Even camped out one night on the sidewalk."

"That's dedication." Jake didn't sound like such a horrible dad to her. She took a deep breath to ask him more about his childhood, only knowing his dad had been a cop, too, but Jake whistled and gestured out the window.

"We're going to start heading into the nice area now."

"The whole area looks nice to me."

"Wait until we go past the Huntington Library toward Lacy Park. That's where the Behrs are."

"Leave it to Wexler to cultivate friends in high places." She didn't need her client Monica Wexler to tell her about the mayor's ambition, which was one of the sticky points in their marriage. Everyone in LA knew the mayor had his sights set on bigger and better prizes.

As Jake turned down the Behrs' street, Kyra wrinkled her nose at the stately mansions a discreet distance from each other, sporting golf-course-worthy lawns with velvety-green grass even at the end of one of the hottest summers on record.

"I don't know. In the realm of multimillion-dollar homes, I prefer yours and Quinn's to these show-offs."

Jake gave a short bark of a laugh that sounded very much like Quinn's. "Neither Quinn's nor my house can compare with these."

"Maybe not pricewise, but your houses have these beat in character."

Jake pulled into the circular driveway of a white mansion, the blandness of it relieved by a riot of colorful flowers bordering the house and running up either side of a long walkway that cut through the grass. It all looked too cheerful for the visit.

When Jake cut the engine, Kyra put a hand on his arm. "Remember, they aren't suspects. This isn't a typical interview."

"Got it." He pinched her knee. "Have I told you I'm glad you're here?"

Kyra tried to wipe the smile off her face as they walked up the two steps to the double doors. The doorbell they pressed rang deep inside the house. Kyra almost expected a butler in tails to answer its call.

When a petite woman with fluffy blond hair opened the heavy door, Kyra blinked at her.

Straightening his jacket, Jake said, "Mrs. Behr?"

A smile touched her lips and she dabbed her red nose with a tissue. "That's right. You must be Detective McAllister, and you're Kyra Chase."

Jake stiffened beside Kyra, and she held her breath, hoping that Mrs. Behr wouldn't blurt out how she knew her name.

"That's right. I'm sorry for your loss, ma'am."

"Thank you, Detective." She stepped to the side and widened the door. "Please come in and join us on the patio. You can remove your jacket, Detective. It's cool enough in the back, but it feels like we're having one of those extended summers, doesn't it?"

"It sure does, ma'am, especially with the Santa Ana winds last month and those wildfires blazing."

Mrs. Behr, looking crisp in white capris, a blue-and-white polka-dot blouse and white sandals, led them through a great room that opened onto the patio. A pocket wall had been fully retracted so that there was no division at all between the inside of the house and the outside except for a track on the floor that separated the wood of the great room from the pavers on the patio.

Okay, maybe this was a little nicer than Quinn's beach cottage on the Venice canals.

As they stepped onto the patio, Mr. Behr rose from a chair, shunting his laptop to the side and running a hand through his thinning hair, where the salt was beginning to take over the pepper.

"Darling, this is Detective McAllister and Kyra Chase. She's the—"

Mr. Behr interrupted his wife. "I know who she is. I'm Michael Behr. Thank you for coming."

Jake shook Mr. Behr's hand. "I'm sorry for your loss, Mr. Behr. We're doing everything we can to catch Mindy's killer."

A jagged sob escaped from Mrs. Behr's lips, and Kyra launched forward and took her arm. "Let's sit down."

Mr. Behr motioned Jake into a chair.

"We don't want special treatment, you know. That was the mayor's idea. There were two other victims before Mindy, and I'm sure you didn't make personal visits to their homes." He peered up at Jake from his clasped hands.

"We're always available to talk to all of the victims' families, and Kyra is part of the task force and on call if anyone, even the detectives, needs to talk."

"Th-that's nice." Mrs. Behr crumpled her tissues in her fingers. "Really, we just want an overview of the investigation. Surely, that's something you can share with all the families, can't you?"

She shot her husband a look from beneath wet lashes, and he set his jaw.

It was clear who had arranged for this meeting. Mrs. Behr may have even gotten the idea from Monica Wexler, who in turn encouraged her husband to reach out.

Jake sat forward in his chair. "We can absolutely tell you the status of the investigation—up to a point. Certain things we keep from the press and even the families, if we feel those things will help us solve the case faster. Does that make sense?"

"It does," Mr. Behr answered as he waved his hand at someone in the great room.

A short Latina with worried eyes and her own tissue crumpled in her hand scurried out to the patio. "Yes, Mr. Michael?"

"Elena, could you please bring us some drinks?" Mr. Behr's gaze darted between Jake and Kyra. "Lemonade, iced tea, both?"

Kyra smiled at Elena. "I'll take a lemonade, please."

"Same, thank you." Jake nodded at Elena, who didn't ask what Mr. and Mrs. Behr wanted.

This kind of money secured you workers who probably knew your needs before you did.

When Elena disappeared, Jake launched into an overview of where the LAPD stood on the case. He included the detail of the playing card between the lips, but left off the severed finger. The families would learn about that indignity later when they got back their loved ones' bodies for burial or cremation.

Jake did a good job of sanitizing the descriptions, and he trailed off when Elena came back with a tray of four tall glasses filled with pale yellow liquid with ice tinkling inside like delicate wind chimes.

When he resumed his narrative, punctuated by questions from the Behrs, Kyra noticed he also declined to mention the latest development with the video. Didn't want to give false hope or just didn't want news getting out yet.

When he wound up, Kyra started her job. She asked

the Behrs questions about Mindy and encouraged them to talk about her—not to help the investigation but to help themselves. They hadn't had two seconds to grieve, and they needed to start that process.

Mrs. Behr was the one who ended the meeting by putting her glass aside and shifting in her seat. "We appreciate your visit so much, don't we, Michael?"

Jake's thorough discussion of the investigation had brought Mr. Behr around, and he also seemed to understand how important it was for his wife.

By the time she and Jake got back to his car, Kyra felt drained, as if she'd just facilitated a two-hour group session. She collapsed in the passenger seat, leaned her head back and closed her eyes. "I'm exhausted."

Jake tapped her shoulder, and she opened one eye, focusing on the phone he held out to her. "What?"

"Too tired to drive out to Santa Monica and talk to Yolanda?"

She bolted upright in her seat and scrambled for her own cell phone. "Inez called you?"

"Almost right after we sat down with the Behrs and I turned off my phone." He squinted at it now. "About two hours ago. Said Yolanda was at the library."

Kyra's fingers closed around her phone, and she pulled it free from her purse. "She texted me, too. Same thing. Let's hurry. We might catch her in the library."

Jake put on the speed, but traffic wouldn't cooperate. Kyra had put in a call to Inez, who hadn't responded yet.

As they got off the freeway and veered onto Lincoln, Inez returned Kyra's call. "I'm sorry. Yolanda just left. I sent you and the detective texts as soon as I saw her here."

Kyra made a face at Jake. "Thank you for that. Do

you know which direction she was headed? Do you know where she stays at night?"

"I think she stays at the women-only shelter in downtown LA sometimes, but not always. When she leaves the library she sometimes goes down to the pier to get food from the restaurants there."

"Thanks, Inez. We'll try that, or we can catch her another day."

"She hasn't done anything wrong, has she?"

"Not at all. We just want to talk to her about someone she might have met. Have you ever seen her talking to a man in the library?"

"Yolanda will talk to anyone who talks to her, but I've never noticed anyone in particular."

"Okay, I'll let you know if you need to keep a lookout tomorrow, too."

Jake idled at a stop sign. "Let's try for another day. We're so close to your place. If you don't need anything from the station, I can just drop you off at home and take you back in the morning."

Kyra turned her head to look at his slightly flushed face. Did he mean he'd drive all the way back to his place in West Hollywood after dropping her off and then come back in the morning to pick her up? Or did he mean he'd spend the night and the two of them would go into the station together?

She broke off as the wail of a siren swooped down on them from behind.

"Whoa." Jake rolled forward a little bit and veered to the right to clear the way for the ambulance and cop car.

Kyra stared at a crowd of people up ahead on the corner of Ocean, across the street from the pier, and her heart pounded in her chest. "Inez mentioned that Yolanda sometimes went to the pier after the library to scrounge for food. Let's look there first before giving up today."

"Okay, but in case you haven't noticed, it's kind of a mess up there." His hands resting on top of the steering wheel, Jake pointed at the clutch of people and emergency vehicles.

"You're in your LAPD car. When have you ever shied away from parking this thing illegally?" She waved a finger at a red curb in a bus lane ahead and to the right. "Stop over there. I want to see what's going on. I have a bad feeling about this."

"About this?" He nodded at the scene on the corner.

"Yeah. Just humor me."

The sedan lurched forward into the intersection and cruised to a stop on the red curb that would give anyone else a ticket in a minute flat.

Before Jake even cut the engine, Kyra had the door open and was scrambling from the car. As Jake called after her, she broke into a jog and hung on the edge of the crowd clumped around an accident scene in the street.

Her breath catching in her throat, she asked everyone and no one in particular, "What happened?"

"Car versus pedestrian."

"Hit and run."

"Some homeless lady."

"Think she's dead."

With her head swimming and the blood pounding against her temples, Kyra shimmied and ducked through the lookie-loos until she staggered to the front, bordering the street.

A body, already covered with a white sheet, lay in the street. One edge of the sheet had flipped back, and in the revolving red and blue lights, Kyra could make out the logo for Santa Monica College on the dirty gray sweatshirt.

Chapter Fifteen

Jake ran to catch up with Kyra and, peering over the crowd, could see her blond head. What the hell was she doing gaping at the scene of a hit and run?

He cupped his hand around his mouth and yelled, "Kyra!"

He had to try a second time before her head whipped around, and he staggered back at eyes as big as saucers on her face and her mouth open in a perfect O. She looked like she'd seen a ghost.

She turned her body in his direction and battled the crowd to reach him.

She fell against him heavily. He wrapped one arm around her and pulled her close to his chest, where he felt her heart hammering against him.

"What is it? What happened?"

She planted her hands against his chest and looked up into his face, whispering, "It's her."

He glanced at the uniforms doing crowd control and the ambulance parked at an angle in the middle of the street. "Yolanda? You're telling me that the hit-and-run victim is Yolanda?"

"Yes." She grabbed the front of his shirt, nearly ripping it off his body. "He did it. I know he did it. He took care of Matt, too. Think about it."

"Slow down a minute." He had to practically drag her away from the scene. Amid the chaos, nobody even noticed their drama. "Sit here."

He'd pushed her into a plastic chair at a fast-food restaurant's outdoor patio. A number of patrons had already abandoned their food and tables to get a look at the accident scene.

"How do you know that's Yolanda? As far as I could see, the body had already been covered."

"Not completely. The sheet had hitched up on one side and I saw her clothing."

"You recognized the clothing of a homeless person you saw once?" He didn't want to believe her, didn't want to face the consequences of her truth, and was throwing everything he had at her.

"It was distinctive." She grabbed the straw stuck in a drink and, with her lips puckered, pulled it toward her until he slid the cup away from her.

"That's not your drink."

She blinked and released the straw. "She was wearing a gray sweatshirt from Santa Monica College. I noticed it because I teach classes there sometimes. Yolanda went on about working in the fashion world, so, of course, I checked out her clothes. The woman lying dead in the street is wearing the same sweatshirt."

The corner of Jake's eye started twitching, and he smacked himself on the side of the head to stop it. "You think La Prey had something to do with Yolanda's death."

It wasn't even a question. Of course Kyra thought that. Didn't he?

Ignoring her tilted head and pursed lips, he plowed on. "What were you saying about Matt?"

"When you set up that meeting with Matt at the motorcycle shop in Van Nuys, he was going to tell you who paid him off to plant the cards for me, wasn't he?" She folded her hands, trapping her fidgety fingers.

"I think he was also planning to tell me that you'd killed Buck Harmon. I mentioned he had dirt on you. I didn't suspect *you* of killing Matt."

"Didn't you?" She raised her eyebrows at him and then grabbed a French fry.

He slapped her hand. "Those aren't yours."

"Ugh." She pushed the half-eaten food away from her. "Matt is about to reveal information to you about La Prey and he dies of a drug overdose, which is not a surprising way for him to go out. Yolanda might tell us who paid her to send me that email and she dies in a hit-and-run accident, which wouldn't seem too suspicious for a transient to meet her end that way. Quinn always told me…"

They recited together, "There are no coincidences in police work."

Holding up his hand, Jake said, "But was Yolanda going to tell us anything? And how would La Prey know if she was?"

"Stop being such a…detective." She flailed her hands in the air. "How does he know anything, Jake? He just does."

He got up from the uncomfortable chair and aimed a finger at Kyra. "You stay here—and don't eat or drink anything from this table. It's not yours."

He stalked back to the accident scene, clutching his badge in his hand, and found the Santa Monica PD sergeant in charge, Campos. As way of introduction, he said, "Jake McAllister, LAPD Robbery-Homicide, Sergeant Campos. Is the victim a homeless person named Yolanda?"

The sergeant puffed up his pumped-up chest until Jake thought the buttons would pop off his uniform. "What's your interest here?"

Jake sucked a breath into his mouth and expelled it from his nose, briefly closing his eyes behind his sunglasses, grateful to the late sunsets that he still needed them. He didn't feel like getting into some kind of contest with this guy.

"I'm not interested in stepping on your turf. I had a few questions I wanted to ask Yolanda related to a homicide I'm investigating. If you could verify for me that Yolanda is the victim and give me anything you got on witnesses or the car, I'll be on my way."

This de-escalation stuff really worked. Campos seemed to deflate and ducked in toward Jake until he could smell the sergeant's cheesy cologne.

Campos replied, "No positive ID yet, but we've heard a few names and Yolanda is one of them. The car was a white SUV. We got the plates, called it in immediately, and the owner reported it stolen earlier today. Probably why the guy took off after the accident."

"Probably." Jake pressed his card into Campos's hand and said, "Impressive work. Call me if you have any more information."

Campos nodded and strode off to the call of one of his officers.

Car theft, murder. La Prey was more than a stalker. Was he a serial killer, too? No. He'd been taunting Kyra during the Copycat Player killings, and that serial killer had turned out to be barista Jordy Lee Cannon, a geek who lived at home with his mother.

When he got back to the patio of the fast-food place, a couple was sitting at the table munching their food.

"Psst." Kyra waved at him from the other side of the

patio. When he joined her, she thrust a soda in his hand. "They kicked me off their table."

"They probably would've done worse if you'd eaten all their food." He sucked down some soda. "Thanks."

"What did you discover?"

"They haven't ID'd the victim yet, but the name Yolanda is floating around. They *did* ID the car already. A witness got the plates, and it's a stolen car."

She shook the ice in her cup. "I can't believe it. No, I can believe it. He's not going to get caught that easily, is he? Poor Yolanda. I wonder how he figured out she was going to rat on him."

"We don't even know if she was...and neither did he. He could've just as easily offered her more money for keeping quiet."

"If you'd met Yolanda, you'd know that would've been a tricky proposition."

"Then he knew it, too, and killed her." Jake slurped up the rest of his drink and tossed it into the recycling bin. "I'm starving. I haven't eaten since breakfast, and that's the first drink I've had since that lemonade with the Behrs. Can I interest you in dinner?"

"We can pick up food and drop in on Quinn. I haven't told him any of these new—"

"No."

Her head jerked back and her blue eyes widened.

"As much as I like Quinn and as much as I appreciate his insight on these cases, I'm done for the day. I need to turn off my brain. I need to breathe."

A little smile haunted her lips. "That's good advice for your anger management."

"I thought that stuff was supposed to be confidential."

"I can make deductions." She patted his cheek.

"Wipe that scowl off your face. I'm down with dinner for just the two of us, and I'm sure Quinn would approve."

"I seem to remember a funky steak house down on Ocean, Chez Jay. Is that still there?"

"It's still there, and I haven't been in years." She tugged on his sleeve. "We can walk from here, but you can't leave your car parked in the red forever."

They made their way through people still milling around the accident scene. Jake picked up his pace when he saw something flapping beneath his windshield wiper.

Kyra crowed. "You got a parking ticket."

Jake snatched the fluttering sheet of paper and scanned the note. He crumpled it and shoved it into his pocket. "It's not a ticket."

As he opened the passenger door for her, she raised her eyebrows at him. "What did it say?"

He grunted before answering. "'Welcome to Santa Monica. Park illegally in your own city.'"

KYRA SIPPED THE last of her red wine, its warmth cruising through her bloodstream and melting her bones. Since halfway through her second glass, she hadn't thought about Yolanda's violent death or how La Prey knew his email emissary had been discovered and was about to be questioned.

She eyed the wine bottle on the table through a pleasant fog. Jake had suggested ordering the bottle with their steaks, and he'd had less than two glasses, his second half-full, the ruby liquid shimmering in the candlelight.

Tapping his glass with her fingernail, she said, "Are you trying to get me drunk?"

"Someone has to drive. Besides, you needed it more than I did." He rubbed the back of her hand with his thumb. "Feeling better?"

"A little wine won't make it go away—not even a lot of wine."

"I know that better than most, but at least your face has lost its pinched look and your fingers aren't busy pulling threads from the tablecloth."

"That bad, huh?"

"Understandable. Are you ready to leave?"

She swallowed and nodded, the haze lifting as she thought about the short ride back to her place in Jake's LAPD sedan, her car stuck at the station and both of them going to the same place in the morning. It only made sense for him to stay at her apartment.

"I'm ready." She dropped her napkin onto the table beside her plate.

On the drive to her apartment, Kyra shot a quick glance at Jake. She'd been the one to break things off twice before just when things had gotten interesting. She should be the one to make the first move now.

As his car crawled down her block, she realized he was actually looking for a legal parking space. That could only mean one thing—he planned to stay the night.

He parallel parked with ease and opened his door. "I'll walk you up."

Just walk her up? Did that mean he didn't intend to stay?

Suddenly she had never wanted anything more in her life than to feel Jake's body next to hers—convenience be damned, first-move protocol be damned.

For a change, she waited in the car while he came around to the passenger side like she knew he would.

When he opened the car door, she got out and fell against his chest, wrapping her arms around his neck. She breathed against his warm, slightly salty skin. "You're spending the night—and I don't mean on the couch."

He put one hand on her lower back and tipped up her chin with the other. "Is that the wine talking?"

"Wine doesn't talk. This is me." She grabbed his face with both hands and planted a kiss on his mouth.

He reeled beneath her sudden assault, then recovered quickly and kissed her back until he'd sapped her strength. That wasn't the wine, either.

His arm around her and her hand grasping the front of his shirt, they staggered down the sidewalk to her apartment building, looking like a couple of drunks on a bender, but it was desire for each other, not alcohol, that fueled their intoxication. At her door, she scrabbled for her keys, dropped them and then banged heads with Jake as they both reached down to retrieve them.

This mishap ended in another soul-searing kiss at the front door, the keys forgotten on the ground between them. Spot meowed and brought them to their senses.

Rubbing the side of his head, Jake said, "Let me."

He picked up her key chain, and it took him three tries to get the key in the slot.

As she bumped open the door with her hip, she grinned and said, "I was hoping your aim would be better than that."

He chuckled, a low sound that reverberated in his chest and practically lifted her from the floor as he swept her inside, slamming the door on a grumpy Spot. "You're too sassy for your own good."

As punishment for her sassiness, he sealed his

mouth over hers and pushed her against the wall in the short hallway.

If they had to stop and kiss like this every few feet before they made it to the bedroom, she wanted a preview of coming attractions. She yanked at the buttons on his shirt and freed it from his slacks. She skimmed her hands across the tight-fitting, V-necked T he had under his dress shirt, the thin material clinging to his muscles.

Pinching the material off his chest, she yanked the T-shirt from his slacks. Her hands wandered beneath the shirt and splayed across the ridges of his pecs.

His hands had been busy, too, and her blouse gaped open. His fingers skimmed the edge of her lacy bra as he kissed her throat.

He murmured against her throbbing pulse. "I need a shower."

"Not cold?"

"Definitely not cold."

"This is an old apartment. I'm not sure my shower is going to be big enough for the two of us, but we'll have to make do 'cause I'm not letting you out of my sight." She stepped back and crooked her finger at him.

He needed no more encouragement than that. He followed her into the small bathroom, dwarfing everything in it.

Kyra whipped aside the shower curtain, and the blue mermaids hissed and sighed in response, the clacking of the shower curtain rings sounding like applause from their tiny hands.

She cranked on the water to warm it up and turned to grab Jake's belt. "Normally, people are naked when they take showers."

"That's what I'm counting on."

The two of them scrambled out of their clothes, bumping their elbows against each other and the walls in their haste.

With Jake standing naked in front of her, she ran her hands down the front of his body, stopping just shy of his erection. She tickled her fingers over the tattoo on his left arm, the tiger fully visible now.

Jake shivered and lifted her off the ground with one arm, placing her in the shower. He climbed in after and she soaped up his massive frame.

He kept grabbing her wrist to stop the exploration of her hands, and finally growled, "There's not enough room in here for what I want to do with you."

As he washed her body with his rough hands, she imagined all the disappointment, pain and horror of the day sloughing off her skin and circling down the drain.

His hands caressed her soapy breasts, sending tingles cascading through her body. She wrapped her arms around his waist to stay upright as her legs wobbled, and his erection brushed her belly.

With a groan, Jake turned off the water and grabbed a towel from the rack outside the shower.

"I forgot to get another towel for you."

"Do you have a problem with sharing? Because I plan to share a lot more than a towel with you."

He patted her dry with the towel first and then swiped it over his own body when she stepped out of the shower.

She backed up into her bedroom, where her king-size bed dominated the room. As her knees hit the edge of the bed, her stomach dipped and she covered her mouth. "I—I don't have any condoms."

He grabbed his pants from the bathroom floor and pulled his wallet from the pocket. He held up two foil squares in his fingers. "At least one of us was thinking ahead."

"Always keep some handy, do you?" She twirled a lock of her hair around her finger, relief and jealousy warring in her breast.

"Ever since I met you." He descended on her, and they fell to the bed together, a tangle of arms, legs and tongues.

As Jake made love to her body, her mind opened to him completely. He knew her. He'd scaled all her walls, stared into her face, unblinking—and he hadn't looked away.

When he entered her, she closed around him. Her tongue tasted the soap on his skin. Her fingers traced the hard muscles on his back and buttocks. She sighed against his shoulder, baring her teeth against his flesh as he drove into her.

His frame shuddered and he whispered hoarsely in her ear. "Look at me."

She turned her head and met his eyes, losing herself in the dark, murky green as his climax claimed every inch of his body...and hers.

His thrusts slowed down, and he squeezed his eyes closed as if savoring every last moment of their connection. When he rolled to her side and nuzzled her throat, she felt a profound and immediate loss.

She burrowed her head into the crook of his neck and twined her legs around his to prolong their contact. As she skimmed her hand across his damp chest, she had a moment of panic. What if he left her, too?

WITH THE SUNLIGHT streaming through the blinds the following morning and Jake still solidly by her side, Kyra took a moment to stretch her toes to the end of the bed and luxuriate in the moment, sort of like Spot after a saucer of milk.

Her head lolled to the side, and she idly stuck out the tip of her tongue to taste Jake's shoulder. Her gaze fell on the glowing digital numbers of her clock on the nightstand and she shot up.

Jake mumbled and slung a heavy arm across her waist.

"Jake!" She prodded his arm. "It's late. We slept in."

Opening one eye, he cupped her breast and toyed with her nipple. "You have someplace to be?"

She sucked in a breath and squirmed, and then she broke away from him and planted her feet on the floor. "We both do, and I'm not traipsing into the war room with you—late for all the world to see."

"I'm gonna have to wear the same clothes as yesterday, unless I have time to run home at lunch." He rubbed his eyes. "I suppose breakfast in bed is out."

"I have yogurt and granola bars if you want something quick." She twisted her head around. "Okay if I shower first?"

"Sure you don't want me to join you?" He wiggled his eyebrows up and down.

"Not if we ever hope to make it out of this apartment today." She wriggled beyond his reach as he grabbed for her.

She took a quick shower, left Jake a clean towel and returned to the bedroom to dress.

Jake was sitting on the edge of the bed, his phone to his ear, the tangled sheets pulled into his lap. He jumped up when he saw her, the sheets falling to the floor. Despite his glorious nakedness, it was his face that commanded her attention, every plane alive with excitement.

"Billy found something in the tapes?"

A wide smile claimed his lips as he nodded. "Two cars, license plates and everything, in Crystal's neighborhood, and two very similar cars in Andrea's area. Looks like we have a couple of suspects."

Chapter Sixteen

Jake sat across from the first suspect, his stomach plunging by the minute. No way was Trevor Beard their neat, anal-retentive killer. The guy couldn't even keep the doughnut crumbs from falling onto his paunch.

"So, tell me again, Mr. Beard. Why was your car in this neighborhood?" Jake drilled a finger into a still photo of Beard's car taken from a security camera a few blocks from Crystal's house.

"Like I said—" Beard took a gulp of soda and wiped the back of his hand across his mouth "—I was picking up my kid."

"At two in the morning?" Billy cocked his head and Jake could tell his partner was trying with all his might not to focus on the coffee stain on Beard's T-shirt.

"Yeah, two in the morning. My ex won't let me pick up my girl when the babysitter's there. So, I waited, and the ex didn't stumble in until around two. Figures— anything she can do to get me in trouble."

"I hear ya, brother." Billy shook his head and whipped out the other photo, the one near Andrea's place with no clear license plate. "What about here? Is this your car?"

Beard bent over the metal desk and squinted. "I don't think so. Hard to tell. Where was it?"

Jake answered, "Canoga Park."

"No way." Beard leaned back and folded his arms on his belly. "I don't never go there."

Both Jake and Billy had already given Beard their cards.

Jake nudged Billy's foot with his own. "I think we're done here, Mr. Beard. We may call you again if we have any more questions."

"Fine by me. I didn't do nothing. Should be a crime to pick up your sleeping kid at that time of the morning, but what're you gonna do when your ex is out partying?"

"Nothing. Absolutely nothing." Billy planted his hands on the desk and pushed up. "Detective McAllister will walk you out."

Jake shot Billy a dirty look from beneath his lashes.

Beard grabbed his can. "Hey, do you have any more of those little doughnuts I can have on my way out?"

"Sure." Jake ushered Beard out the door and rolled his eyes at Billy.

When he came back, Billy was brushing crumbs from the table into his palm. "That guy would've left a trail of bread crumbs at the crime scenes."

"Yeah, not our guy."

"Which is a good thing we can eliminate him, because we got nothing, partner. No judge is going to give us a search warrant based on a car on an LA street in a video. We can't get anything from these guys."

"I'm aware." Jake slipped out of his jacket and draped it over his arm. "When's the next guy coming?"

"About fifteen minutes. He informed me that he had to leave work early for the interview."

"What's he do?"

"Engineer at an aerospace company, so basically a

rocket scientist." Billy leveled a finger at the jacket. "Didn't you wear that suit yesterday?"

"I like the suit. I wore it for the visit with the Behrs and thought it would be good for the interviews." Jake shook out the jacket again to avoid Billy's eyes.

"You were late this morning, too."

"Not like I haven't been working sixteen-hour days. Who are you, my mother?"

"If I were, I'd be telling you not to spend the night at a girl's house on a school day." Billy shook his finger at Jake, and Jake displayed another finger to Billy before he walked out of the interview room.

"I'm going to grab a couple of drinks for the next guy."

Fifteen minutes later, Jake returned to the interrogation room with two sodas and a file folder tucked under one arm. He stowed the items on the table and lingered by the door. Billy had gone downstairs to meet the second suspect, or at least the man who owned the other car caught on video, and Jake always liked to watch them walk. You could tell a lot about a man by the way he walked.

Billy knew what his partner was doing and allowed the subject to walk ahead of him down the hallway.

Mr. Cyrus Fisher had good posture. He dressed his wiry frame in khaki pants with a short-sleeved light blue button-up shirt, no tie. He swung his arms at his sides, but as he approached Jake, he stuck his hands in his pockets. The crepe soles of his shoes made zero noise on the linoleum, and he inclined his head and pursed his lips when he reached the room.

Jake stuck out his hand. "Mr. Fisher, I'm Detective McAllister. Thank you for taking time out of your day to answer some questions for us."

"Certainly." He grasped Jake's hand with his own, and despite the sinewy muscles of his forearm, Fisher's grip was weak.

Jake stepped aside and gestured Fisher to the hot seat—the one bolted to the floor so that suspects couldn't turn it in a different direction. They had to face their inquisitors head-on.

Fisher eyed the other two chairs before bending his knees and lowering himself to the chair.

Jake shoved a soda across the table. "Would you like something to drink?"

"No, thank you." Fisher's sharp nose appeared sharper as he lifted his chin and peered down at the can.

"Coffee, then?"

"I never drink coffee at the end of the day, Detective McAllister." Fisher held up one bony finger. "One cup in the morning is all I allow myself."

Jake shrugged and cracked the tab on his can of soda, but his nostrils flared and his pulse ratcheted up a notch.

"No soda, no coffee. Anything else? We've got some killer doughnuts in the break room." Billy straddled the other chair.

Again, with the pained look on his face, Fisher said, "I don't eat doughnuts, Detective Crouch."

"Okay, nothing to eat or drink, then." Billy gave Fisher an appraising look. "Do you work out? You're in good shape."

Fisher allowed his thin lips to crook into a smile. "I'm a biker, Detective Crouch."

Billy slapped the desk between them with his hand. "Are you one of those guys who rides around with the bright-colored Lycra shorts? Damn, you gotta admire a man who goes out like that."

Fisher did not reward Billy with another smile. "You called me in here because you saw my car somewhere?"

"We did, Mr. Fisher." Jake flipped open the folder and with the tip of his finger dragged the photo, which showed Fisher's car caught in the vicinity of Crystal's house the morning her body was discovered, to a spot on the desk in front of Fisher.

Fisher didn't touch the photo like Beard had done. Instead, Fisher put his hands in his lap and hunched forward a little.

Billy asked, "Is that your car, Mr. Fisher?"

"Well, you know it is, Detective, because there's my license plate, clear as day and the reason why I'm here instead of finishing up work at the office."

Jake eased out a breath he'd been holding. "Can you tell us what your car was doing in that area at two in the morning?"

"Certainly I can. Can you tell me why you're asking?"

"It's near the scene of a homicide that we believe took place around that time." Jake took a sip of soda so he could hide his own face while he watched Fisher's over the rim of the can.

Fisher's expression never changed. "Terrible. My car was there because it's a shortcut I take to work sometimes."

Jake's eye twitched. Not what he was expecting.

Billy burst out with the time again. "You're going to work at two in the morning?"

Fisher tapped a badge inside his front pocket. "It's a secure building, Detective Crouch, and I work in a closed area. I'm in and out at odd times of the day. When an idea strikes, I need to act on it."

Billy gave him a look as if he were an escapee from

an insane asylum, but the three of them spent the next ten minutes looking at a map that included Fisher's house, where he lived alone, the area where his car was spotted and the location of his office.

As Jake suspected, that street could be used as a shortcut. As he also suspected, Fisher's alibi would most likely check out.

When Billy sprang the second photo on him, Fisher pursed his lips again and studied the picture carefully, again never touching it. "That could be my car, but I doubt it. I don't recognize that area."

Jake said flatly, "It's Canoga Park."

"Then no. That's not my car." Fisher's gaze traveled from Jake's face to Billy's. "Is there anything else, Detectives?"

They asked him several more questions, but Fisher stuck with his original story, his cool, precise demeanor never cracking.

"All right, then." Jake stood up suddenly with a loud scrape of his chair, hoping to startle Fisher into grabbing the table or his own chair.

He didn't.

"We'll be checking with your office about the time you arrived to work that day." Billy smiled and spread his hands. "Just to dot our *i*'s and cross our *t*'s."

"Very good, Detective." Fisher made a move for the door. "I can find my way out."

"I'm sure you can, but you can understand protocol." Billy hesitated at the door to see if Fisher would grab the handle.

He didn't.

After an awkward pause of several seconds, Billy yanked open the door and Jake called after Fisher's squared shoulders. "Thanks again, Mr. Fisher."

By the time Billy came back to the interrogation room, Jake had been pacing and working up a steam. He grabbed Billy by the shoulders. "I think that's our guy, Billy."

Billy cracked a grin. "Certainly."

"The bastard wouldn't touch a thing in here. Wouldn't leave his DNA on anything, either." Jake cocked an eyebrow at Billy. "He didn't use the men's room, by any chance, on his way out?"

"Too careful for that." Billy scratched his chin. "You know his office is going to verify his hours."

"I know that."

"We got nothing, brother."

Jake held up his hands and wiggled his fingers. "We have his print. We just need to match it to him."

KYRA SHADED HER eyes as she peered up at Jake in the parking lot of the station, the setting sun creating a glare and giving him a halo. After his performance last night, he definitely didn't deserve a halo...or maybe he did.

She coughed. "You can't just ask him for his fingerprints?"

"No. All we had was his car on a home security video in the area. The car wasn't even in front of Crystal's house, and we already verified his story with his employer. His manager confirmed that Cyrus works odd hours. They don't care as long as he puts in forty hours a week, and he usually clocks more than that. The guy's something of a genius, and they're happy to let him do what he wants. That is not enough to get his prints. He's not a suspect on paper—only in our minds."

"And he didn't leave any prints in the interview room." She chewed on her bottom lip. "Suspicious."

"Very suspicious. We've seen it before—persons of

interest come in to talk and won't touch a thing. We even had a guy one time who crushed out his cigarette, bagged the butt and stuck it in his pocket, so we couldn't get his DNA when he left."

"You're rushing off now to get his prints? How do you plan to do that?"

Kyra had run into Jake in the parking lot when she'd returned to the station to grab files she'd forgotten. He'd waved her down and told her all about the rocket scientist, Cyrus Fisher. She'd been around Quinn long enough to know that cops had to trust their guts.

"I have his address."

"You said it yourself. You can't get a warrant and bust into his place. You don't have enough evidence. You don't have any evidence."

"People put their trash out, don't they? Touch the lids, toss out containers." He lifted his shoulders in the suit jacket he'd dumped on her bathroom floor and worn two days in a row, definitely looking a little worse for wear.

"You plan to skulk around in that?" She jabbed a finger at the black Crown Vic that had *police* written all over it even though it was unmarked. "He's a rocket scientist. He'll spot you in two seconds, especially if you rang any alarm bells with him by trying to get him to eat and drink in the interview room."

"I don't know if we did." Jake scratched his unshaven chin. He obviously had never made it back to his place this afternoon to freshen up after spending the whole night at her place.

"Sociopaths often think they're the smartest ones in the room, and with Cyrus's IQ, he probably believes that double. It always makes them slip up."

"Straight from the extremely kissable, luscious lips of a therapist, but I've done stakeouts before."

Her lips buzzed. "This is more than a stakeout. I'll tell you what. I'll let you use my completely nonthreatening, unofficial-looking car for this adventure on one condition."

"It's not an adventure, and I already know the condition. You want to tag along."

"I deserve to tag along. What if Cyrus Fisher is La Prey? Besides," she said as she put her hand on his arm and batted her eyelashes, "this is not a dangerous mission. You're going to pick up some garbage while I drive the getaway car."

"All right. One piece of trash, and we leave." He shrugged out of his jacket and slung it over his shoulder. "Lead the way."

As Kyra traipsed to the civilian side of the parking lot, she cranked her head over her shoulder. "Why isn't Billy with you?"

"He's picking up his kids, but he knows what's going down. He had the same feeling about Cyrus as I did."

When they got into Kyra's car, Jake put Fisher's address into his phone and she started following the voice. The sun set fast as they drove east, and dusk had fallen by the time they reached Fisher's neighborhood—neat and well-ordered, just like Fisher himself, according to Jake.

They crawled toward his block and Jake said, "Damn."

She slammed on the brakes. "What's wrong?"

"Hey!" He steadied his hands against the dashboard. "Are you *trying* to call attention to your car?"

With her heart still pounding, she squeaked out, "Sorry. You startled me."

She wouldn't tell Jake this, but her nerves had started jangling, and all they were doing was retrieving a piece of trash. She couldn't imagine what it would be like to go in for an arrest.

He tapped the window. "It doesn't look like it's trash night. Nobody has bins out. I can't exactly waltz onto the guy's property and grab a flowerpot or a garden hose."

"Maybe find out when this neighborhood puts out trash and return. Do you have enough to put surveillance on him in case he goes out…hunting again?"

"Nope. We don't have the manpower for that, and I don't want him to suspect anything." He drummed his fingers on the dash. "Get closer to his address and pull to the curb. I have binoculars with me."

Kyra licked her lips as she drove onto Fisher's block. Luckily she did not have to make a U-turn to park across the street and several doors down from his tidy house with its manicured lawn.

She cut the engine, and Jake reached for his bag in the back seat of her car, withdrawing a pair of small binoculars.

Raising them to his eyes, he said, "I just want to see what I can see."

She pulled back a little to allow him a clear view of Fisher's house.

"No trash bins and none on the side of his house, either, not that I could use that evidence anyway. Man, I don't think that guy has one twig out of place. It matches with his crime scenes."

"Is he someone you could see stalking me? Killing Yolanda?"

"No, but that doesn't mean he didn't do those things." He took a sharp breath. "He's coming out of the house."

"He is?" Kyra slumped in her seat. She could see a

dark figure in the driveway of Fisher's house. "What's he doing?"

"He's leaving."

She shot up. "Jake, we have to follow him. What if he's going to plan another attack or, God forbid, kill someone?"

"Okay, okay. Easy. He's in his car."

Lights flashed in the driveway as Fisher turned on his car. Kyra ground her teeth together, hoping he didn't come this way.

Jake said, "He's going the other way. Don't start your car yet. He'll see the lights behind him. There— he turned right. Now go ahead and turn right."

Kyra started her engine and took off after Fisher's silver hybrid SUV. When she turned the corner, she could spot his headlights up ahead. "Tell me how close to get."

"You're fine. It's not too late. There are still cars coming and going in this area. He shouldn't notice anything."

She trailed behind Fisher with occasional instructions from Jake, and when the silver SUV got into the left-hand turn pocket to a major boulevard, she sighed. "That's better."

"Slow down. Don't get right behind him. Let these two cars go."

She chugged along until the two cars behind her got frustrated and wheeled around her, slipping behind Fisher's car in the pocket. Kyra stayed in the far right of her lane in case Fisher decided to study the cars behind him in his rearview mirror.

The green arrow flashed on and the car in front of her dawdled so long she almost missed the light.

Fisher's car zoomed ahead of her and then got in the right lane and slowed down.

Jake lowered the binoculars. "He's gonna park. He's gonna park."

"Where's he going?"

"I think we're in luck. There are a couple of take-out restaurants, a nail salon and a mobile phone store. I doubt he's getting his nails done or buying a cell phone."

They drove past as Fisher parked his car in the small parking lot of the strip mall.

Kyra pounded the steering wheel. "I think he just took the last spot in there."

"That's okay. We're in no hurry. Circle around the block."

She made a sharp turn around the corner and circled back around to the busy street. She turned right and slowed down.

Jake said, "Pull over to the curb ahead and idle. I'm going to see if I can look into the restaurants. I think he went into the Thai place."

She scooted into a metered parking place on the street ahead of the driveway to the strip mall parking lot. "Can you see in there?"

"His car's still here." Jake put the binoculars to his eyes, his mouth beneath screwed up at the side. "I can't get a good look. Wait!"

She clutched the steering wheel. "Do you see him?"

"Pay dirt, baby." He dropped the binoculars from his eyes, which were shining in triumph. "He's coming out of the Thai restaurant with a plate of food and a drink, and he's heading for the small patio. He's going to eat and drink and toss, and we're going to move in for the evidence."

"You're going to take it out of the trash? How will you know it's his?"

"I know he's eating from the Thai place, and we'll

watch the trash can after he leaves to see who else throws something away. We got this."

They waited in the car, and Kyra's eyes burned with tears as she kept focused on the man eating from a to-go container and tapping on his computer.

She asked Jake, "What do you think he's doing on that computer?"

"He could be working, but we're going to find out when Forensics gets ahold of it. Do you know they're still not done going through Jordy's computer?"

"Finding anything on his?"

"Not that I know of, but Jordy spent a lot of hours on his laptop." He jabbed her thigh. "Here we go."

She squinted at Fisher wiping his hands on a napkin, closing his computer and bagging his trash. Her heart skipped a beat at the thought that he might take it all with him.

With the binoculars glued to his face, Jake said, "He's heading for the trash can. He's going to throw away his bag. Done."

Jake sounded like he'd been giving a play-by-play to a game and Fisher had just scored—or they had.

The sun had gone down completely, and Fisher's reverse and brake lights flashed in the parking lot as he started his car and backed out.

As he pulled out, Kyra cracked open her door and the dome light sent a pool of light into the car.

Jake told her to wait at the same time she gasped and pulled the door closed. Fisher drove past them on the other side of the street. She turned to Jake. "Do you think he saw us?"

He shrugged. "Two people in a car on a busy street. You don't need to come with me."

"Oh, yes, I do. Thai food is beginning to sound pretty good about now."

They both exited the car and marched up to the trash can at the edge of the dining patio. Kyra hadn't taken her eyes from it and knew nobody else had put garbage in it.

Jake bent over the can with his phone and took a picture of the plastic bag. He pulled out a glove and slipped it onto his hand. Then he reached into the receptacle and pinched the handle of the plastic bag between his fingers, pulling it free.

He swung it from his gloved hand. "Got it."

He placed it on the table where Fisher had been sitting and nudged it open. "There's the container, his fork and his cup and straw. He's gotta have his prints all over this stuff."

As he stuck his camera in the bag to take more pictures, a movement to her right caught Kyra's eye. She jerked to the side and gasped as her eyes met those of Cyrus Fisher, a slight smile on his pale lips, his hand in his pocket.

"J-Jake."

Jake spun around, and his hand went to his weapon on his hip. With his eyes never leaving Fisher's face, he said, "Fisher."

"Good evening, Detective. Are you looking for something?"

Jake's hand moved to the plastic bag on the table and the crinkling noise sounded like a bomb going off in the still silence among them. "I think I found it."

"Left my prints at one of the scenes, did I?" Fisher clicked his tongue and reached for his front pocket.

Jake's fingers twitched over his weapon, but Fisher held up a tablet. "Just a breath mint, Detective. I suppose you'll want me to do a lot of talking."

"Are you confessing now, Fisher? Because I can take you in along with your prints here."

Fisher popped the mint into his mouth and bit down on it. "I don't think so, Detective."

The blood roared in Kyra's head. She had a feeling Fisher wasn't going to come along quietly, despite his current demeanor.

Fisher chewed for a few seconds as if contemplating his choices. Then his body stiffened, and he clutched his chest.

Jake lunged forward, drawing his gun. "Stop!"

Kyra stumbled back, her hand grabbing for the back of one of the metal chairs at the table.

Fisher gurgled and dropped to his knees, his face turning purple as he gasped for breath. He fell onto his side, and his eyes rolled back as foam spewed from his lips.

"The pill! It's a suicide pill. Stop him, Jake."

Jake crouched beside Fisher, now clawing at the neck of his shirt, veins popping out on his forehead. "It's cyanide, Kyra. He's dying."

"No!" She dropped to her knees and grabbed the front of Fisher's shirt. "Why'd you do it? Why'd you copy him?"

Fisher's eyes seemed to focus for a second before his gagging ceased, and Kyra could've sworn the bastard smiled.

Epilogue

Billy kicked his feet up on his desk, tipping his chair back at a dangerous angle. "It just doesn't make any sense to me. Why would the guy off himself? He didn't even know whether or not we actually had his prints from any of the crime scenes."

"He saw me when he drove away, and must've known at that point he was in trouble."

With a lump in her throat, Kyra raised her hand, wiggling her fingers. "That was my fault. I opened the door before Fisher drove off, and my dome light attracted his attention. He didn't know me, of course, but he recognized Jake and circled back to the restaurant."

"Okay, I get why he went back to see what was up, but why the confession on the sidewalk? He didn't know what we had. He could've gone home, cleared out any evidence he had at the house and claimed he had no idea how his print wound up on that piece of tape. The DA would've required more from us than that for a big case like this."

"Billy, my man, maybe he just recognized our superior detective skills in the interview and figured he was done for." Jake kicked Billy's shoes off the desk and his chair thumped to the floor.

"Yeah, I'm sure that was it." Billy slid his jacket from

the back of the chair and grabbed his laptop case. As he looked around the room, he said, "I hope this means we can finally dismantle the task force. Castillo is beaming. Chief can't stop smiling for the cameras, and Mayor Wexler is ready to hand us the keys to the city. I'm going to go home and relax for a change."

When Billy left the war room, Kyra took his chair next to Jake's and twisted her ponytail around her hand. "That was a horrible way to die, quick but far from painless. Fisher would've rather met that end than spend his life in prison? I'm with Billy. I don't understand why he did it."

"He's a killer, Kyra. Do you understand anything he did?"

"We do have profiles of serial killers. We understand a lot behind what drives them. Did the suicide pill even make sense for Fisher's personality? I'm not sure it did."

"He took it. We both saw him, and the prints we took from his trash matched the print on the tape in Mindy's bedroom. We also found the victims' locks of hair hidden in his home. He killed those women, and we had him dead to rights. Maybe he couldn't face the shame." Jake circled his finger in the air where several cops on the task force were still working, despite the fact that Fisher had died a week earlier. "I'm sure we'll find out more as we sift through the rest of his belongings. We got him. I'm just sorry he died before he could tell us anything about why he copied The Player."

"Me, too." She flicked her ponytail behind her. "Do you think Fisher was La Prey?"

"I guess we'll find out." He glanced over his shoulder at the preoccupied task force members, then leaned forward and brushed his lips across hers. "I'm sorry you didn't get your answers."

"It's almost like they don't want to be questioned, isn't it?" She twisted her fingers in her lap. "I mean, Jordy had to know you were going to shoot to kill when he tried to stab me."

"Yeah, it is." He wheeled his chair back to his own desk and started packing up. "We'd better get going if we want to pick up dinner and get to Quinn's before he falls asleep. He'll want all the latest."

She rose from Billy's chair and placed her hands lightly on Jake's shoulders. "Thanks for keeping Quinn in the loop. He loves it more than he lets on."

"I know he does." Squeezing her fingers, he whispered, "Dinner at Quinn's and then dessert at your place?"

A pulse throbbed in her throat and she purred, "Too bad we're at the station, or I'd straddle you right now."

"Now I really want to get going." Jake jumped from his chair just as Brandon Nguyen burst through the conference room door.

"I'm glad you're still here, J-Mac."

Jake rolled his eyes at Kyra. "Not for long, son. State your business."

"Oh, you're gonna want to hear this." Brandon stood at attention, clutching a folder to his chest, which looked about ready to burst.

Kyra grabbed Jake's sleeve and she didn't care who saw.

Jake's body stiffened beside her. "What did you find, Brandon?"

Brandon waved the folder in the air and crowed. "We found a connection between Jordy Lee Cannon and Cyrus Fisher. They were in contact."

* * * * *

COMING SOON!

We really hope you enjoyed reading this book.
If you're looking for more romance, be sure to
head to the shops when new books are
available on

Thursday 13th May

To see which titles are coming soon, please visit

millsandboon.co.uk/nextmonth

GET YOUR ROMANCE FIX!

MILLS & BOON
— *blog* —

Get the latest romance news, exclusive author interviews, story extracts and much more!

MILLS & BOON
MEDICAL
Pulse-Racing Passion

Set your pulse racing with dedicated, delectable doctors in the high-pressure world of medicine, where emotions run high and passion, comfort and love are the best medicine.

MILLS & BOON
Desire

Indulge in secrets and scandal, intense drama and plenty of sizzling hot action with powerful and passionate heroes who have it all: wealth, status, good looks… everything but the right woman.